A m_____ _gar and Shamus Award-_____ _____ Lutz is the auth___ __ er f___ __ __ _ __ __ _eks *Same* was r__ ___ the hit __ __ __ __ _nale. He lives in St Louis _ _ soup_.

D0320119

Also by John Lutz

*Mister X
*Urge to Kill
*Night Kills
*In for the Kill
Chill of Night
Fear the Night
*Darker Than Night
Night Victims
The Night Watcher
The Night Caller
Final Seconds (with David August)
The Ex
SWF Seeks Same

*featuring Frank Quinn

SERIAL

John Lutz

ROBINSON

Constable & Robinson Ltd
55-56 Russell Square
London
WC1B 4HP
www.constablerobinson.com

First published in the US by Pinnacle Books,
Kensington Publishing Corp., New York, 2011

Published in the UK by Robinson,
an imprint of Constable & Robinson Ltd., 2011

Copyright © John Lutz 2011

The right of John Lutz to be identified as the author of this
work has been asserted by him in accordance with the
Copyright, Designs and Patents Act 1988

All rights reserved. This book is sold subject to the condition
that it shall not, by way of trade or otherwise, be lent, re-sold,
hired out or otherwise circulated in any form of binding or cover
other than that in which it is published and without a similar condition
including this condition being imposed on the subsequent purchaser.

A copy of the British Library Cataloguing in
Publication data is available from the British Library

ISBN 978-1-78033-172-0

Printed and bound in the EU

3 5 7 9 10 8 6 4 2

For Barbara
As are they all

PART 1

I would I were alive again
To kiss the fingers of the rain,
To drink into my eyes the shine
Of every slanting silver line . . .

> —EDNA ST. VINCENT MILLAY,
> "Renascence"

I hear a sudden cry of pain!
There is a rabbit in a snare . . .

> —JAMES STEPHENS,
> "The Snare"

1

Millie Graff's feet were sore. She was a hostess at Mingles, a new and popular restaurant on West Forty-fifth Street near Times Square, and hadn't sat down for over five hours. After work, it was a three-block walk and a long concrete stairwell descent to a downtown subway platform. In the crowded subway, someone would probably step on her toes.

She didn't mind the work or the time at Mingles. Her paycheck was big enough that she'd soon be able to move out of her cramped Village apartment into something larger, maybe on the Upper West Side. Her job was secure, and there was still a chance she could land a spot in an off-Broadway chorus line.

Dance had been Millie's first love. It was what had brought her to New York City from the small town her folks had moved to in New Jersey. Dance and dreams.

She'd kept her weight down and was still built like a dancer: long-waisted, with small breasts, muscular legs, and an elegant turn of ankle that drew male glances.

In fact, as she jogged up the concrete steps to the entrance to her building, holding level a white foam takeaway container from a deli she'd stopped at on her way home, a middle-aged man walking past gave her a lingering look and a hopeful smile.

Not till you grow some hair on your head, Millie thought—

rather cruelly, she realized with some regret, as she shoul-
dered open the door to the vestibule.

She saw no one on the way up in the elevator or in the
hall. Pausing to dig her keys out of her purse, she realized
again how weary she was. Just smiling for seven hours was
enough to wear a person down.

After keying the locks, she turned the tarnished brass
doorknob and entered.

She'd barely had time to register that something was
wrong when the man who'd been waiting for her just inside
the door stepped directly in front of her. It was almost as if
he'd sprung up out of the floor.

Millie gasped. The foam container of chicken wings and
brown rice dropped to the carpet and made a mess.

The man was so close that his face was out of focus and
she couldn't make out his features. She thought at first he
was simply shirtless, but in a startled instant realized he was
completely nude. She could smell his sweaty male scent.
Feel his body heat. She was looking up at him at an angle
that made her think he was about six feet tall.

He smiled. That frightened the already-stunned Millie to
the point where her throat constricted. She could hardly
breathe.

"You know me," he said.

But of course she didn't. Not really.

"I have a gift for you," he told her, and she stood in shock
as he slipped something—a necklace—over her head carefully, so as not to disturb her hairdo.

She was aware of his right hand moving quickly on the
lower periphery of her vision. Saw an instantaneous glint of
silver. *A blade! Something peculiar about it.*

He was thrilled by the confusion in her eyes. Her brain
hadn't yet caught up with what was happening.

The blade would feel cold at first, before pain over-whelmed all other feeling.

He was standing now supporting her, a length of her in-testines draped in his left hand like a warm snake.

He thought that was amazing. *Incredible!* The expression on Millie Graff's face made it obvious that she, too, was amazed. Her eyes bulged with wonder. He felt the throb of his erection.

Despite the seriousness of her injury, he knew she wasn't yet dead. He lowered her gently to the floor, resting her on her back so she wouldn't bleed so much. Carefully, he propped her head against the sofa so that when he used the ammonia fumes to jolt her back to consciousness, she'd be looking down again at what he'd done to her.

She'd know it was only the beginning.

2

"Why would you invite anyone sane to see this?" Quinn asked.

But he had a pretty good idea why.

New York Police Commissioner Harley Renz wouldn't be at a bloody crime scene like this unless he considered it vitally important. Renz was standing back, well away from the mess in the tiny living room. The air was fetid with the coppery stench of blood.

The commissioner had put on even more weight in the year since Quinn had seen him. His conservative blue suit was stretched at the seams, rendering its expensive tailoring meaningless. His pink jowls ballooned over the collar of his white silk shirt. More and more, his appearance reflected exactly what he was, a corpulent and corrupt politician with the fleshy facial features of a bloodhound. He looked like a creature of rapacious appetite, and he was one.

"Look at her," he said, his red-rimmed eyes fleshy triangles of compassion. "Jesus, just look at her!"

What he was demanding wasn't easy. The woman lay on her back on the bloodstained carpet, with her legs and arms spread as if she'd given up and welcomed what was being done to her so the horror could end. Quinn knew it had taken a long time to end. It looked as if the tendons in the crooks of her arms and behind both knees had been severed so she couldn't move other than to flop around, and her abdomen had been opened with some kind of knife. Small circular burns indicated a cigarette had been touched to her flesh. Shreds of flesh dangled from her corpse in a way that suggested it had been violated with a blade and then peeled from body and bone with a pair of pliers.

Quinn figured the butchery for an amateur job, not done by anyone with special medical knowledge. The killer's primary goal was to torture. He'd burned her and stripped away skin for no purpose other than pain.

He must have done this while she was still alive.

Pink bloodstained material, what appeared to be the victim's panties, was wadded in her mouth. The elastic waistband of the panties was looped around her neck and tightly knotted at the base of her skull.

Quinn looked over at Renz.

"Nift says she was alive and what was done to her took hours," Renz said. "The stomach was done first." His voice broke slightly. Not like him.

For the first time Quinn noticed the usually loquacious and obnoxious little medical examiner, Dr. Julius Nift. He was standing alongside a wall with a uniformed cop and a plainclothes detective with his badge dangling in its leather folder from a suit coat pocket. A crime scene tech wearing a white jumpsuit and gloves was over near the door. Everyone seemed to be standing as far away as possible from Renz.

"That's why there's so much blood," Nift said. "A stomach wound like that looks horrible, but the victim doesn't necessarily die right away. Whatever her condition, he somehow managed to keep her heart pumping for quite a while. There's a slight ammonia smell around her head, too. Could be he used ammonia like smelling salts, to jolt her around whenever she lost consciousness. So she'd feel everything."

Quinn could hear a slight hissing and realized it was his

own breathing. Being here with the dead woman, where there had been so much agony, was like being in a catacomb with a saint. Then he understood why he'd made the comparison. Clutched tightly in the victim's pale right hand like a rosary was a silver letter *S* on a thin chain that was wrapped around her neck. Careful not to step in any of the darkening puddles of blood, Quinn leaned forward to more closely examine the necklace.

"Kinda crap you find in a Times Square souvenir shop." Renz said.

"That's where it might have come from," Quinn said. "It says 'New York' in tiny letters on the back."

"I noticed," Renz said, probably lying.

Quinn straightened up and looked around. The living room was tastefully decorated, with wicker furniture and a large wicker mask on one wall. On the opposite wall was a framed Degas ballerina print with "MoMA" printed on the matting. Not expensive furnishings, but not cheap. The apartment was cramped, and the block in this neighborhood in the East Village wasn't a good one.

Quinn wondered what made this a big case for Renz. Major money didn't seem to be involved. This woman appeared to have lived well but modestly. Politics might be at play here. Maybe the victim had been somebody's secret lover. Somebody important.

No. If that were true Renz would be using it for leverage. He seemed emotionally involved here. It wouldn't be because of the goriness of the crime. He'd seen plenty of gore in his long career. He—

Nift was saying, "You wouldn't know it to look at her now . . ."

Careful, Quinn thought, knowing how Nift was prone to make salacious remarks about dead female victims.

". . . but she was kind of athletic, especially for her age," Nift finished, avoiding an explosion from Renz.

"I wanna show you something else," Renz said, ignoring Nift. He led Quinn from the bedroom and into a small bathroom.

There was a claw-footed porcelain tub there, and a washbasin without a vanity attached to the wall. Everything was tiled either gray or blue. White towels stained red with diluted blood were jumbled on the floor and in the tub. The tub, as well as the washbasin, had red stains that looked like patterns of paint applied by a madman.

"Bastard washed up in here after he killed her," Renz said, "But more than that." He pointed at the medicine chest mirror, on which someone, presumably the killer, had scrawled in blood the name *Philip Wharkin*.

"The killer?" Quinn asked.

"Maybe. The kind of asshole who's daring us to catch him. It's happened before. They're out there."

"Don't we know it."

Quinn moved closer to the mirror and leaned in to study the crudely printed red letters. "I don't think he's one of those. He was careful. This was written with a finger dabbed in blood, and it looks like he had on rubber gloves." He backed away from the mirror. "If nothing else, this is a passion crime. Maybe the victim had a thing with Philip Wharkin and it went seriously bad."

"That's how I figure it," Renz said. "If she did, we'll sure as hell find out."

Quinn could see Renz's jaw muscles flex even through the flab. This one was important to him, all right. Maybe, for some reason, his ill-gained position as commissioner depended on it.

They left the stifling bathroom and returned to the living room. The techs were still busy, having taken advantage of the extra space created when Renz and Quinn had left. Nift was down on one knee packing his black bag, finished with the body until it was transported to the morgue.

The corpse was unaffected by any of it. Its pale blue eyes, widened in horror, gazed off at some far horizon they would all at some time see. Quinn felt a chill race up his spine. Hours ago this bloody, discarded thing on the floor had been a vital and perhaps beautiful woman.

"How old do you estimate she was?" Quinn asked Nift.

It was Renz who answered. "Twenty-three. And it's not an estimate."

"You got a positive ID?" Quinn asked.

"Yeah," Renz said.

He leaned over the corpse and lifted it slightly off the carpet, turning it so Quinn could see the victim's back.

Her shoulders and the backs of both arms were covered with old burn scars. Quinn had similar scars on his right shoulder and upper arms.

"The killer didn't do that to her back," Renz said, returning the body to its original position.

Quinn looked again at the victim's features, trying to imagine them without the distortion of horror and the scarlet stains.

He felt the blood recede from his face. Then he began to tremble. He tried but couldn't stop the tremors.

"It's Millie Graff," Renz said.

3

After the body of Millie Graff had been removed, Quinn walked with Renz through a fine summer drizzle to a diner a few blocks away that was still open despite the late hour. They were in a back-corner booth and were the only customers. The old guy who'd come out from behind the counter to bring their coffee was now at the other end of the place, near the door and the cash register. He was hunched over as if he had a bent spine, reading a newspaper through glasses with heavy black frames.

Renz looked miserable, obviously loathing his role as bearer of bad news. Quinn was surprised to find himself feeling sorry for him. Though they held a mutual respect for each other's capabilities, the two men weren't exactly friends. Renz was an unabashed bureaucratic crawler fueled by ambition and unencumbered by any sort of empathy or decency. He'd stepped on plenty of necks to get where he was, and he still wasn't satisfied. Never would be. Quinn considered Renz to be an insatiable sociopath who would say anything, do anything, or use anyone in order to get what he wanted. Renz considered Quinn to be simply unrealistic.

"I haven't seen Millie in almost fifteen years," Quinn said.

"She healed up, grew up, and became a dancer," Renz

said. "Saved her money so she could leave New Jersey and live here in New York. She was gonna break into theater." He sipped his coffee and made a face as if he'd imbibed poison. "I got all this from her neighbors. She worked in the Theater District, but was waiting tables in a restaurant." He shrugged. "Show biz."

"How long's she been in the city?" Quinn asked.

"Five months."

Quinn gazed out the window and thought back to when he'd first seen Millie Graff. She'd had metal braces on her teeth and was screaming with her mouth wide open and mashed against the closed window of a burning car.

He'd simply been driving along on Tenth Avenue in his private car, off duty, when traffic had come to a stop and he'd seen smoke up ahead. Quinn had gotten out of his car and jogged toward the smoke. When he got closer to the gathering mass of onlookers he saw that a small SUV was upside down, propped at an angle with its roof against the curb. It was on fire.

The vehicle was not only on fire. Its gas tank was leaking, and the resultant growing puddle of fuel was blazing. The crowd, sensing an explosion any second, was moving well back, occasionally surging forward slightly, pulled by curiosity and repelled by danger. The woman who'd been driving the SUV was upside down with her head at an awkward angle. Quinn figured her neck was broken.

The girl pressing her face against the window and screaming was eight-year-old Millie Graff. She'd apparently gotten her safety belt unbuckled and was trying to crawl out. But the door was jammed shut and the window remained closed. He saw the frantic girl make a motion as if she was trying to open the window, and then shake her head back and forth, desperately trying to tell someone looking on that the window was jammed.

Quinn moved toward the car and felt someone grip his

shirtsleeve. A short man with brown eyes popped wide was trying to hold him back. "It's gonna blow any moment!" he yelled at Quinn. "Smell that gas! You can't go over there!"

When Quinn drew his big police special revolver from its belt holster the man released him and moved back. That was when Quinn saw the blue uniform over by a shop window. A young PO standing with his back pressed against a wall. Quinn waved for him to come over and help. The man didn't move. A New York cop, frozen by fear.

Forgetting everything else, Quinn ran to the SUV and began pounding on the window with the butt of his revolver, holding the cylinder tight so it remained on an empty chamber and wouldn't allow the gun to fire accidentally. The girl inside pressed her hand against the glass and he motioned for her to move back.

She did, and a series of blows rendered with all his strength broke the glass. It didn't shatter much, but enough so that he could grip the shards and pull them out. He removed his shirt and used it so he wouldn't cut his hands as he tried to pry the rest of the window out.

The girl caught fire. She began screaming over and over, trying to beat out the flames with her bare hands. Quinn could see the flames spreading across the back of her blouse, reaching for her hair.

The sight gave him strength he didn't know he had, and what was left of the window popped from the frame.

He reached through the window, grabbed the girl's arm, and dragged her from the vehicle. Pain made him realize he was on fire, too. Both of them were burning.

That was when Quinn glanced beyond the girl, to the other side of the car. And through his pain and fear he saw a distorted miniature face and waving tiny hands in an infant seat. A screaming child. A baby.

Aware now of more flames in the street around him, more burning gasoline, he slung the wriggling young girl over his shoulder and ran with her across the street. He gave her to reaching arms. Hands slapped at him, and someone threw a shirt over him to smother the flames.

He saw the young cop still frozen against the wall. Quinn screamed around the lump in his throat: "There's a baby in there, other side, rear, in an infant seat!"

The man didn't move, only stared straight ahead.

Quinn shoved people away and ran back toward the burning SUV, ignoring the pleas for him to stay away. He was aware of sirens. Fire trucks down the street, a block away. *Too far away.* The flames inside the car were spreading. The vehicle was filling with smoke.

He glanced back and saw the young girl he'd dragged from the wreck huddled on the sidewalk, surrounded by people. A man was bending over her, maybe a doctor.

Quinn continued running toward the burning SUV.

The explosion knocked him backward. He remembered being airborne, then the back of his head hitting solid concrete.

Then nothing was solid and he was falling.

When he regained consciousness the next day in the hospital, he was told the girl he'd pulled from the SUV had second-degree burns on her upper back and arms, but she was alive. The driver of the vehicle, a teenage sister, was dead. So was the infant in the backseat, their little brother, ten months old.

Quinn had been proclaimed a hero, and the *Times* ran a photo of him posing with the family of the dead and their one remaining child—Millicent Graff.

The young officer who'd gone into shock and been unable to help Quinn, and perhaps rescue the infant, was fired from the NYPD for dereliction of duty.

The NYPD had sort of adopted Millie Graff. Renz had

used the charming child as a political prop, but that was okay because it was obvious that he also felt genuine affection for her.

And now—

"Quinn."

Renz, across the diner booth, was talking to Quinn.

"Sorry," Quinn said. "Lost my concentration for a minute."

"Where'd you go?" Renz asked, with a sad smile.

He knew where.

Quinn felt the beginnings of another kind of flame, deep in his gut, and knew what it meant. In a way, he welcomed it.

This killer had taken away forever something precious that fifteen years ago Quinn had saved. Now he had to be found. He *would* be found. Quinn wanted it even more than Renz might imagine.

This was personal.

4

Renz tried the coffee again, put the cup back down, and shoved it away. "Camel piss." He looked hard at Quinn across the diner table. "You and your investigative agency want this one?"

"Can you convince the higher-ups to turn it over to us?"

"I *am* the higher-up," Renz said. "You might be off the force, along with your retread detectives, but when it comes to serial killers no one can top you. I'll make it clear to everyone from the mayor on down that nailing this sicko is priority number one and we have to use our best. If we don't, and there are more murders, there'll be plenty of blame for all the people who wanted a second-rate investigation. That's a smelly political albatross to have hanging around your neck in this city."

So Renz had his own political motives for wanting this killer brought down fast. Well, that was fine, if it put Quinn on the case. "You sure we got a serial killer?"

"You know we do, Quinn. We both know this guy will kill again, and probably soon. The way he . . . the things that were done to Millie, that kinda asshole is gonna be a repeater."

"Probably," Quinn conceded.

"And this case interests you. It needs you like you need it.

Like I need you. It'll be like before. We're not bypassing the NYPD. The city will employ you and your agency on a work-for-hire basis to aid in the investigation. Of course, you'll be running it."

Quinn knew that what Renz needed or wanted, he would get. Renz was the most popular police commissioner the city had ever known. Not to mention that he had something on almost everyone above him in the food chain. In New York, even if it meant going to jail later, a popular police commissioner with that kind of leverage wielded real power.

But Quinn did have some reservations.

"Because of Millie, I've got a serious personal interest in this case, Harley. We've never done anything like this exactly."

"Nothing is ever like anything else exactly. Think snowflakes."

Quinn sat drumming his fingertips on the table. There really was little doubt that Millie's killer would strike again.

"Don't give me all that contemplation bullshit," Renz said. "We both know you're in. I'll write up the contract we had before, only for more money. I want this bastard in the worst way, Quinn."

"I can see that, Harley. But you don't want him more than I do."

"So we got a deal?"

Quinn stopped with the fingers. "Yeah."

"Your coffee's getting cold."

"Let it."

5

It was almost 2 A.M. when Quinn let himself into his apartment on West Seventy-fifth Street. The apartment comprised the first floor of a brownstone that was two buildings down from the building where Quinn had lived for a while with his now ex-wife May, and then for a shorter period of time with Pearl.

He was trying to get Pearl to leave her tiny apartment and move into the brownstone with him. She wasn't high on the idea. She would spend time with him there, and had even slept over a few times on the sofa, when it was late at night and the subway had stopped running. She'd never had sex with him there, or anywhere else, since her fiancé Yancy Taggart had died saving her life.

Quinn was moving slowly and carefully with Pearl. She was still grieving for Yancy, even though almost a year had passed since his death. Quinn understood that, and he took it into account whenever Pearl acted up.

Yancy had been a good man. And he and Pearl might have made a go of their marriage. Quinn had been sorry about what happened to Yancy, too. But time passed, and life continued beyond the point where Yancy had died saving Pearl's life.

And though it might be bad form and a mistake, the truth was that Quinn wanted Pearl back.

Something rattled upstairs. Then came a metallic ping, and what sounded like a board dropping flat on the floor. Quinn chose to ignore the noise. He'd investigated such things before and found nothing. The old building was prone to make unexpected, unexplainable sounds.

The brownstone had been built in 1885, and it showed its age. Quinn had bought it with some of his settlement from the city. He'd seen it as an investment, and was rehabbing the upstairs, converting it to two spacious apartments that could be rented out to make the mortgage payments. However, if Pearl eventually moved in with him, only the top floor would be rented. The second floor, with its turned oak woodwork and beautiful original crystal chandelier, would be theirs on a daily basis.

Quinn had even from time to time considered offering one of the apartments to Pearl to rent. It would bring her physically closer. Another step toward them moving in together.

Sometimes even Quinn wondered if that eventuality was possible. He didn't underestimate the obstacles.

He and Pearl were both difficult to live with, because neither could completely overlook the other's faults.

Or maybe they were characteristics. Even virtues. Quinn was obsessive in his work, a solver of the human puzzle and a dedicated, even merciless hunter. He might have stepped from the pages of the Old Testament, only his religion was Justice. He was controlled and patient and relentless.

Pearl was equally obsessive about her work, but not as controlled, and certainly not as patient.

Quinn might be mistaken for a plodder, until you realized that not one step was wasted or taken in a wrong direction. Then you knew you were watching a deliberate, heat-seeking missile, and God help his target. When whoever he was hunting moved this way or that, Quinn could be fooled only for a short while. He was tireless, he was inexorable, and, ultimately, he could be deadly.

Pearl, on the other hand, seemed to have been born with a burr up every orifice. She was direct and tough, and her moods ranged all the way from irritated to enraged. While Quinn was slathering his phony Irish charm on a suspect, Pearl would be waiting to kick the suspect where it hurt the most. Suspects seemed to sense that.

Quinn went into the bedroom, sat on the edge of the bed, and removed his boxy, size-twelve black shoes. Sometimes, in the faint glow of the nightlight, he would imagine that Pearl was there asleep. Though in her early forties, she looked almost like a child. Her raven black hair spread like a shadow on her pillow. Even in repose her strong features and dark eyebrows, her fleshy red lips, were vivid and gave Quinn moments of breathlessness. She was a small woman, slightly over five feet tall, but beneath the thin white sheet that covered her, the curves of her compact, buxom form were the timeless landscape of love. She was Quinn's everywoman, yet he knew that in all the world there was no one else like her. She helped him to understand the contradictions and power that women held, though she might not completely understand them herself.

Their relationship, their love, was worth recovering. And once recovered, worth nurturing.

Quinn quietly stripped to his Jockey shorts, and slowly, so as not to wake the imaginary Pearl, moved to the other side of the bed and slipped beneath the sheet.

Am I going crazy? Do I love her this much? To construct her in my imagination when the logical me knows she isn't here?

The bedroom was hushed but for the constant muted sounds of the city. The distant rush of traffic, punctuated by sirens and sometimes faraway human voices, filtered in from the world on the other side of the window.

There was a click, then a hum that built in volume and command. The window-unit air conditioner cycling on. Quinn felt cool air caress his leg beneath the sheet. He moved a bare foot outside the sheet, taking advantage of the breeze. He didn't think the hum or sudden circulation of air would awaken Pearl. He remembered that usually she was a deep sleeper.

Pearl, who wasn't there.

The phone rang at 2 A.M. Quinn fought his way awake and pressed the receiver to his ear. He hadn't checked to see who was calling and was almost surprised to hear the real Pearl. But she was in the habit of sometimes calling him at odd hours.

Does she lie in bed and think about me? Does she construct an imaginary Quinn?

But that would mean—

"What'd Renz want?" she asked.

He swallowed the bitter taste along the edges of his tongue. "It's past two o'clock, Pearl. I'll tell you tomorrow."

"I'm awake 'n so are you," she said. "I don't like it when I ask a question and the answer's hours away."

Quinn yawned, almost displacing his jaw. "Since we're both awake, you wanna meet someplace for coffee, maybe go dancing?"

"Now you're being a smart-ass."

"Yes, I am. I guess it's just in me."

"Talk, Quinn."

He talked. Knowing he'd never have a more attentive listener. When he was finished, Pearl said, "I don't like anything about it except for the money."

Quinn said, "I'm not thinking about the money."

"Yeah. Renz needs it, and you have a mission, so we're stuck with it."

"We are. But it's not such a bad thing, Pearl. Q and A doesn't have anything else going at the moment. Because of the economy, maybe."

"We're supposed to be a recession-proof business."

"Well, maybe we are. Maybe that's why we've got poor Millie Graff."

"Then it is, Quinn."

"Is what?"

"Such a bad thing."

"You're exasperating, Pearl."

"I guess it's just in me."

Quinn wondered if they would ever get to the point where their conversations didn't turn into competitions.

"We're gonna need sleep, Pearl. Breakfast at the diner?"

"Eight o'clock," she said, and hung up.

Quinn squinted at the clock by the bed. He was wide awake now. Eight o'clock seemed an eternity away.

Over breakfast at the Lotus Diner—veggie omelet for Pearl, scrambled eggs and sausages for Quinn—Pearl said, "How are we going to play it today?"

"I'll send Sal and Harold to meet with the liaison cop Renz is giving us. They can pick up whatever information the NYPD has. It's still early for there to be much of that. Millie's body's barely cold."

Pearl took a bite of egg-sheathed broccoli and chewed thoughtfully. She sipped her coffee, also thoughtfully. "Maybe this whole thing will be easier than we think. Could be Millie was having an affair with Philip Wharkin and he turned out to be a nutcase. They had an argument. Then everything went all pear shaped, as the British say. It was a one-off thing."

Quinn looked at her. "You've been to England?"

"Been to the BBC."

"Would it be that simple on the BBC?"

"Never. The inspector would have nothing to do."

"There we are," Quinn said.

"Where?"

"Pear shaped."

They were finishing their second cups of coffee when Pearl's cell phone sounded its four opening notes of the old *Dragnet* theme. She pulled the instrument from her purse and automatically flipped up the lid, completing the connection without thinking to check to see who was calling.

"Pearl? Are you there, dear? It's important."

"Hold on a minute," Pearl said. She moved the phone well away from her, beneath the table. "It's my mother, out at Golden Sunset," she said to Quinn. "This is gonna take a while. Why don't you go ahead without me and I'll see you at the office."

Pearl's mother lived at Golden Sunset Assisted Living in New Jersey, only she didn't quite see it as living.

"Tell her I said hello," Quinn said, and took a last sip of coffee.

Pearl watched him pay at the cash register and wave at her as he walked from the diner.

"I'm back, Mom," Pearl said. "Now what's so important?"

"Did I hear that nice Captain Quinn, dear?"

"You did. He was just leaving. And he's no longer a captain. What's so—"

"Pot roast," her mother said. "You know how, when you too seldom visit here at the nursing home—"

"Assisted living."

"—you coordinate it with pot-roast night? Well, many others have and do and would like to continue. Traditions are much underrated and important, even life-sustaining, like in that song in *Fiddler on the Roof.* . . ."

"What's happened, Mom?"

"Pot-roast night. They have moved pot-roast night."

Pearl was bewildered. "Can't you . . . adjust?"

"They have moved it from Tuesday evening to Thursday evening. People like yourself come to visit on pot-roast night because—and here you will agree—the pot roast is the only digestible food they serve. And to make things worse, not in the gastronomical sense, Thursday evening is SKIP-BO night. The choice for the inmates—"

"Residents."

"—will be either conversation with their visitors, or SKIP-BO."

SKIP-BO was a card game Pearl didn't understand and didn't want to learn. Or talk about. "Damn it!" Pearl said.

"Don't curse, dear."

"My phone's blinking, Mom. Battery's going dead. I forgot to charge it last night."

"A string tied around the finger . . ."

Pearl held the phone well away from her.

". . . not so tight as to leave an unattractive indentation in the skin . . ."

"Fading and breaking up," Pearl said.

Pearl snapped her phone closed, breaking the connection.

"Quinn says hello," she murmured, and finished her coffee before it was too cool to drink.

6

Quinn was seated behind his desk, clearing away yesterday's mail, when Pearl walked into the Quinn and Associates
office on West Seventy-ninth Street. The office was still
warm, even though the air conditioner had been running
awhile. There was a trickle of rust-stained condensation
zigzagging down the wall beneath the window housing the
unit. Pearl was wearing the expression she usually wore after
a phone conversation with her mother. Quinn could understand Pearl's aggravation, but he rather liked her mother.

Sal Vitali and Harold Mishkin were already there. Vitali
was seated at his desk, making a tent with his fingers.
Mishkin was standing over by the coffee machine, gazing
down at it with his fists propped on his hips, as if to hurry it
along. Vitali was short but with a bearlike build, swarthy
complexion, and thick black hair going gray. He had a voice
like a chain saw.

"Harold brought doughnuts," he grated.

Over by Mr. Coffee, Mishkin smiled and nodded. He was
slight, and with the beginning of a stoop. His brown hair was
thinning and arranged in a comb-over, his chin receded beneath a narrow mouth and enormously bushy graying mustache. Mishkin was everybody's idea of a milquetoast.
Everybody would be mostly right, except for when Mishkin

knew he had to do something extremely difficult. Then, hands quaking, mustache twitching, stomach knotting, Mishkin would do it. "True courage," Vitali often growled, defending his longtime partner.

"I'm coming from a big breakfast," Pearl said. "You've gotta let us know the day before if you're gonna bring doughnuts, Harold."

"They're the kind you like," Mishkin said. "Cream-filled with chocolate icing."

"You trying to talk me into one to soothe your conscience, Harold?"

"You read too much into it, Pearl," Vitali said. "He's just trying to make you fatter."

Pearl picked up a silver letter opener and held it so morning sunlight glinted into Mishkin's sensitive eyes. Mishkin took off his glasses and turned away.

"He's being nice to you, Pearl," Vitali growled. "He figures you can eat breakfast and have a doughnut for dessert. It's not against the law."

"If I wanted a doughnut—"

"For God's sake!" Quinn said, thinking it was amazing how Pearl could walk into a room and change the mood, even the temperature. "Has anybody looked up the killer in the phone book?"

Vitali appeared surprised. "Huh?"

"Philip Wharkin. The guy who wrote on the victim's mirror with her blood."

"We don't know he's the killer," Pearl pointed out.

"Do we know he isn't? Do we know he's not some psycho with an irresistible urge to leave his name at murder scenes?"

"I guess not," Mishkin said, and sampled his coffee. He made a face as if it was too hot.

"Then let's find out. I know it's unlikely somebody named Philip Wharkin is actually the killer, but there's some reason that the killer left a name behind, even if it's only so we waste our time. Only it's not a waste of time." He walked over and stood in front of his desk, facing everyone but Mishkin, who was off to the side. "Sal, you and Harold find all the Philip Wharkins in the New York–area directories. Talk to them and find out where they were when Millie Graff's murder was committed. Pearl will use the computer to help you locate them. For all we know, the killer's got a website where he brags about what he's done. When Fedderman comes in, he and I are gonna drive over to Millie's neighborhood and interview anybody who might have seen, heard, tasted, touched, or smelled anything that might possibly be connected with what happened to the victim."

Vitali stood up and began stuffing pens and papers into his pockets. Mishkin worked a plastic lid onto his coffee cup so he could take it with him. Pearl was sliding into her desk chair, ready to boot up her computer.

Quinn and Associates' office was set up a lot like a precinct squad room, a large space without dividers between the desks. Everybody working for the agency was a former NYPD detective, so they felt right at home and fell to work immediately when they were given assignments. Old habits died hard, especially if they were perpetuated by Quinn.

Quinn, Pearl, and Fedderman had always been in one of those thorny relationships where they regularly inflicted minor pain on each other. When things went too far, Quinn usually played the role of peacekeeper. He didn't mind. The verbal jousting between Pearl and Fedderman kept them sharp and contributed to their efficiency. The funny thing was, since Vitali and Mishkin had joined the team, they'd fallen into the same kind of verbal bickering with the others, but not so much with each other. As they had in the NYPD, they acted as a team, with Vitali sometimes protective of the sensitive Mishkin. Whatever acidic chemistry existed at Quinn and Associates, it worked. It seethed and bubbled sometimes, but it worked.

Quinn glanced over at Pearl. She was intently tracing her computer's mouse over its pad, staring at the monitor almost in a trance. A new day. Time to get busy. Morning, murder, and marching orders from Quinn. Another day on the hunt. Despite the fact that she and Quinn were once contentious lovers, Pearl responded exactly like the others.

Argumentative though she might be, in ways that were essential, she could become an efficient, integral part of an investigative team, responding to orders instantly and without question. Pearl could be counted on.

The door opened and Larry Fedderman came shambling in. There were spots and crumbs all over his dark tie, and he was gripping a grease-stained white paper sack.

"I got us some doughnuts," he said.

Pearl glared at him. "Take your doughnuts and—"

Quinn stepped in front of her and showed her the palm of his hand, like a traffic cop signaling stop. She did stop, in midsentence.

Quinn walked over to where Fedderman stood by the door. Fedderman, looking bemused, clutching his perpetually wrinkled brown suit coat wadded in his right hand. There were crescents of perspiration stains beneath his arms.

"Let's go, Feds," Quinn said. "We're gonna drive over to where Millie Graff was killed, find out if any of her neighbors remembered anything important, now that they've slept on it."

As he was hustled toward the door, Fedderman tossed the white paper sack. "The doughnuts are right here on my desk. Anybody can help themselves."

The sound of the car doors slamming on Quinn's big Lincoln filtered in from outside. He left the Renz-supplied unmarked Ford for Vitali and Mishkin to use when they had enough Philip Wharkins to interview.

With Quinn and Fedderman gone, the office seemed suddenly and unnaturally hushed, as if there were no air in it to sustain sound.

Pearl, Vitali, and Mishkin looked at each other.

Pearl made sure her computer was still signing on, then got up from behind her desk and walked over to Fedderman's. She rummaged delicately through the grease-stained white bag and found a chocolate-iced doughnut with cream filling.

She carried the bag over and placed it where Vitali and Mishkin could reach it, along with their cache of doughnuts.

Time for teamwork.

And time to wonder if, this time, teamwork would be enough.

7

Quinn and Fedderman split up. Quinn knocked on the door of the apartment adjoining Millie Graff's, while Fedderman went upstairs. Millie's apartment was a corner unit, so there was no one on the other side of her. The apartment directly beneath her was vacant.

The woman who lived next to Millie was in her sixties, dressed as if she were young and living *in* the sixties. She had on faded jeans with the knees fashionably ripped, a red, blue, and green tie-dyed T-shirt, and rings of every kind on every finger. No makeup. No shoes, either. Her thinning gray hair was straight and hung almost to her waist. Her toenails were painted white with intricate red designs on each one. Quinn considered giving her the peace sign and then decided against it.

He explained why he was there and then double-checked his notes. "Margaret Freeman, is it?"

"My friends call me Free," she said, with a Mary Travers kind of smile.

"Okay, Free," Quinn said, thinking, *Oh, wow*.

She stood aside so he could enter, and he was surprised. The apartment was furnished traditionally, even with a sofa and chairs that matched. The floor was polished wood, with woven throw rugs scattered about. A flat-screen TV reposed placidly in a corner like a god. No beaded room dividers, no rock-star posters, no whiff of incense, no sign or sound of high-tech stereo equipment.

She motioned for Quinn to sit on the sofa, which he did. Free asked him if he'd like anything to drink, and he declined. She settled across from him in one of the matching gray chairs. "I've already talked—"

"Yes," Quinn said. "I read your statement."

"Then you know I use my largest bedroom for an office, so Millie's bedroom is right on the other side of the wall."

She sat back and knitted her fingers over one bare knee, as if waiting for him to ask questions.

"Why don't you tell me what, if anything, you saw or heard?"

Free drew a deep breath. Her breasts were surprisingly bulky beneath her kaleidoscope shirt. "Around ten o'clock, when I was working late, I came in here to lock up and thought I heard someone knocking on Millie's door. Then I heard male and female voices, like when she answered the door and they talked, and then nothing. It seemed to me she let in whoever it was."

"Why would you assume that?"

"I would have heard him walking away in the hall if she hadn't let him in. That's just the way this building is."

"Did it sound as if they were arguing?" Quinn asked.

"No, nothing like that. I went back to my office but didn't go back to work. Instead I stretched out in my recliner to read. I wasn't too surprised to hear the same voices, at lower volume, coming from her bedroom on the other side of the wall."

Quinn wondered if she'd stayed in the office hoping to overhear pillow talk.

"Still friendly voices?" he asked.

"I really couldn't say, they were so faint." She looked off and up to the right, the way people do when they're trying to remember. "I sat there reading my Sara Paretsky novel, only halfway aware of the voices, and after about twenty minutes I heard something I recalled *after* I gave my original statement to the police."

Quinn looked up sharply and felt his blood quicken. But probably this would be something inane and of no help at all. They weren't in a mystery novel.

Free reined in her gaze to include Quinn. "There were no voices, and no other sounds for about twenty minutes. No— more than that. Then, just past ten-thirty, the man said something loud enough that I heard. His voice seemed raised, but not necessarily because he was mad. More like he was trying to make a point. It wasn't until this morning that I went over again in my mind what I'd heard and it became intelligible."

"And what did he say?" Quinn asked, realizing Free was drawing this out for dramatic effect.

"He said quite clearly, now that I recall it vividly: 'You deserve it.' "

"But he didn't seem angry?"

"No, not even upset. It was as if Millie had asked a question and he was answering her."

Quinn knew Millie would have had to ask the question with her eyes. The wadded panties would have been in her mouth.

"And then?" he asked.

Free shrugged. "No more voices. No sound of any kind. I carried my book into my bedroom and went to bed and read myself to sleep."

"You weren't curious or concerned about what you'd heard?"

"Not at the time. Like I said, the man didn't seem angry. He might even have been telling Millie she deserved something good that had happened to her."

Quinn doubted that.

"Can you show me your office?"

"Of course." Free unwove her meshed fingers from her knee and stood up. Quinn followed her down a short hall and into a room about ten by twelve. The word *organized* sprang to mind. A computer was set up on a wooden stand. Broad wooden shelves supported a printer/copier/fax machine, and neat stacks of books and magazines. Most of the books were mysteries, and some were on forensics and blood analysis. Several were on firearms. On a wall was a framed paper target with six bullet holes clustered around the bull's-eye.

"That's my score from the police target range out on Rodman's Neck."

"You're a gun enthusiast?" Quinn asked, somewhat surprised.

"I'm a gun writer and editor of *Firearms Today* magazine and blog. I've given expert testimony in court."

Quinn didn't know quite what to say, and it showed.

"That's okay," Free said. "It often takes people a while to process that."

Quinn grinned. "Yeah. To be honest, I was more prepared to see a gun with a violet sticking out of the barrel."

"Oh, that's not a bad idea, either," Free said.

"Are you the renowned sixties liberal who got mugged?"

"No, I grew up on a farm in Iowa. My dad hunted and plinked and got me interested in guns when I was a kid. I stayed interested. Simple as that."

Quinn walked over and laid his hand on the back of a leather recliner set precisely in a corner. "Is this where you were when you heard the voices between ten and ten-forty-five?"

Free nodded.

He glanced at the apartments' common wall. There was a small louvered vent near the baseboard, painted the same light beige as the wall.

"Were you picking up sound through that vent?" he asked.

"Mostly."

Quinn gave a final glance around.

"Anything else you recall?" he asked. "Sometimes talking about one thing triggers another."

"I'm afraid not this time."

Quinn wandered back into the living room and Free followed. He thanked her for her time.

At the door, he paused and turned. "You're sure of his words."

"Yes. 'You deserve it.'"

"Anything else?" he asked again. You never knew.

Free smiled. "Wanna share a joint?"

Quinn's face gave him away. She had him.

"Just kidding," she said.

"I knew that."

"Yeah, you did. But I was just thinking how I know a lot about guns, and somebody gets murdered next door with a knife."

"Funny world," Quinn said.

"Not so funny."

"You just offered a cop a joint."

"Nobody laughed."

"Peace," Quinn said.

As Quinn waited for Fedderman to meet him down in the building's vestibule, he thought that if they needed to talk to Free again, he'd send Pearl.

8

Quinn, Pearl, and Fedderman were in the office later that day when the door opened and an emaciated-looking man in his forties burst in and stood swaying. He was average height and dressed in dirty gray pinstripe suit pants and a jacket that almost matched them. His white shirt was yellowed, his tie loosely knotted and layered with stains. His shoes were scuffed and one of them was untied. He made Fedderman look like a clotheshorse.

The man steadied himself by resting one dirty hand against the wall and said, "Quinn." His gaze roamed red-eyed around the room.

"You're drunk," Pearl said. "Get the hell out of here."

"I'm drunk, asshole, but I'm not going nowhere till I find Quinn."

"I'm here and I'm found," Quinn said. He stood up and moved around his desk, peering at the man. From the corner of his eye he saw Fedderman also stand, in case the obviously inebriated visitor started trouble.

"I'll asshole you," Pearl said, and came up out of her chair.

Quinn raised a hand and she stopped. Something was going on here beyond a drunk finding his way through an unlocked door.

The man removed his hand from the wall, leaving a dark smudge, and stood almost humbly before Quinn.

"I know you," Quinn said. "Jerry Lido." He saw again the young, uniformed cop standing frozen by fear against a brick wall, watching a child burn.

"I didn't wanna come here at first," Lido said. "Wasn't sure what was gonna happen. Were you gonna listen to me or beat the shit outta me?"

"I'll listen," Quinn said. He wasn't sure how to feel about Lido. He abhorred what the man had done—rather *not* done. On the other hand, how could he not feel sorry for him? Quinn had suffered debilitating guilt because he hadn't at first seen the infant in the car seat. What had guilt done to Lido?

"I don't feel like I deserve a chance," Lido said, "but here I am anyway."

"Why?"

For a few seconds Lido looked as if he was wondering that, too. "You mighta heard I got interested in computers, got good at using one."

"I heard you were a genius at using one, sometimes illegally, but you were too smart to get caught."

Lido chanced a rueful smile. "Too smart to admit it, too."

"Okay," Quinn said. "So why did you look me up?"

"I saw in the paper what happened to Millie Graff," Lido said. He writhed slowly as he spoke, as if suffering great internal pain. "Wanted to do something about it, so I read all about the case in the news. Then talked to some guys I know who are still in the NYPD. Then I set to work with my computer. You're looking at a man who don't have shit, Quinn— except for my tech equipment. I spent every dime I begged or borrowed on that, and I can work it like I'm conducting an orchestra. You wouldn't believe—"

"Let's get to the point, Jerry."

Lido moved farther into the office and was standing near

Pearl's desk. "I worked the Net, learned something about Philip Wharkin. You gotta—" As he spoke he gesticulated with his left arm and knocked Pearl's empty coffee mug off her desk. It bounced loudly on the floor but didn't break.

"Clumsy alky!" Pearl said, her temper flaring. She stood and reached over her desk, shoving Lido backward.

Lido knocked her hand away. "Don't you ever goddamn touch me, you pussy cop!"

Pearl was around the desk, after Lido. He used his arm to sweep everything from her desktop onto the floor; then he snarled and went at her.

Pearl didn't back up. Lido swung at her and missed. Pearl started to punch back, but Quinn had both her arms pinned to the side within a few seconds. Fedderman grabbed Lido by his belt and shirt collar and yanked him back so he and Pearl were out of punching range.

"Calm down now, damn it!" Quinn shouted. He spun Pearl to face away from Lido, staying between them. "You calm?" he whispered in her ear.

"Don't I seem calm?" She was actually vibrating in his grasp.

He walked her over and forcibly sat her back down in her desk chair. Then he looked over and saw Lido curled in the fetal position on the floor.

Fedderman, standing over him, shook his head. "He ran out of gas in a hurry." He looked over at Pearl. "You okay?"

"She's got it together now," Quinn said, hoping saying it would make it true.

"Who's gonna pick up all that shit he knocked on the floor?" Pearl asked.

"I am," Fedderman said, and began doing just that.

His actions did more than anything to cool Pearl's temper. She breathed in and out deeply.

Lido was sitting up now but stayed on the floor, his arms folded across his chest as if he were freezing. "I'm sorry.

Jesus, I'm sorry." He crawled over and started helping Fedderman. Found Pearl's initialed coffee mug and placed it carefully on her desk. "You gotta forgive me!"

"I don't gotta do shit," Pearl said.

"Jerry, stand up," Quinn said, figuring a first-name basis might be a mitigating factor here. He went over and helped Lido to his feet. Lido felt as if he weighed about ninety-eight pounds. Quinn led him over and plopped him down in one of the client chairs.

"What is it you've got to say, Jerry?"

"I wanna help you on this case. I've gotta do that, for my own self-respect. I need enough of it so I can at least shave once in a while without wanting to cut my throat." He looked ready to cry, dabbing at his eyes with a dirty knuckle. "I'll work mostly on my own, but I could at least drop by here now and then and report what I find out. And you can tell me what you need to know and I can find it. I can go places on the Internet you wouldn't believe. Databases you never heard of 'cause they're top secret."

"Illegal places?" Fedderman asked.

"Don't make me walk some fine goddamn line," Lido said. "All I wanna do is help. I'll just drop by here now and then. Report in. What's it gonna hurt?"

Quinn looked at the mess on the floor that Fedderman was still picking up, the mess on Pearl's desk, the furious glint in Pearl's dark eyes, the smudged wall where Lido had leaned.

"Nothing, I guess, Jerry," he said.

Pearl said, "Jesus!" under her breath.

"What were you about to tell us, Jerry?" Quinn asked.

"This guy whose name was written on the mirror, Philip Wharkin. I fed his name in everywhere I could."

"The bloody name on the mirror never appeared in the press."

Lido waved an arm. "I told you, I got connections in the department. Other places."

"Illegal Internet connections?"

"It don't matter. Anyway, you know where Wharkin's name came up? On an exclusive members list for Socrates's Cavern in the sixties." Lido raised his voice, as well as the level of the alcohol fumes he exhaled. "You remember what that place was, Quinn. A sort of high-class S and M club where kinky business types went to let their hair and whatever else down. I checked the other Philip Wharkin. It's not a common name. One's in his eighties living in Queens. Another one's a nine-year-old black kid goin' to school in the Bronx. Then there's our guy, used to be a Wall Streeter, sold bonds for Brent and Malone—they're outta business now. Our Wharkin retired in nineteen-eighty, and died of a heart attack in Toms River, New Jersey, in nineteen-eighty-two."

Quinn thought over what Lido had said. It wasn't much, but it could easily be checked and might save some legwork. And Lido was desperate to help solve this murder. Quinn could understand that part.

"I'm not sure how this helps us, Jerry."

"You know how, Quinn. It's a piece of the puzzle. It introduces S and M into the case. It's a goddamned lead!"

"He's right," Fedderman said. "And there's the letter *S* on the victim's neck chain. Could stand for Socrates."

"I'm with Feds," Pearl said. She picked up a paper clip and threw it at Lido as hard as she could. He flinched as he might before incoming artillery fire.

"Okay, Jerry," Quinn said. "You're on. And you get paid."

"I don't want any pay," Lido said. "Not now. Not yet, anyway."

"Don't play the martyr, Jerry."

"I'm not playing, Quinn. You gotta know that."

"Yeah, I do."

"I'll learn more for you," Lido said. He struggled up out of his chair, almost tipping it over. "I'll be back. Report in."

"Do that, Jerry," Quinn said. "We'll set you up with a case file so you have more to work with."

Lido sniffled and wiped his nose. "That'd be great. I thank you, all of you. I really do."

He stumbled toward the door, bracing himself against the wall again, leaving more smudge marks, brushing a framed photo of the New York skyline and knocking every building crooked. He managed to open the door and half fell through it, and somehow closed it behind him.

The three detectives stared after him.

"There goes a walking powder keg," Fedderman said.

"Too bad we don't have an umbrella stand," Pearl said. "He could have knocked that over, too."

"So what was Socrates's Cavern?" Pearl asked.

"It was on the West Side," Fedderman said. "All voluntary, or so they said. Bad girls and boys in cages, bondage and discipline, flogging." He finished stirring the coffee he'd gotten, along with a fresh cup for Pearl, and laid the spoon on a napkin alongside the brewer. "Some weird shit went on there, games for consenting adults. Even more than that, was the rumor. Believe the whispers and they were into some heavy action."

"You talk like you were there," Pearl said.

"I was. Not long before the place closed in the seventies. An assault call. But when we got there we couldn't find a victim. Well, I mean about half the people we talked to were victims. A good percentage of them wanted to be handcuffed and taken in just for the experience. I had a young partner, DeLancy. He asked some dominatrix dolled up in black leather what a golden shower was. They started having fun with him, and he didn't seem to mind. We left without arresting anybody."

Pearl leaned back in her chair, away from her computer that by some miracle Lido hadn't knocked off the desk. "So what did you think, Feds? I mean, you think the sex devil was at work there big-time?"

"My sense of the thing is that the same behavior that was going on there is still going on, only then it was more . . ."

"More intellectual," Quinn said. "That gave it an air of semi-respectability and upper-class clientele."

"Like the Playboy Clubs?" Pearl asked.

"Like the Playboy Clubs with handcuffs and whips," Quinn said.

"Is it possible our killer just happens to be named Philip Wharkin?"

"And just happened to write his name in blood on the bathroom mirror?" Fedderman asked.

"More likely," Quinn said, "he's somebody who knows who Philip Wharkin was and is using the name. Fashioning himself after Wharkin, maybe as a way to rationalize his crimes."

"Maybe there's a new, modern version of Socrates's Cavern," Fedderman said, "and we're just now learning about it."

"Or that's what he wants us to think," Pearl said.

"I'm halfway there," Fedderman said, "thinking that's what it is."

"Wishful thinking," Pearl said scornfully. "And not with the part of you where you wear your hat."

Fedderman ignored her. "I remember when we raided Socrates's Cavern. There were women there leading men around on leashes."

"DeLancy," Quinn said.

"Yeah. My old partner. Freddy DeLancy."

"As I remember, he got tangled up with a woman from

Socrates's Cavern. Broke enough regulations they had to make up new ones to cover what he was doing. He left the NYPD and moved out to California."

"Became a nudist," Fedderman said. "The club must have influenced him."

"That's not really the same thing," Pearl said. "Socrates's Cavern and a nudist colony."

"Oh, DeLancy didn't belong to any kinda colony. He was what you'd call a lone nudist, and in public places where it wasn't a good idea. Like on buses."

"Back to the point," Pearl said, "we've got what might be a modern version of Socrates's Cavern, or we got a nut operating on his own who knows about the club and is imitating it."

"Or he's not so nuts and wants us to think there's a new Socrates's Cavern," Quinn said.

Fedderman said, "I'm thinking there is a new one."

"You're hoping," Pearl said.

"So what if I am? Detective work can be interesting sometimes, right?"

"You're easily led."

"Me and DeLancy," Fedderman said.

Pearl said. "I don't like to think about it. Or maybe I do."

9

Nora Noon stood near her booth inside the brick school building on the West Side, where the weekly flea market was held. It was warm and drizzling beyond the door at the end of the long corridor, slightly cooler but dry inside the school.

The rain was bad for the market in general, where most of the antique and specialty booths were lined up out in the schoolyard. But for Nora it wasn't bad at all. The small woman with the big, good-looking guy had strolled past her booth three times, the woman eyeing a one-of-a-kind cotton wrap designed and created by Nora. She knew what the woman was thinking: She and Nora were about the same size, and both of them quite shapely, so if Nora sewed something that looked good on her, Nora, it would look good on most women Nora's size and build.

The woman and the good-looking guy slowed and approached the booth. The guy gave Nora the up-and-down glance she knew so well, but she didn't mind. Hell, she was used to it and kind of liked it, now that she was pushing thirty. A silent compliment.

Standing at Nora's display of light coats, the good-looking guy kept his distance while the small woman reached out and stroked a light gray cashmere and cotton creation with a matching sash and scarf that doubled as a collar. She was quite pretty up close, with blond hair and dark roots, like Nora's hair, and almost startlingly beautiful dark eyes, unlike Nora's blue eyes. The woman fondled the label.

"This is you?" she asked. " 'Nora N.?' "

Nora smiled and nodded.

"You have a shop?" the good-looking guy asked, having moved a few steps closer. He was broad-shouldered and had a neatly trimmed gray beard.

"I have places where I display," Nora said. "Sometimes I'm my own model."

The good-looking guy smiled. He was something for as old as he must be. His wife, or whatever she was, looked twenty years younger.

"I work in a space near where I live in the Village, and I sell at places like this and over the Internet. Everything is one of a kind, and I design for real people, not six-foot, one-hundred-twenty-pound models."

"With eating disorders," the good-looking guy said.

Nora smiled. "Sometimes."

"I sure like this," the small woman with the dark eyes said, slipping into the coat. And she should, Nora thought. It looked great on her.

"Made for you," Nora said, "even though we haven't met until today."

They played out the familiar scene then, the small woman being reassured by Nora and the good-looking guy that yes, she looked terrific in the coat.

And you do look great, Nora thought. It would be a pleasure to sell to this woman. She thought back over the work that went into the coat's design, and then the hours getting the cut and stitching just right. She knew the woman was going to buy the coat. Right now, Nora felt so good about what she was doing. She was in the right business and would make a major go of it. Someday the Nora N. brand would sell to the major buyers, be in the finest stores. No doubt about it, if she just kept working. And she would keep working; she was getting better and better at the design end of the business, and developing an accurate sense of what would sell.

"How much is it?" the good-looking guy asked. He asked it like a man ready to be generous to his lady.

"Three hundred dollars," Nora said.

The shapely dark-eyed woman, looking sexy as hell in the soon-to-be hers coat, gave him a look calculated to melt. The good-looking guy shook his head and smiled in a way that made Nora like him. "Okay by me, if it's what you want."

That was it. The guy had too much class to try to talk her down; he knew the coat was a bargain at three hundred.

Nora gave him a smile. *You've got faith in the Nora N. brand, too.*

The good-looking guy paid with Visa, and Nora watched the happy couple walk away, the small, shapely woman clutching the coat in its plastic bag tight to her side.

It might be raining outside, but Nora was inside where the sun was shining.

By the time the antique and flea market closed, the rain had stopped. Mark Drucker, who sold furniture he repaired and refinished at the flea market, used his dented white panel truck to drive Nora and her merchandise to where she rented space in a former produce warehouse near her Village apartment. When they were finished unloading clothing, they used part of the day's proceeds to buy a pizza at K'Noodles and then parted. Drucker drove back to Chelsea, where he lived alone, as Nora did, and Nora sat for a while and sipped a second Diet Coke.

She watched people passing on the other side of the window, the men, mostly. Nora thought about Mark Drucker and the good-looking guy. She knew Drucker, though not a matinee idol, was a quality man, and she could sense the same gentleness in the good-looking guy. *Men aren't all bad*, she thought, *even though they're all men*.

Nora thought about her father, and her brother Tenn, before Tenn was killed in that auto accident. The car that rammed into Tenn's had been stolen and driven by a black man who'd had too much to drink.

A black man.

Maybe that had been part of the problem, the man's color. Nora had many black friends. It was wrong to see them all in a different way because of what had happened. It had nothing to do with political correctness. Racism simply didn't make sense. It wasn't logical and belonged in the last century. She wasn't a racist. She knew she wasn't.

Or maybe she was. It would explain a few things.

She suddenly didn't feel as optimistic as she had a few minutes ago, before Mark had left the restaurant and driven away in his rattletrap panel truck.

Nora moved her glass aside on the tiny table and stopped staring out the window at the people who were not like her, who did not have her kind of problem. Instead she rested her head in her hands and closed her eyes, almost but not quite crying. She was sure she wouldn't cry. That, at least, was one thing she could control.

I really screwed up!

I was so sure.

My God, how could it have happened?

Whether she understood it or not, it *had* happened. And there was nothing Nora could do to change the past. Nothing she could somehow alter to escape what she'd done.

The past was like a goddamned trap.

If only it all happened some other time, before Tenn was killed . . .

She pulled her hands away from her face and stared at the glistening wetness of her palms.

Those are tears.

I am *crying.*

I really screwed up.

Will I ever stop paying the price?

10

Pearl and Fedderman searched everywhere in Millie Graff's apartment for pornographic material or other evidence that she was involved in a deviant lifestyle. Quinn had instructed them not to tell Harley Renz what they were doing, or why, unless they found something. There was no point in unnecessarily stirring up Harley.

Except for the aftermath of murder, the apartment was neat. Millie had been a tidy housekeeper. The sink held no dirty dishes. The small, stacked washer-dryer combination in the bathroom held no wadded clothes. The furniture was arranged with symmetrical precision. On the kitchen window-sill was a ceramic planter with bright red geraniums that appeared healthy even without recent care. Pearl thought briefly about watering them, then decided that wasn't the thing to do at a crime scene.

"Something . . ." Fedderman said, holding up rumpled black net panty hose. "Sexy, I'd say."

"Remember Millie was more than just a hostess in a hot new restaurant," Pearl said. "She was also a dancer. We need to keep that in mind. Look in her closet and you'll find high-heeled shoes that look like implements of torture, maybe with steel taps on them."

Maybe they *were* instruments of torture. Quinn hadn't known Millie at all as a grown woman.

"Here's some kind of tight elastic thing," Fedderman said.

"A leotard," Pearl said. "Also worn to shuffle off to Buffalo." She had a feeling she should be the one searching through Millie's dresser.

"Buffalo?"

"Keep looking."

"Whoa!" Fedderman said, after a few minutes. "How about this?" He sounded like a kid who'd found a trinket in a treasure hunt.

He was holding up a vibrator dildo. He'd found it in a padded brown envelope taped to the back of a dresser drawer, a favorite hiding place of many an amateur. In addition to being blue and having buttons at its base, the vibrator wasn't at all lifelike but had ridges in it and a small protuberance near the bottom, obviously meant for clitoral stimulation. Obviously to Pearl, anyway.

"This what I think it is?" Fedderman asked, grasping the object between finger and thumb and handing it over to Pearl.

"It's not to let you know your table's ready," Pearl said.

"So Millie had her fun."

"Yeah, like millions of other women in New York."

"Pearl . . . ?"

"Don't ask," Pearl said.

Fedderman wisely took her advice. He put his hands on his hips and looked around. "We've tossed the place pretty thoroughly." He knew *tossed* wasn't quite the word; they'd be leaving the apartment almost exactly as they'd found it. As if Millie Graff might do an inspection and approve of their work. "So we searched everywhere and this is all we came up with, this— It kinda looks like some weird electrical bird with a long neck."

"Millie was what cable TV would call normal," Pearl said.

Pointing to the vibrator, Fedderman said. "Quinn isn't gonna like that we found it."

"Let's put it back where we got it," Pearl said. "Quinn won't be shocked to know about it. Hell, it isn't whips or chains. It's a woman's private accessory."

"When I think accessory," Fedderman said, "I think purse or maybe scarf."

"Right now," Pearl said, "I'm thinking testicle clamp."

Fedderman winced and then motioned with his head toward the vibrator. "One thing we oughta know about that . . ."

"Yeah," Pearl said, and pressed one of the buttons. The vibrator began to quiver and jumped so violently she almost dropped it. At the same time, it flickered with a dazzling blue light.

"That's really something," Fedderman said in admiration. "I mean, how the hell can we fellas compete with that?"

Pearl switched off the vibrator and handed it to him. "We found out what we wanted to know. The batteries are up and the . . . accessory is in good working condition. Now put the damned thing back where you found it."

"There's no writing of any kind on the envelope it was in," Fedderman said. "So it wasn't mailed to her."

"Not in that envelope, anyway. That one is probably just for storage."

"It might help if we knew where she bought it."

"I imagine the first thing she did when she got it was remove the price tag," Pearl said.

"Or instructions," Fedderman said. He brightened. "Maybe I should look for instructions."

"Put the goddamned thing back," Pearl said. "We'll tell Quinn about it, and tell him we didn't find any handcuffs or leather restraints or masks or what have you. Millie was a good girl. Let's let her stay that way."

"You know a lot about this stuff, Pearl."

"I spent a lot of time with Vice."

"Well, all of us—"

"It's time to get out of here, Feds."

He silently agreed. Pearl watched as he replaced the vibrator in its padded envelope. He slid the dresser drawer back onto its tracks and made sure it was closed all the way. They took a long last look around the apartment. Both of them could feel the strange silence and sadness that lingered at scenes of violent death.

They left the apartment, with its neatness and geometric arrangement of Millie Graff's life, for the landlord and movers to disassemble. Soon every memory or touch of her personality would be gone. Her refrigerator would contain different brands of food. Someone else would be sleeping in her bedroom, soaking in her bath, hurrying to answer the buzz of her intercom. She would be totally gone from the still point and center of her existence. Her home would belong to another.

Pearl thought that if Millie Graff could somehow know about it she'd be horrified.

Quinn rang the bell of the rehabbed brownstone not far from where he lived on the Upper West Side and waited. An intercom crackled and a male voice asked who was at the door. Quinn found the talk button and identified himself.

The same crackly voice told him to come in, and a raspy buzzer sounded. He opened the heavy door with its built-in iron grille and stepped into a small, carpeted vestibule that smelled faintly of cat urine.

A door beside him opened, and a small, stooped man with a wild sprout of curly gray hair stared out at him. Quinn immediately thought of Albert Einstein, but he said, "William Turner?"

"Bill will be fine," the man told him in a high, phlegmy voice. "You said you were a detective?"

"Yes. Name's Quinn."

Watery blue eyes brightened. "Ah, the renowned serial-killer hunter."

"I'm flattered," Quinn said.

"I admire your work. Your entire career, in fact." The hallway's odor—cat urine—seemed to waft also from the man's clothing. "You see, I'm kind of a cop groupie. I've always admired the police." He emitted a high, peculiar laugh. If birds could laugh, this was how they'd sound. "Listen, I had a good working relationship with the police in my day." Suddenly, as if on a whim, he moved back and motioned for Quinn to step inside. "I won't ask for identification," he said. "I know you from your many newspaper photographs."

"You keep a scrapbook?"

The high laugh again, not quite a giggle. "No, I don't go that far in my idolatry."

Quinn stepped into what could only be called a parlor, and suddenly it was 1885, about the time the brownstone was built. And the year when Quinnn's own brownstone was constructed. The ceilings were at least twelve feet high, with intricate crown molding. Long red velvet drapes puddled on the patterned hardwood floor. The walls were a soft cream color, and a large brick and tile fireplace was flanked by floor-to-ceiling shelves full of ceramic pottery.

"I collect the stuff," Turner said, observing Quinn's interest. "Nineteenth-century American."

"Impressive," Quinn said. He noticed that Turner's clothes were expensive but threadbare, and one of his shirt buttons was missing. Around his scrawny neck was a red paisley ascot.

"Sit down, please," Turner said. He motioned toward a flowered beige sofa with wooden inserts in its upholstered arms.

Quinn sat and looked around again. "Nice place. I've got an old brownstone myself, trying to bring it back."

"Great ladies, worth preserving," Turner said.

Quinn's gaze fell on an antique Victrola record player with a crank and louvered mahogany doors. "You collect old records, too?"

"Not really. Mostly furniture, when I'm not buying pottery. That's what the Victrola is to me—quality antique furniture, wood with a patina you can't find on anything new. But she still plays." Turner did a little old man's shuffle in leather moccasins, as if dancing to the musical strains of the Victrola. Quinn saw that the moccasins were actually house slippers with fleece linings. "Would you like something to drink?"

"Nope," Quinn said, "just some answers."

Turner smiled with yellowed teeth, but his eyes grew brighter. Not Einstein, maybe, but there was an active intelligence behind those eyes.

"Back in the sixties and seventies, you managed Socrates's Cavern on the West Side," Quinn said.

"Sure did. I was manager and part owner." Turner sat down on the edge of a brown wing chair that looked as if it might engulf him if he leaned back. "Listen, the kind of business we were in, I saw a lot of the cops. But we never stepped over the line. Nothing illegal. Consenting adults only. That was something we diligently checked."

"Ever see any of your old friends from those days?"

"Naw. We were just in business together. Then the business kind of ran its course. *Our* business, anyway, not the S and M business." He gave a hapless shrug with narrow shoulders. "Hell, the way it is now, with the Internet and all, everything's changed." Caught in another of his sudden mood swings, he waved his arms exuberantly. "S and M's gone international!"

"Like the House of Pancakes," Quinn said. "Anything like your club still operating in the city?"

"Oh, you know how it is. Sex clubs are here and there. Always will be. But nothing as big as we were. In some ways, society was lots more open back then." He squinted at Quinn. "You look old enough to remember."

"I do remember. Especially that place over on East Fifty-ninth that was doing snuff films."

Turner raised both hands palms out. "None of that in my end of the business. Not for real, anyway." He shook his head in disgust. "Jesus!" He sat even farther out on the chair's large cushion so that it looked as if it might flip up and hit him in the back. "Listen, most of this stuff is with, for, and about grown-ups. You follow me? Alternative lifestyles. We Americans like to exercise our freedom to pursue happiness however we want. Long as we don't get in the way of somebody else's parade and there's no kids or animals involved. Free country, thank God!"

"Amen," Quinn said.

Turner stared at him to see if he might be joking and seemed to decide he wasn't.

"I'm here to investigate a murder," Quinn said, "not find out who was whacking who on the ass in your club back when people were wearing Mao jackets."

"Yet you ask me about the club."

"Yet I do. The name Philip Wharkin mean anything to you?"

"No . . . can't say it does."

"He was a registered member of Socrates's Cavern."

"So were lots of people. Folks you'd never imagine."

"Somebody—maybe another Philip Wharkin—wrote his name in blood on the bathroom mirror in Millie Graff's apartment after he killed her."

"You don't say? I never read that in the paper."

"It hasn't been released to the press."

"Well, if you want, I'll keep mum. I was always ready to work with the cops. Hell, you'd be surprised the off-duty cops that came into the club."

"I doubt that I would," Quinn said. "But don't spread the name Philip Wharkin around. What I *would* like is for you to contact some of the old friends you told me you didn't have, and ask if they know anything about Millie Graff."

"If I can locate them, I'll sure do that. Was Millie a bad girl?"

"Straight as Central Park West, far as we can tell."

"That don't mean anything," Turner said. "People outside the S and M world don't have a clue."

"That's why I want you to ask around inside," Quinn said. "Find me a clue."

He stood up from the sofa with some difficulty, understanding why Turner didn't scoot all the way back in his chair. He gave Turner one of his cards. "Leave a message if I'm not in, okay, Bill?"

"Sure, I will. Cops and me, we were always tight. Fun was what it was all about in those days. A certain kinda fun, anyway." The frail-looking little man stood up with surprising nimbleness and escorted Quinn to the door. "Listen," he said, when Quinn's hand was on the knob. "You're on this case because of the police commissioner, right?"

"That's so."

Turner adjusted his brightly colored ascot as if it might be tightening like a noose. "I mean, he ain't gonna have my ass if he finds out I'm asking around about this Millie Graff, is he?"

"Not a chance," Quinn said. "He's very understanding." And in a lower yet harder voice: "So am I."

11

Wham! Milt Thompson hit a home run into the left-field upper deck of Busch Stadium in St. Louis and the crowd stood and roared.

So did Roy Brannigan.

Beth Brannigan watched her husband sit back down and guzzle the last of his can of beer as he watched the Cardinals–Pirates ball game on their old console TV. He was slouched on the sagging gray sofa. On the wall behind him was a huge, roughly hewn wooden crucifix that had been created with a chain saw. He'd bought it at a flea market for ten dollars. Beth had seen him pray before it for the Cardinals to win. Jokingly, he pretended, but he didn't fool her. In Roy Brannigan's mind, it wasn't the cardinals in Rome who counted. They couldn't hit a curve ball.

Beth was a sweet-looking woman with a heart-shaped face and guileless blue eyes. She had a brown fleck in one eye that gave her a kind of intense look that somehow added to her appeal. Her figure was trim and shown to advantage in a red tank top and short Levi's cutoffs. She was barefoot. Beth had once overheard a man describe her as fetching. She thought that was fitting, the way she fetched for Roy.

Roy's idea of marriage was based on the Old Testament,

and he spun it with his own interpretation. He insisted they attend church every Sunday, as they had this morning. After church they'd have a big meal at home, and Beth would clean up afterward. If the Cardinals were playing a day game, which they seemed to do most Sundays during the season, she'd make sure the kitchen was cleaned up before Roy finished smoking his after-meal cigar out on the porch. She'd have a cold beer waiting when he came back inside to watch the game. Religious though he might be, he had no qualms about Beth working on the Lord's day.

Nor did religion keep Roy from accumulating a large cache of pornography, of which he thoroughly disapproved. He fancied himself a student and critic of erotica. He would from time to time write reproachful letters to the publishers, excoriating them for publishing such filth. But he bought most of his collection by mail, and often an order form and the letter to the publisher would be posted simultaneously.

This televised contest was a night game, part of a twilight double-header to make up for a rainout earlier in the season. Beth had been busy most of the day, and they'd had snacks as well as their usual midday meal.

She was used to tending to Roy's needs. Beth didn't really mind the hard work, when he treated her well. When he was gentle with her.

Which wasn't all the time.

Her mom and dad over in Hawk Point had suspected Roy might be abusing Beth. But her dad had lung cancer, and her mother was too afraid of Roy and the bleak future to interfere other than to warn Beth not to let things go too far. They never had come right out and said what "things" were. But then, neither had Beth.

Even the impotent support of her mother and father disappeared last October when both Beth's parents were killed in an auto accident on Interstate 70. Their car had run head-on into a pickup truck speeding the wrong way. The driver of that vehicle had been killed, too. The autopsy showed he'd been legally drunk.

Beth had mourned hard and been comforted by Roy and his well-worn Bible. They'd prayed together fiercely at home, and with the tiny congregation at the Day of Heavenly Atonement Church.

And then one day Roy acted as if he'd decided she'd mourned enough. It was time to get on with life, he'd informed her, and quoted the appropriate verse in scripture.

Not about to challenge the Bible, Beth had allowed her relationship with Roy to resume its bumpy course.

The pain of grief had lessened, but the course never smoothed. It had led here, to the squalid living room of their ramshackle house and a ball game televised from St. Louis.

"You want some more beer, hon?" she asked.

There was crowd noise from the TV and he didn't hear her. He was suddenly up again from the sofa, in a fury. He hurled his empty beer can so it bounced off the screen door.

"That wasn't a foul ball!" he yelled, pointing at the TV. "That umpire's gonna burn in hell."

"All of 'em, probably," Beth said.

"Yeah."

She thought he was agreeing with her, then realized he'd meant that yeah, he wanted another beer.

"Well," she said, "we're all out."

"Man's gotta be blind not to see that wasn't a foul ball," Roy said.

"I thought all umpires *were* blind," Beth said. "Figured it was a requirement for the job."

Roy was pacing, still angry at the bad call in St. Louis. "Blind or crooked, is what they are. Doggone all of 'em!"

"God'll see they get what's comin' to 'em," Beth said. "Or the devil." At this juncture, God appeared to favor the Pittsburgh Pirates.

"Do I have to tell you?" Roy asked.

"Tell me what?"

"You say we're outta beer, so go get some more. There's money in my wallet on the dresser."

Beth was already on the way. Roy's anger at the umpires might easily be redirected toward her.

Her blue-soled rubber thongs flapping on her feet, and a ten-dollar bill tucked low in the back pocket of her Levi's cutoffs, she set off along Pick Road toward Willis's Quick Pick Market. It was about a quarter of a mile away, near the sometimes busy county road. Though it was dark and shadowy along Pick Road, she could see the combination convenience store and gas station ahead like a bright oasis of light in the night.

Pick Road was paved, but the blacktop had broken up, and Beth couldn't make out some of the cracks until she'd stubbed a toe or come close to turning an ankle. It was no place to walk with floppy thongs. She moved off the narrow road and made better time on the grassy shoulder, but it was still slow going.

In the dark woods that spread out behind the store, a man stood in the dim moonlight and watched Beth's progress. He was wearing tight jeans and a sleeveless T-shirt. A bulky man, he had long dark hair hanging lankly to below his shoulders, and a big belly that overhung his jeans.

As he watched Beth, he shook his head in wonder on his bull neck. What the hell was a piece like that, with those legs and tits, doing out wandering around by herself at night? She could be a hooker who worked the trucks that stopped at the convenience store or to gas up. That was always possible. But she didn't look like a hooker, didn't walk like one. Wasn't even carrying a purse, like almost all hookers did.

No, she didn't look like a working girl.

What she looked like was what he needed. He took a swig

of beer, watching the roll of the woman's hips, and smiled. *Nice . . .*

Then he thought, *The hell with it.* What the girl looked like was trouble.

But trouble appealed to him. That had been his problem all his life. It was almost as if he had to get himself in trouble to validate the kind of screwup he was. Trouble always tugged at him like a magnet, even though he knew in his heart that trouble was . . . trouble.

And this leggy creature in the Levi's shorts certainly represented trouble.

At least she was the kind that could be avoided. If a man wanted to avoid her.

He retreated back into the shadowed woods in case she might glance over and see him.

Wouldn't want to scare her away.

When Beth reached the store, Willis smiled at her as he always did. He was old enough to be her father, but she'd seen him glance at her in that way now and then, so she was careful around him. She acted like a lady. Didn't want any kind of negative word getting back to Roy.

"Six-pack do you?" he asked, when she plopped down a carton of cold beer on the counter.

"It'll do Roy," she said.

Willis laughed. "Won't he drink a brand comes in a carton with a handle? That's six-pack's gotta be plenty heavy, by the time you walk all the way back to the house."

"Get real, Willis. Six little beers?"

"Well, you ain't no Charles Atlas."

"Who's that?"

"Before your time," Willis said. "Unfortunately, not before mine." He rang up the six-pack of Wild Colt beer and fit it into a paper sack so it would be easier for her to carry.

Beth stuffed the change, including the coins, into a back pocket, then smiled a thanks to Willis and went out the door, carrying the beer tucked like a football beneath one arm. He could see the outline of the coins against the taut denim that covered her ass.

That religious nut Roy doesn't know what he's got, he thought, wishing he were twenty years younger.

Ten, even.

Beth hadn't gone far when she realized Willis was right—the beer *was* getting heavy. And Pick Road was just as rough to walk on going back toward the house as it had been going toward Willis's. And the weedy, rocky ground along the shoulder was just as uneven. Burrs now and then worked between her rubber thongs and the soles of her bare feet, causing her to stop and balance on one leg while she let the thong dangle and shook her foot until the burr dropped out.

But worst of all, because she was making slow time, the beer was getting warm.

Roy didn't countenance warm beer. In fact, he liked it cold enough that there were tiny flecks of ice in it.

She stopped and looked up at the moon. It was half full and tilted like a luminous boat. There should be enough light for her to take the shortcut through the woods. She might pick up a few scratches from branches, but she could reach the house twice as fast that way.

But what really made her decide to take the shortcut was that despite herself she felt a little afraid of the dark woods, and she resented that fear. She was afraid of Roy, but that was different—he was her husband. And she had to admit that the punishment he meted out was just and not applied very often. There were only so many things in life that Beth would or *could* allow herself to fear. The woods at night wasn't one of them.

She was nearing the narrow path leading into the trees, so there would soon be no turning back. That would make less sense than anything she might do.

The phrase entered her mind: *Point of no return.*

With another reassuring glance up at the moon floating in the cloudless summer sky, she entered the woods.

12

Nora Noon rode the subway to within two blocks of her apartment. All the way on the crowded train, she'd had the feeling she was being observed.

And of course she was. Any attractive woman on a packed New York subway train was the object of male attention. Bodies pressed bodies. Sometimes, when the train jerked or swayed on its tracks, supposedly accidental contact was made. Nora was used to that kind of thing.

But this was different. Or maybe she felt that way because she was tired, and because of her rapist being released from prison.

She still found herself trusting her memory and doubting the DNA evidence. DNA used in criminal trials couldn't be as foolproof as defense attorneys would have people believe. Nothing, even in science, was that certain. Maybe especially in science. Not that long ago science was telling people to avoid the night air and go to barbers to have their blood drawn when they were ill.

But everyone else accepted DNA as absolute proof, and Nora felt the weight of that, the crush of disapproval. With her wrong identification, she had caused an innocent man to spend over five years in prison. She should pay for that. *Somebody* should pay.

The train lurched. Nora slid a few inches across the plastic seat until her body met that of a man reading a folded *Times* in his lap. He didn't seem to mind. She found herself staring at the newspaper. She'd heard that perverts on the subway used newspapers to conceal their erections.

Don't be an idiot! Don't believe everything you hear. This guy's probably a clerk or accountant or editor, taking the train home to his wife and kids.

Besides, I can take care of myself.

She wasn't sure about that last part. Six weeks of karate lessons had made a difference, but not *that* much difference. And it had taught her just how strong men in general were. The smallest man could generate more strength than even a large woman. It had to do with percentage of muscle mass.

Hunters. The bastards are hunters.

Knock it off, Nora.

The train's wheels squealed on iron rails as it slowed approaching her stop. She waited for the complete stop and then the sudden backward lurch before standing up and elbowing her way toward the sliding doors and the concrete platform.

Fear slipped away as she pushed through the metal turnstile and climbed littered concrete steps to the upper world.

The evening was still bright and the sidewalks crowded with human energy.

About half the outside tables at Perfect Pizza were occupied. On impulse, she stepped through the opening in the iron fence that separated the dining area from the wide sidewalk and found a table beneath an umbrella. A waitress named Emma, whom Nora knew somewhat, immediately came toward her. They exchanged greetings, and Emma smiled the smile that could break the resolve of a professional mourner. Nora was glad she'd decided to come here.

She ordered a slice of pizza with ham and pineapple on it, and a glass of burgundy.

She sat back and let her gaze roam over the diners. What would really cheer her up was if she could spot a woman wearing a Nora N. original. It had happened once before; a woman in the neighborhood had bought a T-shirt with a sequin design and asymmetrical neck, and a month or so later here the woman had been in Perfect Pizza, flaunting Nora's creation. It could happen again, but the odds were long. Like a writer spotting someone reading his or her book.

After the pizza slice and a second glass of wine, Nora left the restaurant and walked the remaining block and a half to her apartment. She felt better now. Unafraid. The wine could do that, push lingering uneasiness away from the active part of her mind. Useful stuff, wine. She might have a glass or two tonight before bedtime.

When she reached her apartment building, she trudged up the worn stone steps with a cautious look left and right.

Nothing suspicious, she decided.

Besides me.

She reminded herself that she'd decided not to let fear do its inevitable damage. She would keep that commitment.

Nora was actually humming as she worked the three locks on her apartment door. They were all sturdy locks. Two of them set automatically when the door was closed. One of them was a dead bolt. She would feel safe on the other side of those locks.

She carefully locked herself in, then went to the kitchen and, after deciding against actually drinking another glass of wine, downed a glass of water. Walking the streets of Manhattan had made her thirsty, even after the wine she'd had at Perfect Pizza. Maybe it was the saltiness of the pizza. Whatever. She wondered how people who lived on the streets could stay hydrated.

How awful it must be to live that way. And it could happen to anyone. That possibility was why Nora worked so hard at her trade. She, like so many living in the city, felt always close to becoming one of the pathetic people she saw every day, panhandling on the sidewalks. Maybe that was why New Yorkers seemed always distracted and in a hurry; visible all around them were the consequences of living without a net.

The spare bedroom in Nora Noon's apartment was for storage. It was stuffed with clothing of her design, cloth creations draped on hangers affixed to shoulder-high steel racks that were on wheels. There was room for an aisle down the middle of the room, but sometimes Nora had to shift the overloaded rolling racks from one side to the other to reach the garment she wanted.

Tonight what she wanted was a dress that had been bothering her for days. It was this afternoon that she'd decided a higher waistline might be exactly what the design needed. Nora could alter the waist and try the dress on herself in front of the triple mirror at her studio. That was one of the advantages of Nora N. designs being for ordinary-sized women.

It was bright in the room with the overhead fixture blazing, and the air was still and stuffy. Some of the material she touched was warm from the sunbeams lancing in at the edges of the drawn shades. There was a faint odor of mothballs. Too faint, Nora decided. Most of her garments had a high wool content. Moths were the enemy.

She pushed aside two of the swaying, overloaded racks and saw the dress she wanted. Dark green with black piping. Maybe that had been a mistake, too, choosing a dark color for the piping.

She reached for the dress's hanger, and a hand appeared from between the garments on the nearest rack and reached for her.

The sounds of her struggle were muffled among the overstuffed racks of clothing. Every time she tried to escape her assailant's grip, her arms and legs would become entangled in material. She soon became swathed in the stuff. The karate lessons were useless. So were her screams, with her mouth jammed with what she knew was fifty percent cashmere.

Nora regained consciousness in her own bed. It was still futile to try to move her arms and legs. She was on her back, with her wrists bound to the headboard. Her legs were spread wide, her ankles tied to the bottom corners of the steel bed frame beneath the mattress. The rope was knotted so tightly that her hands and feet were numb. She attempted to say something but couldn't utter more than a moan. Her tongue probed and found a rough surface. Her mouth was still crammed with material, but it was smoother.

She raised her head to look around her. That was when she realized she was nude and became really afraid.

Fighting off panic, she let her head loll back. There was no pillow so she was staring up at the headboard and the surface of the wall behind it.

Moving her head had caused a tremendous pain in the back of her neck. She remembered a hand clutching her there, squeezing. A man's grip. No woman could encompass her neck so and squeeze so hard.

She let her eyes roll to the right and her gaze fell on an unfamiliar object on the nightstand by the bed. A curling iron. It wasn't hers, though. This one had a white handle and a white cord that ran from the nightstand and disappeared. She knew the cord would be run to the socket just below where the lamp was plugged in. The metal brace was flipped downward so the main shaft of the curling iron was suspended an inch above the surface of the nightstand. A tiny red light glittered on the white handle. It indicated that the curling iron was turned on.

Nora sensed or heard a movement to her left, alongside the headboard and back where she couldn't see who or what it was. She strained to see but couldn't; the pain at the base of her neck prevented her from turning her head far enough.

Her body gave an involuntary jerk. Fingertips gently caressed her perspiring cheeks and then the vulnerable area beneath her chin. They brushed a strand of hair back off her forehead.

"It's possible that your hair is going to curl," a man's voice said softly. "But the curling iron will never touch it."

13

Michelle Roper was quite beautiful, which made her one of Nora Noon's favorite clients. Michelle had dark hair and eyes, high cheekbones, and a trim and graceful figure. Though not a tall woman, she carried herself with a kind of regal bearing. Surely in her ancestry were kings and queens. With Michelle roaming around New York, wearing Nora N. creations to all the fashionable clubs, Nora had her own walking advertisement.

"I was supposed to meet with Nora at nine," Michelle was telling the super of Nora's building. "It's already nine-thirty."

"She might still show up," the super said. He was a middle-aged guy wearing a green work shirt over a bulging stomach. He didn't seem too interested in Michelle's story, though he did seem to have an eye for Michelle.

"There's no showing up involved," Michelle explained. "She sleeps here. We were going to meet at her apartment so I could look at some swatches, then go have breakfast together. She doesn't answer her phone, and her message machine is off. That's not like Nora. Maybe you can raise her. You're the super—"

"Leonard," the super said.

"What?"

"My name is Leonard." He gave her a broken-toothed smile.

"Michelle."

"Much as I'd like to help you, Michelle," Leonard said, "I got no right to enter a tenant's apartment because she don't answer her phone. You try her cell?"

"Yes. She doesn't answer that one, either." Michelle decided to use what influence she obviously had with Leonard. She put on a concerned look. "This is going to sound funny, Leonard, but I'm half Cherokee, and I have a certain sense about such things. An instinct. I just know something is wrong in that apartment." The Cherokee part was true, but that was all.

"Cherokee Native American? No kidding?" He stared closely at her. "Once you know, it's easy to see it." He gave her a shy smile. "It looks good on you."

"Nora and I are friends, Leonard. I'd know if she simply wasn't home. She doesn't answer at her workshop, either, and I've been in touch with several people she knows and they haven't seen her since yesterday." Michelle touched his arm and he almost melted. "If Nora was having some kind of medical problem in there, Leonard, you wouldn't want to be responsible for her not getting help in time, would you?"

"No . . . 'course not. But . . ."

"So how about if we step inside and call out her name, look around to make sure she isn't in there somewhere hurt and unable to get to a phone. Then we'll leave."

"What if the chain's on?"

"Then we'll call her name through the narrow door opening. If Nora doesn't answer, and we know she's inside because the chain lock is attached, we'll know there might be something seriously wrong. She might be unconscious and need medical attention." She smiled at him with perfect white teeth. "Make sense?"

"Makes sense," Leonard admitted, and reached for the bulky key ring attached to his belt.

Michelle was surprised when there was a brief clatter and the chain lock stopped the apartment door after about four inches. She and Leonard exchanged glances. Genuine worry was gaining ground.

Michelle moved near the door and called Nora's name three times. Then Leonard nudged her aside and put his face up to the space provided by the partly opened door. "Mizz Noon?" he boomed several times.

Silence.

"You got a bolt cutter?" Michelle asked.

Leonard nodded. "I'll be right back, Michelle."

He took the stairs rather than wait for the elevator, and within a few minutes returned with a long-handled bolt cutter.

The thick brass chain on Nora's door didn't stand a chance. It parted, and a severed link bounced noisily on the hardwood floor like a coin. The door swung open.

Leonard called Nora's name again as Michelle let him lead the way inside.

The window air conditioner wasn't running and the apartment was way too warm. Michelle stopped and stood still, touching Leonard's shoulder so he'd stop, too. The two of them stood there. They both smelled the peculiar odor, like something . . . maybe meat . . . had been overdone to the point of becoming charred.

Leonard moved away toward the kitchen. Underlying that smell was a sharp, ammonia scent. Michelle, maybe because she *did* sense something terrible, made herself walk slowly to the bedroom she knew Nora used for sleeping and not storage.

She stood stunned in the doorway, staring at what was on the bed.

Leonard edged up behind her and looked over her shoulder.

"Oh, God!" he said, and squatted down, his head bowed.

Michelle turned to look at him. "If you're going to puke, Leonard, try to do it out in the hall."

Taking deep breaths, he straightened up slowly, carefully not looking again into the bedroom. His face was pale and perspiring, and his features were drawn tight as if he might cry. "I'll be okay," he said.

Michelle had long ago been married to a cop. He had told her about his work. Maybe too much. Too much communication could destroy a marriage. But it could also prepare a woman for what she might see at a murder scene.

She rested a hand on Leonard's shoulder and guided him toward the door to the hall.

"We're getting out of here and then I'll use my cell to call nine-one-one," she said.

"Right," Leonard gasped, as if he were out of breath.

"Don't touch anything," she added.

"I don't need reminding," he said.

14

The woods were dark, but Beth was familiar with them. She was making good time along a scarcely defined dirt path, Roy's six-pack of beer tucked beneath her arm, when she heard a sound off to her right. She'd grown up in the country and spent time in the woods, even had camped in them as a young girl. She knew which sounds were natural and which weren't. No animal moved in such a way, brushing low branches and taking even strides through the crisp carpet of last year's dead leaves. No animal other than human.

Zombies, Beth thought, and she giggled. She'd watched an old zombie movie on TV last night, after Roy had fallen asleep. She hadn't dreamed or thought about zombies since, though, until now.

Zombies on your brain, girl.

She made herself smile and continued her pace along the dirt path.

The sound she'd heard didn't seem to move with her. The woods were silent now. More silent than they should be.

After about a dozen paces, she stopped. She knew she was approximately halfway through the stand of trees. Though there wasn't the slightest breeze, she was aware of shadows on the periphery of her vision in slight motion.

Through the shadows, where the moonlight penetrated the canopy of leaves, she saw something shining. It was dark and metallic.

Beth got a firmer grip on the cool paper sack containing the beer and slowly moved forward.

She was relieved to see, parked off the path ahead of her, a motorcycle. A dark blue or black Harley, by the look of it. Nothing supernatural. No zombies. She heard herself breathe out her relief.

Something struck her from behind and she was on the ground. She'd landed with the sack in front of her, so that the six-pack of beer rammed into her stomach and drove the breath from her. She lay curled on her side, hearing her own half gasps, able to move only to draw her legs up after the shock of being unexpectedly knocked down.

Then, realizing what was happening, she became paralyzed with fear.

She could only occasionally glimpse her attacker in the moonlight as he ripped her shorts and panties and worked them down her legs. She tried to scream but made no sound. Her lungs wouldn't work. He was laughing low in his throat, knowing she was breathless and helpless, without even the means to scream. Taking his time. Being methodical. Enjoying himself.

She got only a brief look at his face in profile, and not a clear look. He had long, stringy dark hair and a full beard. He was heavy, and strong, with a belly that hung over his jeans. His breath smelled like onions and gasoline, though she knew the gas smell had to be from the nearby Harley.

Her head was forced back so her mouth gaped open, and he placed his hand over her mouth in such a way that it stayed in front of her teeth and she couldn't bite him. Struggling not to choke, she tasted oil and grit from the man's palm and thick fingers. The edge of his palm pressed against her nostrils so she couldn't breathe.

Then the man was on her. He weighed so much more than Roy. He was crushing her. His weight lifted momentarily and he pried her bare legs apart. She tried to kick but could only wave one calf helplessly in the air. She heard one of her rubber thongs land near her left ear.

His free hand was between her legs, his fingers oily. A later examination would reveal that oil *was* used as a lubricant for the rape. Valvoline thirty-weight.

He was on her again. *In her!* Piercing deep and hard, moving back and forth inside her. He quickly built up a desperate, driving rhythm. She knew it wasn't going to last long, but it hurt so much. She had her teeth clenched and realized she was breathing again, slightly, through her nose. Because he was letting her.

This can't be happening! Not to me!

She became someone else, moving off to the side, an onlooker who, thank God, couldn't see through the darkness of the night.

She hid from what was happening. Hid in the darkness until it was finally over.

Huffing and puffing noisily, the man partially raised his weight from her. Then he patted her on her bare side, as if she'd done a good job. Was he thanking her for keeping quiet? Weren't you supposed to scream as loud as you could if you were being raped? Beth had read that somewhere or heard it on TV, but she didn't want to imagine what might happen to her if she did manage to scream.

He placed one hand on her head, and the other on her right thigh, using her to brace himself as he stood up. Suddenly his weight was off her entirely. She felt her shirt yanked up to cover her head.

She lay curled and quiet on her side, not attempting to stand.

The woods were silent.

It seemed as if forever passed.

Beth tried a scream and merely choked. Tried again.

This time she emitted a loud screech.

Then several more.

A great roar startled her and she drew her body into a ball.

Another roar. She recognized this one as a motorcycle engine.

The cycle gave two loud, abrupt snarls, as if issuing a final warning to Beth, and then roared intermittently and unsteadily as it made its way along the narrow path. Beth heard the Harley clear its throat like a triumphant beast as it broke from the woods. A few seconds later it emitted a steady yowl as it reached the state road.

Beth screamed some more, and then fell silent.

She continued to lie on her side, motionless. She didn't want to rejoin the world outside the woods anytime soon. The darkness that had been her enemy had now become her ally and protector. Time moved for her, but slowly and in a disjointed manner.

Willis, at the convenience store, heard the scream when he stepped outside to bring in his LIVE BAIT folding sign.

He was sure it wasn't an animal.

15

New York, the present

Mishkin and Vitali phoned Quinn on their way to the Nora Noon crime scene and arrived before anyone other than the two uniforms who'd taken the call in their radio car. One of the uniforms, a guy named Sorkin, had worked before with the two detectives and nodded to them. Sorkin had a long, lean face dotted with moles. His features were pale, making the moles more prominent, and he was perspiring. Vitali knew it would take a lot to bring about that kind of physical reaction in the veteran cop.

They were in the hall outside an open apartment door.

"We got a dead woman in the bedroom," the other uniform said. A black man with a small, neat mustache and sad eyes with a lot of white showing beneath the dark irises. Sorkin nodded as if to show that he agreed with his partner.

Before entering the apartment, Vitali glanced over at a graceful, astonishingly attractive woman with black hair and high cheekbones. Alongside her was her physical opposite, a sweaty, chubby guy in dark green work clothes. They were down the hall about twenty feet, pretty much out of earshot.

"Those two are the building super and a friend of the vic," Sorkin said.

"Which one's the super?" Vitali asked in his gravel-pan voice.

"Not the time to joke, Sal," Mishkin admonished him. He looked at Sorkin with his mild blue eyes. "Go on with what you were saying."

Sorkin bobbed his head. "They discovered the body when they found the chain lock on and nobody answered their knock or call. Michelle, that's the female one, had an appointment with Noon and she never showed. Michelle couldn't raise her on the phone or by knocking, so the super—he's the—"

"We know," Mishkin said.

"Well, he couldn't get in with his key because of the chain lock. Michelle told him to go get a bolt cutter, and he did."

"Who wouldn't?" Vitali growled.

"They smelled something coming from the bedroom, like what you can smell even out here."

"Not barbecue," Sorkin's partner said.

"We'll go in and have a look," Vitali said. "Hold on to Michelle and the super, figuratively speaking, so we can get their statements."

"I get Michelle," Sorkin's partner said.

Mishkin gave him a withering look.

"Everybody on the way?" Vitali asked.

It was Sorkin who answered. "Sure, we called it in. That's procedure. You know that. Crime scene unit's on the way, along with the ME, some real detectives—excuse me, Sal, but I mean, you two guys have gone private."

"Semi-private, in this case," Sal said.

"What exactly does that mean?" Sorkin asked.

"We got special powers even though we're once removed, like a divorced father on visiting day."

Sorkin seemed to think that over and find it adequate.

Mishkin removed a small tube from a pocket, squeezed a

worm of something onto the tip of his right forefinger, and smeared it into his bushy gray mustache. The eye-watering smell of menthol displaced the faint odor of scorched flesh. If he didn't supplant the various stenches of death with the overriding pungency of mentholated cream, Mishkin's stomach sometimes acted up at homicide scenes.

"Ready, Harold?" Vitali asked.

Mishkin dried his finger with a handkerchief, nodded, and they went in.

The first thing they noticed was the blood. It was all over the body. Then it became obvious that some of it wasn't blood, but the red of raw flesh showing at the edges and beneath where skin had been sliced. *Peeled flesh.* The victim appeared to have been partially skinned alive. Some of her pale skin was dangling in shreds, left attached at the top and narrowing to points at the bottom. There was more blood that had come from where skin had been broken on the victim's wrists and ankles, from her struggle against the pain.

Pain showed in every line and angle of her face, as if she still suffered even in death. Like the first victim, her eyes were fixated with horror and staring at nothing. There was a thin silver chain around her neck, bearing the letter *S*.

On the nightstand next to the bed was an electric hair curler. Sal noted that it had been switched off. He also noted the dozens of narrow rectangular burns all over the victim's nude body. Burns where they would hurt the most. *Was she burned before or after the partial skinning?* Any of the injuries would have caused the victim to lose consciousness, but there had been no relief from the pain. As with the last victim, around this one lingered the faint but sharp odor of ammonia. Vitali figured Harold might not have needed his mentholated cream this time.

"Sadistic bastard!" Harold said.

"The window's partly opened over there," Vitali said. "That's why the chain lock was on. He locked her in before going down the fire escape."

Noises behind them made them turn, figuring it was the crime scene unit, or even real detectives.

It was Quinn.

"Feds is out in the hall interviewing the super and the woman who found the body," he said. "Pearl's on the way."

Sirens began echoing through the city's stone canyons. Everyone stood and listened for a moment, and it became obvious the yowling was headed in their direction.

Of course, all that yowling didn't mean the vehicles were making good time in Manhattan traffic. Emergency vehicles could howl and yodel as if they were doing ninety while sitting perfectly still blocked in by cars.

"Bet you Pearl will beat them here," Sal said.

Quinn shook his head. "I wouldn't bet against Pearl."

He strained forward toward the corpse, noticing something, then went over and looked more closely at one of the bound and bloody ankles.

"Looks like something, probably a finger, has been dragged through this blood," he said.

They all glanced around, and then moved toward the bathroom at the same time. The other two detectives fell back in deference to Quinn and let him enter first.

There were bloodstains in the white basin and on white towels. But most of the blood was on the medicine cabinet mirror, where it had been used to write what presumably was a man's name: *Simon Luttrell*.

Quinn left the bathroom and moved through the bedroom and down a short hall to the living room. Sorkin and his partner were still there, the partner leaning in the doorway, Sorkin visible outside in the hall. Guarding the crime scene even though Harley Renz's growing and unhealthy influence had gotten Quinn and his team inside before the yellow tape went up.

Quinn nodded at the two uniforms as he went out into the hall. The sirens were right outside now, some of them growling to silence. They were going to beat Pearl here after all.

Fedderman, standing with pencil and notebook and talking to Michelle Roper, looked over at Quinn.

"Do either of you know or know of someone named Simon Luttrell?" Quinn asked.

"He don't live in the building," said the super immediately.

Michelle gave the question a few more seconds' thought. "I don't think I've ever heard of him."

Quinn nodded and said, "Come on into the apartment when you're done here, Feds."

"Just a few more questions," Fedderman said.

"You hear that a lot on TV," the super said.

Quinn edged his way around Sorkin and his partner and went back into Noon's apartment. Mishkin was standing in the living room. Vitali came in from the hall that led to the bedrooms and bathroom.

"The bedroom she's not in," Vitali said. "It's full of nothing but clothes. I mean *really* full of clothes."

"The second bedroom, you mean?" Mishkin asked.

Vitali stared at him.

"How would you know which is which, Harold?" Mishkin could be a trial sometimes. Vitali bore him like a cross.

"The second one's usually smaller. Did you check to see about size?"

"It's not supposed to matter," Vitali growled. "The thing is, that bedroom's damn near bursting open, what with all the clothes in there. Most of them are on hangers, but some are just piled on the floor. I mean, a hell of a lot of clothes."

"Maybe she was in some kinda clothes business," Mishkin ventured.

"Nothing in there looked secondhand to me, Harold."

"Maybe she was a designer," Mishkin said.

Sal smiled. "Or a master of disguise."

"Wouldn't it be *mistress* of disguise?" Mishkin asked.

"Not unless she was a dominatrix or some married guy's secret girlfriend."

"Couldn't she be both?"

Quinn knew what they were doing, cracking wise to stay sane, to scare away the ghosts. Cops had to learn to do that, if they were going to last.

He stopped listening to Vitali and Mishkin as he heard a commotion in the hall, a lot of clinking and clacking of equipment along with hurried, shuffling footfalls on the carpet. The sirens outside were fully stopped now. The troops had arrived, and in force. Sorkin and his partner moved back as if facing a tsunami to give them a clear route to the apartment.

Pearl was the first one through the door.

16

Michelle Roper had informed Quinn that Nora Noon had a sister somewhere in New Jersey. It hadn't taken long to find her, not very far away in Teaneck. Fedderman waited at the morgue the next morning for the sister, Penny Noon, who was driving in to the city to identify the body.

The victim's sister turned out to be a half sister, an attractive woman with choppy blond hair with dark streaks in it that looked deliberate. There wasn't much of a family resemblance to her murdered sister, maybe because the victim was obviously much the younger of the two. Penny had a fuller face, calm gray eyes with the beginnings of crow's-feet, and full lips with pink gloss. She did have the same deeply cleft chin as the victim. Her demeanor was tense but controlled, her strong features seemingly placid.

After the introductions, Penny, Fedderman, and a guy named Clarkson, from Renz's office, stood and waited for Nora Noon's postmortem photograph to appear on a monitor mounted at eye level on the wall. Clarkson wasn't yet forty and dressed in a sharp gray suit, starched white shirt, and gold-clasped tie, making Fedderman by comparison look . . . like Fedderman.

There were chairs angled around the viewing room, but no one was sitting down. Penny had refused the offer of a chair, and the two men felt obligated to stand with her. She was slightly behind Renz's man and standing on Fedderman's right, about a foot away from him. Fedderman recalled the victim's bulging eyes and horror-stricken expression. He knew what might happen and made himself ready to catch a falling body.

But Nora Noon's head-shot photo was surprisingly without the horror of yesterday in that stifling apartment. Her eyes were closed and her facial muscles worked into a neutral expression. The photo was cropped so it showed none of the burn marks on her neck and farther down on her body. None of the stripped flesh.

"Her," Penny Noon said from somewhere deep in her throat. And in a steadier voice: "That's Nora."

Then she emitted a soft sound halfway between a sigh and a sob, and her body sagged against Fedderman.

He caught her and helped her—carried her, actually—to one of the padded black chairs and lowered her gently into it.

She came around suddenly, as if someone had waved smelling salts under her nose. She looked into Fedderman's eyes, causing something in him to turn over and over, and appeared profoundly embarrassed.

"It's all right," he heard himself say. He watched his arm move independent of thought and his hand pat the back of hers.

He realized he was kneeling down in front of the chair like an idiot about to propose marriage. His knee was sore from supporting his weight on the hard tile floor. For some reason he was afraid to look again into her eyes, as if a part of him knew that something profound might happen. Again.

Listening to his aching knee creak, Fedderman made himself stand and turn at the same time. As he did so he glanced up, and was relieved to see a blank monitor screen rather than the dead woman's photo.

"It's all right," he repeated. "This part's over."

"For Nora, everything's over." He thought she was going to start sobbing, but she bit back any show of emotion or loss of control. "It's so goddamned unfair," she said in a resigned voice.

"It is," he agreed.

"I guess everyone says that."

"Everyone's right."

She looked around slowly, as if gradually waking from a dark dream and finding herself in strange surroundings.

"God!" she said, shaking her head.

"He's in the mix somewhere," Fedderman said, knowing as he heard the words that it was an inane thing to say.

She gave him a closer look, curious, her eyes intent and traveling in brief glances, as if she was mapping his features. He could not look away.

"Are you a religious man?" she asked.

"I have been a few times," Fedderman said, "when I was sufficiently scared."

Her wide lips curved upward in a slight smile that stayed. Her hands were in her lap, turned palms up and trembling, as if she were waiting for her fortune to be told and dreading the prognosis.

"That applies to me, too," she said.

Renz's man had come over and was standing looking down at her. "You okay, ma'am?" he asked.

"Okay enough."

He nodded, gave her a smile that meant nothing, and left the room, his mission as witness to the identification completed.

"There goes a piece of the bureaucracy," Penny said.

"I'm a piece of the bureaucracy, too."

"You don't seem a precise fit."

Fedderman didn't know what she meant by that remark, but he was sure he approved.

"I need something," Penny said.

"A drink?"

"Something warm. Coffee, decaffeinated. I think I saw a vending machine when I entered the building."

"You wouldn't want to drink anything that came out of that," Fedderman heard himself say. "I know a place where we could go."

I must be out of my mind.

She looked at him for several seconds before nodding, as if confirming what he'd been thinking.

17

Despite the early hour, Quinn and Jerry Lido sat next to each other on bar stools at O'Keefe's Oasis. They were the only ones in the place consuming alcohol. The three other drinkers, two men and a woman, were sipping coffee. Quinn had consumed only half of his mimosa—a mixture of champagne and orange juice—when he generously ordered another scotch and water for Jerry. It had been Quinn's idea to come here.

"Better ease up on those," the bartender said to Jerry, as he placed the drink on the bar.

"Not to worry, Jim," Jerry answered with a grin. "I got my desecrated driver."

Jim glanced disapprovingly at Quinn as he moved away down the bar. O'Keefe's was near Jerry's apartment, and Jerry was one of the regulars. Maybe they liked him here. Jerry wasn't a bad guy when he wasn't involved in self-flagellation.

Quinn got Jerry talking about the investigation and his computer expertise, and suggested they leave so Jerry could demonstrate something online. On the walk to Jerry's apartment, they ducked into a liquor store and bought a bottle of J&B scotch, Jerry's favorite. Quinn paid. He knew Jerry was great with his computer when he was sober. Drunk he was brilliant.

After about an hour, Quinn said good-bye and left Jerry's apartment. Deep in an alcoholic and electronic trance, concentrating on his monitor and mouse and nothing else, Jerry barely noticed.

When Quinn entered the office, Pearl looked at him pretty much as Jim the bartender had in O'Keefe's.

"You smell like booze," she said.

"I've been—"

"I can guess what you've been doing. Drinking with Jerry Lido. Where is he?"

Quinn glanced around. "Where's who?"

"Are you drunk, too?"

"Who's too?"

"*Too* would be Jerry Lido, who I'm sure is soused despite the early hour."

"No, I'm not soused. Nor am I smashed nor looped nor plastered. Jerry's on the edge, I'd say."

"You're sure right about that."

"He's working now on his computer. Maybe he'll come up with something."

"Like sclerosis of the liver."

"Don't be so rough on him, Pearl."

Pearl simply stared at Quinn. She made him *feel* drunk, though he was sure he wasn't. She could do that.

He shrugged. "I'll be working," he said. "At my desk."

"Don't try to drive it," Pearl said.

That afternoon Quinn was alone in the office when a short, stocky man wearing jeans and a gray T-shirt entered and glanced around with his head tilted back, as if orienting himself while making sure the air was safe to breathe. He walked directly to Quinn's desk. Quinn figured he was in his fifties, a fit fifties. His hair was buzz cut and his chin was thrust outward and upward. His bearing was that of a small person who'd grown up in a tough neighborhood. If his forearms were larger he would have made a great movie Popeye. He stood in front of Quinn's desk and fixed a calm blue stare on him. Up close like that, Quinn could see the road map of fine wrinkles on his face and upped his estimate of the man's age to over sixty.

"You're Quinn," the man said, in a tone that suggested insult.

Quinn thought it might be a good idea to start locking the street door and requiring people to ring to get in. "And you are?"

"A friend of Bill. You know what that means?"

Quinn nodded. It was the way members of Alcoholics Anonymous identified themselves to each other.

"Another friend of mine's also a friend of Bill. Jerry Lido."

"One of Bill's best friends, I would imagine," Quinn said, wondering now where this was going, and having some suspicions.

"I'm Jerry's sponsor in AA, Quinn. The one he goes to for help if he's having trouble, or if he's fallen off the wagon."

"Jerry's wagon travels a bumpy road," Quinn said.

"Over the last few years I've gotten fond of Jerry."

"He could use all the friends he can get."

"Not friends like you."

Quinn leaned back and held a pencil at both ends in his huge hands with surprising delicacy. "What makes you say that?"

"I went to visit Jerry and he told me what was going on. I

know what you're doing. You know an alcoholic does or learns things when he's drunk, and sometimes he can only remember them when he's drunk again."

"Sobriety's a different world," Quinn agreed.

"And you want Jerry to visit his other world so he might get in touch with certain memories."

"And capabilities. He's a genius on the computer when he's drinking," Quinn said honestly.

"You're using Jerry for your own ends. Taking advantage of him."

Has this guy been talking with Pearl?

"Jerry's involvement in this investigation might save lives," Quinn said. "He wants to help. In fact, he came here begging to help."

"And you took him up on his offer."

"He thinks he can find atonement," Quinn said.

"He searched for that in a bottle and didn't find it, and he's not going to find it by drinking with you and then going online and doing things that could land him in jail." The stocky little man appeared disgusted. "My guess is you don't even really drink with him. You probably pour your liquor into a potted plant when he isn't watching."

"That only happens in movies," Quinn said.

"Jerry's my responsibility, and I'm here to ask you not to be his enabler just so he might ferret out some information that'll help you."

"You say I'm using Jerry. Yes, I am. That's because I know it might be worth it. He knows it, too. That's why he wants to help."

"I think it's simpler than that. I think you're an obsessive bastard who'll stop at nothing."

"To find and stop a serial killer? Yeah, maybe I'm exactly that."

"Well, I'm obsessive when it comes to saving Jerry from the bottle."

"Then we're at cross-purposes. Jerry's a big boy. He wants to aid in this investigation, and we accept his offer." Quinn stood up behind his desk. "I'm afraid that's how it's going to be, at least until we nail this killer."

Seemingly without moving a muscle the little man seemed to grow several inches, though he was still looking up at Quinn. "I'm asking you man to man, politely as possible, to leave Jerry Lido alone."

"I can't do that. And it seems to me that whatever Jerry's doing is up to him."

The man swiped his bare muscular forearm across his lips, making a face, as if he'd taken a bite out of Quinn and didn't like the aftertaste.

"I can't say it's been a pleasure meeting you," he said, and spun and headed for the door.

"He can, you know," Quinn said.

The man paused and looked back.

"Can what?"

"Jerry can find atonement in what he's doing."

"While killing himself with alcohol. Anyway, it's saints that find atonement by dying. And Jerry's no saint."

"One more thing," Quinn said, as the man was opening the door.

"What's that?"

"Your name. You never told me your name."

"My name is Joe Nethers, and don't you forget it."

18

It was 2:00 A.M. when the intercom buzzer grated in the brownstone. Quinn switched on the lamp by his bed, and then struggled into his pants that were folded over the back of a chair. The buzzer sounded again as he staggered toward the intercom in the next room. He leaned on the button.

"Whoozere?"

"It's Jerry, Quinn. We gotta talk. I found—"

Quinn pushed the button that buzzed Lido in downstairs.

As Quinn moved toward the door, he heard Jerry taking the stairs up from the vestibule. Though Lido had sounded sober, there was something about his footfalls on the steps that suggested he wasn't navigating steadily.

When Quinn, a sleepy, grouchy-looking man with bloodshot eyes and wild hair, opened the door, he found himself face-to-face with another sleepy-looking man with bloodshot eyes and wild hair, only Lido was ecstatic.

Imagining the scene, all Quinn could think just then was, *Couple of booze hounds.*

"I hit some databases and found out some shit," Jerry said, pushing past Quinn and leaving a wake of alcohol fumes.

Son of a bitch smells embalmed.

"It's two o'clock, Jerry."

"You'll love this, Quinn." Jerry started to pace. Quinn wondered where he got all the damned energy. He'd had a couple of drinks with Lido at O'Keefe's last night despite Joe Nethers's implicit warning. Rather, Quinn had downed a couple of drinks. Jerry had guzzled half a dozen. So here was Quinn, exhausted and with a headache. And here was Jerry, ready to leap over the moon.

Quinn let himself fall back on the sofa, stretched out his legs, and crossed his bare ankles. "So what am I going to love?" he asked.

Jerry stopped suddenly and glanced around. "Where's Pearl?"

"Home in bed."

"I thought you two were—"

"Not exactly."

"Simon Luttrell," Lido said abruptly.

It actually took Quinn a few seconds to remember that was the name scrawled in blood on a mirror at the last murder scene. He realized he wasn't all the way awake, and possibly the alcohol he'd consumed last night still had his brain addled.

"You found Luttrell?" he asked.

"In a way. He's connected to Philip Wharkin. Just like Wharkin, he was a member of Socrates's Cavern. Gold keys, both of them."

"Gold keys?"

"Sure. You had to join to get into the place. Cost plenty, too. Members were brass, silver, and gold key holders. The golds paid the most to join. Their first drink was always free, and they could go anywhere in the club."

Lido looked around again, as if still searching for Pearl.

"Listen, Quinn . . . you got . . . ?"

"Yeah, Jerry." Quinn stood up from the sofa, trekked into the kitchen, and poured two fingers of scotch into a glass.

He returned to the living room and handed the glass to

Jerry, then slumped back on the sofa. Jerry let himself down hard in a wing chair, accidentally sloshing some of the scotch on the carpet, and took a long sip. He seemed to calm down instantly, a trick of the mind.

"Luttrell was a Madison Avenue adman. Responsible for that dancing shirts commercial that used to be all over television. He joined Socrates's Cavern in 1968, just when the club was getting going. He was a member until June of seventy-three."

Quinn couldn't remember any dancing shirts commercial. "What then?" he asked. "Luttrell let his membership expire?"

"He expired," Lido said. "In Del Rico's restaurant, used to be on Third Avenue. He choked on a piece of steak. I don't think people knew the Heimlich maneuver back then, or he might have been saved."

"No point in trying to talk to him, then," Quinn said. He stretched his body out straighter on the sofa and laced his fingers behind his head. "The names on the mirrors, the letter *S* necklaces . . . our killer continues establishing a Socrates's Cavern theme."

Lido was staring at him like a starving puppy.

"That's damned good work, Jerry. We've established a connection and we've got a definite theme. Names of former Socrates's Cavern members. Now we have to figure out what that theme means."

"Sick jerks like him always have a regular routine," Lido said. "Compulsive bastards. You know that better'n anyone."

"Maybe I do, Jerry." Quinn watched Lido down the rest of his drink. It wouldn't be easy to get a cab this time of night—morning. "How you gonna get home, Jerry? You should be in bed, if you're gonna be worth anything tomorrow."

"If you don't mind," Lido said, "you're sitting on my bed."

Quinn stood up and yawned. "I'll get you a blanket from the closet."

"Hot night," Lido said. "I don't need a blanket. I'll just take off my shoes and catch some Z's."

Quinn hadn't heard that in a long time, *catch some Z's.*

"Okay, Jerry, the couch is all yours. I'll see you in the morning."

"So how 'bout a nightcap?"

Quinn thought about it. "Why not?"

He knew Joe Nethers would disapprove.

Pearl would disapprove.

Quinn should disapprove.

In the morning Quinn got up earlier than he should have. He showered, got dressed, then had toast and coffee standing up in the kitchen. He left Lido snoring on the sofa and walked the few blocks to the office to help clear his head.

Pearl was the only one there. Sal and Harold were out searching for Simon Luttrells with Fedderman. Quinn had decided to let them carry out the task for the sake of thoroughness. Renz would insist that every base be touched. And for all anyone knew, they might find the guilty, live Simon Luttrell, or at least a Simon Luttrell who might have some idea of why his name was used by the killer.

"Coffee's made," Pearl said. She was sitting at her desk, booting up her computer.

Quinn walked over and poured himself a mug of coffee, then added cream. He came back and perched on the edge of Pearl's desk, looking down at her.

"Don't put that down and leave a ring on something," she said, nodding toward the steaming mug in his hand.

"Jerry Lido paid me a visit during the night," he said, and described what had happened, what Jerry had learned.

When he was finished, Pearl leaned back in her chair, thinking.

"So our killer continues to establish a Socrates's Cavern

theme," Quinn said, "maybe for no reason other than to throw us off the scent."

"Has he succeeded?"

"Sure. We have to interview, or at least check into, any Simon Luttrells in the New York area. And that's while we're still looking for Philip Wharkin."

"He's forcing us to waste our time," Pearl said.

"Maybe."

"You think it's a double game—making it look *too* obvious so we abandon that avenue of investigation?"

Quinn shrugged his bulky shoulders. "Been done before."

"Yeah, but not often. And serial killers are creatures of compulsion. They don't like straying from their ritual, even in order to lay down false clues."

"That's what Helen says."

"What any profiler would say."

"But what if we're not dealing with a serial killer? Not a creature of compulsion at all."

"Somebody with a logical motive?" Pearl swiveled her chair so she was looking up at Quinn directly.

"Or a different rationalized sick motive not linked to compulsion."

"It would have to be a strong motive," Pearl said, "considering the way those women were tortured before he released them to death."

"Maybe that's what he *wants* us to think."

"A terrible thing to do to human beings, simply to mislead the police. Not many ordinary men would have the stomach, no matter how devoted they were to their cause."

"The evil that men do . . ." Quinn said.

Pearl gave Quinn an alarmed look. "You going religious on me now, Quinn?"

"That's Shakespeare, I believe." Quinn the avid theatergoer. "Shakespeare was big on men doing evil."

Quinn smiled. "What I'm saying is that we can't rule anything out or in at this point."

Pearl swiveled back to face her desk and got busy again on her computer. "Where's Jerry Lido now?"

"Sleeping it off on my couch."

He didn't rub it in to Pearl that Lido, while under the influence, had come up with a useful gem of knowledge.

With Pearl, you didn't rub things in.

"Just in case," she said, "I'm gonna see if I can run down this Luttrell guy. Make sure of what Jerry found. Narrow it down by eliminating everyone without a heartbeat."

"That'll make things easier for Sal and Harold," Quinn said. It wasn't a bad idea to double-check. After all, Lido had been drinking.

He watched Pearl work for a few seconds before he walked away, thinking she was probably an inch away from climbing all over him for getting Lido drunk again. Thinking how much he loved her and wondering why.

Wondering if there was a cure.

19

Here they were, meeting again. This time for breakfast.

Fedderman sat across from Penny Noon in the Silver Star Diner on Columbus near West Seventy-eighth Street. They were in a window booth with a clear view of the busy sidewalk on the other side of the sun-heated glass. Fedderman had breakfast there often and knew the food was good, just in case Penny's request for hot tea or coffee led to a dinner. . . .

A dinner what? A date? That might not be considered ethical.

Well, so what? She just came in to the city to ID a body. She isn't a suspect. Like when Pearl—

"I think I'll go with tea," Penny said, interrupting Fedderman's misgivings. Well, almost misgivings.

The waiter, a skinny little guy with an impressive black mustache, walked over to their booth and they ordered pancakes and tea for Penny, and scrambled eggs, toast, and coffee for Fedderman.

When the waiter had gone, leaving them alone, Fedderman, not knowing what else to say, nodded toward his coffee cup and said, "I drink too much of the stuff."

"So why don't you cut back?"

"We call it cop pop," Fedderman said. "I'm afraid I'm addicted."

Why am I boring this woman with this banal crap? What must she think of me?

"Are you a fashion designer, too?" Fedderman the sparkling conversationalist asked, no doubt reminding her of her sister, whom they'd recently seen dead at the morgue. Not to mention that Penny was dressed today in faded jeans and a clean-looking but slightly threadbare sleeveless blouse.

He sighed hopelessly and grinned. Honesty was the best policy. He knew that. He was a cop. "You've gotta excuse me for making an ass of myself. I'm not used to talking to attractive women under these circumstances unless it might lead to me putting the cuffs on them."

No! I didn't mean it that way.

"Well, there's a novel approach," she said.

She stared at him seriously, smiled, and then laughed an abandoned, throaty laugh that he liked a lot.

Their conversation yesterday in a Starbucks a few blocks from the morgue had been strained and not without Penny's tears. She'd told Fedderman she was surprised by how deeply depressed she felt, since she and the victim hadn't been all that close.

That was something Fedderman decided to explore, now that Penny was less depressed. And it pertained to the case, lending to his comforting delusion that he was working here.

"You mentioned yesterday that you and Nora weren't all that close."

"This gonna be Q and A?" Penny asked.

Fedderman was surprised. Then he said, "That's what we call our business sometimes, for Quinn and Associates Investigations." He smiled. "We do Q and A, Penny, but that's not what I'm doing this morning."

"You're taking a break from the case?"

"A short one. With you."

"Your boss Quinn is an impressive man, but he's also frightening."

"He's on the hunt," Fedderman said. The last thing he wanted was to talk about Quinn.

The waiter came and Penny added cream to her tea and then stirred in the contents of a pink packet of sweetener.

"I suppose Nora and I weren't close because we were ten years apart," she said. "Our father left us a few days after Nora was born. He was an NYU professor who ran off to Mexico with one of his students. A month later they were both killed when a bus they were in ran through a barrier and rolled down a mountainside."

"Still," Fedderman said, "Nora was your blood relation. That means something."

"Apparently it does," she said. He thought she was near tears again, but this morning she disdained them. "We only saw each other on holidays or other family get-togethers. About five years ago, my mother died of pneumonia, and I doubt if Nora and I saw each other half a dozen times after the funeral."

He sipped his coffee and watched her over the arc of the cup rim.

She managed a smile and sniffled. "But what you say is true—blood relationships mean something. Yesterday was harder than I anticipated."

"Identifications of homicide victims are never easy," he said.

She nodded. "But it's over." She drew a deep breath and smiled with a brightness that startled him.

They talked for several hours after that, about everything but Nora Noon and what had happened to her. They talked about each other. Fedderman learned that Penny had back-packed through Europe after college and wanted to return someday to Paris. Penny learned that Fedderman had been a widower for years but still awoke some mornings reaching across the bed for his wife.

Fedderman was still halfway convinced he was working.

You never knew, he told himself, when something seemingly unrelated would strike a chord and prove useful.

"Why did you leave Florida?" she asked.

"It was paradise at first, but I got tired of it. So I came back here to do what I've done all my life."

"Try to find the bad guys?"

"Find them and take them down," Fedderman said. A little romance and excitement wouldn't hurt here. He was getting his footing.

The waiter came over and refreshed their drinks. Penny dropped her soggy tea bag back in her cup and played with the tag and string, as if she were carefully maneuvering a tiny fish she'd just hooked.

"You never did answer me when I asked about what you did," Fedderman said. "I'll bet it's something interesting. Maybe even dangerous." He didn't want her to think he was bragging too much, what with his taking down the bad guys remark.

"I'm a librarian."

"Seriously?" He sat back and stared at her, immensely pleased, as if he'd never before laid eyes on a real librarian.

"I'm seriously a librarian. At the Albert A. Aal Memorial Library on East Fifty-third Street."

"Right here in New York?"

"Uh-huh. I carpool in from New Jersey."

"That explains it. You're obviously smart."

"Because I carpool?"

"No, no, the librarian part."

"Ah," she said, and sipped her tea. "I'm impressed that you're impressed."

"What exactly does a librarian do these days?" Fedderman asked. "I mean, what with all the electronic readers and such?"

"Sometimes I think we mostly sit around and wait to become obsolete," she said. "People still do read paper and print books, and a lot of them. But once we computerized our system, librarians started becoming less necessary."

"Damned computers," he said.

"They must make your job easier."

"Like they make yours easier."

"I bet all those rich widows in Florida were always after you," Penny said.

Fedderman fought hard not to blush. "Not so's you'd notice."

She fiddled around with her tea bag some more.

"I believe that if I were a rich widow, I'd notice you," she said.

He smiled. "I'd be honored to be noticed."

They sat silently for a while, Fedderman looking at Penny, and her staring in the direction of the window but obviously looking inward. The sun coming through the glass laced her streaked blond hair with highlights and lit up her eyes. Pensive eyes. So calm and considering.

Fedderman realized it didn't really matter what they talked about. They were for some reason comfortable in each other's presence. Dinner wouldn't be a bad idea, he decided. A date.

"What are you thinking about?" Fedderman asked.

"The Dewey decimal system."

"I miss it, too," Fedderman said.

20

Willis from the Quick Pick convenience store heard the screaming as soon as he stepped outside into the hot night. He knew right away the screams were coming from the woods behind the store.

He folded the LIVE BAIT sign he'd come outside to bring in and laid it on the concrete near the door. Would there be more screams?

The night was quiet now. He stood with his arms dangling limply at his sides, his head cocked to the left so as to bring his good ear into play, listening for sounds other than the buzz of insects in the woods and up around the pump lights.

The next thing he heard that was louder than the cicadas was a roar. It was uncertain and stuttering at first, rising and falling. Then, about a hundred yards away, he saw a motorcycle burst from the woods onto the county road. It turned away from him, running without lights until it straightened out and had a level stretch in front of it. It roared louder, as if its spirits were lifted by the black ribbon of road ahead. A big Harley—he could tell by the distinctive sound of its engine.

As it receded from his vision, he studied it in the moonlight. It was a dark-colored bike, ridden by a big hefty guy wearing what looked like jeans and a black T-shirt. He had on a dark-colored helmet. Willis saw long dark hair sprouting out from under it, and it seemed that the guy had a beard.

That was it, the image that stayed with Willis as the lone cyclist passed from moonlight into the darker night and was gone.

Then he heard another scream. A woman. He thought about Beth Brannigan, who'd left the store not that long ago, lugging a paper sack containing a six-pack of beer for her husband, Roy. Fearless young Beth, who might have taken the shortcut through the woods. Roy would be on the other side of the woods watching TV from his beat-to-crap recliner, like he always did when the Cards games were televised. Willis wondered if Roy had heard the screams.

The screams continued, ending in a keening wail almost like an animal would make.

Maybe there were others besides the man on the motorcycle. Maybe whatever was going on in the woods hadn't stopped.

Willis ran back into the store and snatched the twelvegauge Remington shotgun from where he kept it propped behind the counter.

After checking the gun to make sure it held shells, he went back outside, locked the store's glass door, and headed for the woods. He found himself feeling oddly elated as he moved at a fast jog toward the source of the screams, holding the shotgun out in front of him crossways with both hands, the way he'd been trained to do back in 'Nam.

Thirty-two years ago. Not so long a time.

Sheriff Wayne Westerley kept the Ford cruiser's accelerator flat on the floor during much of the drive to Willis's

Quick Pick convenience store. He wanted to get there before Beth Brannigan's husband showed up. The big car seemed to chase the converging headlight beams probing the darkness out in front of it.

Roy Brannigan had a temper at the best of times. The fact that he was a religious fanatic didn't seem to have influenced him to try settling matters peaceably.

Willis had carried Beth into the store before calling the sheriff's department. When Brannigan arrived there and was told what happened, he might immediately go after his wife's attacker and trample the crime scene even more thoroughly than Willis probably had, Roy having more at stake.

But Westerley didn't see Brannigan's battered old Plymouth anywhere as he pulled the cruiser into the Quick Pick's gravel lot and parked near the door.

The inside of the store was brightly lighted. When Westerley tried the door he found it locked. It only took a few seconds for Willis to appear inside and open it.

Willis's thinning hair was hanging over his forehead, giving his face depth and shadow in the overhead fluorescent lighting. He looked distraught.

"She's in back," he said.

Westerley had always liked Beth Brannigan. In truth he was kind of attracted to her, maybe especially so because she didn't deserve a nutcase husband like Roy. A drunken Roy tended to preach all the more fervently and defend his view of the Lord with his fists. Westerley sometimes wondered if he used those fists on Beth.

She was in the storage room, reclining in one of the webbed aluminum lawn chaises that Willis sold in the summer. Beth had a terry-cloth beach towel over her that featured a likeness of Elvis in his later-years Las Vegas regalia. The towel came up to her neck. Her bare feet and ankles showed at the other end, where Elvis's head was. Beth's feet were dirty on their soles and turned in toward each other. Nearby on the floor was a wad of rumpled clothing. Some torn jean cutoffs, a ripped T-shirt, and pink panties.

Westerley didn't like Willis messing up the crime scene and its evidence, but on the other hand he couldn't have left Beth suffering and unconscious in the woods. The clothes, though, might have yielded some clues. *They might still.*

Willis noticed the way Westerley had glanced at him.

"Well, hell," he said, "I couldn't leave her layin' there on the ground. And I had to cover her up. The son of a bitch that got her's the one that tore off her clothes."

Beth didn't say anything. She was staring straight ahead, probably in shock, trembling even though it was warm in the storeroom. A bruise was beginning to take colorful form below her left eye.

"I got an ambulance coming from Fulton," Westerley said. He knew they'd use a rape kit on Beth at the hospital, begin the process of accumulating evidence, building a case that would hold up in court. *If we can find the bastard.* "Did you call her husband?" he asked Willis.

"Nope. I thought I'd wait till you got here."

Westerley noticed a shotgun leaning against the wall near the storage room's rear door. "Were you fixing to use that twelve gauge?"

"Would have if I could have," Willis said.

"You gotta—"

"Willis! You in here?"

Roy Brannigan's voice. Willis hadn't relocked the door after Westerley had arrived. He and Westerley looked at each other. Westerley nodded.

"Back here, Roy. In the storeroom."

Brannigan entered and looked around. He saw his wife in the lawn chair, barely covered by a towel. He aimed a dark and puzzled scowl at Willis and the sheriff.

"What in God's name is goin' on here?"

"Beth was attacked," Westerley said. He could smell beer on Brannigan's breath.

Brannigan stared at him as if he'd spoken Chinese. "What do you mean, attacked?"

"I'm sorry, Roy. Not long after she left the store to go back home, Willis heard somebody screaming in the woods. He went to see what was going on, and he found Beth on the ground and hurt. So he brought her here and called me."

"She musta been taking the shortcut back to your place," Willis said. "I was just about to call you."

Brannigan's intense features were bunched, but his eyes were huge and unbelieving. He was trying to comprehend what he'd just heard.

"What do you mean, attacked?" he said again.

"We'll get her to a hospital, Roy," Westerley said. "Then we'll know more. We gotta find out how bad she's hurt."

Brannigan stared at his wife, who lay gazing at nothing as if she were alone on a distant island. Her teeth were chattering.

"I told her and told her not to take that shortcut at night," Brannigan said. His anger was growing, simmering right now, but it might boil over. "They don't listen. They don't damn listen!"

Gravel crunched outside in the lot as another vehicle pulled in and parked. Westerley thought it might be the ambulance and paramedics, but instead his deputy, Billy Noth, appeared in the storeroom doorway. Westerley had told him what happened, so he wasn't surprised to see Beth in her condition. Billy looked at Brannigan, then at Westerley.

"She okay?" he asked.

"We'll find out soon," Westerley said.

"Who did this?" Brannigan asked.

"We don't know yet," Westerley said.

"We'll find the son of a bitch," Billy said.

"God had best find him before I do," Brannigan said.

"We'll do the looking," Westerley said, remembering Willis's shotgun. He knew Brannigan owned several guns. *Too many damned guns around here.*

More gravel crunched out in the parking lot. This time it was the ambulance. Tight metal doors *thunk*ed shut almost in unison, and shortly thereafter came the sound of somebody entering the store.

"Back here!" Westerley yelled.

Two burly paramedics in white outfits came into the storeroom, making it suddenly seem small and cramped and very warm. Westerley was perspiring heavily and could feel the taut material of his tan uniform shirt sticking to his back.

He told the paramedics briefly what had happened, and they hurriedly set about bringing in a gurney and transferring Beth onto it. As they shifted her weight, the towel came half off her. There were leaves and dirt sticking to her nude body. One of the paramedics got a blanket over her in a hurry and kicked the towel to the side. Elvis's eyes showed, somewhat rumpled, and seemed to be observing everything with mild interest.

"Lord, Lord . . ." Brannigan said in a choked voice. "I'm goin' with her to the hospital."

The paramedics looked at Westerley.

"He's her husband," Westerley said. For a moment he wondered how it would have felt to say he was Beth's husband. Westerley's own wife had left him three years ago, unable to stay married to a cop.

"You can ride in back, sir," one of the paramedics said to Brannigan.

"Make absolutely sure they do a rape kit on her," Westerley said softly to the other paramedic.

The paramedics rolled the gurney through the store and outside, handling it gently. Everyone followed. The night was dark but for the island of light where the convenience store stood. The ambulance's flashing red and blue roof lights seemed inadequate, surrounded by all that vast darkness and silence. Moths flitted like stunned spirits before its headlights.

As the gurney's wheels were raised and Beth was loaded into the ambulance, Brannigan walked about ten feet away and stood staring up at the sky. He suddenly howled, startling everyone. His jaws spread even wider and the tendons in his neck tightened like cables as he howled again, louder.

Then he calmly walked to the rear of the ambulance.

"The Lord doth have his reasons," he said, and climbed into the vehicle after Beth.

One of the paramedics shut the ambulance's rear doors. As he walked around to get in the passenger's seat, he looked over at Westerley and rolled his eyes.

Westerley didn't respond, thinking about Beth.

The three men stood and watched the ambulance spray gravel, then break from the lot. A couple of hundred feet down the road, its siren cut in.

"I'd like to know what those reasons are," Billy Noth said. He turned his head off to the side and spat.

When the ambulance was out of sight and could no longer be heard, Westerley laid a hand on Willis's bony shoulder.

"Take us to where this thing happened," he said.

21

New York, the present

"I figured that sooner or later I'd see my good buddy Detective Quinn again," William Turner said.

Quinn was back in the brownstone vestibule that smelled faintly of cat urine. Turner, the former manager and part owner of Socrates's Cavern, had opened the door and was staring out at him, grinning. He didn't look so much like Einstein today. With his meaty lips and gapped teeth, he had what could only be called a lascivious grin. It went so well with his former business that Quinn wondered if it might be practiced.

Turner wasn't wearing a blazer and ascot today. He had on a shimmering purple silk kimono and the same fleece-lined leather house slippers he'd worn during Quinn's last visit. His curly gray hair still looked as if it would overwhelm any comb. His blue eyes were alight with amusement, as if Quinn had just told a joke. Or maybe Turner regarded Quinn simply being there as a joke.

"I heard on the news you found another Skinner victim," Turner said, "so I suppose you're here to ask me about Simon Luttrell." The New York media had already tagged the killer the Skinner. He was going to be valuable to them.

Turner opened the door wider and moved aside so Quinn could enter. "Ask away, Detective."

"Do you have a cat?" Quinn asked.

Turner grinned wider and appeared quizzical. "Pardon me?"

"A ca—"

"No, no. I don't much care for them."

Quinn didn't tell him why he'd asked. The acrid scent in the vestibule that seemed to clog the bridge of the nose. Well, maybe it was some kind of antiseptic cleaning fluid.

He sat down as he had before on the flowered beige sofa, facing Turner's pottery collection. "It didn't take long for the news media to pick up the name Simon Luttrell."

Turner stayed with his grin, but it became knowing as well as lewd. "Prompt coverage is what you might expect, considering the name was scrawled in blood on the bathroom mirror, like with the last victim. And we both know how the NYPD leaks information."

"Not every compartment is watertight," Quinn admitted, "but the ship sails on."

"Poetic and true."

"Do you remember Simon Luttrell?"

"Never laid eyes on the man, that I can recall. No surprise. Our membership numbered well into the hundreds."

"He had a gold key."

"Ah, you've been doing your research."

"Do you recall him now?"

"No. Sorry. Gold-key membership also numbered in the hundreds. It wasn't as exclusive a club within a club that the members assumed." Turner strode to a chair and sat down, causing the kimono to work up and reveal thin, bluish ankles. The reflective purple material was so full of static electricity that it actually struck sparks. "Look, Detective Quinn, all Simon Luttrell is to me is ancient history that I'm not particularly interested in and don't even remember. And as far as I know, he isn't part of the New York S and M world now." The gap-toothed, nasty grin again. It came and went so easily on his fleshy face. "What I think," he said, "is that someone clever is playing with your mind."

"We've considered that," Quinn said.

"And we both know it isn't me." Turner shrugged his narrow, rounded shoulders beneath the kimono. "But, when you've got dead tortured women, one after the other, and sexually adventurous men like Philip Wharkin and Simon Luttrell, or someone pretending to be their ghosts, who you gonna call? An old porn king, that's who." He sighed. "Hell, I guess it's only natural. But it's misguided."

"How did you know Simon Luttrell was dead?"

"That leaky boat we talked about."

Quinn decided not to comment. He stood up, not really surprised that he'd drawn a blank here.

Turner also stood. It took him a while, as a man grown old and slow. "You know the one part of me that doesn't get stiff these days?" he asked.

"I don't know and I don't want to guess," Quinn said as he moved toward the door.

His dismissiveness prompted Turner to further proclaim his innocence.

"I've got nothing to do with those killings, Detective Quinn, and I don't know anyone who'd do such a thing. Hell, I've got a daughter myself." He motioned with his head toward a photo in front of his pottery in the bookshelf. A bright-eyed young girl with springy dark hair grinned crookedly at Quinn from a tilted wooden frame.

Quinn wondered if she knew about her father's earlier life. He almost asked, then decided it wasn't relevant. If it ever became relevant, he'd ask.

"We in the porn industry dislike it more than anyone else if some animal's out there stalking and killing women,"

Turner continued. "It brings heat. Like this visit. And all when you should be directing your efforts toward finding the killer." The silk kimono swished and sparked rhythmically as he escorted Quinn to the door. It made a faint sound like cellophane crackling. "You believe me, I hope."

"It's not that I don't believe you," Quinn said. "It's more that I'm not sure you speak for everyone in the porn industry. To them, women are product and profit."

"Not dead women," Turner said, opening the door to the vestibule. "They're trouble."

He offered his hand for Quinn to shake, but Quinn ignored it, fearing electrocution.

Outside on the sidewalk, Quinn wondered if he could believe anything Turner had told him.

22

Westerley and Billy used their flashlights and were helped by whatever moonlight filtered through the leaves. Willis stood off to the side, as instructed. Now that they'd reached their destination, he switched off the flashlight he'd brought from the store. He had no idea where to shine it, anyway.

Obviously Beth had put up a struggle. The brown carpet of last year's half-decayed leaves had been violently stirred so that here and there bare earth was exposed. The leaves were thick enough that they prevented footprints, and there were none in the bare spots. Westerley noticed a small strip of torn fabric that looked as if it had come from Beth's T-shirt. He kept the beam of his flashlight trained on it while Billy stooped and used a tweezers to lift the fragment and bag it.

Off to the side of where the main struggle seemed to have taken place was a ripped paper sack. Next to it was a six-pack of Wild Colt beer, also ripped open. Westerley went to it and saw that it contained three cans. There were no empty beer cans lying about. Westerley guessed the rapist had punched Beth in the eye in an attempt to quiet her screams. When that didn't work, he hurriedly grabbed three beer cans for the road and tucked them wherever they'd fit in his pockets or on his motorcycle before fleeing the scene.

"This the brand of beer Beth bought at the Quick Pick?" Westerley asked Willis.

"Yeah. That's all Roy will drink."

"The guy you saw speeding outta here on a motorcycle, he look like he was carrying anything?"

"Nope. Had both hands on the grips. I'm sure of that. Coulda had something tucked in his saddlebags, though."

"I'm figuring that," Westerley said, knowing he was making a lot of suppositions without much evidence.

"I'm sure it was a Harley he was riding," Willis said. "I used to own one and I know how they sound, 'specially when they're idling. Potato, potato, potato."

"Huh?"

"You say potato over and over fast and that's what a Harley sounds like."

"Uh-huh."

Westerley told Billy to cordon off the scene with yellow tape so he could come back tomorrow and examine it in daylight. Nobody was likely to come along and disturb it anyway, until the rape found its way into the newspapers and on TV, and that would take a while. This wasn't St. Louis or Kansas City.

When Billy was finished cordoning off a rough square by winding crime-scene tape around four trees, the three men trudged from the woods, following the wavering flashlight beams. Willis walked out ahead, leading the way as if he were guiding an expedition.

When the convenience store lights were visible through the trees, Billy leaned close to Westerley and said, "Potato, potato, potato."

Early the next morning Westerley returned to the crime scene alone. He surveyed the area of the struggle carefully. About ten feet from where the rape must have taken place, he found marks where a motorcycle had been parked. There was a clear indentation from the cycle's kickstand. He searched for tire tread marks but couldn't find any.

When he was about to leave, he saw what looked like a dark stain on a dry brown leaf. He stooped low and examined it carefully. It was no more than half an inch across, but he thought he could detect a splatter pattern. He was pretty sure it was blood.

Beth hadn't bled much, if any, so it might not be her blood, but that of her assailant.

He carefully lifted the entire delicate leaf with tweezers and managed to slide it into one of the plastic sandwich bags the sheriff's department used for evidence bags. He sealed the top of the bag carefully.

The hospital had been unable to obtain any blood from beneath Beth's fingernails, though she'd said she'd scratched her attacker, so this blood could be valuable evidence if it was the same type as the suspect's.

If they had a suspect.

Westerley recalled the words of a former Missouri politician about a wordy but ineffective bill that had passed the legislature. *Now if we had some bread and we had some mustard, we could have a ham sandwich, if we had some ham.*

23

New York, the present

On Quinn's instructions, Vitali and Mishkin revisited the apartments of both Millie Graff and Nora Noon. Something might have been overlooked. Something that linked one or both women to the New York underworld of seamy sex, or to each other.

The two detectives were in Nora's apartment. It was bright and warm from sunlight beaming through the windows.

Vitali was sorting through the stifling second bedroom, stuffed with hangered garments and bolts of fabric. Mishkin, in the other bedroom, was carefully removing, then replacing, intimate wear in the dresser drawers. He handled the dead woman's silk and lacy items with his fingertips, a faintly disturbed and embarrassed look above his bushy gray mustache. Sal, glancing in now and then from the room across the hall, reflected as he had many times that his partner shouldn't have become a cop. The tedious and often repugnant part of the job too often got to Mishkin.

The results were in from the NYPD nerds who'd explored the victims' computers. Millie Graff's hard drive was mostly full of dancing and dancers. Restaurant hostess though she might have been, her dream of professional dancing was still strong. There was a site about "the art" of pole dancing, but it actually did seem to concentrate more on the techniques of dancing with a pole than on eroticism. Her e-mail account was mostly about business matters, and discussions of dancers' progress or lack of same. Her personal account suggested she didn't have a lot of friends in the city, and at the time of her death no romantic involvement. While online, Millie visited the Drudge Report almost daily and read the digital version of the *New York Times*. Fair and balanced.

Nora Noon also had visited the *Times* online. In fact, it was her home page. Illustrations from several fashion magazines were on her computer, along with a downloaded book by Susan Isaacs. She had visited an online dating service a few times but hadn't signed up. Like Millie, she had a business e-mail address as well as a personal account. The business account was completely about business. The personal account revealed nothing helpful. Nora had also been on Facebook, but most of her input was a thinly disguised ploy to establish business contacts.

"These women," Mishkin said loudly so Vitali would hear in the other room, "seem to have been normal human beings, but very, very busy."

"It's a wonder they found the time to get killed," Vitali rasped. Lint or something in the air of the crowded little room kept making him *almost* sneeze.

"They were career women," Mishkin said. "A dancer and a designer."

"Wannabe dancer."

"Same thing. Just a matter of timing." Harold the optimist.

"Everybody's got a career, Harold. Even if they just call them jobs."

"I mean more than a job, Sal. More like a calling. That's why both victims led such busy lives."

Sal shoved his way out of Nora N.'s storage room. Or

oversized closet. He wasn't sure what to call it. Whatever, it was sure full of lint. He sneezed as he entered the other bedroom, where Mishkin toiled.

"God bless," Mishkin said. He was holding up a black thong. "This isn't part of a swimming suit, Sal. It's too fragile."

"Those thong things are popular as underwear, too, Harold. Which is what that one is. Probably most women under seventy have got at least one in their wardrobe."

"How do you know that, Sal?"

"I just do. Like I know red buttons often turn things on."

Mishkin found something else interesting in Nora's dresser drawer. "What are these things that look like halves of hollowed-out cantaloupes with foam in them."

"That's a bra, Harold. It's used when women wear a gown that doesn't have straps."

Mishkin held the attached shallow foam cups out at arm's length and studied them. "They don't look as if they'd support anything."

"They do, though, Harold. And they make it possible to have bare chest, back, and shoulders above the dress without a brassiere strap showing."

"Got it," Mishkin said. "They work on the principle of the cantilever. Like those houses on the hills in California, where half the place hangs out over a long drop to the valley below."

"Harold."

"Yeah?"

"Put the damned thing back in the drawer and let's get out of here."

Mishkin did that, and was shutting the drawer when he noticed something on the floor. A slip of lined paper that looked as if it had been torn from a small spiral notebook. He picked it up and looked at it.

"Here's something, Sal. It must have dropped on the floor

when I was pulling stuff from the drawers. There's writing on it. A man's name and a phone number." He beamed at Vitali. "I think it was in the same drawer as the thong and cantilever bra. Maybe we got something big here, Sal."

"If he isn't an insurance salesman or plumber," Vitali said.

He liked to keep Mishkin's expectations low. Harold could be crushed and depressed for days when something this promising didn't pan out. A real pain in the ass, given to brooding.

Vitali slipped the folded piece of paper into his shirt pocket so Mishkin wouldn't think too much about it.

24

Things had changed. Candice Culligan could afford to take a cab home from the office now. She'd recently been made a managing partner in Kraft, Holmes, and Deloitte, a law firm specializing in corporate research and litigation.

Candice (never *Candy*) might look like a showgirl, with her tall frame and hourglass figure, not to mention generous lips that looked like but weren't the product of collagen. Her long hair was lush and red, her eyes large and blue. And there was something in those eyes that kept people at bay, especially all but the most adventurous men on the make. Like there was a certain pride in her chin-up, long-strided walk. But Candice wasn't only for show, despite the fact that she was a show wherever she went. Candice was smart.

It hadn't taken Marty Deloitte long to figure out how smart, because Marty was no dummy himself. Soon after Candice joined the firm four years ago, Marty had made her his protégé. Both of them ignored the snickers. Marty, sixtyish and too bowlegged even to look good in his four-thousand-dollar suits, was happily married and had four teenage sons who were constantly in trouble because he ignored them so he could work long hours. Margie, his wife, didn't question or complain about his dedication to his work. Not even after she'd met Candice. It wasn't so much that Margie was trusting (though she was). Their rambunctious sons kept her busy visiting neighbors, schools, and sometimes police precinct houses and courtrooms, setting things in order to shrink the fines and prevent incarcerations. She didn't have time to worry about whether Marty was screwing somebody else. If he was, she'd eventually find out, and then she'd castrate him.

Kraft, Holmes, and Deloitte was one of the most successful and wealthy firms in the city. They could afford to pay well, and they did. They could also be slave drivers, mercilessly pushing their employees for more and more billable hours. Within a month at the firm, Candice had gotten sick of the term *billable hours*.

As a managing partner, Candice was now beyond all that. She'd gotten the commensurate big raise and bonus. And the caseload. She'd usually worked her cases with Marty Deloitte at her side, sometimes proffering his advice. And the right cases, like that well-publicized child-abuse custody battle, had come her way. Everything had broken just right for her.

She'd recently moved into a new condo in SoHo. Also, she'd begun dating Riley Carter. He was single, handsome, and the co-producer of the new cable TV quiz show *Fingers and Toes*. The idea was that contestants had to type their answers, and each time they were wrong one of their fingers was taped to the finger next to it. This impeded their typing, so those with the most wrong answers wound up slapping at the typewriter with what might as well have been mittens, which allowed slower-thinking contestants to catch up. That made for some tight contests. Toes had nothing to do with anything except, as the unctuous host endlessly proclaimed, making it easier to count your winnings. Candice thought the whole thing was stupid and unwatchable, but she never told Riley. Why should she? *Fingers and Toes* was one of the highest-rated shows on cable television.

Her cab zoomed and veered and did everything but fly as it made its seemingly reckless way down Broadway toward her new condo. Confident that there would be no collision, that she was lucky in all things, Candice leaned her head against the cab's seat back and smiled.

Half a block away from her condo, the rush-hour traffic finally clogged the avenues and came to a stop. Or maybe there was an accident or construction up ahead. Her cabbie, a young guy with a beard and turban, twitched behind the steering wheel and drummed his palms on the dashboard, impatient to fly some more. Candy knew exactly how he felt. She used to feel that way when things weren't moving fast enough for her.

When vehicles had finished inching up on one another, getting as close as possible to gain precious pavement, it was obvious that traffic wasn't going to move. Not for a while, anyway.

Candice paid her cabbie, tipping generously, and climbed out of the cab. Walking would get her home faster than staying in the vehicle. Other taxi passengers were following the same plan. They were familiar with traffic this time of evening. The subways would be packed, too. And it wasn't a bad evening for walking, even if still on the warm side. People emerged from at least half a dozen cabs lining Broadway and joined the throngs on the sidewalks. The forward motion, at last, was exhilarating.

Along the avenue Candice strode, now and then catching a glimpse of herself reflected in a show window. She couldn't help but smile wider at the woman smiling back at her. She had a great job, an interesting love life, a new condo unit that was everything she'd dreamed it to be, plenty of money. And a future almost too brilliant to comprehend.

Candice understood and fully appreciated her luck. She had everything she could possibly want, and in the greatest city in the world.

She also had a shadow.

The shadow had a knife.

25

The morning after the rape of Beth Brannigan, Sheriff Wayne Westerley carefully placed his meager findings from the crime scene in the trunk of his cruiser. They consisted of a series of Polaroid shots, a quick-set plastic cast of the motorcycle kickstand indentation in the earth, and a plastic bag containing the dried brown leaf with the blood splatter on it. Not much, unless they also had a suspect. Westerley knew the odds were long on that, and getting longer with each passing hour.

He took a last look around the crime scene, thinking it was odd how a residue of emotion seemed to linger where great violence had occurred. As if somehow the very air knew that the harm done extended far beyond the victim. He tried to imagine what had gone through Beth Brannigan's mind last night, but decided he couldn't. What he should be doing, anyway, was trying to figure out what had gone on in the assailant's mind. That might provide some help in apprehending him before he did even more harm.

As soon as Westerley settled himself in behind the steering wheel of the cruiser and bent forward to twist the ignition key, he received a radio call. It wasn't his clerk and dispatcher, Ella; it was his deputy Billy Noth.

"Ella picked up a highway patrol call, Sheriff," Billy said. "Some young boys searching the woods for arrowheads came across a man stretched out on his back. They figured he was hurt, so they went and got their dad, who was waiting back by their car. He went with them to the scene and saw that the man was drunk or stoned unconscious. Also saw who his description fit. He went back to his car with the kids and drove to a phone, where he called the highway patrol. They're on their way."

"To exactly where?" Westerley asked, feeling his pulse quicken.

"State Road GG, just east of the Interstate 44 turnoff. The highway patrol dispatcher said the guy was behind a big deserted barn, about a hundred yards into the woods."

"That's less than five miles from where I am," Westerley said.

He didn't hear what Billy said. He'd already gotten the cruiser's engine turned over, the transmission in drive, and the siren switched on.

After a couple of miles, he switched the siren off but kept the roof bar lights flashing. That was enough to cause traffic to part in front of him so he could hold his speed. Within a few minutes he was turning onto the narrow blacktop road that was State GG.

The barn came into sight almost immediately, a blight off to his left. It was huge and gray and weathered and leaned so it appeared it might collapse any second. Vertical bars of light showed between some of the boards.

Westerley pulled the cruiser off the road and parked about twenty feet from the barn, near its black and cavernous entrance where the doors used to be. He switched off the engine and got out of the car without slamming the door.

It was suddenly very quiet. Westerley stood still in the tall grass and could hear the buzz of insects, the occasional rush of a car passing on the Interstate well beyond the trees. A soft breeze came up, causing the grass to sway and the old timbers of the barn to creak. He understood why somebody wanting to rest or sleep would choose the woods instead of the barn; the damned thing didn't provide much in the way of shelter and really might collapse any second. The breeze stiffened, and Westerley actually saw the structure sway.

It *was* possible that the suspect had moved and was now inside the barn, but Westerley didn't think that was the case. He unholstered his .45 Colt revolver and checked to make sure it was loaded, and then he worked the action once to move one of the rounds in the cylinder into the breech that he usually left empty for safety's sake.

He turned his head to the side and listened closely. No sirens in the distance. Of course, that didn't mean the highway patrol wasn't close. And getting closer. Like Westerley, they'd probably run silent in their approach to where the suspect had been seen.

Keeping the revolver at his side, pressed flat against his right thigh, he moved around the barn and entered the woods.

There was a narrow dirt path, somewhat overgrown but easy to follow. Probably quite a few arrowhead expeditions, and maybe some lovers' trysts, had occurred here. The woods were mostly in shadow, cooler than out by the barn in the blazing sun, and quieter.

He saw the motorcycle first, a midnight-blue Harley-Davidson resting on its kickstand in a small clearing that the sunlight barely touched. In the center of the clearing, with the single sun patch almost to his head, lay a husky man with a dark beard. He was wearing a black T-shirt, dirty jeans, and brown leather boots with run-down heels. A beer can lay on its side near his limp right hand. Two identical cans were on the ground near the motorcycle. Wild Colt beer. The brand Beth had bought at the Quick Pick before the rape.

Westerley could hear the man snoring and breathed easier himself. Deep sleep. Just what the situation called for.

Reaching for the handcuffs hanging on his belt, Westerley moved in. He watched the man's face closely as he advanced, observing a wisp of the suspect's long and ragged beard stir slightly with each snore.

When he was about five feet away, he saw a glint of something. Eye white. The man's right eye was partly open.

Even as Westerley realized the sleep and snores were feigned, the man was up and on his feet. He shook his head and beard, sending grass and bits of leaves flying, and he saw that Westerley was wearing a uniform. He must not have noticed the gun, though, because he spun on his heel and ran.

Westerley was immediately after him. The man seemed to come all the way awake and lengthened his stride. He was picking up speed as they entered the woods, pulling away from Westerley, his long black hair whipping side to side like a metronome.

"Halt!" Westerley yelled. "Sheriff's department! I'll shoot! I'll shoot your goddamned heart out!"

The suspect ran faster.

Shit!

Westerley stopped running and spread his feet wide. He leveled the gun then raised it slightly to fire a warning shot.

It was at that moment that the fleeing suspect glanced back to see where Westerley was and ran hard into a tree.

He was groggy and struggling to get back up when Westerley reached him, kicked his legs out from under him, and cuffed him.

"That made an ugly sound," Westerley said, "when you hit that tree."

"Didn't feel too good, neither," the man said, gasping. Both of them were fighting for breath.

"I was ready to put one into you," Westerley said, hefting the revolver.

"What for? Sleepin' under an elm?"

Westerley got a good handhold on the man's shirt and belt and lifted him to his feet. He gave him a shove.

"What're you doin'?" the man asked.

"Keep walking toward the barn," Westerley said, shoving him onto the narrow path.

"Why'd you chase me?"

"Why'd you run?"

"Where we goin'?" Answering a question with a question. The way guilty people did.

"Walk."

"I got rights!"

"I know," Westerley said. "Soon as I catch my breath, I'm going to read them to you."

By the time they'd reached the cruiser, Westerley had introduced the suspect to Mr. Miranda. He secured him in back, behind the cage, and got in behind the steering wheel.

Less than a minute after he'd turned the cruiser off GG and onto the Interstate, he saw the highway patrol. There were four cars with lights on but sirens off, across the median and heading at high speed in the opposite direction.

"What about my bike?" the suspect whined from the back of the cruiser.

"I don't think you'll need it anymore," Westerley said.

26

Quinn and Pearl had lunch in Quinn's brownstone over on West Seventy-fifth Street, only a short walk from the office. They often did that, stopping at a deli to pick up carryout food.

In the brownstone, they could relax and talk freely, and not always about whatever the agency was working on. Sometimes the talk was about converting closets to bathrooms, about wainscoting or crown molding, or what kind of tile should be in the entry hall. Quinn could catch the news on TV if he felt like it. Pearl could kick off her shoes and stretch out on the couch for an afternoon nap. The kinds of things you couldn't do in a restaurant.

Sometimes after lunch they would climb the narrow stairs leading up from the vestibule and visit the construction crew to see how the renovations were going.

Pearl was becoming more and more interested in the renovations. Quinn hoped that meant she was becoming increasingly interested in the brownstone, and maybe in moving in with him. He thought that in a lot of ways it made sense. He didn't know for sure what she thought.

They didn't stay long in the brownstone today. Even through the thick walls and floors, they could hear the tympani of hammering and the angry whine of power tools. It sounded as if this was the day the workmen had decided to tear down a wall.

Not an ideal place to hang out.

Back in the office, it didn't take Quinn and Pearl long to fall again into the rhythm of work. Quinn was at his desk, Pearl at her computer, when Vitali and Mishkin entered. Both were in shirtsleeves and with loosened ties, Vitali short and decisive in his movements, Mishkin slightly taller and languid, looking like Mr. Milquetoast with his soup-strainer mustache.

"Finished searching the victims' apartments?" Quinn asked.

Both men nodded. Mishkin walked over to the small refrigerator and got a bottled water. Vitali poured himself a cup of coffee and left it black.

"Show them what we found, Sal," Mishkin said.

Vitali drew a folded slip of paper from his shirt pocket and handed it to Quinn. Pearl got up from her desk and crossed the room to peer over Quinn's shoulder.

"We found nothing previously overlooked indicating either victim played around with S and M or had any connection to anything called Socrates's Cavern," Vitali said. "But we did find this."

Quinn looked at what appeared to be a page torn from a small spiral notebook. It had the name Andy Drubb scrawled on it in dark blue ink, along with a phone number.

"It was in one of Noon's dresser drawers," Mishkin said, "along with some thong underwear and a peculiar brassiere."

Pearl looked at him. "Peculiar how?"

"Not all that peculiar," Sal said. "It was for holding up boobs without straps. Harold was unfamiliar with that model."

"Sort of propped them up," Mishkin said. "Cantilevered."

Pearl rolled her eyes.

"Did you cross-directory this guy Drubb and get his address?" Quinn asked.

"Yeah," Vitali said. "He lives down in the Village. We called the number but got no answer, and no answering machine. Drubb won't know who called. We used a public phone in case he had caller ID."

"Go see him," Quinn said, "but don't call first. See how he takes to being surprised."

"That's what we were on our way to do," Sal said. "Wanted to check it with you first."

"Maybe Drubb was in a red hot S-and-M relationship with Nora Noon," Mishkin said. "I mean, with the thong underwear and all. And that bra thing." He glanced at Pearl, his gaze lingering on her large breasts.

Pearl glared at him. "Are you for real, Harold?"

"Funny you should ask. What I was wondering—"

"Never mind, Harold!" Quinn and Vitali said in unison. Nobody wanted to see Pearl erupt.

"We've got a printout of the Socrates's Cavern membership list," Pearl said. "I'll check it and see if Drubb's on it." She went over to her desk and pulled some stapled sheets of paper from a drawer. "It's alphabetical, so this'll only take a few seconds."

"He'd probably be too young," Sal said.

"Then maybe his father," Pearl said

"That's an ugly thought," Mishkin said.

"And wouldn't mean much if it turned out to be true," Sal told him.

"Doesn't matter," Pearl said. "Drubb's not on the list."

"If you don't find Andy Drubb at home," Quinn said, "ask around the neighborhood and see what you can learn about him. It won't hurt if he hears about it and gets nervous." He glanced at his watch. "Stop and grab some lunch on the way downtown."

"Wanna join us?" Vitali asked.

"We already had lunch at my place," Quinn said.

"In the middle of the day?" Mishkin said.

"That's when people eat lunch, Harold," Vitali said.

Mishkin was staring at Pearl's breasts again. Pearl was sure she wouldn't like the reason why.

The Albert A. Aal Library looked like a miniature court building. Though it wasn't all that wide, it had shallow concrete steps leading to half a dozen columns framing five tall wooden doors outfitted with brass kick and push plates. One of the doors had a sign warning that it was automatic, as if anyone getting too close to it might be flipped back down the steps. Fedderman chose that one. The others looked too heavy to move.

The library was surprisingly spacious inside, and well lighted. While it might be narrow, it was long, with rows of steel shelves laden with books. Off to the side was an arrangement of armchairs and wooden racks of magazines and newspapers. A blond boy who looked too young not to be in school was slumped in one of the chairs, reading a car magazine. Fedderman could see only a few people browsing the stacks.

A gray-haired woman, long and narrow like the library, sat behind the wooden counter where books were checked out and returned. She had on round metal-framed glasses trailing a thin braided loop that was buttoned to her blouse. There was no way she could misplace the glasses, Fedderman thought. He'd bought reading glasses but could seldom find them so had stopped looking. He could still see well enough without glasses, if he held whatever he was reading at arm's length and squinted. That was good enough for him because it had to be, unless he happened to stumble across his glasses by sheer luck. But with glasses like this woman's . . .

"Help you?" the woman asked. Fedderman realized she was staring at him with narrowed eyes. Her expression was faintly disapproving.

"Research," Fedderman said. He was uncomfortable around librarians. Had been since as a teenager he'd returned *Lady Chatterley's Lover* three months overdue and—

"What is it you'd like to research?"

Fedderman sure wasn't going to tell her that. "Something in an old newspaper."

She observed him as if he were a mildly interesting insect. "We have newspapers on microfiche," she said. "Our research room is straight down and to your left at the end of those aisles. Someone back there will help you."

Fedderman thanked her and wandered off in the direction she'd instructed. Never a scholar, he still very much liked the unique musty scent of old books. And many of the library's books were old. Only about half seemed to have dust jackets, and some of them were faded.

He had no trouble finding the research room. It had three walls and four viewers, and a wall of shelves on which were stacks of small cardboard boxes with writing on them in black felt-tip ink. A scholarly looking man in a saggy brown corduroy jacket and sloppily knotted pink tie sat at one of the viewers, intent on what was sliding past sideways on the glowing monitor. Fedderman noticed that the corduroy jacket had leather elbow patches. He had never owned anything with elbow patches.

At the far end of the room was the librarian Fedderman had been told would help him. She was reaching up to replace one of the boxes that held a cartridge when she glanced over and saw him. And smiled.

Penny Noon.

She looked more like a librarian today, wearing light gray slacks, a darker gray blazer, and what looked like a man's miniature tie over a white blouse. A large white button with red lettering was pinned to her blazer's lapel. It read *Save the Book*.

"More questions about Nora's murder?" she asked.

"You know me," Fedderman said, though she didn't know him all that well. "Always working."

"So it seems."

"I thought we'd . . . gotten more trusting of each other. That maybe we should see each other again."

"I've been thinking about that. I'm the victim's half sister. Isn't there a conflict of interest there?"

"If there is," Fedderman said, "I don't care. When certain situations occur, when you meet certain, special people, you should take advantage of them."

"Of the special people?"

He felt a flicker of annoyance and embarrassment. "Is this what's known as verbal fencing?"

"No, it's a way of avoiding the subject. We are the subject. Rather, our relationship, brief as it is. I apologize. I'm being evasive and you're being direct."

"There isn't that much time to say what's on your mind," Fedderman said. "For any of us. I know that because of my work. You should know it because of . . . what's happened."

They were both quiet for a moment. Both thinking about Nora. Both knowing that the last thing Fedderman had come here for was to discuss the murder case.

Fedderman began to perspire. He had to break the silence, change the subject. He wasn't good at this kind of patter, especially in the presence of this woman who made him tongue-tied.

"The book," he said, nodding toward her lapel button. "Who's it need saving from?"

"Oh, so many people. Most of them with e-books."

"Huh?"

"Electronic readers."

"Those things can't be much fun," Fedderman said.

"Someone closer than you imagine might disagree with you."

"How do you turn pages with them?"

"I'm afraid pages are becoming obsolete. Like librarians."

"Save the librarians," Fedderman said.

The guy in the corduroy jacket gave him an annoyed look, like a man on the verge of growling. Instead of growling, he gathered up some papers, and then glanced in Penny's direction and stood and left the research room. What? Had they been talking too loud?

Penny walked over and switched off the viewer Mr. Corduroy had left on. Fedderman enjoyed watching her do that. Maybe too obviously.

"Did you come here to save this librarian?" she asked.

"Yes. From the electronic book."

"Is that what you told Ms. Culver?"

"The woman at the desk? No, I told her I wanted to find something in an old newspaper."

She smiled and moved closer to him. He noticed she was wearing perfume. He couldn't place the scent, but it smelled better than old books.

"Was that a fib?" she asked.

"Who would fib to Ms. Culver?"

"I bet you would," she said. She absently buttoned his shirt cuff, then stood on her toes and kissed him lightly on the cheek.

He embraced her and brought her close, held her tight, kissed her on the lips, felt her tongue warm and soft against his own.

Their hands were all over each other, there in the research room.

27

It was easy to get into Candice Culligan's apartment. When the doorman was about half a block away, hailing a taxi at the busy intersection for some tenants, the Skinner simply entered the lobby and crossed to the elevators. Even if the doorman returned immediately, the killer wouldn't be seen, as the elevators were around a corner and out of sight from the building entrance. Not that it mattered, because there was an elevator at lobby level. He stepped inside, pressed the close-door button, then the button for Candice's floor. He leaned his shoulder blades against the back wall of the elevator and relaxed as he rose.

New York, New York, it's a vulnerable town.

The Skinner had done his research. It hadn't been difficult to obtain Candice's address.

The next step, gaining entry to her unit, turned out to be less of a problem than he'd anticipated. This was the second time he'd been in the building. The first time he'd watched her stretch and reach to the top of the doorframe, where she had a key to her door hidden. Amused, he'd watched her use the same key to unlock a knob lock and a dead bolt set about ten inches above the knob. Two locks, and maybe a chain lock visible only from inside.

Can't be too careful, he'd thought, as he watched her place the key back dead center on top of the door frame.

And there the key was again today, square in the middle on top of the wooden lintel.

New York, New York . . .

This time he took the key inside with him and made a wax impression. There was a key shop in another city where he could have a duplicate made.

Knowing Candice was working hard uptown at the offices of Kraft, Holmes, and Deloitte, he leisurely wandered through the condo unit. Since she hadn't moved in all that long ago, the place still wasn't completely furnished, so it was easy to find her files and important papers, to get a *feel* for her life so he wouldn't be killing a stranger. He hadn't felt that way at first, but yes, he was beginning to enjoy killing, especially if he knew the woman as a person. That business about seeing women only as interchangeable sex objects didn't always apply. The feeling of absolute control and power over women he knew, of playing God with the fools who believed in God—that applied.

He was careful not to touch most things and not to leave a fingerprint.

An hour later, he still hadn't found where Candice kept the password to get online at her desk computer. Her word processor was accessible and contained mostly legal documents or letters. *Boooring*. And yet they showed a side of Candice that was organized and precise. It was a side that would soon die like all her other sides. She existed now only because he let her.

When he was ready to go, he glanced around. He'd been sufficiently careful. She wouldn't suspect that anyone had been here in her absence.

But did he want that?

He'd have a key next time he visited, so what did it matter

if she had something to think about? To worry about? Something she'd recall, when the time came, as a portent she shouldn't have ignored?

He returned to the bedroom and flopped down on his back in the middle of the white duvet on her king-size bed. He stayed there a few minutes, not moving, and then got up carefully and looked at the bed, at the impression he'd made in the duvet. Candice would notice it and realize someone had lain there in her absence. Someone larger than herself. Certainly the impression described the outline of a man. In her bedroom. On her otherwise pristine white bed.

Let her think about that.

He'd leave the door unlocked when he left, but replace the key precisely where he'd found it. When she realized the door was unlocked, Candice would assume she'd forgotten to lock it when she'd left for work that morning. She wouldn't be too concerned. Not until she went into the bedroom and noticed his impression on her bed.

He smiled, picturing the expression on her face, imagining the fear that would lance through her.

He knew what she'd do next. She'd steel herself and search through each room to make sure no one was there. To reassure herself that she was alone.

But she'll know someone has been here.

Let her think about that.

And think and think . . .

28

"I don't like pressuring you," Harley Renz told Quinn, "but you know how it works, how it gets passed along like stomach gas."

Quinn thought that was one of Renz's most memorable analogies.

"So who up near the esophagus is pressuring *you*?"

"Seems like everybody in the goddamned city who wears a suit and tie." Renz sat opposite Quinn's desk, hunched low in one of the client chairs, his pink jowls spilling over his white collar. "Think way up where the food is chewed, Quinn, and that's where it all starts." Renz wagged a pudgy, manicured finger. "Nobody, but nobody, wants another Skinner victim."

"Especially the victim," Quinn said.

"Don't be difficult, Quinn. I'm only doing what I've always done, prying the monkey loose from my back so it can ride yours for a while."

"Heavy monkey."

"That's the idea. In order to get rid of it, you'll lean hard on your people."

"On Pearl?"

"Maybe not on Pearl."

Quinn thought of things to say, but he reminded himself

that the killer's first victim, Millie Graff, had been someone Harley and a lot of other cops shared a special bond with; and now they shared a special desire for justice.

"We're doing everything possible," he said, "following every lead, talking to everyone."

"Such as?"

"The victims' friends, colleagues, neighbors, relatives. People who for whatever reason might be able to put victim with killer. William Turner. Remember him?"

"Jog my memory."

"Whips and orgasms, about thirty years ago."

"The Socrates's Cavern guy? That was longer ago than that. Jesus! Black leather. People in cages, or tied up, or both. You're wasting your time there. Millie didn't have anything to do with that kinda bullshit."

"We've gotta touch the bases as we make the turns," Quinn said.

"You gotta hit the ball first. In fact, I gotta convince people above me that you're friggin' A-Rod. That you're returning the investment. I'm telling you, Quinn, for both our sakes, you better come up with something to show."

Quinn leaned back in his chair and crossed his arms. "Or what? The NYPD's gonna fire me? Again? Or try to prosecute me? Again? Or they're not gonna pay me?"

"Ha! You think that's an idle threat?"

"Which one?"

"You think this city's actually paid everyone it owes? Read the papers, Quinn. You're in line somewhere behind Roach Control."

Quinn sighed and dropped forward in his chair so he was sitting up straight. "What I think, Harley, is you've got some pressure, but it's mainly you where the pressure on me starts."

Renz stood up and moved to the door. He looked back at Quinn.

"Pressure's pressure," he said. "Wherever it comes from. And pressure crushes things. And people."

Quinn sat silently and watched him go out the door.

Okay, Harley, play the tough guy. Maybe in your place that's what I'd be doing.

And you're right about pressure.

Vitali and Mishkin were approaching the door to Andy Drubb's walk-up apartment building in the Village when they saw a thin, dark-haired guy in his forties bound up the steps toward the entrance. He was moving fast, giving the impression he was racing his shadow neck-and-neck. He was fishing in his pocket as he climbed, as if for a door key. Every smooth and familiar move he made suggested he lived in the building.

"Might we be so blessed, Sal?" Mishkin asked Vitali.

"We deserve to be," Sal said. "And there are only six units in the building."

"Five to one," Mishkin said.

"I've bet on horses running at those odds."

"Have they ever finished in the money, Sal?"

"Never."

"Then that's probably Drubb going into the building," Mishkin said. "You can't finish out of the money every time at those odds. It's the law of percentages."

That was what Vitali liked about Harold. He actually thought there *was* a law of percentages.

This time, of course, Mishkin was right. The law of percentages asserted itself.

He and Sal simply followed Drubb into the building, waited while he looked in vain to see if he had any mail, then tailed him straight to his door.

He looked frightened when he saw the two of them standing so close to him and realized they hadn't simply been going in the same direction. They'd been following him.

"If you're looking for money . . ." he said, his eyes wide. People were mugged in the city every day. Maybe it was his turn.

They showed him their identification.

"If we're looking for money, what?" Mishkin asked.

Vitali stared at him.

"Then you came to the wrong place," Drubb said.

"I figured you'd say that," Mishkin said. "The law of percentages."

Vitali gave Mishkin his back-off look. "If you'll invite us in, Mr. Drubb, we'd like to talk with you for a few minutes."

Drubb finished unlocking his door and opened it, then stood aside so they could enter first. Vitali led the way, while Mishkin hung back and entered after Drubb.

"It's about Nora Noon," Drubb said.

"How'd you know that?" Mishkin asked.

"Law of—"

"Let's just sit down and get this over with," Sal interrupted in his gravelly voice. It was an incongruously commanding tone for such a short man, like a truck air horn on a sports car.

Drubb sat in a worn-out wing chair, Vitali on a wooden chair with curlicue arms that looked as if it belonged in a dining room. Drubb sat in a corner of a cream-colored sofa that could use a good cleaning. The place was a mess, with a pile of newspapers on the floor alongside the sofa, a half-full coffee cup on a table where it would leave a ring, one of the wooden slat blinds hanging crookedly. It was reasonably cool in there, though. A new-looking window air conditioner was humming along efficiently. On the floor directly beneath the air conditioner was a pair of well-worn jogging shoes, one of them lying on its side.

"I guess you can see I'm a bachelor," Drubb said. He was a powerfully built little man with wide-set blue eyes and a jaw that looked as if it could stamp steel. In his late thirties. Somehow not a bad-looking guy. Good head of black hair, combed straight back and held in place by some kind of grease. A straight nose and even teeth.

"We already knew that," Vitali said. "We checked after we found this." He held out the slip of paper with Drubb's name and phone number on it.

Drubb accepted the paper and stared at it, then raised his dark eyebrows questioningly. Mishkin suddenly wondered if Drubb's eyebrows and hair had been dyed.

"We found that in Nora Noon's dresser drawer," Mishkin said. "With a number of other things."

Drubb got halfway up from the sofa so he could reach forward and return the paper to Vitali. "This must be at least a year old."

"Why's that?" Vitali asked.

"It's been at least that long since I saw Nora."

"You were friends?"

"More than that."

"Were you and she in a relationship?"

"Were we screwing? Yeah."

"Serious about each other? I mean, beyond the in and out?"

"I was serious about her. She was serious about her work."

"How'd you two meet?" Mishkin asked.

"Through her work. I'm a salesman for a fabric distributor. I sold Nora some bolts of cloth for her fashion design business, and one thing led to another."

"Who left who?" Vitali asked.

"Nora broke it off. She told me she was no longer emotionally involved the way she had been. Said she couldn't help how she didn't feel. I believed her. I'd sensed for about a month she'd been losing interest."

"Sensed how?"

"Oh, you know. . . . She seemed to be less involved in what I was saying, sometimes looking past me and obviously thinking of something else. She just . . . seemed not to care about *us* anymore." He looked from one of them to the other. "I suppose I'm supplying you with a motive, but you're going to find out everything anyway. I don't see that I have much choice other than to tell the truth."

"So you'd lie to us if you could?" Mishkin said.

Drubb flashed an uneasy smile. "Only if I absolutely positively knew I could get away with it and no one else would be hurt."

Mishkin looked over at Vitali. "That seems like an honest answer, Sal."

"I don't figure I have a very strong motive," Drubb said. "It's not as if Nora would leave me, and I'd get jealous and kill her after more than a year."

"Oh, you'd be surprised," Mishkin said. "On a percentage basis—"

"We need to ask you some personal questions," Vitali said hastily, cutting off Mishkin and keeping the interview on track.

Drubb shrugged. "It's been a long enough time that questions about Nora and me won't seem personal. Besides, she's dead. I'd like to help nail the bastard who killed her."

"When the affair was on the front burner," Vitali said, "did it involve anything the unenlightened would regard as kinky?"

Drubb gave a short laugh that was almost a snort. "Kinky sex with Nora? Not a chance, Detective. Everything was as straight as if she'd learned it by reading a church manual. Not that she was undersexed. She was a good Catholic girl."

"Like Mary?"

Drubb knew what Sal meant. "No, she wasn't a virgin. And I don't mean to give the impression she was deeply religious. It was more like . . . well, as artistic as she was with her fashion designs, her imagination wasn't all that inventive when it came to lovemaking."

Sal made a mental note of that word. *Lovemaking.* It wasn't the way a man would describe sex with a woman he'd killed.

Mishkin must have been thinking along the same lines. "Are you still in love with her?" he asked.

"No," Drubb said. "We both knew it was over. I'm in another relationship now."

"Is this one more imaginative?" Mishkin asked.

"Considerably."

"I'm assuming you met some of Nora's friends. Were any of them rumored to be kinky?"

"God, yes! They were all fashion people. Nora was the different one."

Sal said, "Did Nora give any indication that she'd ever been forced against her will into any sort of kinky sex?"

"Definitely not," Drubb said. "All Nora seemed to think about was woof and warp."

Mishkin seemed to consider that, as if it might refer to some sort of sexual practice of which he was unaware.

"That's the two different directions threads run in material," Drubb said, seeing his confusion.

"Woof and warp," Mishkin said, as if digesting the information. "You must know a lot about materials like the ones in Nora Noon's apartment."

"Well, I do."

Vitali sighed and stood up from his uncomfortable little chair. "We'd like you to give us a list of names, Mr. Drubb. The people you remember as Nora's acquaintances."

"I'll do the best I can."

Drubb stood up and went over to a small desk that appeared to have been beaten with chains to make it look like an antique. It looked like a cheap desk that had been beaten with chains. He moved various detritus out of the way, then opened a drawer and got out an address book and pen and paper. "I'll give you addresses and phone numbers, too, if I have them."

"We'd be grateful," Vitali said.

Drubb set to work while they watched.

"We might need you later as a material witness," Mishkin said.

Vitali looked at him, wondering.

29

Vincent Salas's appointed attorney, Jack Murray, had never before defended a rapist. Alleged rapist. The wily old prosecutor, Maurice Givens, was having fun with the young attorney.

Murray, an affable fellow and not without persuasive powers, had been able to get a change of venue on the grounds that everyone in Hogart and the surrounding county wanted to torture and kill Salas. The jury not only might have been biased, they might have been hard to hold back.

Even with the Jefferson City jury, the trial was going poorly for Murray—and of course for his client, Vincent Salas.

Not that Salas was helping his cause. He'd refused to get a haircut and shave off his beard, and Murray couldn't talk him into wearing a coat and tie. For some reason Salas had rejected the simple strategy of looking unlike a motorcycle thug who would rape a young housewife.

Salas wore a blue work shirt, a clean pair of Levi's, and his black engineer's boots. He'd at least shined the boots. Murray was a little bit proud of having talked him into that.

"Of course," said Givens in his smooth southern Missouri

glide, "the defendant's real problem is that *aaall* the evidence points to his guilt."

Murray was a skinny young blond man with untamable short hair. He leaped to his feet to protest. He seemed to leap when he did everything. Even before his objection, he got a weary "Sustained" from the judge, but the jury had heard. And Murray had to admit, Givens was right about the evidence being a mountain under which Vincent Salas was all but buried.

Now Givens got to the point. He turned to Beth Brannigan, who was dressed in an ankle-length pleated skirt and high-necked white blouse with ruffled trim.

"My dear Mrs. Brannigan," he said at slightly higher volume, "is the man who raped you present today in this courtroom?"

Beth was so nervous she had to consciously force the words from where they'd stuck in her throat. "Yes, sir. He is."

"And would you point to him, please."

Beth's arm snapped up even though her hand and the finger that pointed were trembling. She was pointing at Vincent Salas, who stared back at her with the mock deadpan expression of a man who knew the deck was stacked, and that he'd had a losing hand even before the cards were dealt.

"Let the record show . . ." Givens was intoning.

Jack Murray had known from the beginning that the case was hopeless. There had been his client, sleeping and drunk, a few miles from where the victim had been raped, and a few feet from empty beer cans of the brand that had been stolen from her when he'd fled the scene. There was his motorcycle parked nearby, a Harley-Davidson, just as the witness who'd seen him flee had described. There was Murray's client, dressed as his victim had described. There were scratches on his face, and his victim had described how she'd scratched him.

Now there he was in court, with his dark hair and dark beard, as his victim had described. And the prosecution's expert witness had already testified how Salas's blood type was the same as that found at the scene of the rape. From the scratches on his face, no doubt. The ones Salas claimed had been made by a feral cat.

"Ah, the feral-cat defense," Givens had muttered, barely loud enough for the jury to overhear.

Salas had even figured out a way to make things worse for him. He'd run from the law.

Not just from the law, but from Sheriff Wayne Westerley, who was a hero in the county and had won reelection to his office by a landslide two years ago. Murray had cross-examined Westerley yesterday. The sheriff, a handsome man to begin with, appeared in court wearing his tailored uniform, looking like a movie star, making Murray feel like the paparazzi. Westerley had sat there calmly while the flustered Murray leaped around as if electrified. The contrast wasn't lost on the jury. When Murray had sneaked a peek at them, he had the distinct impression they thought he was needlessly badgering Westerley, who was merely stating the facts.

At least when Westerley was finished with his devastating testimony and walked past the jury on his way out, no one had asked for his autograph.

What I should have done, Murray thought, was go to engineering school. Built bridges or something. Or maybe done stand-up comedy. A couple of times he'd managed to make the jury laugh.

It helped some that after the guilty verdict, Maurice Givens had taken him aside out in front of the courthouse and told him not to worry, this had been his first murder trial; Murray was young and had the makings of a top-notch trial lawyer.

The next week, after sentencing, Givens again approached

Murray outside the courthouse and slapped him on the back. "If the scumbag had anybody else for a lawyer—but me, of course—he'd have gotten fifty-five to sixty."

Salas had been sentenced to thirty-five years in the state penitentiary in Jefferson City. If he managed to survive, it would seem like an eternity. Murray didn't feel good about it.

"Don't be downcast," Givens had told him in parting. "We both know the bastard's guilty."

If Salas was downcast, it was difficult to know it. When he'd been sentenced, he'd worn the same stoic expression he'd displayed when found guilty, almost as if he were bored. Even when Murray visited him later in the lockup and they discussed the appeals process, Salas seemed disinterested. Both men knew where that short road would lead.

Murray told himself that what Givens had related to him outside the courthouse was true. Not just about him having the stuff to become a top-notch trial lawyer, but about Salas's obvious guilt. The evidence had certainly been there. And Salas had certainly acted like a guilty man. Now it was time simply to go through the process of appeal. Automatic motions that would mean nothing.

Time to chalk this one up to experience and think ahead, Murray told himself. And not just to this evening, when he had a date with a sexy court stenographer.

In two weeks he was going to defend in court some members of an organization called Humane Commandoes, who'd blown up a chicken coop, chickens and all, for no apparent reason. The ACLU wouldn't touch that one. The commandoes would have Murray as their lawyer.

It had been a small coop. Only a few chickens had died.

Murray figured maybe he had a chance.

30

Candice Culligan knew immediately upon entering the apartment that she wasn't alone. Her senses informed her of what her mind didn't yet know. Subtle movement in the air, a scent, a geometry unlike the one she'd left when she'd gone to work this morning, slight sounds of a frequency felt rather than heard.

After seeing what *might* have been the impression of a man on the duvet on her bed, Candice had become more cautious in everything she did. It was amazing what fear could do. The go-getter woman of supreme confidence had been replaced by someone meeker and milder. She'd come more and more to see her apartment as a refuge, a sanctuary from fear.

So powerful was the sum of these sensations that she actually turned to leave.

Her hand was reaching for the doorknob when she heard a man's voice say, "You're here now. You might as well stay for a while."

For the rest of your life.

She was still frozen by fear when he moved in close to her. His breath was warm on the back of her neck. She hadn't even had time to whirl and see who'd spoken.

He turned her around slowly, using only the tips of his

fingers on one hand to guide her, almost as if they were dance partners. With the slight movement she felt some of her fear slip away.

Candice had shifted her attaché case to her left hand to unlock and open her apartment door. Now, as she turned, she moved it to her right. It was leather, stuffed with legal briefs, heavy and with brass corners. A weapon. She drew her breath, planning to continue revolving her body, moving away from her assailant, coming up and around with the attaché case. Fast. Hard. *Visualize it and you can do it.*

Make it count!

As she coiled her body and made the beginning of her turn, her eyes snapped to the knife he held before her face. It had a knobby wooden handle and a short, wide blade that curved in on itself and ended in a sharp point.

Visualize it.

What she found herself visualizing was the knife parting her flesh, loosing torrents of scarlet blood.

If it hadn't been for the knife she might have made the initial moves of resistance. At least put up a struggle. But her resolution wilted within her and she heard herself whimper as she let her arm holding the attaché case drop. She couldn't make out her assailant's features through her fear and tears, but she could see that he was smiling. He was smiling and she was paralyzed.

Goddamn him, he was smiling!

Her willpower seemed to flow from her in exact proportion to his sadistic amusement.

That's all I am to him—something amusing.

He encircled her wrist with a powerful hand, squeezed, and she heard rather than felt her attaché case drop to the floor.

"I brought a case of goodies, too," he said. "It's in the bedroom. Let's go there and I'll show you."

He marched her slowly but steadily toward the short hall

leading to her bedroom, guiding her by her aching wrist, the cool knife blade now resting against her throat.

She glanced back and got a glimpse at his face. He didn't look like the man she'd mistakenly identified as her rapist years ago. Or, as far as she could tell, like the man who actually had raped her. And yet . . .

The mind could play such tricks.

His fingers dug into her arm and she whimpered again, and at the same time felt a hot coal of anger deep inside her. She wouldn't let herself be led like this, like a goddamned lamb to slaughter.

I know tae kwan do. Took the concentrated course in self-defense. I can beat this bastard in a fair fight.

But there was the odd little knife, and at that moment all she really knew was terror. One abrupt motion of his arm and her blood would flow.

The ember of anger refused to become flame. She would do what he said. It was her only chance of survival. And she clung to the belief that she *did* have a chance. That she'd be talking about this at the law office tomorrow, that she might even be testifying against this man in court.

She tried to tell him he was ruining his own life by what he was about to do, but the words wouldn't come. And what *was* he about to do? What crime *was* he about to commit?

Rape? Murder? Both?

Maybe he knows the risk he's taking, and is willing because this isn't the first time. Maybe he's done this before.

Maybe he's that killer.

The Skinner!

She struggled to speak, to plead with him, but her throat was so dry that she could only croak. Which made him smile again. It was the smile that struck her numb and dumb, that controlled her. *Control.* That was what he wanted. What all the assholes of the world wanted. That was why she'd become an attorney. She was the one who was supposed to be in control. The law controlled everyone. It was fair, or at least logical. She was a representative of the law.

And the person who had her was a representative of the devil. There was a force emanating from him that seemed supernatural, that dwarfed her own feeble efforts and made them meaningless.

He sat her down on the bed, pushed her back. The killer attorney might as well have been a humanlike doll in the hands of this real killer. His plaything. On the bed was the attaché case he'd mentioned, not so unlike her own. Except for the contents, which were visible because the case was opened so he could get what he needed in a hurry.

With quick, practiced motions, he deftly ripped off long strips of silver duct tape and bound her ankles, then turned her onto her stomach and taped her wrists behind her back. Rolled her over again so she was lying on her back, staring up at the ceiling.

He disappeared from her view for a moment and her strength and courage began to clear away some of her terror. She could do more than croak now. She could scream. She could scream loud!

She drew in her breath and tried, but merely whined.

She heard him laugh.

He was back, but she still had a chance to scream. She saw that he'd been to her closet and had one of her stiletto-heeled red pumps. As she stretched her jaws wide to shriek, he jammed the shoe's pointed toe deep into her mouth, pinching her lower lip against her teeth. The shoe's dirty, gritty sole lay hard against her tongue, its toe touching the back of her throat. The sound she made was more like a gargle than a scream.

Still pushing the leather toe down her throat, he bent the rest of the shoe upward, so it was shaped as if it were on the rear foot of someone taking a gigantic stride. The shoe's curved back rim dug into her forehead just above the bridge of her nose, while her nose was in the shoe itself. She could barely breathe, and the sole of the shoe was exerting leverage and forcing her lower jaw down so far it felt as if it might become unhinged.

Quickly he wound duct tape around the shoe and her head so that everything was firmly in place as one piece and the pressure forcing her mouth wide was constant.

He stood back with his arms folded and surveyed his work. The firmly taped shoe was immovable, its stiletto heel protruding from the center of her forehead like the horn of a unicorn. She could barely see beyond each side of the shoe.

He smiled as he thought that was what she'd look like if he applied more tape—a mummified unicorn.

But as it was, she closely enough resembled a goat.

He drew from his pocket a long silver chain with a silver letter *S* dangling from it. He held the chain before her so she could see it around the shoe, and then looped it over her taped head. It lay on her bare neck and chest like ice.

Then, seemingly ignoring her, he began to undress.

When he was nude, he used the knife to cut away her clothes. It took a while, and her clothes were ripped as much as cut cleanly. While this was occurring she closed her eyes and her mind and sent herself away. This wasn't happening to her, simply because it couldn't be. Somebody else. It was somebody else in this bed.

My bed!

Candice felt her bladder release. The warmth of her urine between her thighs and beneath her was strangely comforting.

But when he held the knife before her eyes, her horror made everything dark, darker, and she welcomed losing consciousness. She wanted nothing more in this world than to slip into nothingness.

Almost instantly she was choking, gagging. The stench of ammonia made her nauseated.

She saw the small bottle in his hand, with the tight cotton

wad stuffed in its neck, and knew immediately what he'd done. She could imagine him holding the bottle beneath her nose, near the deformed shoe.

He brought me back! Damn him! He brought me back!

"I don't want you to miss anything," he said, reading her mind. He gave her a smile that was eerily beatific. "Aren't you sorry now for what you did?"

Keeping the ammonia at the ready on the nightstand, he began to work with the knife.

He was quick, deft, engrossed.

Even as the pain roared through her blood she recalled a case where a woman's throat had been slit but not deeply enough to kill her. The victim's blood had coagulated faster and thicker than usual and she'd survived.

It *could* happen.

That was the one slender hope she clung to as she slipped into, and was yanked back from, unconsciousness. Again and again. Journeys in and out of pain.

And again.

Very calmly, he drew a pack of cigarettes from his pocket and lit one. Like a character in an old movie, he let the cigarette dangle from where it was stuck on his lower lip, so that it waggled when he talked. The scent of burning tobacco mingled with the smell of ammonia.

"It's funny, isn't it?" she heard him say. "We both want the same thing now. For you to stay alive as long as possible."

She moaned.

He giggled. "Well, I didn't mean funny *ha-ha*."

He held up the bloody knife so she could see it grasped in his rubber-gloved hand.

"Aren't you sorry now for what you did?"

But she observed the dreaded knife only briefly.

During those times when she was conscious, she could not look away from his eyes.

PART 2

Hell is empty,
And all the devils are here.

—WILLIAM SHAKESPEARE,
The Tempest

31

Quinn and Pearl stood among the Crime Scene Unit techs, medical examiner, and police photographer, looking down at the dead body of Candice Culligan. In the corner of his vision Quinn saw Pearl absently cross herself. She was given to spells of Catholicism.

Dr. Julius Nift, the ME, was still bending over the bed on which Candice lay. He was feeling and probing, his jaw set, his eyes intent. Repugnant though the little ME might be, Quinn had no doubts about Nift's competence.

"Last night around midnight, give or take two hours," Nift said, in answer to Quinn's question about time of death. "That's all I can give you right now. It looks as if he started in on her hours before she died."

"Stringing it out," Pearl said through clenched teeth.

"Exacting torture," Nift said, "with periods of rage. The way she's so tightly taped indicates that. And look at the careful and precise stripping away of the top layer of skin so it dangles in shreds. Almost as if he were decorating her."

Quinn forced himself to look again at what was left of Candice Culligan.

"Observe how those small cut marks and cigarette burns were done with such deliberation," Nift continued. "Now look at her pubic area, the way it was slashed. Those long, curved cuts. This was a crime of passion. Sometimes cold passion, but passion nonetheless."

"What about the shoe used as a gag?" Quinn asked.

Nift shrugged. "You tell me."

"The way it's taped to her face, so the spiked heel looks like it's coming out of her forehead, makes it look almost like a unicorn horn."

"So why would he give up on the wadded panties used as a gag?" Nift asked.

"He's not satisfied with just pain," Pearl said. "He wants to humiliate his victims. He's getting more violent, more dangerous, if that's possible."

"Why all the dried blood around her mouth?" Quinn asked Nift.

"Shoe toe mighta been jammed in there so hard it took some teeth out. I'll know more when I get her on the table and we get intimately acquainted."

Pearl felt her stomach turn. It was all she could do to hold herself in check and not physically attack Nift.

"The name on the mirror this time is Nathan Devliner," Fedderman said, walking back into the spacious bedroom. He'd been in another part of the apartment, checking for bloody writing. "I guess we have to check the Socrates's Cavern membership again."

Quinn said. "We still have the chain with the letter *S*."

"We were speculating about the shoe jammed in her mouth, and bent and taped over her face so it looks like she's grown a horn," Pearl said.

"Unicorn horn," Fedderman said.

Pearl glanced at Quinn.

"Great minds in the same channel," he said. But the stiletto heel *did* resemble a unicorn horn.

"Maybe a reference to a goat," Fedderman said. "A unicorn is a kind of goat."

"Sacrificial goats," Pearl said. She looked at Quinn and

Fedderman. "Who knows what goes on in the minds of these sickos?"

"Isn't it sacrificial lambs?" Fedderman said.

"Lambs don't have horns," Pearl said.

"They do if they're rams."

"Then they're not lambs."

"Enough," Quinn said.

"Maybe the killer just happened to find the shoe handy and figured it would make an effective gag," Fedderman said.

"The shoe's mate is in the closet," Quinn said. "He must have taken time out while she was unconscious or too scared to scream, and gone to get it and bring it back over to the bed. He was looking for effect. Whether he was thinking of sacrificial lambs—or goats—is hard to say."

"Or unicorns," Pearl said. "They're mythological, and maybe that's what our killer wants to become. That's what most serial killers want to become—myths." She did a double take and gave Fedderman a keen, appraising look. "What's with the new suit, Feds? I miss your baggy brown outfit. You keep wearing those Armani threads and people will stop thinking of you as a sartorial disaster. The rumor is that you abuse your suits before you wear them so you'll look like a suspect after a rough night in the lockup. It makes the riffraff identify with you and open up in interrogations."

"That's only a myth," Fedderman said.

Quinn looked more carefully at Fedderman. He, too, had noticed something different about the potbellied, lanky detective. Fedderman's obviously expensive blue suit made him look as if his mismatched body was made of matching parts, which was a triumph of tailoring.

The suit *was* a pip. Quinn could think of only a few reasons why Fedderman might suddenly have become a virtual *GQ* model. He didn't like any of them.

After the techs left, Quinn and his detectives went through the apartment methodically. They were sure the lab wouldn't come up with a useful fingerprint or palm print, and there would be nothing distinctive about the gloves the killer wore. The Skinner was nothing if not careful.

Quinn made it a point to check Candice Culligan's address book. It contained no Nathan Devliner.

There was no Nathan Devliner in any of the NYC directories.

"Give me a minute," Pearl said, from where she was seated on the sofa working her laptop. "I'll check the Socrates's Cavern membership list Lido came up with."

The others stood silently while she bent closely over her computer.

"Here it is!" she said after a few minutes. "Devliner was a member."

She raised a finger, asking for more time.

They gave it to her. More than a few minutes this time.

"Okay," she said finally, looking up from her computer. "Nathan Ernest Devliner was a Socrates's Cavern gold-key member from January, 1970, to September, 1975, when he moved out of the area. He died in Kingdom City, Arizona, in April of 1986. A cerebral hemorrhage. He was seventy-four. I guess he retired and moved west."

"He retired and then some," Quinn said. "What he didn't do is torture and kill Candice Culligan. What he *isn't* is the Skinner."

Leaving them with the same puzzle they'd set out to solve.

32

Jock Sanderson had done time for raping Judith Blaney. It had been hard time. A small man, with fine features and a lean, muscular frame, Jock had fallen victim to sexual abuse in prison. Half a dozen gang members had in fact made him their own, passing him around like depreciating property.

It had been a nightmare, and it had lasted until the team of Legal Aid lawyers, campaigning to overturn wrongful eye-witness rape convictions, used DNA evidence to prove that someone else had raped Judith Blaney.

Late last year, Jock Sanderson was pardoned.

The real evidence had been skimpy to begin with. Jock had simply been in the wrong place at the wrong time, and Judith Blaney had been the wrong woman. She'd wrongly identified him in a police lineup, and again in court. She more than anyone had caused him to live his nightmare. To live it over and over for more than five years.

So what was left of Jock had been freed to walk in a world that still thought him unworthy. He'd begun to drink, an old habit that soon became an addiction. Now he was a regular at AA meetings and had been dry for months.

The only job he'd been able to find was with Sweep 'Em Up Janitorial Service, sweeping and cleaning entertainment venues, from sporting events to Broadway and off-Broadway theaters, the days after evening performances. A weekly paycheck had enabled him to leave the halfway house and the constant pressure of church services and one-on-one attempts to convert him to Christianity. Jock dealt with that by doing what he figured most Christians did—pretend. Prison had taught him well how to do that.

He could sometimes even pretend and fool himself.

The way Jock figured it, he'd been done wrong. Somebody owed him. That somebody was Judith Blaney.

He hadn't raped Judith. He'd been home in bed alone, suffering with a cold, on the evening of her rape. Of course he had no witnesses to corroborate his alibi. Usually you didn't welcome company when you were flat on your back with a fever and congested chest.

Jock had never seen Judith before his arrest. But he dreamed about her a lot in prison. He'd seen her face almost every night in his dreams. Her nightmare lived within his nightmare.

Often, some of the things that had been done to him in prison, he did to Judith Blaney in his dreams. His muffled screams became hers. Also his humiliation. His pain. She would beg him with her eyes to stop. But he didn't stop. Not in his dreams.

Sometimes, he thought, dreams meant something.

Jock had been following Judith for almost three months. He didn't mind if now and then she noticed him. Let her wonder.

After the first month, she'd obtained a restraining order. He was forbidden by law to harass her, or even to approach within a hundred feet of her.

He knew what a hundred feet meant. He could measure the precise distance in his mind. So he continued to follow Judith. He would be far enough away that she couldn't do anything about it. She would know he was there though. Not always, but she could never be sure when he was observing her. At times she'd forget and feel safe. Then she'd glance behind her and there on the crowded sidewalk, or perhaps across the street watching her pull away in the back of a taxi, there he would be, and any joy would drain from her features and an expression he interpreted as fearful would come over her. That would give him a cold satisfaction.

But most of the time she didn't know he was tailing her. That also gave him satisfaction. He was becoming expert at watching her without her knowledge. Sometimes even moving close to her, inside the protective hundred-foot legal distance. Like a trespasser on a dare.

Like tonight. He'd been on the same crowded subway car, then only ten feet behind her on the teeming platform. He'd been nearby her on the escalator. He kept a more prudent distance behind her on the sidewalk on the way to her apartment. She would often glance behind her, especially if the night was dark and the sidewalks not crowded.

He was close enough tonight to hear the tapping of her high heels. If he stayed tight to the buildings, keeping an awareness of light and shadow, he could haunt her like a ghost whose presence she would barely sense.

Now and then he'd deliberately let her catch a glimpse of him, let her know she wasn't alone in this fear-filled world that only the two of them inhabited and that she had helped to create.

Jock knew Judith now better than she could imagine. The way hunters knew the thing they hunted.

It was almost an hour after dusk. They were on a long block that was almost deserted. Only the two of them. *Tap, tap, tap* went her heels on the hard concrete. Echoing in the street and in his mind.

Can you feel my eyes on you?
Sense my thoughts?

I already served time for raping you. Maybe I have a free one coming. Maybe more than just rape. I paid. You should pay.

Her stride was brisk and rhythmic, hurried but not panicked. Not yet.

Tap, tap, tap . . .

Faster now. She was picking up her pace. Afraid of something. Did she know he was here? No, she couldn't. She couldn't be sure.

He was certain she hadn't spotted him.

He dropped back, confused by her obvious uneasiness, and saw a figure detach itself from the shadows and fall in behind Judith. The figure was that of a man. Medium height. Medium build. That was all he could be sure of from this distance.

Jock slowed his pace and tailed the man who was following Judith. Unquestionably, the shadowy figure was acting furtively. What was going on? Was Judith getting plain-clothes protection? Had she gotten the police interested in him again?

No, he was sure the police would have approached him or come to his door and warned him. Since the day Judith had pointed her finger at him in a lineup, he'd been close acquaintances with the police, with the prison system, with the thugs that kept the order. They were all alike.

Sometimes they wore uniforms, sometimes not. But he was positive the figure ahead wasn't a policeman. The police didn't work that way. Didn't look that way. Didn't *feel* that way.

Jock watched the man following Judith stand across the street from her as she entered her apartment building.

The man tilted back his head and stared up at the correct window and waited patiently until it became illuminated. Then he put his hands in his pockets and walked away. His gait was different now. More relaxed. The intensity had gone out of him.

Excitement rippled through Jock like a chill. Something strange was happening here. Someone else had entered their private, fearful world.

He wasn't the only one stalking Judith.

33

It was a few minutes past eleven the next morning. Quinn was alone in the office, a quiet cocoon in the maelstrom of Manhattan. The sharp ring of the phone was startling. He squinted at caller ID. Nift from the morgue. Quinn reached for the receiver.

"I won't keep you in suspense," Nift said, when Quinn had picked up. "Official cause of Candice Culligan's death was a heart attack."

Quinn was slightly surprised. "Pain did that to her?"

"More likely the thought of more pain. Under the kind of torture she underwent, sometimes the body and mind simply can't endure any longer. If Candy hadn't had the coronary event, she would have soon bled to death from the knife wounds. The partial skinning process."

Candy. Not only was Nift on a first-name basis with the woman's corpse, he was using a nickname. Quinn wondered sometimes about Nift's relationships with his female subjects. Pearl had voiced suspicions about the obnoxious little ME, and Pearl had an annoying way of being right about people.

"What about the way her throat was cut open?" Quinn asked, trying to shake the creepy feeling that sometimes came over him when he was talking with Nift.

"A sharp, broad, and curved knife blade did that in two

intersecting cuts, probably done slowly. The cutting wasn't as deep or damaging as it appeared. The throat wound might have been the final one inflicted, and the killer thought it was the coup de grâce. But she was already near death when her throat was cut. I say *near* death because her heart was still pumping when the injury was inflicted. The wound bled enough to indicate that."

"Was the same knife used to inflict all her wounds?"

"It looks that way. A handy little blade. And by the way, there was no damage from the necklace chain with the *S* charm. And apparently it was put on the victim before her death."

"I don't suppose there was anything of the perpetrator on her."

"Not even a hair. And the only blood on her was her own. There was no flesh beneath her fingernails. No saliva or sperm anywhere. Just the marks of long and arduous torture, mostly of peeling off her top layer of skin and leaving it hang in shreds, until finally her heart gave out. I've been over every inch of her, Quinn, and I can tell you this little tootsie went the hard way."

Little tootsie. Jesus, Nift!

"There were twelve carefully placed cuts on her body, used to initiate the peeling process, and twenty-seven stab wounds in and around her pubic area. The knife penetrated her vagina at least twice. Not far, but it did great damage."

"Raped with a knife blade," Quinn said. "Was she dead at the time?"

"No, those injuries were all antemortem."

"He's one sick bastard," Quinn said. "What about the blood around her mouth. The shoe do that?"

"No," Nift said, "her tongue was cut out."

"God! I hope he didn't do *that* to her while she was still alive."

"She was dead, or there would have been even more

blood. And maybe we'd have gotten lucky and she might have bitten him. That would have given us some DNA to work with. He's one careful killer, Quinn."

"And angry."

"The tongue might have been removed by the same knife he used to skin her. Actually, it did a neat job, like it had a hook blade and was made expressly for removing tongues."

"People eat calves' tongues. Do slaughterhouses use a special kind of knife to remove them?"

"I don't know. Your department. Go question some cows. If you don't have any more questions, I'm going to terminate our conversation, Quinn. I got another hot date waiting. Well, cool date."

"I'll call you if I think of anything," Quinn said.

"I was just about to suggest that," Nift said, and broke the connection.

The street door opened with a draft of warm air, and Fedderman came in wearing his brand-new suit and a fresh white shirt. He walked like a model in need of a runway. "There's no Nathan Devliner in the New York phone directories," he said.

"No surprise there," Quinn said.

"Also, I talked with all the residents in Candice Culligan's building. Nada for my efforts." He strutted over and poured himself a mug of coffee, careful not to drip anything on his sleeve. "What the animal did to her couldn't have made much noise."

Fedderman went to his desk and slouched in his chair, ruining the suit's effect so that he was once again the familiar Fedderman. Quinn told him about Nift's phone call.

"Cut her tongue out?" Fedderman's face screwed up as if his own tongue ached in sympathy.

"'Fraid so," Quinn said. "Nift said the Skinner did a neat job of it. Probably with the same knife that inflicted the other wounds. Happened after she was dead. Killer probably knew there'd be too much blood if he tried it while she was still alive. Besides that, she might have managed to bite him."

"Killer's smart," Fedderman said. "He leaves us nothing to work with except what he chooses. Sends us the way he wants us to go."

"Toward Socrates's Cavern," Quinn said. "The members' names written in blood, the letter *S* on or near the victims, maybe even a victim resembling a sacrificial animal . . . it all points too clearly in that direction. By now the killer must know we're not buying into it."

"Oh, I dunno," Fedderman said. "He might think we're not very smart."

"I can't imagine what would give him that idea," Quinn said, "except he's getting away with murder."

"Maybe he believes in ghosts. All the suspects he's given us are dead."

Fedderman stood up from his chair in seemingly disjointed sections, the way he always did; even the Armani suit couldn't disguise that. He walked over to the rack and removed his suit coat, then draped it carefully on a hanger.

"Why the new threads?" Quinn asked, as Fedderman returned to his desk chair. He picked up some papers and idly scanned them, then dropped them back, as if he might not have heard Quinn.

"I thought it was time," he said at last.

"I didn't notice any patches on your old clothes," Quinn said.

Fedderman sighed and met Quinn's gaze directly. "You aren't gonna let this go, are you? You or Pearl?"

Quinn smiled. "Sorry, Feds."

"Okay. I'm interested in somebody, and she seems interested in me. I figured, in her honor, I oughta replace at least one of my old detective suits."

"I would think you'd save the Master of the Universe outfit for when you weren't working."

"When am I not working?"

"You've got a point. In fact, you need another suit."

Fedderman shrugged. "I got a couple of sport jackets that'll get me by."

"Do any of us know this woman who wields such sartorial influence?"

"I don't think so." Fedderman squirmed in his chair. "You know her name, though. Penny."

"I don't think—" Then Quinn remembered. "Penny Noon?"

"We've gone out a couple of times." Fedderman made a backhanded, dismissive motion with his long fingers, as if the assignations meant nothing of importance.

Quinn knew better. "I dunno, Feds. A victim's sister . . ."

"Are there rules and regulations?" Fedderman asked.

"No, no . . ." Quinn leaned back in his chair, almost toppling, and laced his fingers over his stomach. Fedderman was right. Penny Noon wasn't all that close to what had happened to her sister Nora. Or didn't seem to be. It wasn't as if she was a suspect or an eyewitness. And this wasn't the NYPD. He lifted his feet and let the chair tilt forward. "No problem, Feds. Live happily ever after."

"Well, thank you very much, Your Honor."

"Thanks for what?" Pearl asked.

Neither man had noticed her enter. She wandered over and got her morning mug of coffee. Third mug, actually. Her lush black hair was still mussed, almost the way it was when Quinn had left the brownstone this morning and she was tumbling out of bed.

As she moved toward her desk, she glanced in the direction of the coatrack, then at Fedderman. "You got an ascot goes with that thing?"

"I don't need a mascot," Fedderman said.

She plopped down in her desk chair, ostensibly uninterested in what he had to say. She got out the Swiss Army knife she kept in her drawer and used as a letter opener, and deftly sliced open an envelope she'd plucked from her post office box on the way to the job. Maybe she was going to forget about the portion of the discussion she'd overheard on entering the office.

"Thanks for what?" she asked again, absently.

Quinn said nothing. He and Fedderman knew Pearl was on the scent and would one way or another get an answer to her question.

"Penny Noon," Fedderman said, in quick surrender.

"Penny Noon what?" Pearl asked, glancing at what looked like an ad that she'd slid from the envelope.

"Nora Noon's sister," Quinn said. "Feds is seeing her."

"She's been invisible?"

"No. *Seeing* her."

"In a romantic way?"

"Yes."

"Explains the amazing dream suit," Pearl said. She crumpled envelope and ad and dropped them into her wastebasket. She looked deadpan at Fedderman. "Penny short for Penelope?"

"I don't know," Fedderman said.

"Must be serious."

Quinn thought it was time to change the subject before Fedderman could come up with a retort. "Nift called about the postmortem," he said to Pearl. He told her about the phone call and about Candice Culligan's tongue being removed. Even tough Pearl blanched when she heard about the tongue. But she seemed to regain her equilibrium quickly.

"That's sick, Quinn."

"Don't I know it? All in all, there's not much we can use. The victim was methodically tortured and then stabbed twenty-seven times in and around the pubic area."

"The things we do for love," Pearl said.

34

No one spoke for a while. Pearl booted up her desk computer and fed something into it with a flash drive she'd brought with her and dug out of her purse. She seemed, in her mind, to be alone in the room.

Quinn wondered why she had to hound Fedderman so persistently. She did that to almost everyone she knew. Quinn could love her because he understood that these were defensive actions. Preemptory strikes, but defensive.

There were other, more admirable, facets to Pearl's personality, and she was so damned smart. That last part was what made her at least bearable to her fellow detectives. There was no denying her talent. Or her doggedness.

Still, she could make life miserable for Fedderman. And for Vitali and Mishkin when they were unable to avoid her.

And, let's face it, sometimes for Quinn.

"I did a few hours' work on my laptop before coming in," she said. "Made a discovery."

"About our latest victim?" Quinn asked.

"Yeah. Six years ago Candice Culligan was beaten and raped. They caught the guy and he got fifteen to twenty at Elmira. Five months ago he was released because DNA evidence established that even though she'd identified him, he couldn't have been the rapist."

Pearl took a slow sip of coffee. Quinn knew she had more to say and was stringing it out. Fedderman was glaring at her, maybe still angry about the remark about not knowing Penny Noon's full name.

"So she was a rape victim," Fedderman said.

"They all were."

Quinn leaned forward. "Say again, Pearl."

"*All* of the victims where there were Socrates's Cavern clues were at one time or another rape victims. And the accused and convicted rapist in each case was released when DNA evidence overturned his conviction."

"So that's the relevant common denominator," Quinn said. "Not Socrates's Cavern."

"It would seem so," Pearl said. "We've been had."

"The bastard was playing us," Fedderman said. "Using Socrates's Cavern's old membership list to lead us down the wrong road."

"We suspected it," Pearl said. "At least, I did."

Quinn laced his fingers behind his head and leaned back, back, back in his swivel chair. Pearl and Fedderman were used to Quinn tempting disaster. He'd never actually tipped the chair, only almost.

"Bears thinking about, doesn't it?" Pearl said.

"Sure does," Quinn said. "It's too much of a coincidence that all these falsely accused and released rapists would all at once set about killing the women responsible for putting them behind bars."

"And ruining those men's lives," Fedderman said, "breaking up their families, blackening their reputations, costing them their employment . . ."

"Yeah, yeah," Pearl said. "You're thinking these guys have actually all gone bonkers at once and are getting their evens with the women who messed up their lives?"

"It's barely possible," Fedderman said, but not as if he believed it.

Pearl got a comb from her purse and ran it through her hair. "We're talking about a serial killer here, Feds. And a torturer. Not many people—even pissed-off falsely accused men—have that kind of monster living inside their skins."

"But one of them does," Quinn said. "One who knows he'll be the prime suspect when his accuser is murdered. The initial victims and the Socrates's Cavern connection are subterfuge. A forest so we won't notice the tree. He's killing the others so his intended victim will be just another corpse, part of a string of serial-killer victims."

"And if he's arranged for a halfway plausible alibi," Pearl said, "we'll never get onto him."

"Oh, we will," Quinn said. "Sooner or later we'll nail the bastard."

"I like the imagery," Pearl said.

"I wonder how many other women are out there in the same positions," Fedderman said, "with the men they falsely identified as their rapists recently sprung from prison."

"According to Blood and Justice—" Pearl began.

"What's that?" Quinn asked.

"The organization of attorneys dedicated to using DNA evidence to right legal wrongs. I used their website statistics to work it out. The number of mistakenly identified and convicted rapists released in the last five years in the New York area is thirty-two."

"You're joking?" Fedderman said.

Pearl finished with the comb and put it back in her purse. Her hair was still disheveled. "DNA doesn't joke."

"Assuming all those women are still in the area," Quinn said, "they're all in danger. We need to talk to them."

"And the men who did time because of them," Fedderman said. "One of them is probably the Skinner."

"I'll print out the list of women," Pearl said. "Then I'll work up the list of their exonerated alleged rapists."

"Names, addresses, whatever else you can find out," Quinn said.

Pearl was smiling. "I was just thinking, the safest of those women is the one the murderer doesn't want to harm until he's ready to risk drawing attention to himself—the woman who mistakenly identified the Skinner."

"If she isn't dead," Fedderman said. "One of the early victims."

Quinn shook his head no. "To be on the safe side, our guy will wait and take her down somewhere in the middle of his trophy hunt. He'll want the camouflage."

"Crazy old world," Fedderman said.

"It is if you're mooning about Penelope," Pearl said.

Fedderman was about to say something when Quinn caught his eye. Fedderman let out a long breath and sat back. *Some things,* said the look on his face, *you simply have to endure.*

Like Pearl and inclement weather.

"First thing we need to do," Quinn said, "is talk to the three men who were falsely accused of raping the first three victims."

"Keeping in mind," Pearl said, "that part of what we believe could be bullshit, and we might be talking to the killer."

Pithy Pearl.

"There is one other job I figured I'd give to Feds," Quinn said. "We need somebody to go to a slaughterhouse and find out if they use a special knife to remove calves' tongues. If so, see if they'll give you one." Quinn grinned. "A knife, that is."

Fedderman got up and deftly slipped on and buttoned his suit coat, as if he were about to model it. "Somebody's gotta look into this tongue thing, so why not me?"

"It'll keep your mind off Penelope," Quinn said.

Pearl said, "God, I hope so."

When Fedderman had left, Quinn phoned Renz at One Police Plaza.

"A breakthrough on the Skinner case?" Renz asked.

"Any second now," Quinn said. "Did you talk to Nift or read his report?"

"Yeah. The thing with the tongue—that's new. Give you any ideas?"

"Symbolism, maybe," Quinn said. "The victims talked at a trial and sent people to prison for rapes they didn't commit."

"*All* of the victims?"

"So far, yeah. And there are twenty-nine more women out there who might fit the profile. They need to be offered protection."

"They will be," Renz said.

The phone was silent for a few seconds.

"Then the entire goddamned chain of murders is symbolism," Renz said. "I don't see why we should settle on the tongue."

"The killer apparently took it with him. Maybe that means something."

"Or not." Renz was thinking about what else might not mean something. Protecting as many as twenty-nine women around the clock. Three eight-hour shifts times thirty-two. *Yeah, find me ninety-six cops with nothing to do, Quinn.*

Renz would do what he could.

"Either way, let's keep this tongue business from the media," Quinn said. "Only the Skinner and us will know about it. That way we can use it to test for false confessions and weed out all the crazies."

"Good idea, Quinn. Seems like everybody and their cousins are confessing to these murders, except for the real killer. Keeps our phone lines burning. And sometimes people actually walk into precinct houses and confess. Why the hell do people do that?"

"Maybe the same reason they confess in church," Quinn said.

"There," Renz said, "is a scary thought."

It wasn't as scary as the ones Quinn was thinking.

35

"You're *what*?" Roy Brannigan asked his wife. He jumped out of his chair as if lightning had struck nearby.

It was a warm summer night. The sky was still a faint purple, and dusk had sent its advance scout shadows among the trees. Crickets were chirping. Beth and Roy were on the porch. Beth had thought this would be a good time and place to tell him. Good as any, that is. She was pretending to sip ice water, and Roy had just finished drinking his second beer. Beth thought two beers might make him mellow enough that he wouldn't turn mean when she . . . surprised him. She sure didn't want to wait and take her chances with five or six beers.

She said the word again, realizing it was like dropping a stone into a calm pond: "Pregnant."

Roy paced three steps this way and that on the plank porch, a man walking nowhere, banging his heels so they made a lot of noise. "For the love of Jesus, Beth!"

She remained seated in her rocking chair, knowing that if she stood it might escalate whatever was going to happen.

"Roy, please! It's not like it's my fault."

He stopped pacing to face her with his fists propped on his hips. "How were you dressed? What were you doing taking a shortcut I told you over and over not to take? And at night! What were you carrying under your arm? How'd you just happen to cross paths with that Vincent Salas?"

"How do you know—"

"That it isn't mine?" He turned his head to the side and spat. "I haven't touched you since you became unclean in the eyes of the Lord. I hadn't touched you the month before the . . . thing with Salas."

You never touched me enough, she thought, and was immediately ashamed of herself.

"You got inside you a child with the mark of the beast," Roy said.

"Don't talk like that, Roy. I need you."

"Oh, you got what you need. Dressed like a whore, with alcoholic drinks on display, and wandering through the dark woods. What did you think might happen? What did you *want* to happen?"

"Not what happened, Roy! I swear it."

"You got nothin' left to swear to," Roy said, and hurled his empty beer can far out into the night.

"When you get raped," Beth said, remembering the ER nurse's words, "it's something that happens *to* you. You have no control over it."

"Like you got no control over lots of things once you start tempting fate and the devil."

"But I didn't start—"

He stomped inside the house and slammed the door after him. It made a sound like a gunshot. An execution.

She looked in through a front window a few minutes later and saw him seated at the desk reading his Bible. The hand that wasn't turning pages was clenched in a fist.

The devil was very real to Roy.

They exchanged no more words before going to bed and lying with their backs turned to each other. Beth couldn't stop crying and lay with tears tracking down her face and making her pillow damp. Outside the house, insects buzzed loudly and seemed to be accusing her, as if they knew what she was and disapproved. As if all of nature disapproved of her.

When she awoke in bright morning light, only seconds passed before dark dread began smothering her again, tightening her throat and making her sick to her stomach.

The baby . . . !

She felt with her right hand what might already be a swelling of her abdomen.

Too early. Too early for that.

A slight noise made her raise her head and look around. She was alone in the bed. Roy was fully dressed and standing over by his dresser. He had a suitcase propped on a chair and was stuffing clothes from the dresser drawer into it.

"What're you doing, Roy?"

"Just what it looks like."

"You're packing."

"That's what I'm doing," he said, not bothering to glance her way. "I'm packing."

Within five minutes she heard the front door slam, and then the car door outside like a belated echo.

The car's engine kicked over and immediately roared. Tires crunched on gravel and spun faster, casting rock and dirt as if sowing seed.

When the sound of the car had subsided, Beth climbed out of bed and plodded into the living room. The house was silent and felt empty, as if even *she* weren't there.

Absently dragging her fingertips over furniture, reassuring herself as to its substance, she wandered across the room to the desk and opened the top drawer.

The Bible, King James Version, with its worn red leather cover, wasn't in its usual place, tucked in the front right corner of the drawer.

She slid open a bottom drawer. There was no sign of the plain yellow envelopes containing Roy's pornography collection.

Roy was gone.

She was alone.

36

New York, the present

Adam Wright lived in a basement apartment in Lower Manhattan that wasn't fit for rats. He was a man in his forties, but he looked older. His face was the color of slate. His eyes were only slightly darker and refused to be still, though they were always downcast. The way his facial bones seemed about to pierce his flesh suggested that once he might have been a handsome man. Now he was wasted as if by some persistent disease.

After Pearl had knocked on his door and shown him her ID, he'd offered her the only chair. It was a rickety, wooden straight-back with wriggly armrests and lots of spindles. On it sat a blue, absolutely flat pad decorated with a faded New York Mets team logo. Pearl settled down carefully on the chair, hoping it wouldn't collapse beneath her, and got out her notepad and her gnawed yellow pencil. Wright sat slumped on the edge of the unmade bed. She didn't have to tell him why she'd come.

He said, "I felt as bad as anyone when I heard about Millie Graff being killed."

"How *did* you hear about it?" Pearl asked. The stench of stale perspiration and something she couldn't identify made her want to jump up and flee from the tiny efficiency. There was no stove, only a hot plate with a dented old pressure cooker on its double burner. Maybe Wright had been cooking something that produced the rotten smell.

"I saw it in a newspaper somebody threw away. Soon as I read it, I got scared. I think you know why."

"How'd it happen?" Pearl asked.

"The murder?" His pale eyes remained downcast, roaming this way and that, as if he were trying not to stare at her breasts.

She waited patiently until he looked up at her face. "Not the murder," she said. "How'd you get the bad collar on the rape charge?"

Eyes down again, focused somewhere to the right of her knees. "I was working on a construction crew over on Tenth Street. Repairing a stone fascia. It was hard work, but it paid good. I'd just been transferred there after a roofing job in SoHo. The others had been there over a week. The guys I was working with talked a lot about Millie Graff, though none of us knew her name then. She had great legs, they said, and whenever she walked past, she'd put on a kind of show for us. Tried to get a reaction. You'd be surprised how many women do that."

Pearl wouldn't be surprised by how many construction workers *thought* that. "Maybe it was in your imagination about Millie Graff. She was a professional dancer, so she'd have great legs and a certain way of walking."

"Yeah, she sure as hell had that. Those. Anyway, the guys that appreciated her pointed her out to me one day, and it seemed to me she gave me the look."

Pearl raised her eyebrows. "*The* look?"

"That one. So I didn't think she'd mind if I put a move on her next time she passed. You know, just talked to her."

"According to the court record, you suggested oral sex, only not in polite language."

"Yeah, I guess that was kinda outta line."

"Dumb, too."

"Sure. But not punishable by five years in prison for a crime I didn't commit." His eyes were steadier now, more injured than angry.

"I agree."

"Sure you do, now, when it's too late."

"I'd apologize if it'd do any good," Pearl said.

Despite herself, she was beginning to like Adam Wright. Or at least beginning not to *dis*like him. It was easy to see what he'd been, and might be now, if he'd had better luck. Beneath the grime and stench was a decent man approaching a premature middle age and the abyss all humans feared. He had been picked up by a whim of fate and plunked down here in a crappy life, and his future looked even worse.

"What do you do now, Adam?" she asked.

"Do? You mean to survive? I get a Social Security disability check because I fell off a ladder a few months ago washing windows. Messed up my back."

"What's in that sack over there?"

Immediately she wished she hadn't asked. Wright began to tremble. He attempted a smile. "You got a search warrant?"

"I don't want a warrant," Pearl said. "I'm not gonna look in the sack."

She made an obvious show of *not* writing in her pad. She'd be damned if she was going to report some poor wreck for selling aluminum cans to augment his disability payments. All so he could pay the rent for this shit hole.

Wright nodded gratefully. He tried to shrug but seemed too weary even for that. "You get outta prison, and even if it's DNA evidence that sprang you, people still associate you with rape. Now, even with murder. I had a good job doing construction work. Since then I haven't been able to find anything. I know why, and even understand. Hell, I wouldn't hire me." He looked so disgusted he wanted to spit, and probably would have if he wasn't entertaining company. He dragged a hand with ragged fingernails across his lips. "It's easier to lose a reputation than to find one."

"What about the night Millie was murdered?" Pearl asked.

"I was in the hospital, watching hour after hour of *South Park* reruns."

"My God, Adam."

"I didn't kill Kenny, either. Not even once."

"Get serious, Adam."

"Okay. That was the night I had my rare bit of luck. I'd bent over earlier that day to pick up a . . . to pick up something, and I couldn't straighten up. This happened up at Fifty-fourth Street and Lexington, and a lot of people gathered around me. Some guy with a cell phone called for help and I got taken to a hospital emergency room. They helped me some but not much, and I spent the entire night there, watching TV and driving the nurses crazy, trying to get them to give me more pain pills. Angels of mercy—bullshit!"

"They might turn out to be angels after all," Pearl said, "if they give you an airtight alibi."

"That's what the other cop said."

Pearl paused in her note taking.

"What other cop would that be?"

"The one who was here a few days after Millie Graff's murder."

"What was his name?"

"Her name? Hell, I don't know. She wasn't as pretty as you. She had an NYPD badge, though. She was all business."

"Don't think I'm not," Pearl said.

"No, ma'am."

"I can see how you got into trouble."

For the first time, Wright smiled. Briefly he looked ten years younger and Pearl saw again what he might have been, and it made her sick.

She put away her pencil and notepad in her purse and stood up, careful not to lean her weight on the chair's spindly arms.

"That's it?" Wright asked.

"It."

He looked disappointed. Probably he never got visitors unless someone in the neighborhood was raped or murdered.

"I was told my alibi checked out," he said, as if struggling to maintain conversation, to keep her there. His starvation for human contact had overwhelmed his fear. Again Pearl felt a thrust of pity for him. To be such an outcast, to be shunned, could in itself be a disease.

But what could she do? She couldn't give him back his reputation. His five years.

"How's your back now?" she asked.

"Not good. I need an operation to repair some ruptured disks. Tell me the city's gonna pay for that."

"I would if I thought it'd help."

"But it won't."

"It won't," Pearl said, and left him alone in the ruins.

"Wright is just a poor schmuck," Pearl said, sitting at her desk in the Q&A offices. "My gut tells me he couldn't kill anyone."

"Anyone under the right circumstances can kill anyone else," Quinn said. He was standing, with his sleeves rolled up, drinking a diet Coke.

"You really believe that?" Pearl asked.

Quinn wiped foam from his chin and stared at her, wondering how she could think otherwise, considering the experience she'd had as a cop. "Yeah. I don't like it, but I believe it."

Pearl knew he was right, but she didn't feel like giving Quinn the satisfaction of agreeing with him. Besides, she was still feeling sorry for Adam Wright.

"Wright was in the hospital the night Millie Graff was killed," she said. "He'd been collecting aluminum cans and hurt his back."

"That's his alibi? He hurt his back picking up an aluminum can?"

"Well, he didn't admit he was a can collector, but I'm sure he is. The important thing is, he hurt his back and was hospitalized at the time of Millie's murder."

"You feel for this guy, Pearl?"

"His life is a load of shit. But aside from that, he really does have an alibi."

"Did you check out his story?"

"No. I will." Pearl had no doubt that hospital records, along with eyewitness accounts, would substantiate Adam Wright's alibi. Still, she should be reserving judgment until she verified his alibi. Was she getting soft?

"You getting soft, Pearl?"

Damn it! Thinking parallel thoughts again. It angered her. It was almost as if her privacy was being invaded.

"You should move in with me permanently," Quinn said. "We could be like an old married couple that finishes each other's—"

"Sentences," Pearl interrupted. She smiled and shook her head. "I don't think so, Quinn."

"We're sleeping together some of the time, anyway, even if we are practicing celibacy." *Yancy Taggart, even dead, is still in the way.*

"Almost celibacy," Pearl said. Things had changed lately, and were still changing, but slowly.

"I said *practicing*," Quinn said. "And I'm redecorating the brownstone for you."

"That place is an investment," Pearl said. "And eventually it'll be a good one. That's why you're rehabbing it."

Quinn smiled. "Pick a room and choose a color."

"Your room, black." She laughed. "Never mind. Anyway,

if I moved in with you, my mother wouldn't approve. She still calls it shacking up, like I'm young Barbara Stanwyck in one of those movies where she winds up in an electric chair."

"Could happen," Quinn said.

"Yeah, to anyone. You told me so just a few minutes ago."

"Barbara Stanwyck. Didn't she usually get last-minute reprieves in those movies?"

"Not all of them."

"Think about it, Pearl. Please."

"I have. And my gut feeling is that Adam Wright didn't kill anyone."

Quinn sighed, making sure it was loud enough for Pearl to hear. "Okay. Just check his story before we strike him from the list."

"Of course," Pearl said. "Quinn?"

"Yeah?"

"The brownstone tonight wouldn't be a bad idea."

"Your air conditioner broken?" Quinn asked.

"I'll break it if you want."

37

The day had started off unseasonably warm. Now brief snow flurries formed droplets on the windshield, so that occasionally the wipers were needed. Sheriff Wayne Westerley steered his Ford Crown Vic cruiser up the bumpy driveway from the county road to Beth Brannigan's ramshackle frame house. The driveway, more of a road, really, was once graveled, but over the years mud and ruts had claimed most of the rock.

If Roy Brannigan hadn't lit out on Beth when he learned she was pregnant, Westerley would have been on him to regravel the drive, just to save the suspension on the cruiser. But Westerley wasn't about to utter a word that might cause more hardship for Beth.

He parked in front of the plank porch and sat for a moment behind the wheel while a stiff breeze blew flecks of snow almost horizontally across the windshield. When the bare tree limbs stopped swaying, he opened the door and climbed out.

Beth had heard his arrival and came out onto the porch. She was wearing a sacklike blue dress that hung from shoulders hunched against the cold. He saw that her feet were clad in fuzzy blue house slippers. Her hair was streaked red where the cold sunlight struck it. She wore no makeup that he could discern, and her eyes were the blue of her skirt. Normally a graceful woman, she stood somewhat awkwardly with her feet planted wide. It was late now in her pregnancy.

As Westerley approached from around the other side of the car, he absently started to put on his eight-point cap.

Beth smiled. "You don't put *on* a hat when you're about to enter a house, Sheriff."

Westerley smiled back. This woman, with all she'd been through, and how she'd looked on the night of the rape and later in court, caused his throat to tighten up so words didn't come easily. "Since you called and left a message with the dispatcher," he said, "I figured it was an official visit."

"Well, I guess it is. But it can be a hatless one."

She held the front door open for him and he edged inside past her, smelling the fresh scent of perfumed soap or shampoo. It struck him that despite what had happened to her, a woman like Beth would get lonely with her husband gone. Then he cautioned himself not to think that way, even though Roy was a grade-A prick to have deserted his wife after what happened, just when she needed him most. Westerley reminded himself that this was an official visit, cap or no cap.

"You want some hot tea with lemon in it?" she asked. "I already got the water on."

"Love some."

Westerley lowered himself into a creaking green vinyl sofa and watched her walk into the kitchen, heard her clatter around in there. In a few minutes she returned carrying a tray with two steaming cups on it. There was a napkin on the tray with a stack of five Oreo cookies.

He thanked her for the cup as she handed it to him. She placed the tray on a table within his reach and then picked up the other cup. Westerley sipped and made a big deal out of sighing and licking his lips in appreciation.

She grinned. He saw that she wasn't drinking her tea, but had put the cup back on the tray. Maybe something about being pregnant. Maybe in her state it tasted bad. She unconsciously touched her extended stomach, as if picking up his thought waves.

"You mentioned trouble on the phone," Westerley said. "What kind you got?"

"Letters."

She reached into a pocket in the voluminous dress and withdrew a stack of white envelopes with a rubber band around it.

"They're from the penitentiary," she said, handing the letters to him.

He leaned forward and placed his cup on the tray. "From Vincent Salas?"

"'Fraid so."

There was a total of nine letters. He peeled off the rubber band and saw that the top five envelopes had been neatly slit open. The others were still intact.

"He's been writing regular. The first letters were kind of pleading with me to change my story, claiming he was innocent. I swear, he does seem to believe it."

"Don't let him fool you," Westerley said.

He removed the folded letter from the top envelope and read. It was written in a neat hand with a blue felt-tip pen. The first part was a litany of how hard life was for Salas in prison. The rest of the letter was a desperate plea for Beth to change her story so he might be able to win an appeal. Salas's signature appeared tight and neat at the bottom.

"In a letter I got last week," Beth said, "he seemed like he'd given up all hope of getting out, and he blamed me for what he called his predicament. Then he got nasty, Sheriff. Threatening. I didn't open any letters after that. After a while, when he kept writing, I called your office."

"You did right," Westerley said. "He's got no business harassing you like this. I'm gonna take care of it. As for any more letters that might already be in the mail, you just ignore them. Don't open the envelopes. I'll talk to the warden in Jeff City and see that Salas stops writing you."

He didn't tell her he intended to talk to Salas personally. Scare the holy bejesus out of him. As if Salas could make good on any threat.

"I wasn't gonna call you," Beth said. Again she touched her stomach lightly, as if it might be about to burst. "But I figured I didn't need any more stress in the form of letters. Not at a time like this."

"No reason for you to feel stressed. Salas can't harm you in any way from where he is." Westerley rebanded the letters and tapped them hard with his forefinger. "This kinda thing isn't unusual. Losers like Salas find themselves where they need to be and don't like it. They got nothing to do and nothing to lose, so they write letters. Might be he's trying to gain your cooperation, through lies or fear, and get you to write back and say something his lawyer might be able to use to impress an appeals court or parole board. It's an act played by many a guilty prisoner. You were right to call me." He picked up the banded envelopes and waved them. "You forget about these. They'll stop coming. They're not your problem anymore. Far as you're concerned, Vincent Salas is as gone as yesterday."

She was looking at him as if he'd just preached a sermon and pronounced her saved.

He smiled, a little embarrassed. "Sorry. Didn't mean to make a speech."

"It was a speech I needed to hear," Beth said.

Westerley finished his tea, then picked up his cap and stood up out of the creaking sofa.

"I do thank you, Sheriff."

He held his cap in both hands, grinned, and motioned with his head toward her bulging belly. "I don't doubt we'll see each other soon. And if I'm not on duty, my deputy Billy Noth will drive out and transport you to the clinic."

"That's awful kind of you. You and Billy both."

"You're a taxpayer," Westerley said. Instantly he realized it had been a stupid thing to say. Beth had no doubt been on welfare since Roy cut out after learning of her pregnancy. Westerley doubted if Roy had picked up any of the medical bills. It was more like him to preach about charity than to practice it.

Westerley moved toward the door, putting on his cap and tugging it low so the visor almost concealed his eyes. Beth hadn't moved. With his hand on the doorknob, Westerley looked back at her. He nodded again toward her advanced pregnancy. "Everything . . . in there all right?"

She smiled the way she used to. Before what had happened to her. The tiny dark fleck in her left eye caught the light. "Couldn't be better," she said. "And I thank you for asking."

"Speaking of asking, do you know . . ."

"The baby will be a boy," she said.

Westerley didn't know quite what to say to that. He gave her a lingering last look before leaving, as if fixing her in his mind so she'd stay as long as possible in his imagination, like an image burned into a TV screen. Then he went out the door.

It was snowing again. Much harder. The kind of snow that coated everything and made it pure and cold, but not forever.

38

New York, the present

Harley Renz had nicked himself with his razor this morning. Quinn was glad.

Plastered to Renz's bulging pink jowls were two small tan adhesive squares that were supposed to be invisible and might have worked if Renz had been Hispanic. The nicks could have been what put him in a bad mood.

The office had a window that looked out on a potted tree. Its leaves were as still as an oil painting. Morning sun blasted golden glory through the tilted blinds and warmed Quinn's bare forearm resting on the chair facing Renz's desk.

Renz inhaled deeply before speaking, puffing out his jowls and looking for a moment like a bullfrog about to croak. "I've got enough to be pissed off about without you coming in here all worked up because Millie Graff's rapist was questioned without you knowing about it."

If Quinn was pissed off, he didn't appear so. He seemed to choose those rare times when he displayed anger, so that in retrospect it was difficult to know if it had been real. That was one of the things about Quinn that infuriated Renz. This morning Quinn's voice was flat and carefully modulated.

The way it sounded, come to think of it, when he *was* pissed off.

"Exonerated alleged rapist," Quinn corrected.

"Yeah, yeah. Who else might he have raped?"

Quinn shrugged. He didn't want to get into that conversation with Renz. Harley wasn't the only cop with the "everybody's guilty of something" philosophy. Often it was used as a rationalization to bust someone's skull.

"I feel as bad about Millie Graff's shitty luck as you do," Renz said.

Quinn knew that wasn't true. "What about the other Skinner victims' released alleged rapists?"

"I don't feel bad about them."

"You know what I mean."

Renz drummed the fingertips of both hands briefly on his desk. He wanted this office visit to be over. "Weaver just finished interviewing them, too."

Quinn sat forward. "*Nancy* Weaver?"

"The same." Renz blinked and swallowed. He obviously regretted mentioning Weaver's name.

"Jesus, Harley! You think Weaver's gonna keep these interviews away from the media? The way she sleeps around, she's probably trading pillow talk with half the journalists in town."

"Best you remember she's Lieutenant Weaver now, an aide to the commissioner."

"Harley—"

"She's earned the position, Quinn. And not in the way you might think in your dirty mind."

"*My* dirty mind? You're the one who's gotten down and shamelessly rolled in shit in order to get ahead."

"And don't you forget it."

"I grant you Weaver's good at her job, and I don't care about her sexual adventures. What I do care about is you sending her around to interfere in the investigation you gave *me* to run."

Renz thought it might be a good time to pretend to be angry. "Listen, Quinn, I'm the goddamned police commissioner. If I want to monitor an investigation, I will."

"As long as I know about it, Harley. If I'm gonna run an investigation, I want one hand to know what the other's doing, and whether there's a third hand."

"That sounds reasonable, Quinn, but you gotta understand there are political ramifications here. I got everybody on my ass about this case. You might insist on doing everything your way, but this is happening on my watch, and if things go crappy and slippery, I take the fall."

"I wouldn't think political ramifications would matter, considering the nature of this killer."

"Political ramifications always matter."

"Would Millie and the others understand that?"

"You bet they would. To make a go of it in this city, you have to step on some toes, and you have to avoid the toes of the people you got no choice but to dance with."

"No denying that," Quinn said.

"I can tell you that Millie and those other women wouldn't want me slapped down by some dimwitted, deal-making sleazeball with mayoral ambitions, just because of what happened to them."

"You're not a dimwit," Quinn said.

Renz leaned forward, his elbows on the desk. "Listen, Quinn. Two of the released rapists—"

"Wrongly convicted men."

"Okay. Two of them have solid alibis for the times of death of at least one of the Skinner victims, if not the victim they were wrongly convicted of raping. One of them is back in prison on a burglary rap. Another hanged himself last year in a barn in Iowa. Left a hearts-and-flowers note in his pocket.

Claimed he couldn't find work, couldn't adjust to society after prison, and the woman he was seeing jilted him."

"Poor bastard."

"Friggin' loser," Renz said. "But that's not what we're talking about. If you read Weaver's notes and listen to her interviews, it starts you to thinking that maybe this Socrates's Cavern thing is nothing but a diversion. The killer wanting to off some victims safely before he nails his primary target."

"We're thinking that's the game," Quinn said. "He's one of the convicted rapists who were freed on DNA evidence, and he wants his particular finger-pointer and the object of his revenge to be simply one of many Skinner victims."

"So he'd be just another face in the crowd," Renz said. "And one who's already been wronged and would have a dumb-ass jury's sympathy if he did happen to get marched into court."

"Weaver tell you this?"

"Weaver tells me facts. I pass them on. You're the lead detective. You draw the conclusions."

"I think Weaver is right," Quinn said. "It's the same conclusion we reached. And the killer is intelligent. He knows that by now we've figured out the DNA prisoner-release connection between the victims. That won't stop him. The Socrates's Cavern thing was probably just a stalling tactic anyway. He'll continue to kill until he's accomplished what he set out to do. Each victim will have a singular likely killer. One of them will be the Skinner, but we might never be able to separate him from his fellow suspects. Not if he plays it smart."

"I don't like that kind of defeatist talk," Renz said.

"You're the one in love with facts, and the fact is, we've got a new starting point because we let ourselves be led down a dead-end path by the killer."

"*You* let yourself be led."

"It's on your watch, Harley."

Renz pursed his lips and nodded several times, causing his jowls to quiver. One of the little adhesive patches rubbed on his white collar and dropped from his neck to reveal a nasty razor nick. Quinn hoped it stung.

Quinn sat silently, waiting for Renz's reaction to this new direction in the investigation.

"Science," Renz said at last. "Goddamned science has caused all this trouble."

Quinn didn't want to hear any more of Renz's lies or rationalizations. He stood up and left.

Behind him he heard Renz say, "I got a new cell phone, and I don't even know how the damned thing works!"

Join the club.

39

When Quinn got back to the office, Weaver was waiting for him.

Pearl had banished her to a chair over by the coffee brewer.

"You got an emissary from Renz wants to talk to you," Pearl said.

Weaver had seen Quinn and stood up. She'd helped herself to coffee and walked toward him, the steaming mug held in front of her in one hand, with her thumb on top of the rim to help hold it steady. Quinn smiled inwardly when he saw that Weaver was using Pearl's personalized cup with Pearl's initials. Weaver was holding the cup so the initials were plainly visible.

Deftly, Quinn moved into Pearl's line of vision so she might not notice the mug, and motioned for Weaver to take one of the chairs angled toward his desk.

She swiveled neatly on a high heel and settled into the chair. She was wearing dark slacks and a white shirt, a blue blazer. It was an outfit Pearl often wore. Not today, though, thank God.

Weaver wasn't a classic beauty, but she was attractive. Compactly built (something like Pearl only not as busty) and easy to look at, with a twinkle in her brown eyes that suggested she was up for anything. As Quinn sat down behind his desk to face her, he noticed a cinnamon scent of perfume.

"I understand you've been doing things behind my back," Quinn said.

"Sex is sex," Weaver said. There went that twinkle.

"Don't smart-mouth me. I've got Pearl to deal with, and that's enough."

"Okay, you made your point and I'm sorry. What I've been doing is obeying the orders of my superior."

"Meaning?"

"I had no choice. But that part of my assignment is over. I came here to tell you that from now on I'm acting as a liaison officer reporting to Commissioner Renz."

"Isn't that another way of saying informer?"

"Not in this case. Now all our dealings will be aboveboard, and I'm to be an integral part of the investigation. The commissioner figured you needed help."

"We met this morning," Quinn said, "and he didn't mention anything along that line."

"I know. He briefed me on this morning's meeting." Weaver took a sip of coffee, then leaned to the side and set the mug on the floor so it wouldn't leave a ring on the desk. "Listen, Quinn, I don't want to cause you grief. I like you. You were one of the few friends I had on the force. I'd like for us to stay friends. You always understood me. I've got an active libido, but so what? Other people have red hair or are left-handed. There are plenty of male cops who lead active love lives and it doesn't seem to harm them or hurt their chances for advancement. There's a double standard."

"Sure there is. I thought you'd learned to live with it."

"I have. That's how I made lieutenant."

Quinn didn't want to know the details. "So Renz understands you?"

"He understands my ambition."

"Because he's ambitious?"

"Because we're ambitious in the same way."

Quinn leaned back and looked her in the eye. "Can I trust you, Nancy?"

"Of course you can't. We both know I'm working for Renz and I'm always going to have to come down on his side of the fence. But I can promise I'll walk that fence carefully and try to do you as little harm as possible." She gave him a wan, helpless smile. "Those are the positions we find ourselves in."

Meaning you can't trust me completely, either.

"I understand," Quinn said. He gave her a smile much like hers in return. "We can learn to coexist."

"I would like one condition," Weaver said. "I don't want you to use me to feed misinformation to the commissioner."

"We've got a deal," Quinn said.

"And I do have a question right off," Weaver said.

Quinn waited.

"Fedderman over there. Why's he dressed like he's graduating from primary school?"

Quinn smiled. Weaver didn't miss much.

"His old suits finally wore out," he said.

Part of the truth.

That was what made the world go round. Partial truths.

Quinn and Weaver talked with their heads close together at Quinn's desk and then left for an early lunch. They asked if Pearl wanted to join them. She said only if she could bring her own knife.

Quinn gave her the look, as if he was headmaster and she was twelve years old and had been caught reading porno with the school janitor.

After deciding to dine alone, Pearl left the office and walked toward the Eighty-first Street entrance to the park, where she could get a hot dog and Diet Coke from a street vendor and sit on a bench and brood while she ate. Mostly because of Nancy Weaver's arrival at the office, she was in a dark mood. *Moody.* She felt a twinge. Her mother had always described her that way when she was a child. Pearl would overhear her talking to some of her lady friends: *She's such a smart child, but so moody. Some days she's so prickly she shoots quills.*

The man she loved (most of the time) and lived with (part of the time) was having lunch with a professional sex machine, and here was Pearl thinking about her mother.

And, as so often happened—or seemed to happen—when she thought about her mother, her mother called her on the phone.

When Pearl heard the first four notes of the old *Dragnet* TV show theme and fished her cell phone from her purse, she wasn't at all surprised to see that the caller was Golden Sunset Assisted Living.

She sighed, or maybe it was a growl. She flipped the phone open and pressed it to her ear so hard that the side of her head hurt.

"Hello, Mom."

"Pearl, I've been calling and calling here from the wilds of New Jersey and your message machine is making that shrill sound like it does when it's stuffed too full of messages and I was worried sick about you. For all I knew you were lying dead on the floor."

"You should have called my cell phone number, Mom." *Before jamming up my answering machine.*

"Which at this time I am doing, Pearl. I saw on TV here at the nursing home—"

"Assisted living," Pearl corrected.

"Way station on the road to death. What I saw on the TV was a doctor explaining how, when a woman gets into her forties, it becomes more and more complicated, which is to say dangerous, for her to have a child."

"You mean grandchild," Pearl said, driving to the point. "*Your* grandchild."

"Yes. Little Rebecca, waiting in the wings, in a manner of speaking."

"My wings," Pearl said, wondering how many other women were walking around not even pregnant with the child they weren't going to conceive who was already named. Already Pearl was sick of Rebecca, and the kid hadn't even been born.

"Not that you aren't my own darling angel, Pearl. A mother's love encompasses and forgives."

"Forgives what?"

"So many things."

Pearl squeezed the phone, causing the built-in camera to activate and snap a picture of her hair.

"As for Captain Quinn—"

"He's no longer a captain, Mom."

"He's not getting any younger, either."

"I'll tell him you said that."

"Oh, he'll understand. Your Captain Quinn is a mensch and would, I am sure, make a fine father. You two have been romantically involved for a while now, so I know that marriage is on the near horizon—"

"Not that I can see."

"—and once that happy event occurs, God willing, there still is time, if barely, to create that which you will hold as dear as I hold you."

"Quinn and I are content as we are, Mom."

"You *think* you're content, dear. As did your father and I, until you came along, and like little Rebecca—"

"Mom, stop it. If I get pregnant, you'll be the first to know."

"No, *you* will be the first, and then you'll understand

every word I'm telling you now of a mother's best wishes for the daughter she loves. In an instant it will become clear to you."

"I really don't have time to talk, Mom. I'm helping to track a killer who's murdered—"

"Your eggs, Pearl."

"My *what?*"

"Have you checked to be sure you're fertile? I mean, with a doctor, of course."

"I don't want to talk about my eggs."

"I think we can be reasonably sure that the virile Captain Quinn—"

"You're starting to break up, Mom."

"There is someone I want you to talk with, Pearl."

"About what?"

"You and Captain Quinn. And your . . . arrangement."

"What arrangement?"

"Shacking up, Pearl. To put it crudely but not without accuracy. After all, if you're going to have a child—"

"But I'm not pregnant, Mom. And I don't intend to get that way. And Quinn and I aren't living together."

"Cohabiting, then."

"Sometimes," Pearl said.

"Meaning your clothes are in his closet. I shrug, Pearl."

"Mom—"

"As a favor to your mother, and it's seldom enough that I ask for one, will you just talk to this person, Pearl?"

"Who is this we're discussing?"

"Rabbi Robert Gold."

"I thought you said a person."

"A rabbi is a person, Pearl."

"Rabbi Gold and I have nothing to discuss."

"You can say that never having met the man?"

"I can," Pearl said. "I did."

"Pearl, someday Rebecca—"

Pearl flipped the phone closed, breaking the connection.

Talking to her mother was like a debate with the Spanish Inquisition. Win or lose, it was torture.

40

The room was small and gray and square. A single rectangular wooden table and two wooden chairs were bolted to the concrete floor. The overhead light fixture was made up of two softly buzzing fluorescent tubes encased in a wire cage. It provided the only illumination in the room. The light was pale and ghastly. The temperature was warm. The odor was a blend of perspiration and lingering fear.

Vincent Salas sat directly across from Westerley. A guard in a uniform that was way too small for him stood outside the single door that had a tall, narrow window in it so he could glance in now and then and see that everything was going smoothly.

Westerley had told the guard it was okay to go ahead and remove Salas's handcuffs. There was no reason for Salas to make trouble. And if he did, Westerley would welcome it.

Salas was thinner than when he'd stood trial and had already acquired the dusty gray pallor of the longtime convict. He went with the room. His dark hair was cut military short, and the flesh around his sad dark eyes was finely lined. Westerley thought Salas was one of those cons who would age fast behind the walls.

"Are we here to talk about my parole?" Salas asked in a

husky voice. He still had at least the vestige of a sense of humor.

"We're here to talk about your letters."

"My cigarettes, did you say?"

Westerley gave him a grim smile and pulled two un-opened packs of Camels from his pocket and tossed them in front of Salas on the table. A standard form of prison bribery that never seemed to change. Or maybe by now it had become simply good manners.

"I'm rich," Salas said, and scooped the packs close to him and tucked them in his shirt.

"You didn't say thanks," Westerley said.

"That's because I know they aren't free."

"Something else that isn't free is using the U.S. mail to harass Beth Brannigan."

Salas settled back in his chair, acting like a man in control. "I think I have the right to correspond with whoever I want to on the outside, so long as the letters pass the censor."

"I'm going to see that they don't. And you're not corresponding *with* anyone. The letters only went in one direction."

Salas studied him. "You puttin' the salami to Beth? Because I never did."

"Sure, you're innocent. Like almost everybody else in here."

Salas touched his chest lightly with his fingertips. "But I *am* innocent."

Westerley leaned toward him. "What you're *not* anymore is a letter writer. Not if the letters are to Beth Brannigan."

"What if I get a lawyer and insist on my rights?"

"Your lawyer would tell you that, as a practical matter, you'd better find another pen pal."

"Practical the same as legal?"

"Sometimes. Sometimes not. This is out-state Missouri and we got certain traditions. Even if you behave in here and somehow get out in ten or fifteen years, I might not be sheriff any longer. But whoever my successor is, or his successor, if you write any more letters to Beth, you'll wish you hadn't."

Salas showed no reaction. Penitentiary face already, Westerley thought.

"My guess is you'd make a small mistake that could be regarded as a parole violation," Westerley said, "and you'd be back here like you were snapped back by a rubber band. That's if the parole board never saw your letters and granted you a parole to begin with. You start your stretch by harassing your rape victim via the U.S. mail, and the odds are you'll grow old here and deteriorate along with the buildings."

"I guess you got them letters in your possession."

"I do. And I'm gonna hold on to them. And there aren't gonna be any more of them, or I'll see that you don't have to wait ten or fifteen years to wish you'd never learned to write. You'll limp all the rest of your miserable life."

"A threat?"

"You betcha. An actual physical threat. But just between you and me."

"Maybe Beth likes my letters. Maybe she's in love with me."

"Like she loves garbage."

"Some women do love garbage."

"If she was one, I wouldn't be here. Anyway, she only read the first few letters. She turned the rest over to me unopened."

"But you opened them."

"Sure. I'm the sheriff."

Salas closed his eyes, as if he didn't want Westerley to see the thoughts behind them. Then he opened them and smiled. Westerley was liking that smile less and less.

"Can I smoke in here?" Salas asked.

"It don't matter. I'm leaving shortly." Westerley leaned in close and locked gazes with Salas. Held steady until he won the staring contest. When Salas looked away, Westerley clutched his face by the chin between thumb and forefinger, as you might do with a recalcitrant child, and swiveled his head back so they were looking at each other again. "You write any more letters and I'm gonna see you alone in another room where there won't be a guard within shouting distance. You get my meaning?"

Salas didn't seem scared, but he was paying close attention.

Westerley squeezed Salas's lower jaw harder and gave him a grim smile. "We got us an understanding?"

Salas said something like "Eyah."

Westerley released Salas's chin but made sure their gazes were still locked.

Salas didn't look away this time. His dark eyes were flat and emotionless, maybe the way they'd been when he raped Beth. Westerley knew the distance in those eyes; he'd driven Salas's sick and evil demon well back in its lair.

"If she ain't opening the letters anyway," Salas said, "I don't see any point in sending more."

"I'm glad you got that straight in your mind."

Westerley stood up, then went over and rapped a knuckle on the door as a signal to the guard that he was leaving.

"Go easy on the cigarettes," he said, with a glance back at Salas. "Those things are killing lots of rats on the outside."

41

The Skinner had learned the doorman's routine easily enough. As usual, the man in his absurd quasi-military uniform left his post untended when he bustled down to the corner to hail a cab for someone leaving the building. By the time he was helping his charges into the cab and receiving a liberal tip, the Skinner, unseen, was on his way up in an elevator. Since he was in his deliveryman uniform and carrying a package, anyone glancing at him would have paid him little attention. He was as much a part of the décor as one of the potted plants, and about as memorable.

It was easy for him to slip the apartment door's knob lock with his honed credit card. He then made short work of the dead bolt with his lock pick.

He wasn't surprised when he eased the door open and found that the chain wasn't attached. Judith Blaney was dining out with friends on the other side of town. Probably they would stop someplace else for drinks after dinner. She'd be pleasantly tired when she got home, anxious to kick off her shoes and go to bed. The friends she was with were all women, so Judith was almost certain to arrive home alone.

She'd be surprised when she closed the door behind her and wasn't alone. The Skinner, an expert at his grisly passion, would take full advantage of that surprise and have her helpless even before she had time to cry out.

He tucked the box, in which he carried his tape and instruments, beneath his arm, and with a glance up and down the hall pushed his way into the apartment.

The Skinner locked the door after him but left the chain off, so when Judith came home she'd think everything was as she'd left it and the apartment was inviolable and waiting for her with its comforts and safety. Her world would seem tight and secure and unchanged.

The killer knew how important *unchanged* was.

Familiarity was easily mistaken for security. It made for denial that lasted until the end. Well, near the end.

The Skinner smiled, turned, took two steps, and drew in his breath.

He stood still, staring at the man casually seated on the sofa. The man had his hands folded in his lap, his legs crossed, and was staring back at him.

Not a large man, the Skinner told himself. Slender, but with a coiled kind of look about him suggesting a wiry strength. He was wearing pale gray slacks, a black blazer, and no tie. Almost absently, he slid a hand into one of the blazer's side pockets, but the implication was clear. There might be a gun in that pocket.

The Skinner's mind was spinning, calculating.

The police? Had they somehow guessed Judith Blaney was to be the next victim?

No. I don't see a badge. And only one man.

And not a very intimidating one.

If not the police, who?

Then he remembered the other man he'd seen in the vicinity of Judith. Two hunters on the trace of the same prey?

It was possible.

Given the circumstances, maybe even likely.

The Skinner felt grounded again. Though not exactly in

control, he was sure he could get on top of this situation even though he didn't entirely understand it.

"I'm here to make a delivery," he said amiably.

The man on the sofa laughed. He had neatly aligned features that somehow just missed being handsome. His wavy black hair was combed straight back, as if he were perpetually facing a wind.

"What's funny?" the Skinner asked.

"You coming to make a delivery, when I came here to give something to you."

"What would that something be?" asked the Skinner

"An alibi.

"For what?"

"The murder of Judith Blaney."

"You out of your mind?"

"Like you are. But we want the same thing."

"Which is?"

"Judith Blaney dead."

The room seemed to have developed its own heartbeat. The Skinner was breathing softly and evenly. Whatever the hell was going on, there was wriggle room. He'd be able to work something out, even if it meant leaving here with two dead bodies in the apartment.

"I was released from prison six months ago after serving time for a rape I didn't commit," the man on the sofa said.

"I know who you are now," the killer said. "Judith Blaney pointed you out as the man who attacked her. Your conviction was overturned because DNA proved you were innocent."

"And I know who you are," the man on the sofa said. "I know what you're doing and I heartily approve of it. I know you need alibis for the . . . well, for certain nights. I can provide them."

"Why should you?"

"You're going to do to Judith Blaney what I was going to do."

He drew from his pocket not a gun but a theater ticket. He laid it on the sofa arm, snapping it flat as if it were a card he'd pulled from a new deck. "This is a ticket for a play at the Berman Theater, *Tables Turned*. You seen that play?"

"No. I'm not much for the theater."

"I bought it at the box office, paid cash. It's for tonight's performance. You still have plenty of time to get there before the curtain goes up."

"Why should I go see a play when I don't like plays?"

"So if the police question you about Judith Blaney's murder, and where you were *tomorrow* night, you'll know what you're talking about when you refer to *Tables Turned*."

"Aren't you kind of ahead of events?"

"Yeah. And that's a good place to be. I did hard time in prison because of Judith Blaney. I want her dead. Obviously I can't kill her, because the police will be all over me as soon as she turns up not breathing."

"Then you're the one who needs an alibi. Not me."

"And I can have one, when I know for sure what night she's going to die."

"*Can* you know that?"

"Yeah. Haven't you been listening? It's tomorrow night. I'll be sure and have a solid alibi. Tomorrow evening, you go wait with the ticket holders outside the Berman Theater or in the lobby, and do something to make yourself memorable. Nothing drastic. Maybe pretend to trip over something and almost fall. Or get into a little argument about somebody crowding ahead of you. That kinda thing."

The man on the sofa paused, waiting for the Skinner to say something more. The Skinner didn't.

"But you don't go into the theater auditorium," said the man on the sofa.

"Why should I? I already saw the play last night. Tonight."

"Exactly. Instead you filter away without anyone noticing, and come here, and wait for Judith."

"And?"

"Then you have your fun. Just like you were going to do tonight. Only you can prove you were at the theater. At least a few people from the lobby or waiting outside in line will remember you. You can describe the play. To top it off, you'll have a ticket stub."

"I won't have a ticket stub for tomorrow night's performance."

"Yes, you will. I'm going to give you one. If it isn't a stub, it'll have a bar code on it. They do that so tickets can't be counterfeited or used twice. There's only one bona fide ticket for that seat on that night, and it will have been used, and you're going to have it or its stub."

"What about the people that sat next to that seat?"

"They'll recall that somebody sat there, but they won't remember who, not by the time the police finally get around to checking on you. They won't even recall if it was a man or woman. Besides, you'll have the canceled or torn ticket. And the ticket will have been paid for in cash. There won't be a record of who bought it."

"Where you gonna get this canceled or torn ticket?"

"It doesn't matter. I'll get it, and you'll have it. We'll meet the day after Judith's murder, and I'll give it to you."

"And you get what out of this?"

"Judith dead. As the prospective prime suspect, I can't kill her myself."

"But you know I'm going to kill her anyway."

"That's true."

The Skinner studied the man on the sofa for a long time. Then he came to a conclusion and smiled. "You don't have the balls to kill her."

"That's true, too. My years in prison . . . took a lot out of me."

"I'll bet," the Skinner said. "And I bet I know how. You and Judith Blaney have got something in common now."

"Never mind that. I've been following Judith, trying to scare her, I admit. But she knows I won't hurt her. I can't. The police'll be on me even before her body drops. When I noticed you were watching her, too, I figured out who you must be. I thought of something that'd be good for both of us, and neither of us can talk about it in the future or we'll mess ourselves up. We'll both be safe. I won't have Judith to brood about any longer, and you'll have an alibi for the time of her death. Not a perfect alibi, but one good enough to hold up if they don't have much else in the way of evidence. And I've been reading about you. You don't leave a lot of evidence."

"I don't leave any."

"Still . . ." The smaller man shrugged. "A little insurance . . ."

"You could simply have let things take their course and made sure you had an alibi for the time Judith left the world."

"Let's call having somebody else kill the bitch my insurance. I'm never going back to prison."

The Skinner thought about it and decided he really didn't have much choice. He didn't want to kill this little poof. That would be too messy and complicated. The way to neutralize him was to make him an accomplice.

He walked over to the sofa. The little man might not have balls, but he didn't look scared, only curious. Maybe it was the look of a guy who'd already lost all he had.

The Skinner picked up the theater ticket from the sofa arm and tucked it into his shirt pocket.

"Good," the man on the sofa said.

The Skinner moved toward the door.

"Enjoy the play. Remember it," said the man on the sofa. "It's a musical."

"God!" said the Skinner, and let himself out of Judith Blaney's apartment.

42

Beth Brannigan had never felt so much pain. The contractions were coming closer together, tying her into knots so she could hardly breathe.

The baby is trying to get out. He's trying to be born.

Beth found herself terrified and astonished, as if this were something she'd never suspected would happen. As if she hadn't been waddling around all those months with a new life inside her.

A complete surprise.

The bedroom window lit up with a flash of distant lightning. A storm on the way. Just what Beth needed.

Thunder rumbled through the darkness outside. A few large raindrops struck the window, and then came the steady plinking sound of rainwater dripping against the metal elbow of the downspout.

Beth switched on the bedside lamp and glanced at the numerals on the clock radio. Two-thirty a.m. Babies picked the damnedest times to be born.

If this was the real thing.

Even if it wasn't the real thing, what was she going to do to find out? Wait until her water broke before calling for help?

She reached for the landline phone by the bed and considered calling 911. Then she decided that would probably bring Sheriff Westerley or his deputy Billy Noth.

Beth realized it was Westerley she wanted to come, to be by her side.

She put the phone back in its cradle and rooted in the tiny nightstand drawer until she found his number.

Another flash of lightning illuminated the night. Rain began falling in a torrent.

When Beth picked up the phone again, a strange thing happened. Some of her fear disappeared, and it was replaced by an odd kind of exhilaration. This was really happening. She was about to become a mother.

She made her call, alerting what had obviously been a soundly sleeping Westerley, who came awake in a hurry.

"You sure?"

"I wouldn't have called if I wasn't," Beth said. "You told me—"

"Huh?"

"What?"

"Sorry," he said. "I was putting on my pants. How close together are the contractions?"

"About fifteen minutes."

"We got some time, then. Stay calm."

"I'm glad you know something about this. What was that?"

"Knocked over a lamp. Oww! Damn it!"

"Sheriff? Wayne? You okay?"

"Yeah. Stubbed my toe. You stay calm and I'll be there before you know it."

"Wayne?"

"I'm leaving. I'll see you soon."

There was a crash, and he hung up.

Beth lay in bed smiling, until the next contraction.

* * *

The seven-pound-four-ounce baby boy was born at 6:07 that morning. The birth had been accomplished without complications. It hadn't been easy for Beth, but it was less painful than she'd expected.

Sheriff Westerley had stayed at the clinic throughout the ordeal of birth. He came into her room a few minutes after the nurses had given Beth the infant to hold.

He leaned over the bed, and she thought he might kiss her on the forehead. Instead he straightened up and smiled down at her.

"He look's like he's got all his parts," he said.

She laughed. That hurt a bit, but the pain didn't dent her relief and euphoria. "I'm gonna make you his godfather."

"Fine with me," Westerley said. "In fact, I'm honored."

On the birth certificate Beth used her maiden name, Colson. The space for father was filled in with *unknown*. Beth named the baby Edward Hand, after her grandfather. Her son would be Edward Hand Colson.

Beth, lying in bed with her eyes closed and with an inner peace that she'd never believed possible, was already thinking of him as Eddie.

43

New York, the present

Fedderman and Penny Noon were eating pasta at Vito's Restauranti in Lower Manhattan. The food was a lot better than the neighborhood.

"The angel-hair pasta's terrific," Penny said, winding another bite around the tines of her fork, "but I wouldn't risk coming here alone for it."

"Mean streets," Fedderman said. He had on the new suit and looked better than merely respectable.

Penny paused in her winding and raised her eyebrows. "You've read Chandler?"

"And Hammett," Fedderman said. "We detectives like detective fiction. It gives us a break from the real thing."

"The novels aren't realistic?"

"Sometimes, but not usually," Fedderman said. "Down in Florida, when I was sitting fishing and not catching anything, I read a lot."

"Just detective fiction?"

"Mostly. Connelly, Grafton, Parker, Paretsky, Mosley . . ."

"Those are fine writers."

"I left out a lot who are just as good. There's this guy in St. Louis . . ."

"Something about you," Penny said. "When we met I knew somehow you had a literary bent."

Fedderman took a sip of the cheap house red. He'd never considered himself the literary sort. He realized Penny was doing something for him, lifting him in ways he hadn't suspected possible.

"Sometimes your boss, Quinn, seems like a character out of a book," Penny said.

"A good book?"

"The best. There's something about him. He can make you trust him. And he's handsome in a big homely way. Like a thug only with a brain. It's easy to see that people respect him. And sometimes fear him."

"It can be the same thing," Fedderman said.

"Have you ever seen Quinn angry?"

"Sure have. And sometimes he's angry and you don't know it. That's what's scary. He's tough in ways that are more than physical."

"You obviously respect him."

"I know him. He's a good man. We've been friends for a long time. Rode together in a radio car back in another era."

"Has police work changed that much?"

"Society has. Police work changed along with it."

Penny was going to ask what Fedderman meant by that when his cell phone buzzed.

"Sorry," he said, smiling apologetically as he dug the phone from a pocket and checked caller ID. He delayed making the connection. "It's Quinn."

"Of course. He sensed we were discussing him."

Fedderman pressed TALK. If the call was one he didn't want Penny to overhear, he was ready to remove his napkin from his lap and stand up from the table.

But it was Quinn who did most of the talking, and the call promised to be brief: "We've got another Skinner victim,

Feds. Woman named Judith Blaney." He gave Fedderman Blaney's address."

"On my way."

After breaking the connection and slipping the phone back in his pocket, Fedderman said, "That's something that hasn't changed about police work. We get a call, day or night, and we have to respond." He reached across the table with his right hand and stroked the back of Penny's hand, so delicate and smooth. "I'm sorry."

"We both are," she said. "But I understand."

Fedderman noticed that his right shirt cuff was unbuttoned. He raised his arm to fasten it, at the same time waggling a finger to summon their waiter.

"I'll put you in a cab, then I'll have to drive cross-town," he told Penny. He'd driven them to the restaurant in the unmarked and had it parked outside near a fire hydrant.

The waiter arrived with the check and surveyed their half-eaten food. "Wanna box?" he asked.

Fedderman, who'd planned on spending the evening with Penny in her apartment and wanted to punch someone, felt like telling him yes, he did want to box, but instead declined.

Penny accepted the waiter's offer, but she had in mind angel-hair pasta rather than pugilism.

44

When he glanced across the room, over what was left of Judith Blaney, Quinn saw Fedderman enter the apartment. Fedderman had his designer suit on, causing a few of the uniformed cops and white-clad techs to regard him with new respect. Maybe Fedderman had been elevated to their superior in some way they didn't yet know.

It was a good thing the victim's apartment was spacious. Vitali and Mishkin were also there, along with Pearl. Nancy Weaver, in plain clothes, was also there, and nodded to Fedderman, or to the suit. Nift was at work on the body. The techs were doing the dance of white gloves. The two uniformed cops who'd taken the squeal stood near the door, controlling entrance and egress. They were Bob Stanze and Paul Goldak, two of the NYPD's best. Fedderman wondered if they'd just happened to take the call or they were there by design because Judith Blaney was somebody important. The apartment was big and in an expensive neighborhood—but not *that* expensive for Manhattan.

"Was she queen of something?" Fedderman asked Stanze, as the handsome young cop moved to block the entrance again.

"Office manager for Bleaker and Sunshine, Mad Avenue ad agency."

Fedderman must have looked blank.

"You know, the talking goose?" Stanze said.

"Oh, yeah. The Southern Morgan Bank commercials."

"Blaney must have known everything the goose was gonna say," Goldak said. He was a small man with a big heart, and a kidder. It was impossible to know if he was joking or suggesting a possible motive.

Quinn, wondering what they were talking about, motioned Fedderman over.

"What was that all about, Feds?"

"Talking goose."

Quinn felt like sighing. Did talent for detective work come with a skewed view of the world?

Like the killer's?

"Lots of artistic blade work this time," Quinn said, gazing again at the victim.

The silver letter S and its chain were draped across Judith Blaney's forehead and open eyes instead of looped around her neck and resting on her chest and breasts, as with the previous victims. Part of the reason was that the Skinner had removed both breasts and tucked each neatly in its corresponding armpit. The usual shreds of flesh were there, barely still attached to the rest of the body. This time there were also intricate, curving cuts. Designs. Then the wild stabbing and slashing of the abdomen and pubic area. A wadded-panties gag lay near the victim, presumably removed by Nift, and her mouth was open, clogged with blood that had welled up from her throat instead of a scream.

"No shoe in the mouth this time," Nift said, "like with the last victim."

"Same killer, though," Quinn said. "He's just trying to throw shit in the game. They do that sometimes."

"Or he might not have found a shoe he liked," Fedderman said. "One that would make a good unicorn horn—if that's what it was supposed to be."

Nift nudged Judith's hair aside, and for the first time Quinn noticed something white stuffed in her ear. "What's that?"

"Cigarette butt," Nift said. "He extinguished a cigarette in each ear. Looks as if it happened some time before her death."

"Mother of God!" said one of the techs, who'd overheard.

"Hardly." Weaver's voice.

"Anybody make anything out of those carved designs or symbols?" Quinn asked.

"Just that the Skinner's a head case," Vitali rasped.

"The letter *S* seems to turn up several times," Weaver said, "but that could be because the Skinner just liked to make wavy cuts with his knife."

"Or because you're looking for them," Quinn said.

"They could have some sort of religious significance," Pearl said. "The necklaces with the letter *S*, for Satan." She thought for a moment. "Or for sacrificial goat. Remember the victim with the high heel taped to her head to look like a horn."

Weaver ignored Pearl's brainstorming other than to give a disbelieving little "Hmph." Quinn could see that Pearl didn't like that. He reminded himself again to keep these two separate as much as possible. Not easy to do, since Weaver was Renz's liaison officer.

Screw them! Quinn thought. If they couldn't get over their petty disagreements and do their jobs, they could take a walk.

Of course, he had to live with Pearl.

Wanted to, anyway.

Pearl might have been right about Weaver imagining her own letters on what were random carvings. There seemed nothing significant in the almost elegant cuts other than that the killer was having his grotesque version of fun.

"Did the same knife do the carving that did the rest of the work?" Quinn asked Nift.

The little ME with the Napoleon haircut squatted with his head bowed for a few seconds, pondering. "Yes. I think we can assume the same knife did all the cutting, including the removal of the breasts. And the nipples. Which are, incidentally, beneath the breasts."

Nift stood up and puffed out his chest. Quinn thought he might have actually slipped his fingers inside his shirt à la the famous Napoleon portrait, but for the bloody gloves. "Odd thing about this one. The hate is there. The passion. But there's also a kind of wild exuberance in the random, swerving cutting on the body. More as if the killer was entertaining himself instead of grimly exercising vengeance. And those aren't deep cuts. She was alive and watching and feeling when those were happening. How the Skinner must have enjoyed it!"

Quinn turned away and exchanged glances with Pearl. Nift sounded exuberant himself, and it was sickening.

"When are they gonna—" Pearl began, but Quinn raised a hand to silence her, then led her away.

"I was just wondering when that little prick will finally be fired," Pearl whispered to Quinn.

"He's a city employee," Quinn said, "and he knows the secrets of the dead." He gave her shoulder a slight squeeze to make sure he had her attention. "He's our colleague."

Pearl said something about lying down with dogs and wandered away. Quinn could tell she was seething.

"Girlfriend's got the jumps," a voice said beside Quinn. Nancy Weaver, who'd noticed something wrong between Pearl and him and sidled over.

"Let's all just do our jobs, Nancy," Quinn said. And moved closer to the corpse.

* * *

The Skinner watched the man who'd been in Judith Blaney's apartment approach him where he sat sipping a chocolate latte at an outside table. Traffic streamed past only a few yards away. The Skinner was unbothered by the low haze of exhaust fumes. There was a tilted green umbrella above the table that kept the sun out of his eyes but allowed for a warm slice of light across his bare forearms.

The man came and stood by the table but didn't move to sit down. The Skinner didn't invite him to sit.

The man reached into a pocket and laid a used and canceled theater ticket on the table next to the latte mug.

"Your alibi," he said. "And there's no way to prove you weren't there last night at the time of . . ." He glanced around. No one was seated near enough to overhear. He smiled. "We don't need to say it out loud."

"It was really a crap play," the Skinner said. He returned the smile but in a way that was creepily joyful. "But the encore performance was terrific."

"I'm glad you had a good time." The man turned to walk away, and then hesitated. "You like baseball?"

"The way I like Mom and apple pie. 'Specially Mom. Why?"

"You didn't enjoy the play. Maybe next time we can make it a ball game."

The Skinner didn't like hearing that. Not at all. A "next time" with this potential blackmailer's involvement wasn't what he had in mind. He worked alone. A secret between two people wasn't a secret. People like this, bullies and parasites—he didn't like them at all. They hadn't the right to live.

On the other hand, they were usually smart, and cautious with their information. Someone else knew, or there was a letter with a lawyer or in a safe deposit box. Insurance. The unpleasant man knew he didn't even have to tell the Skinner about such insurance. They both knew he was safe.

The man walked along the street parallel to the curb as he was trying to hail a cab. It brought him close again to the Skinner's table.

A cab slowed and swerved toward him and he pointed a finger at the Skinner, his thumb raised like the hammer of a revolver. Grinning, he brought the thumb down and said, "Yankees fan! Am I right?"

The Skinner said nothing as the man climbed into the cab and it drove away.

Cocky little bastard.

But he'll learn.

45

Quinn was on the sofa in the brownstone, leafing through the autopsy photos of Judith Blaney, studying each one carefully. The workmen were busy on the top floor. Sounds of sawing and hammering could be heard, but barely, muted by the thick floor and walls.

Pearl was standing behind the sofa, leaning over Quinn's shoulder. Her hand rested lightly on his back, weightless as a small bird that had lit there. The hand was either for balance or to display affection. Quinn couldn't be sure which.

They were going to make a lunch of the lasagna they hadn't eaten last night at Ricco's Restaurant. That the gruesome morgue photographs of Judith Blaney didn't affect their appetites suggested to Quinn that maybe they'd been in this business too long.

He glanced back at Pearl, then straightened the stack of black-and-white photos and placed them on the coffee table. Pearl came around and sat in a chair facing him.

"I was studying those wavering cuts in her torso and thighs," Quinn said.

"We both were."

"See anything to them? I mean, in the way of some message being communicated?"

"The message I get is that the Skinner is one sick cookie. Sick and sadistic."

Quinn sighed and leaned back in the sofa. "What kind of knife do you supposed made those cuts?"

"Something sharp and with a fine point. Probably made for a specific purpose. A specialty scalpel?"

"Nift says no. He doesn't think the killer's using any sort of medical implement. But he does admit he can't be certain."

"Maybe something for cleaning fish."

"Doesn't seem likely," Quinn said.

"Maybe it's simply another diversion. We are all agreed that the business with the Socrates's Cavern membership list and letter *S* are simply that. Not to mention the shoe in the mouth."

"Diversions, but we're still forced to waste time checking them out."

"So maybe we're supposed to run around in circles trying to figure out what the fancy cut marks on the victims mean. Or maybe they mean nothing."

"One distinction," Quinn said. "The killer seems to have enjoyed carving designs in Judith Blaney. He apparently spent a lot of time doing it."

"I get you," Pearl said. "It's his pleasure as well as a diversion." She sat back and thought. "The wrong rapist identification factor—now that's a solid connecting thread. I'm sure we'll find it in Judith Blaney's murder."

"That's what the killer wanted to conceal in the beginning," Quinn said. "He must have known we'd eventually tumble to it."

"You don't suppose," Pearl said, "that he's using the rape misidentifications the same way he used the Socrates's Cavern diversion."

"You mean there might be a third, actual motive? You're making my head hurt, Pearl." But he had to admire her mind's reach. "It would require too many victims," he added. "The risk increases with each one."

"He's a psycho," Pearl said. "He might not have done a risk analysis and determined a point of diminishing returns."

"Oh, I bet he did. In fact, I think we can rely on it."

She gave Quinn a level stare. A lock of her dark hair dangled near her left eye, giving her a tousled, sexy look. "Are we getting closer?" Her voice seemed slightly husky.

He didn't want to misunderstand her. "To the killer?"

"Of course." Her strictly business voice now.

He stared at her. She didn't seem to have noticed the double entendre. Or maybe she had and was playing dumb. He wished she'd spend the afternoon with him in bed so he could make love to her, try again to convince her that she should move in with him. Yancy Taggart had died long enough ago that his memory no longer stood in the way. Quinn was reasonably sure of that. If only she could make up her mind. Her heart.

"I feel that we are getting closer," Quinn said, "but I couldn't tell you why."

A persistent high-pitched dinging drifted from the kitchen. The oven timer.

"Pearl," Quinn said, "do you want to stay here after lunch? Maybe spend the night?" ·

"The lasagna's ready," Pearl said. "I'm not."

When they were almost finished with lunch, the brownstone phone rang.

Nift again.

"I thought I should mention what else I discovered when I cleaned all the blood out of Judith Blaney's mouth and throat," he said.

Quinn looked at what was left of his lasagna.

"It seems her tongue was removed," Nift said.

"Removed?"

"Cut out. Back near its base. Very deftly."

Quinn said nothing.

"Am I calling at a bad time?" Nift asked.

"No, not at all. Thanks." Quinn hung up the phone. He looked at Pearl.

"Anything important?" Pearl asked.

"I'll tell you after you finish lunch," Quinn said.

Marinara sauce dripped from a corner of Pearl's mouth. Her tongue darted out and she licked it away. Shrugged. "Whatever."

Pearl, Pearl . . .

46

Pearl was glad she'd drawn this assignment. She'd given her interview with Jock Sanderson a lot of thought. The way she figured it, they were already in the territory where the Skinner might assume the woman who was his main target, the focus of his revenge, would seem to be simply one in a line of Skinner victims, none distinguishable from the others. Thus none of the *suspects* would in any meaningful way be distinguishable from the others. At least that was how the killer would see it. When he thought his safety in numbers was adequate, he would kill the one true object of his rampage.

And of course, his one true object couldn't be distinguished by being the last killed.

Perhaps that one true object had been Judith Blaney.

Sanderson seemed surprised to see Pearl, which struck her as odd, considering they had an appointment. Pearl wondered if he preferred that his questioner were a man. Maybe a woman seeking the killer of women made him uneasy. If so, all the better.

Afraid of women? Sometimes these creeps are deeply afraid.

Jock Sanderson was a medium-height man whose compact build made him appear shorter. It was Pearl's experience that men with that physical characteristic were deceptively strong. But then Quinn was tall and rangy, and he was unusually strong even for his size. Pearl warned herself not to categorize people on the basis of small samplings; in her business that could prove fatal.

Sanderson had the kind of eyes that picked up the dominant color around them, and a full head of wavy black hair. He would have been downright handsome if there hadn't been a crookedness to his features that spoiled the effect. He had a nice smile.

"Please come in," he said, making a sweeping motion with his right arm to invite her grandly into his squalid apartment, as if he were a butler at a posh estate.

Well, the apartment wasn't actually squalid. Though the furniture was a bit worn and mismatched, the place was clean and ordered. So much so, in fact, that Pearl pegged Sanderson for kind of a neatnik.

As she moved past him he did a nifty little dance to get out of her way, as if he wanted to stay on the perimeter of her attention but not too close.

Pearl crossed the living room and sat on a sofa draped with a rose-pattern slipcover. It reminded her of the sofa in her mother's living room when she was a kid. There was what looked like a cigarette burn in it.

"Cool enough in here for you?" Sanderson asked, smiling for about the third time since she'd arrived. He had even white teeth that he obviously liked to flash.

"Just right," Pearl said. Though it was past eleven and the morning hadn't yet heated up, an old window unit was humming away on alert without the compressor engaged. There was a faint odor in the place, as if someone had recently been frying fish. She drew her notepad from a pocket of her linen jacket and found the pencil tucked inside its leather cover. She flipped to the first unmarked page. "You said on the phone that you already knew about Judith Blaney's death."

"True," Sanderson said. "I always watch local news in the morning before I go to bed." He sat perched on the substantial arm of a hulking chair covered with brown corduroy. "The murder of a beautiful woman. Another Skinner victim. That kind of thing doesn't take long to make the news."

"You said you watched the morning news 'before' going to bed?"

"True." As if Pearl had gotten another one right. The white smile. "I work nights. Usually get home sometime around six in the morning. Then I shower, shave, eat a healthy breakfast, and go to bed."

Too much detail, Pearl thought. *Lying?*

"How did you feel when you heard about Judith Blaney's death?" Pearl asked.

"I was glad." No change of expression on the almost-handsome features.

"She was tortured before she died."

"I know a lot about torture."

Pearl raised an eyebrow.

"From being in prison," Sanderson explained.

"Tortured at whose hands?"

"You'd be surprised. A rapist isn't high on the scale of respect when it comes to the other prisoners. And for that matter, let's include the guards. Some of them think the thing to do is to make sure the inmate understands what it feels like to be raped. There are too many unguarded places, times. There's no one to stop them from doing what they want."

"You were raped in prison?"

"Many more times than once." He swallowed hard enough for her to hear the phlegm crack in his throat. The expression on his face caused a pang of pity in Pearl.

"I know it won't help to say I'm sorry," she said, "but I

am." It was odd, she thought, that he'd make it a point to bring up the subject. Other than as an explanation of what he'd had to go through because of Judith Blaney. Didn't he know he was giving himself a motive?

"I was physically what you would call attractive when I went behind the walls," Sanderson said. "I was repeatedly beaten, along with the other indignities. That's why I look now like I might be an ex-boxer."

Pearl didn't think he looked like a former fighter, but she let him go ahead and think she did. His hands were too delicate looking to have been taped and used as blunt instruments.

"You raise my curiosity," she said.

"I'm not gay," he said. "Never was." Sanderson drew a deep breath, as if to steady himself. "But that's not what you're here to talk about."

"No," Pearl said. She tested the pencil to make sure it had a sharp enough point. "Judith Blaney was killed sometime around eleven o'clock last night."

"I've got some coffee on," Sanderson said. "Would you like some?"

"No," Pearl said. This guy was something. "I would like some answers instead of more verbal dancing around."

"Sure. My bad." He actually looked embarrassed. "At ten last night I was working with a crew cleaning up the old Superior Theater on West Forty-sixth Street. Some kind of church or other had rented it for a revival meeting that went until just past ten. We were waiting and started working as soon as the place cleared." He shifted position on the chair arm. "You know the Superior? It's been shut down as a movie theater for years, but it's still in use. Different kinds of events take place there."

"I know it," Pearl said. "It was a porno theater in its later years."

"Yeah. Shame."

"Who employs you, Mr. Sanderson?"

"Company called Sweep 'Em Up. It's a janitorial service that cleans up the venues after sporting events, lectures, political rallies . . . whatever. You can probably tell from this apartment that it doesn't pay well, but you don't get your pick of jobs when prison's on your résumé."

"How'd you get this one?"

"There's a prisoner-placement service, a charity thing. And my AA sponsor Dave vouched for me. So far, it's worked out well enough, but I'd like to get something better someday. Move up in the world, far as I can go, anyway."

Another suspect with a drinking problem. Well, that should be no surprise. "What else does Sweep 'Em Up clean?" Pearl asked.

"Oh, we're a big outfit. We clean Broadway and off-Broadway theaters, hotel ballrooms . . ."

"How long you been working there?"

"Couple of years. It's the only job I've had since I got out. It's helped me stay straight, stay out of trouble."

"Do you attend AA meetings regularly?"

"Now and then, I'd say. I've been sober for nine months now. I won't lie to you. I fell off the wagon a few times. But Dave and my faith in a higher power picked me up and made me sober."

"That's good," Pearl said.

"I try." The wide, white smile. "Gotta keep trying."

"People can vouch for you being at work from about ten o'clock last night until past dawn?"

"Oh, yeah. The whole crew. Six of them, not counting me. And the company locks us in as soon as we set to work. For our own good. Safety. And you know, in the event anything big gets stolen, we don't get blamed. They leave a guard outside one of the doors, so we can get out in case of a fire."

"You worked all night?"

"Somebody sure did. Go by and look at the place. We swept up and bagged all the trash and bottles and condoms. Yeah, condoms even at a revival meeting. You'd be surprised."

"Not me," Pearl said, thinking for some reason of Nancy Weaver. She pretended to scribble something with her pencil. "I will talk to Sweep 'Em Up and the people involved. To check your story."

"I wish you would."

"You said you were glad when you heard Judith Blaney had been murdered. Can you explain that a little more?"

"What's to explain? The bitch was responsible for ruining my life. After what happened to me, I wouldn't be human if I didn't feel glad about what happened to her."

Pearl smiled. "I guess you know that gives you a motive."

"I've got an alibi, too, thank God."

"Tell me, Mr. Sanderson, after you were proven innocent and got out of prison, didn't you even once consider . . ."

"Killing Judith Blaney?" He crossed his arms, and muscles rippled. He shouldn't have been such a pushover in prison. But then some of those cons pumped iron half the day, building themselves into perfect thugs. An ordinary man like Sanderson wouldn't have stood a chance without somebody in the cellblock to back him. And like he said, rapists were on the rung just above child molesters. Even the worst cons had something like morals. "To be honest," he said, "I did think about killing her."

"*Really* think about it?"

"No, not *really*. It takes balls to kill somebody, and I lost those in prison. Figuratively speaking."

"Good," Pearl said. "I mean about the figurative part."

She looked for the toothy white smile, but it didn't appear.

After replacing her notebook and pencil in her purse, she

stood up and thanked Sanderson. He straightened up from where he was perched on the chair arm.

She handed him her card. "If you think of something . . ."

"I won't," Sanderson said. "I don't intend to think of Judith Blaney at all. Alive or dead."

As Pearl left the apartment, she decided she didn't blame him.

"I checked out his story," Pearl told Quinn later that day in the office. "There's no doubt where he was when Judith Blaney was killed. He's got seven witnesses confirming his alibi, including a uniformed security guard."

"So we cross off another one," Quinn said. "Jock Sanderson isn't the Skinner."

"He's another guy with a drinking problem."

Quinn nodded where he sat in his desk chair. "What happened to those men, to be wrongly convicted of rape and then serve time, it figures to drive some of them to drink when finally they do get out and realize they still wear the badge of dishonor."

"I guess," Pearl said. "It's a complicated problem with a simple but damned difficult solution."

"Probably most of the men still alive on our list of thirty-two have a drink or drug problem."

"Maybe the Skinner does."

"No," Quinn said. "I have some idea of what makes him tick."

Pearl remembered that Quinn himself had once been falsely accused of rape.

"Being falsely accused of a heinous crime has its effects," Quinn said. "Instead of drinking, shooting up, or sniffing, the Skinner kills."

"And Jerry Lido becomes a computer maniac."

"Right."

"Trading one addiction for another."

"I suppose."

"And you?"

"Me?"

"Your addiction is that you need a mission," Pearl said. "Is that what you traded for?"

"No."

"Then what?"

He smiled. "That would be you or Cuban cigars, Pearl."

"You've already got Cuban cigars, in your desk drawer."

"That's a fact, Pearl."

Jock Sanderson left the AA meeting alone. It had taken place in a room above a restaurant. There was nothing fancy about it, and it could do with a visit from Sweep 'Em Up. There was a slightly raised platform at one end, and metal folding chairs were lined up facing it. A large framed photograph of a smiling President Kennedy hung on the wall across from the door. No one seemed to know why. The room had a separate entrance with a stairway leading up from a door at street level.

Jock had without doubt been the most interesting member there this evening. He'd stood up and told the others everything about Judith's murder. Well, not everything. He'd almost convinced himself that the torture and murder had occurred as a complete surprise to him. Faking sincerity. He'd long thought that was what got you ahead in life, phony sincerity. If you had luck to go with it. The luck was what Jock had never had, but now maybe things had turned a corner.

Dave, his sponsor, had left the meeting ahead of him and was waiting out on the sidewalk.

"You gonna be okay, Jock?" Dave asked, concern on his alcohol-ravaged face.

"I am," Jock said. "I was tempted, but I denied myself. I'll be okay."

"The devil's waiting to move in on you if you give it half a chance," Dave said.

"And I know it, Dave. But I've got God on my side now."

"That's good. Wanna go for some coffee?"

"I think I need to be alone, Dave. Deal with the grief."

"You suffer grief over the death of a woman who wrongly accused you of rape?"

"I do. I mean, the way she was killed. So horrible. It requires God's understanding, Dave, but I can try. Judith Blaney did nothing to me deliberately. She made an honest mistake."

"You sure of that, Jock?"

"I am. She had no reason to lie."

Dave stepped back and regarded him. "I think you're going to be okay, Jock."

"I am."

"But stay on your guard." Dave hugged him, then turned and walked away.

"On my guard," Jock said after him. "That's me."

But he was thinking it was other people who'd better be on their guard.

47

Beth Colson watched the boxy yellow back of the school bus rumble down the dirt drive to the county road and then turn toward the highway. For an instant the pale face of a student was visible staring out the rear window. Not Eddie, she was sure.

Dust raised by the bus was still hanging in the air when Sheriff Wayne Westerley's cruiser slowed and made a right turn into the drive. It was a gray SUV with SHERIFF lettered on both sides and a roof bar full of lights. There were extra lights mounted on the front, down low and protected by wire guards.

The big vehicle navigated the bumpy dirt drive easily on its oversized knobby tires. Beth moved back to stand by the front porch while Westerley parked near the stand of big oak trees that were showing their golden fall leaves.

He climbed down out of the big SUV and came toward her, smiling. Beth couldn't help but think how trim and handsome he looked in his tan uniform and black leather cross belt and holster. He even had a black tie on today, tucked in between his uniform shirt's top two buttons. Beth had always thought that was an odd way for uniformed men to wear their ties. Either you were going to wear a tie or you weren't.

"Special occasion?" she asked, smiling at Westerley.

He grinned and appeared puzzled.

"You look so dressed up and nice in your uniform."

"Always special when I come see you, Beth." He removed his black-visored garrison cap and stopped and stood a few feet away from her. Behind him dust was still settling. A bird started nattering in one of the oaks. "I saw the bus on the way in. Eddie get off to school okay?"

Beth smiled. "Yeah. He's on the honor roll again this year. Can you believe it?"

"Sure. He's a super kid."

"He is that."

"I got some news," Westerley said. "Thought it best if I came and told it to you in person."

Beth felt a cold weight in her stomach. "This bad news?"

He shrugged. "Depends."

"On what?"

"Who you are, I guess." He removed his cap and held it before his crotch with both hands, as if he'd forgotten to zip his pants. "Now that DNA makes identification so certain, even after years have passed, there's this organization, a bunch of lawyers running around the country reopening old crime cases where there were blood samples taken. Those samples, mostly taken to determine blood type, are still around in old evidence files."

The bird stopped its nattering and the forest around the house was silent. "I heard about that on the news," Beth said. "They started doing that after the Simpson case."

"DNA science has gotten more sophisticated since then. And so have the people using it to free wrongly convicted prisoners."

"Not a bad thing," Beth said.

"Yeah. Well, this organization looked into the state's rape case against Vincent Salas." Westerley moved slightly closer to Beth, as if he wanted to be within range to catch her if she fell. "They determined that Salas couldn't have been the one who raped you, Beth."

Beth did feel dizzy. The sky, the woods, the sheriff himself, seemed to spin for a few seconds, as if the earth had tilted. She felt Westerley's hand on her arm, steadying her.

"That ain't possible," she heard herself say.

"It is, Beth. The DNA proved it. Salas's attorney's been to the state capital, rushing this thing through. They don't want an innocent man in prison one day more than he has to be there."

"Innocent? Can that really be true, that he's innocent?" A thought hit her hard. "If Salas didn't rape me, *who did*?"

"That's something you don't need to worry over, after all these years. Besides, the statute of limitations has expired." Westerley wasn't positive of that, but it had to be close. "Bastard who did it, from way outta state, the kinda things he'd do and the life he musta led, he might even be dead by now. Time has a way of leveling things out. Let that part of the past stay buried in the past, Beth."

Westerley was gripping both her arms now, looking down at her from beneath the visor of his cap. "You must have made a mistaken identification, Beth. It happens. You didn't do it on purpose. You didn't do anything wrong."

"Except send an innocent man to prison."

"There was plenty of other evidence against him."

"How could that be, if he wasn't guilty?"

"It's that kind of world, Beth. That's why a jury needs to find beyond a reasonable doubt. The jury in your case thought it was doing just that, that there was no reasonable doubt Salas was the rapist."

"When's Salas gonna be released?"

"In three days."

Beth began to cry and shake her head sadly. "What did I do? Oh, God, what did I do?"

"Your best," Westerley said. "You believed Salas was the one, or you wouldn't have pointed him out in a lineup, and in the courtroom. None of this is your fault."

"All of it's my fault."

She was suddenly hugging Westerley, and his arms were around her.

"You want me to be with you when he gets out?" he asked.

"You suppose he'll be furious with me?"

"I don't know. I'm not sure how he's gonna feel. I know this: I'm gonna have a talk with him right off. You won't have anything to fear."

"I've got me to fear, Wayne. My conscience."

"I don't see how you could have done anything different, Beth."

"I coulda been more sure."

"It's so easy to say that after the fact. Knowing what you knew, thinking what you thought, feeling like you did, there wasn't much else for you to do."

She looked through a mist of tears up into his eyes. "You really believe that?"

"Damned right I do."

"I wish I could be as sure as you."

She dug her forehead into his shoulder, and her body trembled with her sobs. The woods began to trill with the sounds of insects becoming more active in the building heat. A breeze kicked up, stirring the leaves and moving the dust around.

"You want me to stay with you?" he asked.

She hugged him harder. "Yeah, I want you to stay with me." *I do, and I don't.*

48

New York, the present

Jock Sanderson finished with the tiled floor of the ladies' room at the Uptown Diamond Theater, then used the wringer on the bucket to press and roll out the mop head.

He stood leaning on the mop's wooden handle, surveying his work. The cracked gray tiles gleamed as best they could after so many years. The metal stalls were free of graffiti, if you didn't look too closely at the remains of a lipstick sketch of a huge male organ on one of the stalls. The things women drew and wrote in public restrooms never ceased to amaze Jock.

He made sure he'd put a new plastic liner in the trash receptacle by the door. After a last look around, he backed out of the restroom, pulling the mop and bucket on rollers behind him, making sure the bucket didn't tip as it *thunk-thunk-thunked* over the tiles. It was good to get away from the smelly ammonia-based disinfectant he'd used to swab down the old walls and floor. His nasal passages were clear enough now, thank you.

The Uptown had only recently been reopened and used for off-Broadway productions. The repertoire group that acted there was currently doing *Hamlet*. Not Jock's kind of thing. Too melancholy. Not that Jock walked around with a silly grin pasted on his face. It was just that he believed people could and should do something in this world, make their own way, create their own wake in the water. Like when he was in prison for that rape he'd had no part in. Behind the walls, he'd made himself a cutting tool out of a piece of broken glass he'd found, diligently filing it to shape on concrete and hiding it in his waistband.

He'd used it to cut the first con who'd had a go at him. Then he'd stomped on the glass weapon, grinding it into bits so it could yield no fingerprints. Nobody ever learned who'd opened the assailant's gut so that closing it required thirty stitches.

Jock fell under the protection of a gang of skinheads. He'd been safe then from the gangs of black and Hispanic cons. All it took was keeping quiet most of the time and getting a few ballpoint ink tattoos that identified him as somebody not to bother without damned good reason.

Not that his time behind the walls hadn't been hell. It would be, for a guy like Jock. But he was a fast learner and an operator.

He had to smile as he rolled his bucket along the Uptown's side aisle, careful so the soapy water wouldn't slosh out onto the carpet. Figuring angles, keeping quiet, holding your cards close—he'd learned those things in prison. They were also useful on the outside. They helped him to get things done.

Like Judith Blaney.

He dumped the bucket's contents in the backstage sink, then rolled the bucket and mop toward the lobby. He made his way to the exit. It was six in the morning and already plenty bright and warm outside.

After helping to load the equipment in the Sweep 'Em Up van, he said good-bye to the rest of the cleanup crew and then ambled toward the subway stop that would take him south through Manhattan and home. It was already warm, the time of year when the concrete canyons didn't completely cool off during the sultry nights. He wouldn't smell so good on the subway, but he could put up with the sideways glances and people trying to get some space between him and them. It wouldn't always be that way.

Underground in the subway stop it was cooler. The platform was already crowded. There were working people like Jock, standing back on their heels and tired from their night jobs. There were a few out-and-out alkies who'd fouled themselves and smelled even worse than Jock. Already there were plenty of men and women dressed for the office, some of them toting attaché cases or folded newspapers. Getting an early start. Trying to stay employed in the lousy economy.

Everybody became more alert as a breeze moved over the platform. A train was approaching, pushing the air ahead of it through the narrow dark tunnel. A distant set of lights became visible, and the crowd on the platform moved nearer to the edge, preparing to board the train as soon as it lurched to a halt and the doors slid open.

Jock suddenly became aware of a man standing close to him, actually nudging his arm.

He looked over to give the guy a dirty look, and found himself facing the Skinner.

Jock drew in his breath. "What the hell . . ."

The Skinner smiled grimly and handed him a small cardboard box, the sort of thing a cheap piece of jewelry might come in.

"I thought you should have this," the Skinner said, "as a reminder that it would be best if we kept our secret just between us."

He turned and walked away, losing himself in the mass of people eager to board the train.

Jock knew he'd soon have to board and fight his way to a seat. The train had arrived and was already starting to slow.

He raised the lid of the tiny box and at first didn't know

what he was looking at. Some kind of snail, only too large for that. He prodded it with his forefinger and found it cold and pliable. Some sort of seafood? Dead, thank God.

Then he noticed the contour and color of the object and, staring at it, realized it was a human tongue.

Judith Blaney's tongue!

It must be!

The message was indirect but clear. *This is what happens to people who talk against the Skinner. Who can't keep a secret.*

Jock quickly replaced the lid and swallowed hard to keep last night's doughnuts down. It almost worked. He had to clamp his teeth and lips together and gulp down the sweet and bitter column of bile that rose in his throat.

He slumped on a hard plastic seat molded for the derrieres of extraterrestrials. The train thundered through darkness while he sat holding the tiny white box on his lap with both hands, all the way to his stop.

After he'd climbed the concrete steps to street level, he began walking fast on sidewalks that hadn't yet become packed with pedestrians. He was aware of the hardness of the concrete through the thin soles of his shoes.

He dropped the box in the first trash receptacle he came to. Casually. Not glancing back.

Only then did he slow his pace.

He was perspiring heavily. The odor of his own stale perspiration nauseated him. Bile rose again in a bitter column at the back of his throat.

Judith Blaney's tongue. Jesus!

For a second—only a second—he felt sorry for her.

Then he thought about the detective who'd questioned him in his apartment. He couldn't recall her name. The one with the black hair and eyes, and the big boobs. Despite her femininity, there'd been a kind of toughness about her.

She'd told him that if he came up with any other information he should call her. What if he called her with this? Handed her the box and said he'd found it in his mailbox or some such thing? "Maybe this will tell you something," he could say, not smiling at her, keeping a straight face. A penitentiary face. All the while watching her expression as she slowly realized what she was holding. Pearl. Yeah. That was her name, Pearl something. With her job, she'd seen some shit, so maybe the tongue wouldn't bother her and might even turn her on somehow. You never could tell; women were funny that way.

But he wasn't about to go back and even touch that box again. He wanted its contents out of his life. Forever.

Still, the thought of handing it to the cop with the boobs amused him. It actually made him smile.

The Skinner sat on a park bench near a Central Park play area and searched through the *Times* and *Post*, as he always did after taking a victim. He'd watched local TV news faithfully, too.

Again, there was no mention of the missing tongues—neither Candice's nor Judith's.

There was plenty of other lurid detail in the news reports, especially in the *Post*. He'd looked in the latest giveaway copy of *City Beat,* too. Even though the thin paper was a freebie, it had broken some big news in New York. It must have spies and purveyors of gossip all over the city, calling themselves journalists.

Of course, he knew why there'd been no mention of the tongues. The police were holding back that piece of information so they could be sure they'd have the right man when finally they had a suspect. Only they and the killer knew about the missing tongues. *Our little secret.* The police envisioned an interrogation that would be like a quiz with a trick question. The suspect would have to pass the simple test to be authenticated, and then he would be bona fide and hell bent.

Maybe it would be fun to contact the police, or one of the papers or cable news channels, and mention the tongues himself. Keeping his identity unknown, of course. Taunt the police. Taunt Quinn, who was supposed to be some kind of super hunter of serial killers.

No, he decided; better to let them think they were ahead in the game. Or at least catching up. It was enjoyable, even titillating, to know so much that Quinn didn't. To know that Quinn wasn't half as smart as he thought he was.

In fact, having Quinn as lead investigator was a bonus. The Skinner appreciated Quinn. The famous serial-killer hunter made everything a lot more challenging and interesting than some NYPD drone would have done. A man to match the mountain. Almost.

The Skinner extended his legs as he leaned back on the bench and closed his eyes. The morning sun's heat felt wonderful on his face. He decided he felt good. The turnover of the tongue to Jock Sanderson had gone well. The little bastard would still be shaken by that. He'd been given plenty of reason to guard his own tongue, to make sure it didn't say the wrong thing to the wrong people.

Not that he hadn't had reasons already. But it was always best to give people like Sanderson motivation they could *feel* as well as reason out. The Skinner knew the kind of man Sanderson was. A schemer and a taker, without ethics or shame. A survivor who would do first of all what made the best sense for him. He would not be too prideful or stubborn to be scared into safe behavior. The severed tongue had been effective.

And here was an amusing thought: Maybe the tongue was something Judith Blaney owed Sanderson. A better-late-than-never piece of the entire woman he'd wrongly served time for possessing.

The Skinner relaxed in the warm sunlight, feeling the weight of his tension evaporate.

He assured himself that there was symmetry and justice in the world, and that destiny was on his side.

"He's fixated on it now," Helen Iman said. The lanky red-headed profiler was leaning, all six feet plus of her, with a palm flat on Quinn's desk. Quinn marveled at how long her fingers were. No doubt she could palm a basketball.

"So he figures to remove the tongues of all his future victims," Quinn said.

Helen nodded. "That's the way it usually works in these kinds of cases. Two times in succession means a trend."

"Fedderman checked with slaughterhouses. They don't use the kind of knives to remove calves tongues that were used on the victims."

"Human victims, you mean," Helen said.

Quinn looked at her. "You a vegan, Helen?"

"No, no, just a plain old omnivore. Still, when you think about some of the stuff we eat . . ."

"The trick is not to think about it," Quinn said.

"Maybe the Skinner's mastered that part of it."

At first Quinn didn't know what she meant. Then he did. "Oh, Christ! You don't suppose . . ."

"That the killer might be consuming the tongues? That to him they're a delicacy?"

"I've seen so many things I didn't think possible," Quinn said.

"I doubt that he's into cannibalism, but we can't rule it out. I do know that if he isn't, he might be plenty pissed off if it was in the news that he was probably eating pieces of his victims. Even cannibals don't like to be called cannibals. And being falsely accused might make somebody go crazy with anger and make a mistake."

"Could shake things up," Quinn said. "Whether he's eating parts of his victims or not."

"A win-win," Helen said.

"Do you think it might be more valuable to us that way than holding back the tongue information from the media?"

"That'd be up to you to decide."

Quinn sat back and looked up at Helen's bony face. It was still attractive, but it would become craggy as she aged. She smiled down at him from her lanky height, made even taller by the three-inch heels she was wearing. She should be coaching or starring on a women's volleyball or basketball team. Or maybe even flaunting her tall self on fashion-show runways.

He smiled. "You seeing anybody, Helen?"

"Why? You interested?"

"Somebody worthwhile should be."

"Somebody like Fedderman the clotheshorse?"

"Sure," Quinn said. "Feds is a good man."

He knew Helen had been going out with some creep of a lawyer who specialized in representing cops' widows with insurance claims. Sometimes doing more than simply representing them. Guys like that, it always amazed Quinn that women couldn't see through them, even in times of grief. Maybe it was because they wanted so badly to believe.

Women, he thought. *So easy to fool and difficult to deceive.*

"Want me to give you Feds's number?" Quinn asked.

Helen straightened up her long frame and smiled. "I've already got his number, Quinn. And it doesn't work the combination."

Quinn considered phoning Renz and discussing whether the business with the victims' tongues should be made public, along with the theory that the Skinner was not only a killer but a cannibal. If Helen Iman was right, that kind of publicity might drive the Skinner over the top. It might cause a killer who had raised procedure and caution to the level of art to make the one mistake that was all Quinn and his team needed.

Renz might go along with it. Then again, he wouldn't like the additional heat directed at him for not being competent enough to apprehend a monster like the Skinner.

Quinn reached out and dragged the phone across his desk to him. But he didn't call Renz. He called Cindy Sellers at *City Beat*.

Sellers had no scruples, and she could keep a secret. Probably Renz was already secretly feeding her information about the Skinner murders; she was his favorite media stooge and ally. Renz had used her to plant and manipulate information in a number of cases. But that wouldn't matter. It wasn't as if they were friends. Neither was the kind of person who had real friends. And Sellers wasn't above playing a double game. In fact, it would appeal to her baser instincts.

She seemed to have a lot of those.

49

As the days passed, the weight of Beth's guilt became heavier. Wayne Westerley had told her where Salas was living, in a rundown trailer park fifty miles up the highway, near Lorenton. He wasn't working, as far as Westerley knew.

So what was Salas doing? That's what Beth wondered. Was he simply lying around hating her, blaming her, having good reason to think she'd ruined his life?

That was what Beth couldn't stand, not knowing what Salas thought of this entire tragedy. Of the mistake—if he thought it *was* a mistake—that had cost him his reputation and some of his best years.

As she sat on her porch, in a wooden rocking chair Westerley had bought for her at a Cracker Barrel restaurant, Beth's mind would dart like a trapped insect in a bottle with a cork, where there was no way out, but there was nothing to do but keep trying.

As she sat rocking, gripping the chair's armrests so tightly her fingers whitened, she heard Sheriff Westerley's big SUV turn into the drive. She recognized the sound of its powerful engine and the underlying whine when it switched gears to negotiate the rutted drive beyond the copse of maple trees.

It was sundown, and she was expecting him this evening. She sat quietly, rocking gently back and forth in her chair.

Westerley flashed her a smile from behind the steering wheel and then parked the big vehicle where he usually did, near the back of the house where it wasn't visible from the road.

She heard the SUV's door slam shut, then Westerley's boots crunching on gravel.

Beth smiled as he stepped up onto the porch. He came over and leaned down, and she scrunched up her toes to stop the rocker momentarily while he leaned down and kissed her forehead.

"What were you thinking?" he asked, as she let up with her feet and the rocker resumed its slow rhythm.

"You don't wanna know, Wayne."

"Guess not," he said, looking more closely at her.

She looked toward the orange ball of the sun dropping ever so gradually toward a distant line of pines.

"Eddie around?" Westerley asked.

"I thought I told you the other day, he's visiting his great aunt in St. Louis."

"You did tell me," Westerley said.

He entered the house and came out a few minutes later with a beer can in his hand, letting the screen door slam behind him. "Sip?"

"No, thanks." She rocked. The chair's runners made a soft creaking sound on the porch planks.

"You don't have to worry about Salas," Westerley said. "I got that straight with him the day after he was released. He won't harm you, Beth."

"Did he say he forgave me?"

"I can't tell you that. He wouldn't discuss his feelings toward you. I think he's so busy hating the state of Missouri, he's got no room to hate anything else. He thinks they owe him."

"I think so, too."

"Well, that's not for us to decide, except maybe on election days."

She rocked silently for a while.

"Still and all," Westerley said, "with Eddie away and you alone here, I get uneasy."

"I'm fine here," Beth said. Why tell him about the nightmares she lived in as an alternate world, and the guilt that lay on her like one of those lead aprons that dentists use to x-ray?

"Sun's almost down," Westerley said. "We should drive up the highway and get us something to eat."

"Then come back here?"

"That was my thinking." He smiled at her. "Yours, too?"

"No need to drive anyplace. I thawed out some steaks," she said. "I can make a salad while you're cooking them on the grill out back."

"Yours is the best plan," Westerley said.

He moved close to her again, leaned over her, and kissed her once more in the dying light.

When Beth woke the next morning to a jay raising a ruckus outside her bedroom window, Westerley was already gone. The edges of the shades were illuminated by the brightness of the day. She couldn't remember dreaming, but she must have. Her palms were red and sore where she'd dug her fingernails into them.

What she did remember vividly was last night before she'd slept. She absently reached over to where Westerley had lain and her fingertips explored cool linen.

If only her life had begun last night, instead of—

Just like that, her memories of Westerley's touch, his warm breath in her ear, everything . . . dissipated. Her mood immediately darkened.

Salas. She seemed unable to go fifteen consecutive minutes without thinking about Vincent Salas, and what she had
done to him. Nothing—not even Westerley—could change
that. She wore the past like chains, and she couldn't find a
way to break free.

She felt her face stiffen and begin to contort. Unexpected
and uncontrollable weeping threatened. It never lasted more
than a minute or two, but it was becoming more frequent.
She drew and held a deep breath, keeping it inside her until
she felt her sanity return. The impulse to weep receded. She
knew she had to do something about this. It might occur in
public. She couldn't let that happen.

Face your fears.

That's what she'd been told by the state-assigned psychologist who'd been so much help to her after Salas had—after
the rape.

That's what Beth decided to do this morning, face her
fears and her regrets, in the person of Vincent Salas. She and
Salas both knew that nothing could heal the damage done
because of Beth's mistaken allegation; the only course left
was for Beth to let him know how terrible she felt about
what had happened—no, what she'd done. It hadn't simply
happened like a brief summer shower. She would apologize
to him. It was the least she could do for him. Even if he refused to accept her apology, maybe she'd feel less of a
weight on her during her days, and during her nights when
sleep wouldn't come.

So am I doing this for me?

*Maybe. Or maybe for both of us. It might help to put what
happened behind us.*

She took a quick shower, dressed hurriedly, and brushed
her hair. It seemed that more individual hairs than usual
were caught in the brush's bristles. Were fear and remorse
causing her to lose her hair? She'd seen that happen before,

to an abused woman who used to own the beauty salon in Hogart.

Though she wasn't hungry, she forced down a hasty breakfast of toast and coffee. Before leaving the house, she took a long look at herself in the mirror. The woman staring back at her appeared haggard and older than Beth remembered, as if she were being consumed from the inside. In a way that was happening. Guilt like acid was eating her alive.

Well, it was time to act. To do *something*.

She locked the front door behind her and then left the porch and walked around to the garage. Its wide wooden doors opened to the side, and as she swung the second one on its rusty hinges something buzzed past close to her ear, making her flinch. Hornets had built a nest in the garage, just as guilt had claimed a home in her mind.

When Roy had left he'd taken their late-model Ford pickup truck. Beth was left with the old Plymouth. She still drove it, even though there were over two hundred thousand miles on the odometer. The old car had some rattles, but it still looked okay, and except for a persistent squealing sound coming from inside the dashboard—Westerley had told her not to worry, it was probably a fan motor with a loose bearing—it ran well.

Beth pulled the garage door all the way open, got in the car, and was relieved but not surprised when it started right up. She let it idle motionless for a few minutes and then backed it out of the garage. Though the morning was clear, you never knew about the weather this time of year. Clouds and rain could develop quickly. She got out of the car and closed the garage doors so water wouldn't run in if a sudden shower did blow through while she was gone.

On the road she felt better. It wasn't going to rain. The morning was going to remain glorious. And she and Vincent Salas would have a civilized conversation and come to an understanding.

Once she turned onto the Interstate, she reached Lorenton in less than an hour. It was already almost ten o'clock, so Salas should be awake. Westerley had mentioned where Salas lived in the trailer court—third trailer on the left after you go though the entrance, gray with blue trim. *Pile of crap*, Westerley had called the trailer. Which was about what you could afford, Beth thought, if you recently got out of prison. She wondered if Salas had a job. If not, maybe she could help. She could offer her help, anyway.

There was a lot of making up to do. A lot to talk about.

As the Honda sailed smoothly over the blacktop highway, Beth's thoughts wandered. She created a conversation in her mind, thinking on ways to steer their talk in the right directions.

In a sad kind of way, she and Salas needed each other. He could use her help to find a way up in the world, and she could use his forgiveness.

He shouldn't mind that kind of trade.

After she made the turnoff to Lorenton, Beth had no trouble finding the trailer court. Oak Tree Estates, it was called. Which sounded pretty ritzy.

But it wasn't ritzy. And Beth saw only a few big pin oaks. Most of the other trees were scraggly-looking maples. The gate Beth drove through wasn't an actual gate but a rusty iron archway with broken curlicues and some weedy-looking vines growing halfway up each leg.

There was the trailer, dirty gray with faded blue trim. It had wooden latticework concealing the wheels and tires. The same kind of vine that was growing up the entrance arch was laced into the lattice. Two wooden steps led up to a screen door. The trailer's windows were all tinted, or blocked with shades or drapes. It looked deserted.

Beth got out of the car and walked over hard dusty earth to the steps. There was a clutter of cigarette butts on the ground near the bottom step, as if someone habitually sat there and smoked. She felt the lump of guilt in her gut suddenly turn to fear. Was she out of her mind coming here? This man had every reason to hate her, to harm her.

She might have turned around and gotten back in the car, but a woman's voice said, "He's in there."

Beth turned and saw a heavyset woman with scraggly gray hair walking toward her. She was moving slowly, as if her feet hurt, carrying an ovular blue metal roaster without a lid out in front of her with both hands.

The woman stopped about twenty feet away and stood as if balancing the roaster so liquid inside wouldn't spill out. Behind her was the trailer she must have emerged from. Its screen door was hanging open. It had a tattered green awning over the door, and smaller, newer-looking awnings over two of its windows. A rusty tricycle lay on its side near the steps.

"Go ahead an' knock," the woman urged Beth. "He's in there. I heard him come home last night. Couldn't help but hear." She shuffled carefully to the side about ten feet and tossed a grayish liquid from the roaster into the weeds. "He's in there," she said again, over her shoulder, giving Beth a show of yellowed, jagged teeth. She looked Beth up and down. "He could prob'ly use some company." The woman headed back toward her trailer, holding the metal roaster in one hand now, letting it dangle at her side.

Determined not to let herself be scared away, Beth climbed up on the first step leading to Salas's trailer door and pushed a buzzer that almost certainly didn't work. She knocked three times on the metal frame of the screen door.

There was a faint noise from inside the trailer. Then the door on the other side of the screen door opened inward, and there Salas stood, staring down at her.

He was only a vague shape behind the dark screen, not as big a man as she remembered, but still large. He seemed to have put on weight in the right places while in prison. If he hadn't been wearing a sleeveless white undershirt, he would have been almost invisible in the dimness behind the screen.

"So what do you want?" he asked, in a hoarse voice that suggested Beth had awakened him.

She fought to find words for the ominous dark form towering over her, gazing down at her with a stillness that suggested great calm and a kind of superiority. *She* was the one who had lied. *She* was the one who had caused all the damage. Even her husband Roy had told her that before leaving her.

Salas made no move to open the door and invite her inside, or to step outside and talk with her. This wasn't going at all as Beth had planned.

"I'm . . ." she managed to say.

"I know who you are."

"I thought we should talk."

He was silent for several seconds, then: "So talk."

"I came here to assure you—" Beth said. *God! Did that even make sense?*

The shadowy form behind the screen said nothing.

Beth forged ahead. It was why she'd come all this way. "When I identified you in that police lineup, and in court, I would have sworn I was pointing at the right man."

"You did swear."

"I don't know how I could have made such a mistake. And . . ." She gulped air. ". . . I sincerely apologize."

He said nothing. Didn't move.

"I-I'm genuinely sorry," Beth said. "I know it can't mean much to you now, considering what happened, but I just wanted you to know—"

He closed the trailer door and she was standing alone on his bottom step, staring up at the screen with a blank surface behind it.

She stood that way for more than a minute, arms at her

sides, head inclined, as if gazing up in search of a god that had forsaken her.

When she backed down off the step, she stumbled and almost fell on the hard baked earth.

Beth barely remembered the drive back to Hogart and home. It seemed that suddenly there she was, in front of her garage with the car's engine idling.

She realized she was crying.

She knew that nothing had changed, but that everything must.

After parking in the garage and slamming the car's door behind her, she had to run from the hornets.

50

New York, the present

The Skinner sat hunched over his chocolate latte at an outside table at Starbucks and stared at the *City Beat* he'd plucked from a neutered vending machine a block away. The giveaway paper was lying on top of several newspapers the Skinner had bought that morning. The headline infuriated him.

SKINNER, CARVER, CANNIBAL

What on earth . . . ?

He read on, oblivious to the people streaming past nearby on the sidewalk, the rumble and exhaust fumes of traffic, and the morning sun beginning to shine brighter and hotter on the round metal table. His attention was rapt.

Anonymous sources . . . Unnamed authorities . . . removed his victim's tongues for the purpose of cooking and consuming . . .

He felt sick. He pushed his latte across the table and rested his elbows on the warm iron. How could they possibly believe *that*? What right did they have to jump to such a conclusion? To lie about him?

Cannibalism! The sick bastards!

Quinn! This has to be Quinn's doing. He knows *it isn't true. There's no reason even to imagine such a thing.*

It's so goddamned unfair!

Quinn. He'd somehow gotten the story planted. And this was exactly the kind of reaction he wanted. The idea was to get under his skin. *Under the Skinner's skin.*

Well, it wasn't going to happen. Not in the way Quinn expected. Not with the desired result.

He was calmer now that he had an understanding, or at least a hypothesis, as to what such a breathtakingly absurd accusation was about. And it was in some ways an effective stratagem. What could he do about it? Sue for defamation of character. *No, Your Honor, I did not consume the tongues of those women!* Would the court break out in laughter or in violence?

He felt himself smile. Good. He had a handle on this now.

This was a demeaning and devious move by Quinn, its aim no doubt to infuriate him and make him careless. But it wouldn't work. Let the papers print what they wanted. Let the bubble heads on televised news babble. The Skinner knew the truth. Quinn knew the truth. The two of them were locked in a deadly game, and the game board was the city.

So far, the Skinner was way ahead.

He intended to stay ahead.

Now that he had something of a grip on what had happened, he was breathing less raggedly. His rage had turned cold.

So had his latte.

He carried the mug inside and told the acne-scarred kid behind the counter that the latte had been cool when he'd given it to him. The kid listened to his voice, took a look at his face, and promptly made a fresh latte, very hot.

The Skinner returned with it to his table and sat and read newspapers for a while longer. The *Times* and *Post,* the *Daily News,* the *real* newspapers, hadn't yet picked up on the cannibalism angle. But the Skinner knew they would. It would be irresistible. Then it would be on televised news (if it wasn't already), and people would be talking about it. Tongues would wag.

The Skinner laughed out loud at his unintentional play on words.

Laughter! Is that what you expected, Quinn?

"Is this true?" Jerry Lido asked Quinn.

They were in the office. The air conditioner hadn't caught up with the heat. Vitali and Mishkin had just left to interview two more of the thirty-two prospective killers. Quinn was behind his desk. Lido had just come in. He looked neat this morning—for Jerry Lido. He had on a navy blazer, white shirt, and a red, blue, and gray diagonally striped tie that made him appear to have attended some kind of posh British school. Even his pants were pressed.

"That thing about the tongues and the Skinner," Lido persisted. "Cannibalism. I saw it on TV news."

Already? "It might be true," Quinn said.

"We don't deal in mights, do we?"

"We try not to."

"So?"

Quinn gave him a look. "There you are."

Lido understood. "Hush-hush," he said, winking. "Shouldn't have asked."

"Never hurts to ask," Quinn said.

"I believed that before I got married."

"Yeah. Well . . ."

Lido moved over and sat on the edge of Pearl's desk. He'd become more and more at home in his position as part of the investigative team. "What about you and Pearl?"

"In what way?" Quinn asked.

"Ever think about marriage?"

"Pearl's not hot on the idea."

"How about you?"

Quinn winked as Lido had. "It's hush-hush."

"Ah." Lido glanced around him, as if suddenly surprised to find himself where he was. Quinn knew the look. He knew the sensation, for that matter.

"You had breakfast, Quinn?"

"Sure have."

"Then it's not too early to pop around the corner and have a drink."

"Ten o'clock, Jerry."

"In *this* time zone."

Quinn thought about it. Pearl would arrive soon. It might be a good idea if they were gone when she breezed in. That is, if they were going to ignore time zones.

Pearl would disapprove of morning cocktails at ten. She still didn't like what Quinn was doing with Jerry Lido. *To* Jerry Lido. She had a point, Quinn knew, but not a good enough one. Women had died. More were almost certainly going to die. They wouldn't be pleasant deaths. Quinn and his team were supposed to stop them from occurring.

Simple as that.

"Why not?" he said. "A drink wouldn't hurt us."

"Or two."

Quinn left a note for Pearl saying they'd be back soon. He didn't mention where they'd gone.

Fedderman sneaked up and surprised Penny in Biographies. She seemed pleased to see him. She was wearing a mauve summer dress today that clung to her figure, white pumps with low heels, a thin silver necklace. Fedderman was wearing the suit.

Penny smelled like cinnamon and old books and perfumed shampoo. Fedderman drew a deep breath of that potpourri and committed it to memory.

He kissed her on her forehead. Her flesh was damp with perspiration though it wasn't all that warm in the library. "I thought the research room was your department."

"I'm versatile," Penny said. "We librarians have to be, in the face of technology run rampant."

"Complaining again?"

"I shouldn't. I'm employed." She lightly touched the back of his hand. "And I've got a lot to live for. I think we both do."

"Which is why I came to see you," Fedderman said.

"Oh?" She looked at him curiously, waiting.

"That's it," Fedderman said. "It's why I'm here."

Penny laughed. "Well, it seems to me you should have arrived at work a few hours ago."

"Our hours are flexible." He wriggled his eyebrows. "I'm flexible, too."

Penny shook her head. "I keep seeing new sides of you, Feds. Sides I like. That doesn't mean I like your jokes." She glanced up and down the aisle and picked up a book from a cart and slid it into its assigned space on a shelf, between Truffaut and Truman. "Maybe I shouldn't ask this, but is our relationship diverting too much of your attention away from the investigation?"

"The Skinner? I think you're more important, Penny."

"I don't."

That brought him up short.

"Remember he murdered my sister, Feds."

Fedderman felt a rush of shame. Of course she was right. So elated was he over their affair that he'd forgotten it had come at the expense of Nora Noon's life.

"You're right, Pen. Damn! I'm sorry."

"You don't have to be. It's just that while I care about you,

I don't want to distract you from your work. Especially since it involves stopping the animal that killed Nora."

"Do you think about it a lot?" Fedderman asked.

"Only every other minute. And I don't like knowing the killer is out there walking around free, maybe stalking some other woman. Maybe even me."

Fedderman gave her shoulder a squeeze. "You can't believe that, Pen."

"Why not? He killed my sister."

"We understand serial killers. They murder compulsively. Their urges are triggered in ways they themselves don't understand. It would be highly unusual for a serial killer to claim two siblings in two separate murders."

"You said he acted out of compulsion. If he saw something in Nora that triggered him to kill, maybe he'd see the same thing in me."

"Pen, tell me you don't stay awake nights worrying about that."

"Sometimes I do worry," Penny said. "I know it might sound crazy. . . ."

He bent over and let his lips brush hers. "No, it doesn't sound crazy. Only human. Notions like that can get a grip on you. But believe me, Pen, it isn't likely."

But Fedderman had to admit she had a point. It was something he'd never considered. He understood how, in her position, grieving for a dead sister, she might consider it.

"It only seems possible late at night, in the dark," she said.

"Like a lot of things," Fedderman said, thinking about his own nighttime world between wakefulness and sleep, the violence he'd seen, the blood and the faces of the dead. They came unbidden to him more and more often as the years passed.

Penny gave him a smile that looked as if it wanted to fly from her face. "I don't want you worrying about me."

"In a strange kind of way, I want to worry about you."

She sighed. "Yes, that's how it works. And I want to worry about you. Love and worry are close companions."

He tried to kiss her again, but she turned away, grinning.

"I think it's time for you to go to work, Feds."

"Do you insist?"

"Common sense insists."

"That's been getting in the way all my life." He looked into her eyes. "I don't want you walking around scared."

"I'm not. I'm walking around trying to stay employed."

He nodded, glad she was joking about it now.

Someone had entered the aisle down near the opposite end of the library, so they didn't kiss good-bye, merely touched hands.

As Fedderman walked past the front desk toward the exit, Ms. Culver gave him a disapproving look over the rims of her glasses, as she always did on his arrival or departure. He wondered if she meant it. If Ms. Culver really felt that way about him. It kind of bothered Fedderman to have somebody like that so strongly disapprove of him when they'd only recently met.

It suggested that she knew more about him than he did.

51

Weaver was wearing a cheap plastic raincoat, but it would have to do. It didn't bother her that she had no umbrella to fend off the steady light rain falling from a dark evening sky. An umbrella would make her more noticeable.

Though the evening was still warm, the careless breeze blowing along the city's stone canyons sometimes carried a chill. At least Weaver had found a temporarily dry spot, huddled deep in the doorway of an unoccupied building across the street from Jock Sanderson's walk-up in a bleak brick structure that looked as if it should have been demolished decades ago.

Weaver had read Pearl's notes and report. She was disgusted by Pearl's account of her interview with Sanderson.

Jock Sanderson had every reason in the world to kill Judith Blaney. She'd even had a restraining order issued against him. Sure, he had a seemingly ironclad alibi for the time of Blaney's death, but so what? It was obvious to Weaver that Pearl had been too easy on him.

It was easy to read between the lines. Instead of seeing a wino in a cheap-ass apartment, Pearl had seen an underdog in its pathetic lair. In Weaver's judgment, this asshole had played Pearl like a piano, made her feel pity so he could little by little ease her over to his side.

And that's how the interview had ended. With Pearl almost apologizing for disturbing this good citizen in his meager shelter from a heartless society.

Maybe Pearl was right in assuming Sanderson's innocence so readily. But Weaver thought there was a chance she was wrong, and that he had killed Judith Blaney. Whether he was the Skinner was another question. He might have somehow found out about the severed tongues and used the Skinner as the basis for a copycat crime, made Blaney's death simply look like another in the string of Skinner murders.

As terrified of Sanderson as Judith Blaney must have been, Weaver figured she deserved more than Pearl's half-assed conversation with him, and then a perfunctory dismissal of him as a suspect.

Of course it was also true that Weaver saw this as an opportunity to show initiative and make her fellow officers—especially Pearl—seem incompetent. If she went out on her own, secretly, and nailed the Skinner, her career would be made. Renz would see to that.

Pearl had screwed up. There was opportunity here, and Weaver was going to seize it.

She straightened her posture and then stayed still as she saw a dark figure emerge from the apartment building. A man. Wearing a black or dark blue raincoat and a beret or beret-like dark cap. He stutter-stepped down from the apartment to the sidewalk in a quick, easy maneuver that suggested he was familiar with the wet concrete steps.

When he turned and passed beneath a streetlight, Weaver was sure the man was Jock Sanderson.

He picked up his pace, and Weaver had to hurry to keep up. She barely felt the rainwater finding its way beneath her coat collar and trickling down the back of her neck.

Sanderson went down the steps of a subway stop, used a MetroCard, and passed through the turnstiles. Weaver followed.

The platform was crowded, and a train was roaring and screeching in, still traveling fast as its cars winked past waiting passengers. Weaver knew it would slow down and stop in a hurry.

With a loud, protracted squeal, the train did just that. Its sliding doors opened, and passengers streamed out. Some of the people on the platform waited patiently out of the way, while others began easing in through the sides of the doors.

There was a lot of milling about. Weaver looked around and saw that Sanderson was boarding the car behind the one she was about to get on. She turned away as casually as she could and joined the knot of people waiting to board Sanderson's car.

More passengers than usual streamed from that car, and there was a great deal of pushing and shoving. When Weaver finally fought her way to the door, the car was almost too crowded to get on. She boarded anyway, pressing into the mass of passengers standing and gripping support poles. Several people glared at her. One woman, hugging a cluster of shopping bags to her breast, blithely gave Weaver the finger.

Weaver didn't mind. What bothered her was that she couldn't see Sanderson. The train lurched forward, and the mass of pressed humanity shifted in unison. Weaver didn't like all the bad breath, the body odors mixed with the smells of damp coats and wet hair. She wished to hell that Sanderson had taken a cab. She might be following in a second dry and warm cab. Like in books and movies.

The subway swayed and jiggled though a turn, causing a man to shift position and step on Weaver's toe. Another man almost lost his footing, leaning against Weaver. He didn't seem in a rush to straighten up. She decided he was the source of the bad breath.

The train stopped and took on even more passengers. Weaver watched the sliding doors as best she could and didn't see Sanderson get off. To be sure he was still in the subway car, she leaned sideways and studied the platform through a window as the train pulled away.

There was no Sanderson among the teeming, hurrying riders who had just left the train.

The next stop was Forty-second Street, a busy one. Only a few passengers got off, but many more piled into the cars. Not Weaver's car, though—it was already crowded to maximum. She watched several people begin to board and then change their minds and drift back and away.

So it went stop after stop. Slowly, the passengers leaving the car began to outnumber those getting on. Weaver caught a reassuring glimpse of Sanderson seated toward the rear of the car.

She lost him at the Thirty-fourth Street stop. He rose from his seat and pushed his way out of the car almost immediately when the doors opened. It took Weaver several seconds to struggle to the nearest door and ease her way out onto the platform.

There were simply too many people massed on the platform for her to keep sight of him. She walked toward the steps leading up to the street, thinking this was as good an exit as any.

There was no sign of Sanderson in the stairwell or on the street.

Weaver glanced again in every direction and then stood there, the cool drizzle on her face, and wondered what to do next.

Then she saw Sanderson across Thirty-fourth Street. He was walking into the breeze, holding an umbrella in front of him as a windbreak as well as protection from the slanting drizzle.

Sanderson had slowed down. Despite the rain, he didn't seem to be in a rush. He strolled with seeming aimlessness, from time to time stopping to look into shop windows.

Weaver followed, pretending to look into those same windows.

They walked that way for blocks, with Weaver keeping her distance to avoid being noticed. She was good at tailing, and she was sure Sanderson didn't know he was being followed. He wasn't exactly being evasive, yet his behavior wasn't quite normal. There was something about the way he was walking, slightly bent forward, with his umbrella always at precisely the same angle, concentrating intently on something ahead of him.

Sanderson was following someone with single-minded determination not to lose them. He was focused on his purpose as if his life depended on it. Or someone else's life.

She understood it then. He was stalking someone.

Weaver moved up slightly and observed him more closely, her heartbeat quickening. Sanderson was stalking, all right. Not simply following, but stalking. Everything about his pace and attitude suggested it. Weaver strained to see through the darkness and relentless rain, but couldn't make out anyone up ahead of Sanderson.

That didn't mean there was no one there, considering the weather.

They had turned several corners. There were no shop windows now. The neighborhood was downscale. The block they were on featured a closed dry cleaner, a boarded-up restaurant, a political headquarters now for rent. The peeling poster of the smiling candidate in the window reminded Weaver that things weren't always as hopeful as they seemed. He'd lost big in the last election.

There were only a few people on the street.

And then Weaver noticed that she was alone.

No. Not alone!

She heard a faint rustle and sensed movement behind her and to her left. She began to spin away. Only began. Something slammed into the base of her neck and she was on the wet pavement.

She looked up and saw a man in a dark coat, a balaclava concealing everything of his face but his eyes and mouth. He was holding some kind of club or cudgel in his right hand.

As Weaver scrambled to get up, he jabbed hard with the club beneath her ribs. Pain shot through her right side, but she didn't go down. Instead she clawed at her attacker's face. She missed his eyes but felt her fingernails gouge flesh.

Again he was on her with the club—maybe a nightstick!

Is this guy a cop?

Whatever he was swinging was plenty hard. He slammed it across the width of Weaver's back, making a sound that sickened her. Down again, on her hands and knees, she tried to catch her breath. She caught pain instead.

Then greater pain exploded at the back of her head.

Everything became dim, as if streetlights were going out one by one.

She smelled something like ammonia and felt someone holding her hand. For a second she thought she was being rescued, pulled up away from the darkness that dragged at her. Then she realized what she felt was her assailant cleaning beneath her fingernails that had gouged him. He didn't want his DNA scraped from beneath her nails in the morgue.

Oh, God! In the morgue!

As she dropped into a dark world, her last awareness was of the slushy patter of soles on wet concrete, the faint and rhythmic splash of rainwater. She'd heard the sound often and could recognize it. Someone running away.

Years ago a hospice worker had warned Weaver to be careful about what she said when her mother lay dying in a hospital bed. The sense of hearing was often the last thing to go.

Am I dying?

52

The Skinner sat at a table in the atrium of the Citigroup Building, sipping an egg cream. There were no actual eggs in egg creams, which was one of the things the Skinner liked about them. They were tricky and misleading. Possibly most people who drank them, especially out-of-towners, assumed they'd consumed an egg. He smiled grimly. There were a lot of misconceptions about what people ate in this town.

He sipped and savored. Yes, egg creams were misleading. They symbolized the misleading and mislabeled world people were supposed to live in. But he'd learned long ago there were as many worlds as there were people. Anyone who was smart enough soon figured out it was possible to create and live in a world of your own, and it was just as valid as the one projected by so-called reality. It was the individual world of the spirit and the mind. It wasn't mystical at all, but simply another chosen reality. Not buying into the common delusion; that's what it was all about. The real rules, the ancient, few ones, were the only rules that mattered. The only actual reality, deeply buried in the human psyche, as it was in that of every living being.

He sucked on the plastic straw and it made a gurgling sound that signified the end of the egg cream.

Best to stop thinking bullshit, he decided. Not the place or time for hypothesizing. Concentrate on creating Quinn's reality, keeping the wily cop in a world controlled by the Skinner. Different worlds for different folks. If his and Quinn's worlds met only now and then, and tangentially, everything would work out fine.

He wondered if the lady cop he'd beaten was dead. And if she was alive, had she learned her lesson? Would she be able to go back to her job and be part of the game? Had Quinn lost one of his pieces?

The Skinner had beaten her with a tire thumper, a club-like instrument used by truckers to whap the tires of eighteen-wheelers to make sure they were inflated. He'd bought it in the shop of a highway gas station and restaurant frequented by truck drivers (a sure sign of good food) after noticing how much it resembled an old-fashioned wooden nightstick. It was even weighted at the end like a nightstick and had a leather strap to wind around your wrist so you wouldn't drop it. A crude weapon, but effective. Ask the lady cop.

He gathered his napkin, cup, and crumpled straw wrapper from the table and stood up to leave. Maybe he'd stop in at the bookstore in the building and buy something to read. A thriller of some sort. Escape literature.

As he made his way toward a trash receptacle, he noticed two men seated facing each other at one of the tiny tables, their heads bowed. Their brows were furrowed and their gazes fixed, as they concentrated on a chess board between them.

Lost in a world of their own.

Quinn loomed watchfully, like a rough-hewn and wing-less angel, over Nancy Weaver's hospital bed. His shoulders drooped and his massive hands dangled useless at his sides. Right now he felt useless. Helpless. Before him was a problem for surgeons' hands and scalpels, not cops' hands and guns.

Weaver was unconscious but coming out of it. As Quinn watched, her bruised face contorted in pain and her body twitched in a reflex action to change position, which she couldn't do because she was belted to the bed faceup so she couldn't put a strain on her injured back. She moaned and tried to but couldn't quite open her eyes.

Quinn examined her IV bottles, then adjusted a plastic valve slightly. He waited a few minutes and then stepped out into the hall and hailed a passing nurse.

"I think she's regained consciousness," he said.

The nurse, a portly, middle-aged woman with puffy cheeks and diamond-bright blue eyes, gave him a suspicious look. Her plastic name tag identified her as Rose. "The patient in two-oh-five?"

"Right. Officer Nancy Weaver."

"Ah, the policewoman." Rose shuffled several clipboards she was carrying, found the proper one, and gazed at it. "Hmm . . . you're sure she's regaining consciousness?"

"She asked if she could talk to me," Quinn said. "Mumbled it, but she asked."

"And who might you be?"

Quinn showed her his ID.

Rose looked him in the eye. "You're positive she's conscious? She's receiving a sedative along with her glucose. We're trying to hydrate her. She has several serious injuries."

Quinn moved nearer to Rose. "I've got to confide in you, dear, that it's vitally important that she and I speak. Lives do depend on it."

Rose had heard that one. She shook her head no. "We'll get Officer Weaver well on her way to survival, then you can question her and catch whoever did that terrible thing to her."

Quinn laid a huge hand on her shoulder with a feather

touch. "No, no, dear, you don't understand. Her interest and mine, and I hope yours, are to make sure she's not soon joined by another patient with similar, or perhaps even worse, injuries at the hands of the animal that beat poor Nancy. There is a time-urgent aspect to this matter."

Rose shook her head adamantly. "I can't be responsible for—"

"But you will be, Rose. Responsible for another woman suffering as Officer Weaver now suffers. That is, if you don't let her and I simply exchange a few words. Then she can rest all the better knowing she's done her duty and we know who did this heinous thing to her. I beg you, Rose, to let her finish what she set out tonight to accomplish."

Rose gave Quinn a long, hopeless sigh. He wasn't sure if it meant surrender or exasperation. Rose was hard to read.

Quinn moved closer and lowered his voice even more. "Young as you are, my impression is you've been a nurse for some time. You must know your real responsibilities in gray areas such as this, dear. Vital gray areas. We all know there are rules that must in special times be circumvented to prevent tragedy."

"You are so full of bullshit," Rose said.

Quinn's earnest smile was undaunted.

"You can be in the room with us," Quinn said.

"You're damned right I can," Rose told him, and led the way.

As soon as they were in the room, Rose examined the IV bottles hooked up to the tube leading to Weaver's arm.

Weaver's eyes flickered open. "Quinn . . . ?" she managed to groan from her bed.

He touched her lightly on the forehead. "Don't try to talk, Nancy, unless I ask you something."

"I'm in goddamned pain. The bastard hit me with something that looked like a nightstick."

"Who was it, Nancy?"

"I was following Sanderson."

"Jock Sanderson? Why?"

"I read Pearl's notes from her interview with him. They didn't look right. The guy got to her, gave her a load of crap instead of straight answers."

Quinn had read the interview and didn't see it that way. And not too many people got to Pearl. "You really think so?"

"Yeah. So I decided to tail Sanderson and see what there was to learn. I got the feeling *he* was tailing someone. Stalking her."

"Her?"

"I'm guessing there," Weaver admitted. She took a deep breath. "Damn, that hurts!"

"Sanderson did this to you?"

"Must have. I was tailing him one second, and the next he was pounding away on me with that club of his."

"You saw his face?"

"No. It was dark and he was wearing a balaclava. I could just see his eyes and mouth."

"So you couldn't identify him for sure."

"No. Guess not . . ."

Weaver's voice was wavering. She was obviously getting weaker.

"We're done here," Rose said.

"No," Weaver said. She tried to grasp Quinn's arm but couldn't move her own. "I scratched his face hard under the balaclava. I remember that for sure. I did damage. Then I smelled ammonia—"

"Ammonia . . ."

"That's it," Rose said, and reached for the valve on the IV tube.

"He cleaned under my fingernails," Weaver said. "I could feel the scraping. . . ."

Rose readjusted the plastic valve.

"He might be our Skinner," Weaver said.

"Skinner?" Rose asked. "The animal who's killing those women?"

Quinn nodded. "The very same." He looked down at Weaver, whose eyes were closed again. "Nancy?"

Weaver's breath evened out and her features relaxed.

"She's resting," Rose said, "as she should be. And if I ever find again that you've tampered with medical equipment in a patient's room, I'll sic the authorities on you like a pack of mad dogs. There'll be no more asking me to break the law for you. And you a policeman yourself."

"I—"

"Don't bother to deny it, please. I've heard enough lies." She sighed loudly again. It seemed to be her signature way of expressing herself. "Have you got a card, Quinn?"

He looked at her.

"A business card, man!" Another trailing sigh.

Quinn dug his wallet from his pocket and handed her one of his Q and A business cards.

Rose tucked it in a pocket of her nurse's uniform. "When the patient comes around again and you can count on her actually making sense, I'll straightaway give you a call."

"Thanks, Rose. I'll have someone standing guard on Weaver here at the hospital. If you notify him, it'll be the same as notifying me."

"I hope you catch the murdering psychopath," Rose said.

"We will," Quinn assured her. He moved toward the elevator, and Rose walked alongside him. At the elevator doors, they paused. Quinn smiled his surprisingly beatific smile and gave Rose's elbow a gentle squeeze. "You did the right thing, dear."

"I was told those very words once after extramarital sex. It was a lie then and it is now."

53

Edmundsville, Missouri, 2006

"You almost fell on your you-know-what," May Ann said.

Beth had stumbled during an underarm turn on the crowded dance floor. May Ann had been the last of the group to arrive, and was still playing the chaste Catholic schoolgirl all grown up. Beth knew that was going to change in a big way after a few more drinks. Already May Ann was beginning to laugh too loud and bat her eyelashes.

The place was the 66 Road House, though it wasn't anywhere near the new or old Route 66. The music was Hank Williams. There was sawdust on the dance floor, and the garage band that played the 66 was loud and almost on the beat. Beth was dancing with her friend May Ann Plunkert. The two women's other friends, Gloria Trish and Sami Toyner, were at the table near the Stag Beer sign, sipping bourbon and water on the rocks. That and scotch and beer were pretty much what the 66 served. A drink with a parasol would probably result in a fight.

In the time she'd worked at Arch Manufacturing, Beth had made some good friends. Lots of single women were employed there, and there were plenty of cliques and enough ways to spend time if you weren't too tired after work. Beth had fallen in with a group of about a dozen who called themselves the Sole Sisters. They weren't particularly wild, but they had their fun.

Beth hadn't made any close male friends, but she'd gone out on the occasional date. Nothing worked for her romantically, or for the men passing through her life. It was difficult for her to become involved with someone. The men she'd dated who were interested in more than sex broke off the relationship after learning she had a fourteen-year-old son. Baggage. People Beth's age had baggage, and that was the way some of these jerks saw Eddie.

Beth truly loved Eddie. Tonight he was on a camping trip with his best friend Les and Les's father. Eddie was turning into quite the outdoorsman. He especially loved fishing.

Since she'd left Hogart, things had worked out well. She had a job, a house, a life. Most important of all, Beth had her son to raise. She had all that, and she liked her work well enough at Arch, but now and then she found herself thinking there had to be more in life.

Like Wayne Westerley. Had she been an idiot to break off her affair with Wayne? A part of her didn't want to leave him, but she knew that if she was going to find any happiness and get Eddie away from the fallout of what had happened to her, she had to leave Hogart.

The town wasn't much to leave, anyway, a blink-of-the eye business loop off the Interstate and a dozen tree-lined side streets featuring houses that would have been historic but for the fact they were cracker-box shacks on the day they were built.

From time to time she did miss Wayne, not only their sexual involvement but the quiet times on her front porch, the leisurely walks along Trout Lake. He'd helped her to heal, and it wasn't his fault that the healing could never be complete.

Westerley had driven to Edmundsville to see her several times after she'd moved, but she'd stopped that, too. It was as if he brought a part of the past with him, and it was a past Beth needed to escape. Eddie was the finest and only part of her earlier life she wanted to carry into the future.

Beth spent her hours at Arch working on the line, helping to manufacture orthopedic blanks for shoe inserts. Some of the blanks would be packaged as is, in three sizes, for distribution to retail outlets. Others would be custom-shaped to the prescription orders of orthopedic doctors. Those were the jobs that took expertise, and of course they paid better. Beth looked forward to making that transition one of these days, when she'd obtained enough seniority. Of course there were the more physically demanding warehouse jobs, which paid well, but Beth saw the physical toll those took on women and wanted no part of any of them except maybe forklift operator. But that was a high seniority position and would be years away even if she had a chance at it.

She almost slipped and fell again, and heard May Ann giggle. *Too much sawdust on the floor.*

The music stopped, which was fine with Beth. She was winded and perspiring, and a lock of hair dangled down on her forehead and kept getting into her eye. She and May Ann started back across the dance floor toward the table, which required picking their way among two-steppers waiting for the next song and was almost a dance in itself. A guy in a white Stetson sat down on stage in front of the band and began strumming a regular acoustic guitar and singing. He sounded something like Hank Williams. Beth caught a glimpse of him and he even looked like Hank Williams.

Someone tapped her on the shoulder and she turned around.

The man smiling at her also was wearing a white cowboy hat. He was average height, handsome, and built wiry like Hank Williams, and damned if he didn't resemble Williams in the face even more than the guy onstage. The same sort of dark-eyed sweetness in his lean features. He had a slender, slightly long nose and a sharp chin with thin lips. Dark eyebrows that were sort of angled up at the bridge of his nose to give him a puppy-dog inquisitive look. Not the greatest features, she thought, but they did hang together well.

"I like that," he said.

Beth wasn't sure she wanted to flirt after only one drink. "And what would *that* be?"

"The way you're sizing me up. Shows you're interested."

"I was thinking you look a little like Hank Williams."

"I been told that. 'Fraid I can't sing like him." He grinned. Good teeth. "I could maybe sound better than that guy onstage, though."

Beth smiled. "I just bet you could," she said sarcastically. There was something about this guy. She felt comfortable with him, but maybe in a sisterly way. Of course, that could change. Maybe . . .

No. He'll be just like the others.

"Now, that's a tone of voice I don't like," he said, touching her arm and guiding them away from May Ann and over to the edge of the dance floor, which was getting crowded, what with all the fellas taking advantage of a slow dance. "I don't like that little frown of yours while you're looking at me. I ain't that bad a singer. I cross my heart."

He moved in close to her. As if it was the most natural thing in the world, they were dancing. Barely moving, but dancing.

"I'm Lincoln Evans," he said. "Friends call me Link, so I'm 'Link' to you."

"Beth Colson."

"Now we know each other," he said, and his embrace tightened.

Link wanted Beth to leave the 66 with him that night, but she explained to him that she was there with friends. She even led him over by the hand and introduced him to the others.

"We work out at the plant," she said, a little embarrassed but also pleased by the envious glances from her friends.

He touched the brim of his hat and smiled down at them all, as if his next move would be to sit at the table and regale them with tales of the rodeo. Instead he guided Beth back onto the dance floor. He was holding her even closer now.

"You all work at some plant?" he asked.

"Arch Manufacturing. We make insoles."

"No kidding?" Like it was the most interesting job in the world.

"Shoes," Beth said.

"What? Did I step on yours?"

She laughed. "Insoles for shoes."

"Oh. Yeah, I figured that."

Was he being sarcastic? Beth didn't know how to reply. They had struck the wall of first-date awkward conversation.

"It's not very interesting work," she said. "So what do you do? No, let me guess. You're a cowboy. A real one."

"Unemployed like a real one," he said. "What I been doing is driving around Missouri in my truck, looking for work."

"What kinda work?"

"Any. And I mean any. Jobs are scarce out there."

"So I heard." They danced silently for a while. "Listen," she said. "I've got a little influence at Arch." *Very little.* "I can at least let you know when there's an opening and put in a word for you."

He looked down at her as if he could hardly believe her. "You'd really do that for me?"

That and more. "Sure. Why not?"

"Because you barely know me."

"I've got a good feeling about you, Link."

"Like I've got about you." They danced slower and slower, until they were standing locked in a simple embrace, and then he kissed her.

Beth changed her mind about leaving the 66 with her friends. After the music stopped, she made her way over to the table and told May Ann and the others they could go without her. She had her own car, anyway, and thought she might leave early.

She could feel their eyes on her as she walked out of the 66 with Link Evans.

They sat in his dusty and dented pickup truck for a while and kissed and talked and kissed some more. Then he pulled her close and she felt his hand move up beneath her blouse and onto her right breast. His fingers danced over her nipple and then gave a slight pinch.

God! He knows what he's doing.

As he began unbuttoning her blouse she realized that he'd felt her sudden involuntary resistance.

He released her immediately.

"I don't want to rush things, Beth. Not with you."

"I'm sorry. It's just that. Well . . ."

"If you're not in the mood, that's reason enough for me to wait."

"There's something you oughta know."

"What? You're married?"

"No. Divorced."

"So?"

"I've got a fourteen-year-old son."

He sat back as if he needed a little distance to take her all in at a glance. "No kidding?" He reached for a pack of cigarettes on the dashboard and lit one, coughed, and flipped the cigarette out the window. It made a glowing arc in the night, like a miniature shooting star. "Gotta quit those damned things."

"His name is Eddie."

"Well, Eddie's a lucky boy, with you as his mom."

"What about you, Link? Are you lucky?"

He laughed. "Well, I gotta admit I just now was trying to get lucky."

"You know what I mean. Does what I just told you change things between us?"

He seemed puzzled, but only briefly. "Changes this. I'm very much looking forward to meeting Eddie."

They kissed again, and she felt his fingers tugging at the material of her blouse. This time she helped him with the buttons.

Later, in Link's motel room just off the Interstate, Beth lay wondering what she and Link had just begun. He was a wonderful, gentle lover, and he seemed more than pleased with her.

But Beth was worried. What was happening to her, and to Link, would take a measure of commitment. She had a hunch he was capable of it, but she wasn't so sure about herself.

Somebody clomped around in the room upstairs and then was quiet. The only sound in the night was the distant whine of trucks on the highway, downshifting to make the turn on the dark Interstate instead of heading straight for Edmundsville. Beth thought it might be the loneliest sound she'd ever heard. It almost made her cry.

Hank Williams, what have you started?

Six weeks later they were married in Las Vegas and spent a week in luxury at the MGM Grand. Most of the time Beth felt she was trespassing. Link spent an hour at a slot machine and won almost a thousand dollars. He kissed her and told her it meant their marriage was starting off lucky.

The rest of their time there they didn't gamble. That was the only way you could beat a casino, Link said. Beth agreed with his decision, figuring if they stopped gambling, their luck couldn't change.

54

Whoever answered the phone at Sweep 'Em Up told Quinn that Jock Sanderson was at an uptown YMCA with the rest of a cleanup crew, making fresh again an auditorium where an author had spoken last night about his book on how television pundits were poisoning American society.

"I think I read that one," Quinn said, and told the woman on the phone that if Sanderson happened to call, it would be best if she didn't mention her and Quinn's conversation.

"He'll be too busy with his mop and push broom to call," the woman said. "Anyway, once the daytime cleanup crews are out on the job, nobody calls here except maybe people like you."

"Did Sanderson work last night?"

"No. It was his night off. That's why he's on this daytime job. It's cheaper for our clients if we clean during the day, and venues like the YMCA don't hold events so often that they're in a big rush to clean up afterward."

"How long's it usually take to clean up after something like an author lecture at a YMCA?"

"You mean what time will Sanderson get off work?"

"You're ahead of me," Quinn said.

"They didn't start all that early, so it'll probably be push-ing five o'clock. You want to talk to him, you might be able to catch him when he's on his lunch break around noon. It'd be better for him if the boss and the rest of the crew didn't know the police were visiting him."

Quinn told her that was a good idea, but the moment he hung up he left to drive to the YMCA where Sanderson was working today. He wasn't in the mood to give a damn what Sanderson's boss or his fellow employees thought about the law questioning him.

The YMCA was a modern gray and glass cube on a block of old buildings being renovated. Quinn was directed by an Arnold Schwarzenegger look-alike in a too-tight shirt to the auditorium.

After walking down a hall with glass windows looking in on a swimming pool, an indoor track, and a room full of people working out on exercise equipment, he pulled open a wooden door with a pneumatic closer and stepped into a small lobby. He used an identical door to enter the auditorium.

It was dim and, even without people in the seats, it didn't seem all that large. It smelled musty, in the way of empty auditoriums. Quinn estimated it would accommodate about five hundred people. He wondered what kind of turnout the author of the TV pundit book had spoken to last night. He guessed it would depend on whether the speech was free.

A man and woman in gray work coveralls were moving things from the small stage to an area behind some curtains. Two others, both men, were using long-handled push brooms to sweep the gray painted concrete floor between the rows of seats. One of the broom pushers fit Sanderson's description. Quinn walked to the end of the row he was sweeping and waited until Sanderson looked up and noticed him. He held up his ID and motioned for Sanderson to come to him.

As if grateful for the break, Sanderson propped his broom between two seat backs. He sidled toward Quinn in a way that suggested the seats were occupied and he was worried about stepping on toes. Quinn saw why. The seats hadn't been raised yet on that end of the row to allow room for sweeping beneath them.

Sanderson stopped and stood in front of the end seat, looking expectantly at Quinn. Up close, Sanderson looked shorter than he did at a distance, but he was solidly built—well set up, as old cops used to say. Quinn was disappointed to see that there were no scratches on his face. Weaver had clawed the man who attacked her, and had done so hard enough to come away with his flesh beneath her fingernails.

Quinn identified himself.

"I already talked to another cop—officer," he said. "Pearl somebody or other."

"That's all right," Quinn said, as if Sanderson had been seeking reassurance. "I'm here about something else. A woman was badly beaten last night, not far from where you live." He watched Sanderson's reaction. He'd know the beating took place a long walk or subway ride away from his apartment.

Sanderson maintained his poker face and shrugged. "Well, it ain't the safest neighborhood. I'm thinking about moving."

Quinn stared at him. "Let's talk about this out in the lobby."

"Sure. But remember I'm working. We've gotta finish this up in another few hours."

"This won't take long."

"That's what they tell you when they hang you."

Quinn guessed that was a joke and managed a smile. He remembered a woman who'd hanged herself in her bedroom years ago and hadn't done a good job. It had taken her long, agonizing hours to die in a noose that was too loose, at the end of a rope that was too short. He thought that people who killed themselves had a responsibility to give it some thought first. They owed it to whoever was going to find the body.

The lobby was angular and carpeted in red. Though there was enough glass to qualify it as a greenhouse, the brightness was intensified by overhead track lighting. There was a low black sofa along one wall, but neither man moved to sit down. Quinn got what he wanted, a close look at Sanderson's face in good light. There was no sign of scratches or gouges, or of makeup covering any. This wasn't the man Weaver had clawed.

But that didn't mean he hadn't had something to do with the assault.

"We gotta have time to get those restrooms cleaned," Sanderson said, pointing to a door with the international symbol of a woman in a skirt standing squarely as if she were in a snit.

"You'll have it," Quinn said. "Where were you between seven and ten last night?"

Sanderson rubbed his chin, making a show of trying to remember. "I don't know if I could tell you exactly, but around seven-thirty or so I went out for a walk. I was gone quite a while."

"What's a while?"

"I dunno. Maybe two, three hours."

"You're quite a walker."

"Yeah. It helps to get rid of stress."

"What's stressing you?"

"Same things stressing lots of people. Getting by, getting around, stretching a buck, holding on to a job because it's not easy to get another one if you've spent time behind the walls."

"Woman trouble?"

"Huh?"

"You didn't mention woman trouble."

"Right now, I ain't got any. Not that I didn't have lots of it once. But you know all about that."

"Not all, maybe."

Sanderson shrugged one shoulder beneath his gray uniform. "Well . . ."

"Anybody see you during this walk?"

"Sure. Hundreds, I suppose. You know New York. But I doubt if any of them would remember me." Sanderson smiled. "I mean, I don't remember any of them, do I?"

"Did you go in someplace and get a cup of coffee? Maybe stop to buy a newspaper or magazine?"

Sanderson took a long time to answer, putting on another show of searching his memory. "No, I didn't stop or do anything that anyone might remember."

"These walks you take, do you have any sort of destination when you set out?"

"Never. That's part of why they relieve stress."

"Do you ever pick somebody at random and follow them? Just for something to do?"

Sanderson appeared shocked by the conversational swerve. "Follow somebody? No, that's nutty."

Quinn smiled. "Yeah, I guess it is." He held out his hand for Sanderson to shake. "You can get back to work. Thanks for your time."

"Sure." Sanderson shook the proffered hand.

But Quinn didn't let go. He tightened his grip slowly and powerfully. Not as tight as he might. Just letting Sanderson know he could easily crush all his fingers. "You wouldn't have anything to do with a woman getting beaten up last night, would you?"

Sanderson was too proud to show any sign that his hand hurt. He'd learned in prison not to reveal vulnerability. "It wasn't that cop, Pearl, that got worked over, was it?"

"Why would you think so?"

"I don't think so. I'm asking 'cause I don't know. I kind of liked Pearl, is all. She was nice. I wouldn't wanna think somebody beat the shit out of her." He took a deep breath and let it out, but still didn't change expression. "Say, you wouldn't mind letting go of my hand, would you?"

Quinn acted surprised that he was still clasping Sanderson's hand. "Oh, sorry." He turned the hand loose.

Sanderson grinned. "I need that hand for work."

"And, since you don't have any woman trouble right now, not just for that." Quinn winked and turned to leave.

"Thinking about Pearl," Sanderson said.

Quinn felt a stab of anger and turned back around.

"You never answered me whether it was Pearl that got beat up last night," Sanderson said.

"Somebody else," Quinn said.

"Good. If something happened to Pearl, I'd wanna know myself who had a hand in it."

Quinn stared at Sanderson, wondering if the little bastard was quicker off the mark than he seemed.

"I better get back to sweeping up," Sanderson said.

Quinn nodded. "That'd be your best bet."

As he left the YMCA, Quinn had a better understanding of why Weaver thought Sanderson might be worth watching.

However, Weaver was probably wrong. There was no doubt about Sanderson's alibi for the night of Judith Blaney's murder. And for that matter, no doubt that he *wasn't* the man who assaulted Weaver. Sanderson was just another small-time ex-con with a devious streak and a healthy skepticism, probably a fraction as smart as he saw himself.

Weaver had been right in her suspicions but wrong in her conclusion.

Exactly what Quinn had spent much of his life trying to avoid.

Still, Quinn had respect for intuitive reasoning, and Weaver had demonstrated that quality in other investigations.

It might be a good idea to put a tail on Sanderson for a while.

To make sure.

55

Verna Pound was past the point of waiting until no one was looking. She simply walked up to the wire trash receptacle, which was chained to a light pole at the corner, and began poking through its contents. She saw a roach skitter away from a white foam box. It was the small kind that wouldn't accommodate much food, but well worth a look.

She scooted the roach farther away with the backs of her fingers, and opened the box.

It contained half a hamburger and another cockroach. This cockroach took its leave even before Verna could brush it away or whisk the chewed hamburger and bun from it.

She was grateful. Even if she found nothing more, this was enough food to hold her until breakfast tomorrow morning at the chapel.

She hunched her body around the foam container and limped away from the trash barrel. Her plan was to find a safe place to sit down, eat her meal along with the third-full bottle of wine she'd bought from a friend, and then walk across town to the shelter. She'd rest a few blocks from the shelter and see if she could beg a few more dollars. It was best to get a jump on her tomorrows, assuming she could hide the money safely from the thieves that came in the night. That was a problem at the shelters. That and sex. Why any of those sickos would want to force sex on the sorts of poor and battered women who slept in such places was beyond Verna's comprehension. And it was absurd that any of the street women would want anything to do with the homeless and hapless—and bathless—men who bedded down at the shelters. Dirt and desperation were mood breakers. Not to mention hunger.

There were exceptions, of course. On her better days, Verna liked to think of herself as one. And perhaps inside his ragged clothes and dirt-smeared exterior was a man worth knowing. One who could see beyond Verna's exterior to the beauty inside.

Some women—or maybe all women—never gave up hope.

Verna remembered the man who'd given her a five-dollar bill earlier that evening. That was the money that made possible the shelter bed. He seemed genuinely interested in her. His suit had been old and threadbare, but his scuffed shoes weren't too worn. A guy maybe just beginning the long and steepening slide. He so obviously couldn't afford to spare the five dollars he'd given her that Verna for a moment felt like returning it. For only a moment.

She'd watched him as he strode away. Viewed from behind, at a distance, he appeared as if he possessed some wealth. Not prosperous, but maybe a guy with a job.

She was thinking about the generous donor when a black sedan pulled over to the curb slightly ahead of where Verna was walking.

Her heart jumped. *Police? I'm not staying in one place, panhandling. I'm not dressed so bad that I look like a street person. What the hell . . .*

She decided the car had nothing to do with her.

But as she walked past it, picking up her pace and staring straight ahead, a man called her name.

She looked over and saw the generous guy standing by the car with the driver's side door open.

"Verna Pound," he said again. He was grinning.

"Do I know you?" Verna asked.

"Five dollars' worth."

Now she understood what he expected for his money. "I'm not selling," Verna said. "Only borrowing."

"I don't expect to be repaid, Verna. Gifts aren't meant to be repaid with something of more value. I only want to talk with you."

Verna had been moving slowly forward, and was now about ten feet away from the man. "How do you even know my name?"

Instead of answering, he slammed the car door and cut across the sidewalk so he could be next to her, walking with her. Casually, he aimed his key fob behind him, and the big car's lights flashed as its doors locked.

"You *do* remember me?"

"I remember the five dollars," Verna said. She didn't tell him about her cataracts. Now that he was close, the man was something of a blur to her.

He slowed his pace to hers, and they walked together for a while. They were approaching a small stone church next to a boarded-up brick building. There was a dark passageway in between the two buildings. Verna attempted to change her direction a few degrees so she'd be walking away from the dark passage, but the man from the big car didn't budge and let her bump herself into him. Verna began to be afraid.

"How do you know who I am?" she asked.

"I saw your name in the paper, so I looked you up. Tried to find your address and found that you have no address."

"What is this? Am I owed some money?"

"With what's going on, maybe you could get a book con-tract."

She gave him a dubious look. "Me? What, am I famous? Am I missing my fifteen minutes?"

"Don't you read the papers or watch the news on television?"

"Hah! I haven't read a newspaper in months, and if you see a television set trailing behind me, let me know. Not that I could afford the electric bill."

"You really should read the newspapers," the man said. "About the rapist who served time for a crime he didn't commit."

"What have I got to do with that?"

"You really don't remember?"

"I'm lucky if I remember if I got socks on." They walked on a few steps, more slowly. "Really, how'd you know where to find me?"

"It wasn't hard."

"In *New York*?"

"I'm a cop." the man said. He flashed a badge inside a thin leather folder. "We can find anyone."

"That didn't look like a police badge."

"It is, though."

"I don't understand this," Verna said uneasily. She trusted nothing and no one, and especially she didn't trust this man.

She'd seen his name when he flashed his shield, but hazily. She couldn't recall it. If she remembered it later, maybe she'd check him out tomorrow, phone a precinct house and make sure he was actually a cop.

If he was the real thing, that still didn't mean Verna would talk to him. Right now, cops represented authority, and authority was what had hammered Verna into her present circumstances.

The man grinned over at her. "Whew! If we don't slow down I won't have any breath left to ask my questions."

"Questions about what?"

They were at the passageway between the cathedral and the adjacent building. "Come in here where it's quiet and we're alone together and I'll tell you," he said.

"I don't think so."

He smiled. Shrugged.

That was when a police car came around the corner.

Miracles do happen.

Not that Verna was in any deep trouble; she could handle this guy.

But she couldn't be sure.

She realized he was no longer gripping her arm.

When she turned to talk to him, he was gone.

Must have run down the dark passageway alongside the church. She stared into the dimness, but knew that with her eyes she couldn't see him even if he was back there.

Well, she wasn't going to follow him.

Verna held her head high and strolled past the oncoming police car. The cop who was driving glanced at her and the car slowed slightly. But it didn't stop. That was fine with Verna. Maybe the guy who'd had her arm really was a plainclothes cop and the car was on its way to pick him up in the next block. That was how cops usually worked, in pairs.

Verna didn't want to hang around and figure out any of this. All she'd been looking for was a place to sit down and eat the partial hamburger she'd found. This city was tough. It wouldn't give her even that much.

Then she remembered the five dollars and figured she wasn't so unlucky after all.

56

It required eyes that never quite closed.

Vitali and Mishkin had maintained a loose tail on Jock Sanderson for several days. Sanderson led a dull life. He left his apartment and went in to work about ten o'clock, wearing what looked like gray coveralls. Sometimes he wore regular casual clothes and carried the coveralls in a gym bag. Switching off the task of driving, one of the detectives followed Sanderson as he walked to his subway stop. The other simply drove there and waited, then left the parked car and picked up the tail. The car, and the first detective, would be waiting near the offices of Sweep 'Em Up when Sanderson arrived. Then they would tail the white van that transported Sanderson, along with other members of a cleanup crew, to whatever job they had for the night.

After that came boredom and a long night, with sleeping in shifts. Vitali and Mishkin had done this kind of work plenty of times and were used to it—inasmuch as anyone ever really got used to it. Both had learned the cops' technique of almost sleeping, yet with part of the mind remaining alert and watchful. The watchfulness was accomplished through eyes that never quite closed.

By morning Vitali usually managed not to have been completely exasperated by Mishkin, and not to have injured

Mishkin's delicate feelings. Or Mishkin himself. As for Mishkin, he would seem unaffected except for being tired.

Then would come the daily routine in reverse, as Sanderson left work for home. Sometimes he'd leave directly from the job, and other times he'd return to Sweep 'Em Up in the white van and then go home from there. A normal, everyday, monotonous life. It was nothing like following a showgirl.

"This isn't like following a showgirl," Mishkin said, while watching the unmoving white van in his peripheral vision.

Beside him, Vitali said, "We've never followed a showgirl, Harold."

"I'm imagining," Mishkin said. "You must do that sometimes, Sal."

"You'd be surprised, Harold, some of the things I imagine."

Now and then Sanderson would eat out. Often he'd get takeout from a nearby deli. Sometimes he'd stop in at a small grocery store and stock up on simple food he could prepare in a microwave. He ate a lot of frozen pasta.

Vitali and Mishkin were patient. Varying their routine somewhat, they took advantage of slow-moving traffic that made it easy to follow Sanderson in the air-conditioned, unmarked car, even if he was on foot on his way to his subway stop. That way neither of them had to get out in the hot evening and walk. The traffic was so locked up that sometimes Sanderson, walking, would actually pull ahead of them for a while. They would catch up with him at intersections where he was waiting to cross. This kind of work required patience, as well as ways to counteract the boredom.

Vitali was driving the unmarked blue Ford tonight. He felt tired and irritable and by now doubted that Sanderson was anything but a poor ex-con who'd had his life turned upside down by a mistaken identity. He was on a treadmill of despair, and Vitali and Mishkin were on it right behind him.

Lounging next to Vitali, in the Ford's passenger seat,

Mishkin said, "I been thinking, Sal." He continued watching the unsuspecting Sanderson through the windshield as he spoke. "Wouldn't it be nice if this tail surprised us and panned out? Like maybe if Sanderson met a mysterious beautiful woman and they went someplace and talked like they had a big secret, maybe exchanged a brown package wrapped with string."

"A MacGuffin," Vitali said.

"Huh?"

"That's what Hitchcock used to call packages like that, MacGuffins."

"Who was MacGuffin?"

"Never mind, Harold."

"What I'm talking about is a romantic assignation."

"That isn't going to happen, Harold."

"It does in books."

"We're not in a book, Harold. Try to remember that."

"How do you know we're not, Sal?"

"Not what?"

"In a book."

Vitali said nothing. Had his wrist draped over the top of the steering wheel. His gaze was fixed straight ahead on Sanderson. He knew that as long as the tail lasted, he'd simply have to endure Mishkin's conversational meandering.

"You know that famous athlete that got in trouble because he was addicted to sex?" Mishkin asked.

"Do I know him?

"Of him?"

"Yeah."

Vitali came more alert. Sanderson had stopped walking and was looking into the show window of an electronics shop. Only a few seconds passed before he walked on. Boredom again descended on the car.

"That athlete that checked himself into a sexual-addiction

clinic, Sal. Ever think about sexual-addiction clinics? I mean, really consider them?"

"For myself, Harold?"

"Don't try to be funny, Sal."

Vitali said nothing.

"I been wondering what kind of places those are. I mean, even on the outside."

"Like hospitals, I guess."

"What sort of architecture?"

"Lots of towers, I imagine," Vitali said. He didn't move his head. His right wrist was still draped over the wheel.

"Yeah. I was thinking about the entrances. And the exits. Don't forget the exits."

Vitali gave Mishkin a look.

"Maybe dormers, Sal. Sets of big dormers on the roof."

"Definitely big dormers," Vitali said.

"Those people who get checked in there, Sal, how do you think they keep them apart?"

"I wouldn't know, Harold. The doctors and staff, I guess."

"These are addicts, Sal. What do you think they have for rooms? Do the doors have automatic locks? Are there little individual compounds topped with razor wire? Those people are like rabbits, Sal."

Sanderson had reached his subway stop. He barely broke stride as he descended the concrete steps and disappeared underground.

Like a rabbit going down its hole, Vitali couldn't help thinking.

Mishkin had the door open and was getting out. It was his turn to tail Sanderson on foot.

"I'll pick you up outside Sweep 'Em Up," Vitali told him.

"Try parking where you did before, Sal." And Mishkin was out of the car and jogging toward the subway steps.

Vitali sat and watched Mishkin disappear underground.

Like another rabbit.

Or maybe more like one of those terriers bred to follow their prey into burrows.

"We're sure Sanderson's clean," Vitali told Quinn, after five days on the tail.

Quinn nodded behind his desk. He'd already decided to end the tail. There were only so many suspects you could cover in the case. That was the problem, exactly as the Skinner had planned it. "Get some sleep and I'll put you and Harold on something else."

"Better use of manpower," Vitali said.

"Weaver isn't gonna like it that she was beat to a pulp for nothing."

"How's she doing?" Vitali asked.

"Out of the hospital. Her thoughts are a little scrambled, and she still has headaches. Renz has seen she gets medical leave, and she's going to stay with her sister for a while."

"So she's out of the game on this one."

"Like Sanderson," Quinn said.

57

Beth's recommendation had worked. Link Evans was hired at Arch Manufacturing. He worked for a while on the line, but it didn't take long for his bosses to see he had more to offer. As soon as seniority allowed an opening, he was promoted to forklift driver. Beth liked that. Link wasn't so tired when he got home, and he could spend more time with Eddie.

There was no doubt in her mind that Link loved Eddie. They'd play catch sometimes in the evenings until Eddie got tired of throwing the ball. Link was convinced Eddie had baseball talent. Maybe he was right. Beth was no judge.

As Eddie got older, he hadn't filled out physically in the way Link expected. He remained a spindly kid. Though he could still play ball well, his real talent seemed to be in scholastics. Eddie had been a whiz in Edmundsville primary school, with grades at the top of his class. Not only that, he was an amiable kid well liked by teachers and his fellow students.

High school was only slightly more difficult for Eddie.

That was all fine with Link. He bragged on Eddie's grades. It was obvious that Eddie was going to be more of an intellect than an athlete. Not that he and Eddie didn't still play catch.

In fact, they played catch even more often than when Eddie was younger.

There was something about these relentless games of catch, Beth thought. It was simply tossing a sphere back and forth, yet it forged a bond between father and son that a woman might not understand. Beth didn't, quite. It might have something to do with giving and receiving, and then giving back. Beth wondered, had men played catch with their sons through the ages? Had primitive men and their sons tossed stones back and forth?

She bet they did.

Men were still a puzzle to Beth.

"Don't you guys ever get tired?" she asked one night, from the wooden Adirondack chair they'd bought and Link and Eddie had painted.

Plop! Went the baseball into Eddie's glove. Eddie grinned and fired it back. *Plop!*

"Tired of what?" Link asked. He'd put on a few pounds while working and eating regularly, but he was still a lean man, and athletic.

"You know. Playing catch."

"No, it's natural." Talking to her had made Link glance over and drop the next pitch from Eddie. He bent low to pick up the ball and tossed it back sidearm and hard.

Plop!

"Natural, Mom!" Eddie said, with a touch of braggadocio.

Beth sat back with her eyes closed, sipped lemonade, and listened to the rhythm of summer and growing up. Hers was, she decided, a good life to be living.

Except for . . . small things now and then.

Plop!

Well, maybe the same small thing. It was something she

hadn't yet let crystallize into an actual suspicion. Her mind still danced around it, and only at odd times when the notion caught her off guard. Sometimes it was because of a certain light, or a certain angle, or a manner of speaking.

Acquired, Beth thought. *It all could be acquired.*

But not the angle of nose, the eyebrows, and the dark eyes.

Imagination?

Beth didn't know what to think, what she'd do if she opened the gates and let the suspicion take root. Let it become serious.

The lazy rhythm of the ball zipping from one glove to the other momentarily ceased—a break in the order of the universe—and then continued. Somebody had dropped one.

It had been years, another world, and she'd caught only a fleeting glimpse of her attacker. But people's looks could change over time, especially when they gained or lost a lot of weight. Link *was* about the right age. And the rape had occurred at night. She'd seen her rapist only by moonlight.

But it was true—at least she sometimes told (admitted to?) herself—that with more weight, and with a full and darker beard, Link might fit Vincent Salas's description.

Beth tried, as she too often did these days, to recall the glimpses she'd had of her attacker so long ago, reimagining over and over the bulk of his body, the quick movement of an arm and hand to snare her wrist and pin it to the ground, the line of his bearded cheek as he raised his head to glance around, the quick white glint of an eye in moonlight.

Crazy!

Beth bent her thoughts in other directions. She should be immensely pleased that Link and Eddie got along so well. Link was a wonderful, loving, and attentive father. And husband.

He'd gotten Eddie interested in something beyond baseball and fishing—coin collecting. Link had become something of a serious coin collector, well beyond the stage of wheat pennies and coins with silver content. He'd even begun attending conventions, and after each such gathering of serious collectors, he would return with coins he'd bought (as an investment), and some old coin or other for Eddie. Eddie had a growing collection of his own.

Coins. Eddie and Link would sit for hours arranging and talking about their collections, what Link seemed to see as the romance of rare coins. Beth saw rare coins merely as something else to foster even stronger bonding between Eddie and Link. A bonding and a closeness that threatened to block out Beth.

Is that what I'm worried about? That I'll be odd woman out?

She actually laughed out loud, half amused and half ashamed of herself.

"Something funny?" Link yelled from where he stood in front of the wire fence in case the ball got past him.

"Me," Beth said. She smiled. "Nothing you two guys'd be interested in."

She closed her eyes, sipped more lemonade, and listened to the ball slapping into the oiled leather gloves, back and forth, two-way catch.

Exclusively.

58

New York, the present

Verna Pound had spent all her money in a deli. She'd had only enough for junk food displayed in the racks, and she tried to stretch it as far as possible. The dark-skinned woman behind the counter—maybe Indian or Middle Eastern—didn't even bother with the extra three cents Verna owed her for the day-old cupcakes and apple turnover. She wanted Verna out of the deli as soon as possible. Not after making a big scene. Just out. Verna's presence was bad for business.

On the way out, Verna used her body to conceal that she was stealing a plastic bottle of water. The dark-skinned woman might have said something behind her, but Verna didn't stop to find out. There was a certain cost to doing business in some Manhattan neighborhoods. Besides, water shouldn't be something a person had to steal.

Back out on the sidewalk, lugging the white plastic bag of what for her would be one of her better meals all week, she made her way toward Ben's for Men's. It was a low-to-medium-priced men's clothing store with an entrance that was a dog-legged tunnel of display windows full of suits, coats, and various other men's apparel. The shop was closed until tomorrow, so the windows were dark, but the deep and concealing shadowed tunnel was accessible. The recessed entranceway was one of the few places in the neighborhood where Verna could feel almost completely safe and relax.

Even though it was dusk and still fairly early, Verna was exhausted. But then, that was her usual state. She waited until no one seemed to be looking, then shuffled into the show-window tunnel, going in as far as she could but at the same time being careful not to touch the shop's glass door. There would almost certainly be an alarm system.

Verna lowered her aching body and sat with her back against the brick surface beneath the display windows. She let out a long sigh, wondering if other people ever got this tired. The way she lived must be whittling away at her life, making her old though she was still in her thirties.

Someday . . .

No, Verna cautioned herself. Someday was today, and tomorrow didn't look any brighter. Hope could be cruel. In her circumstances, it was better not to let hope through the door. If hope wanted to hang around outside and taunt her, let it. She knew that you couldn't trust hope.

Hungry as well as tired, she wolfed down one of the chocolate cupcakes and gulped some water.

One of the shadows toward the front of the entranceway moved, startling her. It might have been simply someone walking past, back-lit by the faint glow from the street.

But she knew that wasn't true. She was beyond the crook in the zigzag glass panels.

The shadow moved again, and a man appeared.

From where Verna was sprawled propped against the bricks beneath the glass and a display of blazers, he appeared tall. He was wearing dark clothing, probably black. A light jacket, even though the evening was warm. He was carrying a gym bag.

He obviously expected to find her there. Must have followed her and watched her enter beneath the Ben's sign. Then he'd waited for the right moment to come to her. It was almost completely dark now, time for the monsters to come out and play.

Verna didn't move but kept her eyes trained on the man. She didn't think she knew him. He wasn't one of the neighborhood street people.

Or *did* she know him? He did look vaguely familiar.

He stooped beside her and placed the gym bag nearby. He smiled at her, then unzipped the bag and reached inside. She saw no fingernails and realized he was wearing flesh-colored rubber gloves.

When his hand came out of the bag, it was holding a knife with a kind of blade she'd never seen before. It was short and curved, and looked sharp and wicked.

Verna knew that if she tried to scream she'd be dead or unconscious within seconds. She was too tired to scream, anyway. Too tired to resist.

"You know who I am?" the man asked, placing her plastic water bottle aside carefully so it was a safe distance away and wouldn't spill.

"I read the papers," Verna said, "even if they're a few days old. I know who you are."

He reached into the bag again. "I'm going to put some tape over your mouth," he said. "It's a precaution. Try not to be afraid."

"You don't have to do that. I'm not going to scream."

Very quickly, using both hands yet somehow not nicking her with the knife, he applied the tape. When she raised a hand to peel it off, he grabbed her wrist, then taped both wrists together. He ran a long strand of tape around her waist and arms so she couldn't raise her hands high enough to touch her lips. Her right leg moved reflexively to kick him, but he merely intercepted the feeble effort and pressed her knee to the tiles.

"You're going to scream," he told her. "But this way it won't be out loud." He mashed her knee hard against the concrete, sapping the strength out of her leg. Then he grinned. "By the way, it's okay to be afraid now."

Verna bowed her head and closed her eyes. This man didn't know she was beyond certain kinds of fear. Over the past few years she'd learned to endure. That was her strength, to let whatever was going to happen simply roll over her and happen. Afterward she would assess the damage. Whatever was left of her soul and body, she would drag from the scene after the madness had passed.

And if there was to be no afterward . . . that would be a mercy.

The sharp smell of ammonia jolted her so her eyes flew open. She gagged and choked, her body heaving as the rectangle of duct tape blocked her screams. Her coughing seared her throat and made sounds like a dog trying and failing to bark. The man's powerful hands held her still until the coughing stopped. She could handle this, she told herself. If only she kept calm, she could endure it and then it would be over. She concentrated and forced herself to breathe evenly through her nose. The sharp ammonia scent was still in the air, nauseating her.

The man gazed down at her as if he pitied her. He was so calm and looked so kind. He might have been an angel here to rescue her from everything her world had become. He *was* that, she told herself.

You might not know it, but you are my salvation.

Then she remembered. It had been a long time ago, in her muddled mind, but she remembered. This was the man who'd wanted to talk to her. By the church.

I know you! The cop! You're the one who gave me the five dollars. You helped me!

Kindness meant a chance. If nothing else, a less painful passage into death.

She tried to beg with her eyes, feeling like a bad silent-film actress but not caring. Hope was stronger than she'd thought. Stronger than she was.

He wasn't a cop—that was for sure. Still, he'd given her the five dollars. . . .

"It isn't going to be easy for you," he said.

Very methodically, he sliced away her clothes and then taped her legs tightly together.

You're a friend! You helped me! Help me! Help me!

His betrayal was of a magnitude that crushed her.

Verna understood that she was not beyond pain.

She did somehow manage to hold panic at bay. The kind of mindlessness that would turn her into something less than human. She kept repeating to herself that this would pass. She tried to beg for mercy through the tape but couldn't make more than a low humming sound, over and over.

"That's my favorite tune," the man said, as he used the knife on her.

At first he bent to his task casually, but his concentration grew and the blade bit deeper and deeper and established a repetitive rhythm.

She noticed through the pain and horror that gripped and gripped and gripped her that he'd somehow found the time to light a cigarette.

59

Quinn had phoned Pearl and given him the address. She was driving the unmarked and arrived at the crime scene ahead of him.

The first thing she saw as she pulled the car to the curb was that the sidewalk on the right side of the street was cordoned off with yellow crime scene tape. There was a big uniformed cop standing beneath the BEN'S FOR MEN'S sign, his arms crossed, his head cocked to the side, appearing as if he were contemplating trading in his uniform for the sharp-looking suit displayed beside him in the window.

Pearl parked the car behind an NYPD cruiser, got out into the sun-drenched heat, and ducked beneath the tape.

When the uniform forgot about the suit and came toward her, she flashed her ID. He stepped back into the meager shade and motioned with his arm.

Pearl entered the dogleg tunnel of clothing display windows and heard echoing voices. The maze of glass seemed remote from the rest of the city and smelled musty. There was another smell Pearl recognized and could almost taste. Death assaulted all the senses.

The tech team was at work in its busy and concentrated fashion. Dr. Julius Nift, the obnoxious little ME, was crouched

beside a woman's body like a lascivious troll. His black
leather medical case was open beside him.

Nift looked up at Pearl's approach and nodded. "Our
killer's going downscale."

Pearl looked at what was left of a thin, raggedly dressed
woman. Obviously a street person. A rectangle of gray duct
tape dangled from one corner of her gaping, blood-clogged
mouth.

"The job's fun sometimes, isn't it?" Nift said. He removed something silver and sharp from his medical case
and began poking and probing.

"You touch the tape?" Pearl asked.

"Of course not. I left it for the real inspectors so they
could make brilliant deductions." He used a tweezers-like
instrument to lift a shred of severed flesh from the victim's
abdomen and peered beneath it. "Yuk," he said in a flat
voice.

"Is this finally a female corpse that holds no sexual appeal for you?" Pearl asked Nift. In the corner of her vision
she saw a tech's head turn toward her in surprise.

Nift merely smiled, smug in his insensitivity. "Oh, I
dunno. Maybe when I clean her up."

"You're an asshole," Pearl said.

Nift shrugged. "You asked."

Quinn had arrived and caught the last of the conversation.
His bulk seemed to fill the confined space. "I don't want to
know the question," he said, with a warning look at Pearl.
The big uniformed cop had come into the display tunnel a
few steps behind Quinn and stood stone-faced. He looked as
if his nose had been broken almost as many times as Quinn's.

"She died last night around nine to midnight," Nift said,
happy to change the subject now that Quinn was here. "I'll
give you a closer estimate sometime today."

Quinn stooped near the body for a closer look.

"Ugly," he said.

"I was just remarking on that," Nift said.

"Tortured like the others. Same kind of knife cuts and cigarette burns."

"Same kind of wounds, same kind of knife," Nift said. "Short, sharply curved blade, very well honed."

"But not surgical?"

"Not like any surgical instrument I've seen. For detail work, though, I would say." He grinned. "Like for carving on models. Big models."

"The tape on her mouth was like that when the body was found by the sales clerk who came in to open the store," the uniform said. "I made sure nobody touched it till the CSU and ME got here."

Pearl looked beyond him and saw another uniformed cop standing near the bend in the display windows. A redheaded guy in a cheap suit, whom Pearl recognized as a police photographer, was making his way toward them. Murder was a magnet. The troops had arrived in full force.

"Her tongue . . ." Quinn said, staring at the gaping bloody hole that was left of a human mouth.

"It's been removed," Nift said. "I think very deftly. I'll have to clean her out to be certain of that. And unless she's lying on it, the killer left with the tongue."

"He would," Quinn said. He carefully checked the victim for identification. There was nothing. Not even a scrap of paper in the pockets of the threadbare clothing. He looked at the victim's tangled, bloody hair and figured it had been tangled even before she was killed. There was dirt beneath her jagged fingernails, but no sign that she'd resisted her attacker.

"She have a purse?"

"Not when we got here," the bent-nosed cop said.

"Just another street woman," Nift said, watching Quinn across the dead woman.

"I want her printed as soon as possible," Quinn said, standing up. Feeling it in his legs

"My God!" a man's voice said behind Quinn.

He turned to see a slender, handsome man with spiky blond hair and round-framed glasses. He was wearing a spiffy cream-colored suit that reminded Quinn the inveterate theater buff of Sporting Life in *Porgy and Bess*.

The reed-thin man was at least three inches taller than Quinn and wearing some kind of cologne giving off a scent that didn't mix well with the coppery smell of old blood.

"The officer told me I could come back here," he said. "I'm Ben. You know, of Ben's for Men's. Ben Blevin." He held out his hand and Quinn shook it, noting that the reedy Ben was surprisingly strong.

Quinn thought about going inside the store with Ben and questioning the clerk who'd discovered the body, but that would mean leaving Pearl with Nift, along with a lot of other people who wouldn't intimidate Pearl in the slightest. He glanced at his watch. Mishkin was looking after Weaver in the hospital, but Quinn knew that Fedderman and Sal Vitali would be here soon.

"Let's go inside the store," Quinn said to Ben. "I want to talk to your clerk."

As Ben led the way into the store, Quinn glanced back at Pearl with what she recognized as his *Behave Yourself* look.

Pearl would try.

60

Edmundsville, 2008

Beth sat in the 66 Roadhouse and watched Link dance with her friend Annette Brazel. Annette was a small, attractive woman who was about as susceptible to Link's flirting as a concrete post. She ran a leather-cutting machine at the plant and had a husband who acted in community theater in Edmundsville and had a reputation for meanness. Beth wasn't jealous.

She never worried about that part of her marriage. Though a measure of passion had long since left her partnership with Link, some remained. And she was secure in the knowledge that Link would never leave her if it meant giving up Eddie. Of course, Eddie was fast becoming a young man. In a few more years he'd be going off to college. Hard to believe now, though; he still looked and acted so much like a green kid.

As Beth sat and sipped her Bud Light and watched the dancers, it struck her as it often did how much Link and Eddie resembled each other. Or maybe that was in her mind.

But no, she was sure. . . . When Link spun around and the light hit his face a certain way, it was almost like looking at an older Eddie. Almost as if . . .

Jesus! Get that out of your mind!

The contemporary country music ended, and the band

began playing an old Hank Williams song. It reminded Beth of when she and Link had met here at the 66, when that same song—might have been, anyway—was playing.

Hank Williams, singing about love gone wrong.

Link and Annette stayed out on the dance floor, Link taking advantage of a slower beat. They were dancing close to each other, but not too close. Annette glanced over at Beth and winked.

As Beth sat watching them she noticed the beer can on the table where Link had been sitting. It was a Wild Colt can, the same brand that was found on Vincent Salas's motorcycle the night of the—

Oh, God, stop it!

It was a popular brand locally. Half the men in the 66 were drinking it right now. DNA had proven it was a coincidence that Salas had been drinking it—

DNA can prove, or disprove, lots of things.

Beth told herself, as she had so many times lately, that she was torturing herself because of guilt.

But that didn't mean—

"Annette's got a sore foot," Link said, settling down in his chair, behind the opened Colt can.

"That would be because you stepped on it," Annette said.

Link grinned. "That'd be because you got your feet mixed up between the second and third steps of my grapevine maneuver."

"Your *what?*" Beth asked.

"Mumbo jumbo," Annette said. "That's his escape when he knows he's wrong, talking mumbo jumbo."

"I'm hurt," Link said.

"No, I'm the one with the toe." Annette looked over at Beth. "Wanna go to lunch tomorrow? Might as well. It's gonna rain all day."

"Does most Saturdays," Link said. "The weatherman knows we don't work weekends."

"The weatherman's a son of a bitch," Annette said.

"We'll do it," Beth said. "I'll call you."

"I'm not invited?" Link asked.

"Damned right, you're not," Annette said.

"He's going to Kansas City for a coin show, anyway," Beth said.

Link's passion for coin collecting had grown. "Gonna be an auction of antebellum silver coins," he said. "Some rich guy's estate is selling his whole collection."

"I don't know what you see in that old stuff," Annette said.

Link took a sip of beer. "It's history. And art. And a pretty good investment."

"And an obsession," Beth said.

Link shrugged. "I guess it is, but a harmless one."

"I'm more interested in new coins," Annette said. "The kind you can spend."

The band was swinging into one of Beth's favorite tunes. Link gulped down some more beer then stood up. He offered his hand to Beth.

"Wanna dance to this one? Give Annette's toe a rest?"

Beth smiled. "You bet I do." Trying to get into the mood. To shake her self-destructive suspicions.

Link led her onto the dance floor and they began a two-step with underarm turns. Within seconds the floor was too crowded for turns, and Beth and Link began close dancing.

He held her loosely and confidently, his wife, his lover, his possession. More beloved than his coins in their velvet-lined display folders.

Not more beloved than his stepson.

Annette had her shoe off and was sitting sideways in her chair, rubbing her toe. Beth saw her smile enviously at her and Link. Annette and her husband Mark had no children, and as far as Beth knew didn't want any. Still, here was Beth with a husband who loved her and a child they both loved.

Beth figured that what she needed in life, what she *had*—man, child, home—addressed an emotional void that most women had attempted to fill since the human race began. She was one of the winners.

That was how it must seem from the outside.

Link held Beth tighter, drawing her closer. But it seemed to Beth that now there was a limit to how close they could be.

61

New York, the present

A brief shower had cooled down the city, and the sun, back from behind scudding low clouds, made everything glisten in reflecting dampness. Quinn and Pearl couldn't resist walking the short distance from the office to have lunch at home (as she lately found herself thinking of the brownstone). Besides, the rehab crew was closing in on finishing off the floor directly above, in what had once been the dining room. Quinn and Pearl could go upstairs and check on how things were going while a pizza heated in the oven.

They strolled down Amsterdam and saw by the faces passing them going the opposite direction that most people felt the way they did. This was one of those rare moments after rain when time seems to pause in order to give people a chance to glance around and really see fresh, wet actuality.

What they saw was a city they loved. Nineteenth-century buildings a short walk from glass and stone and poured concrete climbing toward an indecisive summer sky. Quinn appreciated the sights and smells and sounds around them. Twist-tied plastic trash bags huddled bursting at the curb, low-lying exhaust fumes from stalled traffic, a distant urgent siren, two people arguing about who had hailed a cab first, violin music—hesitant and distant. Quinn and Pearl ex-

changed a glance, each knowing what the other was thinking.

The inside of the brownstone was quiet until Pearl walked
across the living room and switched on the window-unit air
conditioner. There was no sound from upstairs. Maybe the
workers had gone to lunch early.

Pearl and Quinn decided they'd have lunch first, thinking
maybe the workers would return by the time they were finished. Pearl put a frozen pizza with sausage and mushrooms
into the oven, then got a bag of pre-cut washed vegetables
out of the refrigerator, along with a tomato, some green
onions, and vinaigrette dressing. While she put together a
salad, Quinn got out silverware, plates, and napkins and set
the table.

He sat in one of the wooden chairs and watched Pearl fid-
get around the kitchen, opening and closing the oven door as
if that would hurry the pizza, tossing the salad for a second
and third time. Sprinkling ground pepper on the salad,
adding bits of cheddar cheese she tore from slices that were
meant for sandwiches. Even a pinch of salt. Not a born cook,
Pearl.

The phone on the kitchen wall rang, breaking the silence
and domestic mood. Quinn scooted his chair a few feet to
the side and reached for the receiver.

He saw on the tiny caller-ID screen that the caller was Sal
Vitali, from the morgue. He mouthed Vitali's name silently
to Pearl, who was staring at him curiously.

"You weren't at the office," Vitali said, "and you had your
cell turned off, so I figured you might be there."

"What've you got?" Quinn asked, eyeing the oven timer
that was closing in on pizza time and a flurry of activity by
Pearl.

"They got a print match on the Ben's for Men's victim,
Quinn. She's—she was Verna Pound, thirty-six years old,
picked up for shoplifting two years ago."

"She on our list?"

"Yeah. Back in 2005 she accused a guy named Tyrone Ringo of raping her. Got a conviction. Tyrone spent his time behind the walls and was exonerated and released from prison two years ago."

"Not that long ago," Quinn said. "Might seem like yesterday to Tyrone."

"No," Vitali said. "He died nine months ago of tuberculosis he contracted in prison."

"Anything else notable about the postmortem?"

"Nothing other than that she was tortured for over an hour by somebody truly screwed up. Sick bastard with his trick knife made her death even more of a hell than her life was. You wanna read it, the whole report's been faxed to the office."

"Actual cause of death?" Quinn asked, not wanting to go back to the office just yet.

"Loss of blood from all the carving he did on her. Damn, Quinn, imagine it, with the cigarette burns and the knife, the bastard taking his time and enjoying himself."

"At least we got her prints," Quinn said. "Maybe she's got family."

"I doubt she has any family that gives a shit," Vitali said, "the way she was barely staying alive on the street. Kind of person that made one wrong move after another because she had lousy luck. Tried to steal a coat and was unlucky enough to choose one with a mink collar. Expensive enough to make it a grand larceny charge. Put on probation, disappeared. Now here she is again, in the morgue, after a layover at Ben's for Men's. Hell of a life."

"She tried to lift a coat," Quinn said.

"Yeah. In January in New York. To survive."

"Hell of a life," Quinn agreed. He hung up.

"What were you talking about?" Pearl asked.

"Death."

The oven timer started its annoying chiming, and Pearl sprang into pizza mode.

After pizza and cold Heineken beers, Quinn and Pearl trudged up the brownstone's steep wooden steps to the floor above.

The workmen were up there. They'd finished lunch and were back on the job. About half of the carpet was laid. It was light beige. Seeing so much of it down made the space seem surprisingly vast. And sound carried differently. Quinn could understand why the work hadn't been audible down in the kitchen.

"Think we got the color right?" Quinn asked.

"I'm sure we did," Pearl said, though she didn't give a shit one way or the other. She knew it made Quinn happy when she went domestic on him and displayed interest in colors and furnishings. In truth she could barely remember the carpet color in her old apartment where she'd lived for years. She knew it had some kind of spatter design on it, but she wasn't positive that wasn't accidental and hadn't accumulated over time.

"Then I'm sure," he said.

"Sounds like closure," she said.

He looked at her. She shrugged.

"Okay to step on it?" Quinn asked one of the workmen, a guy named Cliff who seemed always surly.

"That's what it's made for," Cliff said, and continued crouched on the floor and banging a padded device with his knee to stretch the carpet.

Quinn wandered over to where the job supervisor, Wallace, was down on his hands and knees working the carpet to fit around the door to the next room.

Wallace glanced up and nodded to Quinn. "It's going great," he said, before Quinn could ask. He continued cutting the carpet before working it beneath the recently painted white baseboard.

Quinn felt a sudden chill. "What kind of knife is that you're using?"

Something in Quinn's voice made Wallace stop what he was doing and straighten up to a kneeling position. He held up the knife. It had a blunt wooden handle that looked something like the knob of a bedpost, and a sharply curved blade about five inches long.

"This is a carpet-tucking knife," he said. "Looks somethin' like a linoleum knife, only it's not. It's for fine work around baseboards and thresholds, anyplace that's tricky and requires a touch."

Pearl had seen what was going on and came over, her footfalls silent on the new carpet. "That looks sharp," she said, pointing at the knife.

Wallace grinned. "Gotta be sharp. Carpet, and carpet pad, don't cut easy, 'specially where you're doin' delicate work and can't get a lotta muscle into it."

Pearl said, "Jesus, Quinn."

Wallace stared at her.

"Where would you buy a knife like that?" Quinn asked.

Wallace, still on his knees, shrugged. "Hardware store, I guess. Or commercial tool supplier. I bought this one years ago in New Jersey from some place that was goin' outta business."

"What's a knife like that cost, Wallace?"

Wallace managed another kneeling shrug. "A good one, about fifty, sixty bucks. Thereabout."

"I'll give you seventy-five for that one."

Wallace squinted one eye. What the hell was going on here? What was special about his carpet-tucking knife? "That's too much, Mr. Quinn."

Quinn smiled. "Okay. We can make it twenty-five."

Wallace gave him a sly smile.

"Fifty," Quinn said.

"I ain't one to dicker," Wallace said.

Quinn peeled the bills from his wallet and handed them to Wallace in exchange for the knife. Pearl watched Quinn's jaw muscles work as he hefted the small but lethal instrument in his huge right hand.

"I can finish the job without it," Wallace said. "Cliff's got another one in his tool box."

"Cheaper'n that one, too," Cliff said. He kicked again with his knee at his padded carpet stretcher and gave Quinn a conspiratorial wink. "You can buy mine for twenty bucks."

"Shoulda spoken up sooner," Quinn said. He nodded to Wallace and moved toward the stairs. Pearl gave Cliff a hard look and followed.

Back in the kitchen, Quinn knocked back what was left of his warm beer and called Sal Vitali on Sal's cell phone.

"Got a job for you and Harold," Quinn said, when Sal had answered. "I want you to check on commercial and retail places that handle tools, building supplies."

"What are we building?" Vitali asked in his gravelly voice.

"A case," Quinn said. "Airtight."

62

On the walk back to the office with Quinn, Pearl's cell phone emitted its *Dragnet* theme alert. Still thinking about the carpet-tucking knife, which was wrapped in a paper towel and stuck in one of Quinn's pockets, she flipped up the phone's lid and answered without first checking caller ID.

When she saw that the call's origin was Golden Sunset Assisted Living in New Jersey, it was too late. She was connected to her mother.

"Pearl, I was thinking about you, so I thought I should call."

"I'm kind of busy, Mom. You know, this murderer . . ."

"Busy, shmizzy, when I heard about an offer that would change your world—and such a dangerous world—I knew it was a mother's duty to make sure her loving daughter heard about it and might—"

"What sort of offer, Mom?"

"A job, dear."

"I've got a job, Mom. In fact, right now I'm trying to do it."

Quinn coughed. He would.

"Are you with the mensch Captain Quinn?"

"Matter of fact, yes. But he's no longer a—"

"Longer shmonger. You could do much worse, Pearl. In fact you have."

Pearl thought if her mother mentioned Yancy by name she'd hang up on her. Or break the connection. Whatever you did with cell phones.

"But that's neither here nor anywhere, Pearl. The thing is, this is an interesting and well-paying position you are being offered that allows you to be out and about like you say you like to be as a policewoman."

"Detective, Mom."

"Deschmective."

"Is that your mother?" Quinn asked, glancing over at Pearl.

Pearl nodded.

"Tell her I said hello."

Hello, schmello, Pearl thought.

"I overheard," Pearl's mother's voice said on the phone. "Tell the big mensch to marry my daughter. Stop this shacking up together that in God's eyes, and the world's, will shame you both as long as it continues. What are you two afraid of? Making a commitment to each other like your father and I made and the result—God bless—was you, Pearl?"

Quinn was grinning at Pearl. She wondered how he'd look with the phone in his mouth.

"Women your age, Pearl," her mother said, "women still bursting with vitality, are not too old to bear children. But there is a natural order of things, Pearl, and shacking up is not an accepted part of it. However, grandchildren are."

"For God's sake, Mom! You know I still have my own apartment."

"Where you are not often, considering how seldom the phone is answered. Maybe, God willing, Captain Quinn will gladly be part of a marriage with two wage earners in two separate jobs, both or neither of which would become nonexistent in a worsening economy. Add to this, of course, a small dependent."

"I keep telling you, he's no longer 'Captain Quinn,' Mom. You make him sound like a breakfast cereal."

"He's not a cereal, dear. He's a property owner. Which, the moment of marriage to you, you yourself would become. Now this job that might be yours for the asking was told about to me by Mrs. Katzman, here at the nursing home—"

"Assisted living."

"—but in the strictest confidence. The inside track would be yours because you would be working for Mrs. Katzman's lovely son Aaron, who is a big producer."

"Big how? Obese?"

"Pearl!"

"Sorry. What does he produce?"

"Plays, is what."

"Broadway plays?"

"Close to Broadway. And he is in no way fat, but very trim and manly, except for the ponytail, and close to your age. He said to his mother, Ida Katzman, when I was show-ing them both your photograph—that one where you're just climbing out of the swimming pool in a T-shirt and look just like Sophia Loren in—"

"I was eighteen when that was taken, Mom."

"Nevertheless, what Aaron Katzman said when he saw that photo—and he said it as if he meant it—"

"I don't care, Mom."

"—was that he could guarantee you a job as assistant stage manager. At first it would just be—"

Pearl knew what it would be later on. She decided to take the quickest route back to reality.

"I'll think about it, Mom. Honestly. You can tell Mrs. Katzman I'll consider it, and thank her for me for telling you about it. And thank Alan."

"Aaron. Of Aaron Katzman Productions."

"Okay. Aaron."

"I sense, Pearl, an eagerness in you to end our conversation."

"Mom, I don't—"

"I understand, Pearl. You have a life to live while mine dwindles away here at this stopover on the way to hell."

"You don't believe in hell, Mom."

"I didn't, Pearl, until I found myself in its anteroom."

"Mom, I've really gotta—"

"I understand, I said. And I still do. Say good-bye for me to Captain Quinn."

"He's not—"

But Pearl's mother had terminated the conversation. This didn't happen often. Usually Pearl had to force the issue and hang up first.

Pearl was pissed off, and at the same time felt bruised. She had hurt her mother and felt guilty as hell, and she knew she would call back, probably tomorrow. Or the next day.

"How is your mother?" Quinn asked, seeing Pearl flip her phone lid closed and work the instrument back into her pocket.

"Hurt and in hell," Pearl said. "So am I."

Quinn nodded. "Aren't we all?"

"It doesn't bear thinking about," Pearl said, thinking about it.

Fedderman had sat in or just outside of Weaver's room for the past six hours. Weaver remained drugged up and didn't make sense when she attempted to talk. Fedderman felt sorry for her, but he was getting tired of sitting or standing guard. It happened a lot in books and movies, but in real life not many people were assaulted in hospital rooms except by doctors who graduated last in their class in medical school.

At the end of the hall, the uniformed cop the precinct had

sent over to spell Fedderman stepped out of the elevator and trudged toward where Fedderman sat outside the door to Weaver's room.

Fedderman had known him right away: Jesse Jones, a capable and light-hearted black man with a pencil mustache. Jones was slight of build, but Fedderman knew he was whipcord strong. He'd worked with Jones for a while in Burglary and had been impressed by the man.

Fedderman watched him approach. Within fifty feet of Fedderman's chair, Jones switched his gleaming white smile on like a spotlight.

"You can turn it over to me now, sir, and I'll fill the breach here," Jones said.

Fedderman liked the "sir." Jones wasn't one of the new wiseass guys. He was a little older and had been around and respected his elders. And being retired from the NYPD made Fedderman his elder, even though there wasn't *that* much difference in the men's ages. At least, that was how Fedderman saw it.

He got up slowly from the chair and stretched until he heard his back pop and become less stiff. "I'm ready to be relieved," he said, looking beyond Jones at the long corridor lined with identical doors. The killer would have to know his way around hospitals in order to find and take out Weaver. Fedderman thought there was no place more confusing than a hospital.

Stretching his back, Fedderman realized how tired he was. He shot a glance at his watch to make sure he hadn't been imagining that it was time for him to be relieved.

Yep. Jones was five minutes early. "Let's take a last look at her before I log out," he said.

Fedderman opened the door to Weaver's room and let Jones enter first.

The only sound in the quiet room was the soft in-and-out breathing of Weaver, who lay on her back in bed with her eyes closed. She was hooked up to an IV and to several monitoring machines. Normally tan and vital, she looked like a pale representation of herself, with the taut white sheets pulled up to her neck.

"She any better?" Jones asked.

"You see what I've been seeing most of the day," Fedderman said.

"Bastard musta beat the crap outta her," Jones said in a whisper, as if there was some danger of waking Weaver. "Broke her spirit as well as her bones."

"Not her," Fedderman said. "She'll have plenty left."

Jones smiled. "So she's a game one."

"Yeah. She'll shake this. What we don't want is whoever attacked her coming in here and adding to the damage."

"He won't this day," Jones said. "I can guarantee it."

Both men left the room. Out in the hall, Jones sat down in the chair Fedderman had spent hours in today. He settled in like an airline passenger prepared for a long flight. Glancing down, he dangled a long arm and picked up a magazine from a small stack on the floor, a well-worn *People*.

"You want something else to read before I leave?" Fedderman asked.

Jones shook his head and held up the *People*. "Don't need anything else. This has got it all. Go on home and forget this place for a while, sir."

Fedderman nodded and left to walk to the elevator. Most of the people in *People,* he didn't recognize. Besides that, they all looked like kids.

Outside the hospital, he breathed in air that didn't smell faintly of menthol; then he walked to a small jewelry store that had been in the next block for years. There he stood in front of the display window and studied the array of rings. The engagement rings were set off by themselves in a maroon velvet display case that made the gold or silver in them look like it had just been polished.

They were all expensive, except for two at the bottom of the display.

Fedderman had an hour before he was to meet Penny. He'd never been a man of impulse, but here he was in an Armani suit, mooning at engagement rings. Penny had changed him.

He again went over the calculations he'd made in his chair in the hospital corridor. Retired cops, if they'd been honest cops, weren't among the rich. But he'd been thrifty and had a fair amount in his IRA account that he hadn't touched.

He thought for a moment, settled on one of the rings at the bottom of the display, then went into the jewelry shop feeling the way he'd felt as a kid diving into the untested waters of a lake.

Excited. But you could also drown.

63

Edmundsville, 2010

Since Eddie had gone away to school in Iowa, Link went to coin shows and conferences more often. He'd changed jobs and worked for Krupke Currency Exchange, a large coins and precious metals dealer. Much of the work was done on the Internet, but there was also a lot of travel involved. Link and Eddie were still in close touch via e-mail, and still discussed coins. Eddie would request certain coins for his collection, and Link would often find and purchase them. When he returned home, he'd put them in the drawer along with Eddie's collection portfolio.

Beth watched Link through the window as he stepped down off the porch and walked to where the Kia was parked in front. He would take the car, or sometimes the pickup truck, and leave it at the airport in Kansas City while he was away—this time at a coin show and auction in Cedar Rapids, Iowa. He hoisted his big carry-on into the passenger side of the car and walked around and climbed in behind the steering wheel. He'd packed his sport coat and was wearing a white shirt and paisley tie. Beth noticed that he'd put on a little weight the past few years, and he wasn't so nimble working himself in behind the steering wheel.

The sun-baked red car gave a rumbling roar, telling anyone within earshot it needed exhaust work. Link backed around so he was headed down the long dirt and gravel drive, then shifted to drive and was on his way. Beth stood at the window and watched until all the dust behind the car had settled.

Though they weren't wet, she wiped her hands on the dish towel she was holding. After a slight detour to toss the wadded towel onto the sink counter, she went to the phone and called Sheriff Wayne Westerley.

Within two hours Westerley was parking his SUV, with its red and blue lights on the roof and the big sheriff's badge painted on the doors, exactly where the Kia had been parked. He stepped down from the vehicle and hitched up his belt with the holster and law-enforcement paraphernalia hanging from it. Beth thought he'd put on weight just as Link had, only Westerley still had a flat stomach. His face and shoulders appeared somewhat broader in his tan sheriff's uniform. He moved easily and with his familiar muscular grace as he came up the wooden steps to the porch.

Beth opened the front door and they looked at each other. Beth felt something tugging at her. She hadn't expected that. Or had she?

Westerley was sweating, as if the SUV's air conditioner didn't work. He smiled. "Been too long,"

"It has," Beth said. She wished she'd thought to make some lemonade, something. She returned his smile. "Get you something to drink? Glass of ice water to cool you down?"

"Be fine." He removed his Smokey hat. His dark curly hair looked the same. Not even a fleck of gray.

As she was going into the kitchen she saw him placing the hat on the coffee table as he sat down on the sofa. She could feel herself slipping back in time. It was a pleasant but unsettling sensation.

She came back with a glass of water poured over cubes from the refrigerator ice maker. Nothing for herself. She handed Westerley his tall, clear tumbler and then sat down in the wing chair that was angled toward the sofa.

He sipped his water and grinned. "Just what I needed." He glanced around. "Where's Link?"

"Off to Cedar Rapids to a coin show."

"He's still heavily into that, huh?"

"Heavily. Working for a coin and precious metal company now. Mostly on the computer here at home, but he does some traveling, too."

"And Eddie?"

"Away at school." *Nobody here but the two of us.*

Westerley took another swallow of water. She watched his Adam's apple work in the strong column of his throat.

He observed her with a half smile, as if this was an ordinary visit between old friends. He knew it wasn't, but he couldn't figure out where it was going. He put his glass down on a *Coin Universe* magazine. "You said you had a problem, Beth."

"Did I say that?"

"Gave that impression." He had a hard time keeping his gaze away from her cleavage showing above the scoop-neck white blouse she was wearing with her jeans. The jeans were faded and tight, molded to her body. Dressed for seduction? He realized his breathing was ragged. Took another sip of water. He felt like pressing the cold glass to his forehead but didn't.

Beth squirmed in her chair. Whatever they were going to discuss made her uncomfortable. "I do have a problem, Sheriff."

"Wayne. Name's Wayne, Beth. Remember?"

She began absently wringing her hands in her lap. Her hands looked older, he noticed, though it hadn't been *that* long since he and Beth had last seen each other. Edmundsville and Hogart weren't all that far from each other, and in the same county.

"I do have a problem, Wayne."

Sure. You have a son in college. That was his first guess. "With Eddie?"

"No."

"Not with that bastard Salas?"

"No. Or maybe yes. More with Link."

Westerley leaned back in the sofa and crossed a polished black boot over his knee. "Just relax and tell me what it is, Beth."

She leaned forward slightly, as if to compensate for his settling back into the sofa. "You ever notice how much Eddie looks like Link?"

Westerley drew a deep breath and stared at her. He *had* noticed the resemblance, though he'd never made mention of it. "There's some physical resemblance," he said, "and people pick up the mannerisms of who they're always around. Who raises them."

"It's more than that, Wayne. Like you said, it's physical."

"You do know what you're implying, Beth."

"I do. And I wouldn't imply it to anybody but you."

"But why—?"

"I don't know why, Wayne. Link would be the one to tell you that, if what I suspect is true."

"Jesus, Beth! What do you want me to do?"

She shook her head as if in sudden pain. "I'm not sure. I thought maybe you could tell me."

"You did the right thing. I'm glad you called."

"So am I."

"I think you've given this some thought, Beth. We both know a possible way to make sure. DNA. A paternity check."

"I can't just up and ask Link if we can do that."

"You wouldn't have to ask him. I know people at the state lab where the tests are performed. It might take a while, though. They're always running behind." He ran a finger around the rim of his glass, as if expecting it to sing like fine crystal. "You sure you want to do this, Beth?"

"What do you need?" Beth asked.

"DNA samples of Link. And of Eddie."

"We can find something, I'm sure. Some of their hair, with the follicle still attached."

Westerley sipped his ice water. *She's been reading and learning about this.*

Beth continued: "Link's cigarette butts are still in the ashtray by the porch glider, and maybe someplace else in the house. Eddie keeps his own toothbrush here for when he visits. And we might even get nail clippings from both of them."

Westerley nodded, thinking it all over. She might have already collected those samples. "Has Link been a good father to Eddie?"

"The best," Beth said. "God help me, that's what makes me suspicious—the way he treats Eddie, just like he's his natural son. As if Link knew he existed and couldn't keep away from him, so he married me to raise his own child."

"Your rapist would want to be a true father to your son?"

"His son, too."

Westerley pursed his lips and gave an almost silent whistle. "I can't think of that ever happening, Beth."

"But it *could* happen, Wayne!" Beth bowed her head. He saw tears glisten an instant before her dangling hair concealed her eyes. "Or maybe I'm sick and guilt ridden so I'm suspicious when I shouldn't be."

"You aren't sick, Beth. Guilty, either. And you're right about it being possible." He lifted his glass again and took a long sip of the cold water. Condensation dripped from the glass onto his thigh, spotting his uniform pants. "I'm going to see if there's enough left of the blood sample from the rape scene to make another DNA match. That'd be hard evidence."

"Whatever you say, Wayne."

"No, Beth, it's whatever you want."

She took several breaths and extended a hand with tentatively groping fingers, as if trying to find her balance. "I want to know everything, Wayne."

She lifted her gaze. No sign of tears now. "Even if it means Link is Eddie's biological father, and the man I've been loving and living with is the one who raped me."

"There'd be serious fallout," Westerley said. "You ready for that?"

"Of course not. But I need to know. I need the truth."

"It doesn't always set you free," Westerley said.

"But it doesn't slowly kill you, like a lie."

When Westerley got back to his office, he found Billy Noth watching a guy from the state who looked about fourteen installing a new computer system. Westerley had been satisfied with the last one, but he'd been told it was five years old and hopelessly out of date.

"This is Jimmy," Billy said.

The young guy grinned at Westerley. "You're gonna love this, Sheriff. Put you right inside the heads of the bad guys."

"Just where I want to be," Westerley said.

"This baby's gonna have some RAM," Jimmy said. "New software's gonna be ideal for data mining."

Westerley wondered if Jimmy shaved yet.

"Soon as I'm done here," Jimmy said, "I'll give you a short orientation course. Then, you need any questions answered, all you gotta do is click on *Help*."

And get further confused, Westerley thought.

That was pretty much the way it turned out. The new software was a lot like the old, only with additional speed and
muscle. Trouble was, Westerley forgot how to use those new
muscles almost as soon as Jimmy finished explaining.

"If you're past fourteen years old," Billy Noth said, smiling, "it's hard to remember this crap."

"That's too bad," Westerley said, "because you're gonna
be the department's IT guy."

"What's that?" Billy asked.

Jimmy glanced from one to the other and shook his head
hopelessly. "I'd stay and explain some more, but I've got another one of these to install before lunch." He motioned with
a lean, youthful finger for them to step closer. "C'mere. Before I leave, I just wanna make sure you two know where the
Help button is."

"Button?" Billy said.

After Jimmy had left, Westerley played with the computer awhile, trying to run through some of the routines he'd
been shown. It soon became obvious how much more useful
the new system would be once Westerley, or Billy, mastered
it. Trouble was, that day seemed a long way off.

Westerley left Billy to play with the computer and walked
down to the Hogart Diner for some lunch before he went
mad. He made sure Billy understood the *Help* feature. That
was the key, Westerley thought. Or button.

Norbert Vanderbilt (not a relation to *the* Vanderbilts),
owner and cook at the diner, leaned on the counter and listened to Westerley's computer woes.

After setting up a customer with a cup of coffee in a window booth, he returned to face Westerley across the counter.
"You really need help with anything to do with computers,
you oughta talk to my wife's nephew, Mathew Wellman. Kid's
a genius."

"Comes to tech, being a kid's the first qualification," Westerley said.

Norbert nodded. "Mathew's only twenty-two and already graduated from Northwestern, got a doctorate from Cal Tech."

"Expensive education," Westerley said. "He go on scholarships?"

"Well, when you figure it out mathematically, these places paid Mathew to attend. He somehow worked it out so he made money getting his education."

Westerley was interested. "So he really knows his stuff."

Norbert made a backhand flipping motion with his right hand. "Mathew discusses computers and the Internet, nobody knows what the hell he's talking about."

"Sounds perfect," Westerley said.

"He's on sabbatical for a couple of months, staying at our place, so if you want, I'll tell him to drop by and see you."

"Sabbatical? I didn't think students went on sabbatical."

"Oh, Mathew's teaching now. Back at Cal Tech. Making a fortune for such a young person."

"Jesus!" Westerley said, thinking how nice it would be if he had a sabbatical coming, never mind the fortune. He did have some protracted time off once, after a fleeing felon had slammed an axe handle down on the back of his neck. It took a while for the bones to heal. "Ask Mathew to drop by the office when he has the time," he said. "I'll make out a list of things Billy and I can't cope with."

"Oh, he'll be glad to help. He loves problems almost as much as he loves answers."

64

New York, the present

Fedderman didn't go home after leaving the hospital. He went instead to the Albert A. Aal Memorial Library, where Penny worked. Careful to avoid the venerable Ms. Culver, he sat in a corner of the magazine section and pretended to read *Popular Science.*

That lasted about five minutes, and Fedderman was asleep.

He awoke with Penny standing over him, nudging his shoulder gently, but again and again.

Fedderman sat up straight and looked around. He and Penny appeared to be the only people in the magazine section. He wiped a hand down his face and looked at his watch. *Good God! Almost nine o'clock.*

Penny smiled and leaned close so she could speak softly to him. "The library's about to close, Feds."

He smiled back. "That means you're ready to go home?"

She nodded.

"You hungry?" he asked.

"Starving."

"Me, too."

He became aware of a magazine in his lap and placed it on the chair next to him. Then he unfolded his lanky body from where he sat and touched Penny's arm lightly, as if to make sure she was real. He tapped all the pockets of his new suit to make sure nothing had fallen out, then glanced down to be positive there was nothing of his on the chair cushion.

"So how does Italian sound to you?" he asked.

"Just right."

Ms. Culver was behind the main desk, but with her back conveniently turned. She was looking for something in a cabinet. It seemed to Fedderman that she was pretending to search so she wouldn't have to look at him. Ms. Culver seemed to be that way, where he was concerned.

They went to Delio's, a relatively new restaurant in the lobby of a tall building that contained mostly offices. Soft lighting was provided by artificial candles that looked real in the center of each white-clothed table. A piano was playing somewhere out of sight, and a guy in a suit and wearing a gray fedora wandered by now and then, crooning Frank Sinatra songs. Fedderman thought he sounded more like Bobby Darin, and with the snap-brim hat he looked like Mickey Spillane.

"So how's the case going?" Penny asked, after they'd ordered and were sipping wine.

Fedderman waited for the crooner to drift into another room of the restaurant before answering. He decided his suit beat the hell out of the one on the singer, even figuring in the fedora.

"We're making our usual slow but sure progress." he said. He thought it better not to mention the carpet-tucking knife theory. Not so soon before dinner.

"How's Officer Weaver?"

"Not good. She's slipping in and out of a coma."

"And she never identified who beat her up?"

"Not positively, no. And any other way doesn't count."

"But you've got a good idea who it was."

"Not really. Not the way Weaver's been talking. Her mind's not right yet. Maybe it never will be."

Penny hunched her shoulders and shook her head. "God, what a world."

"Weaver will be all right," Fedderman said. "She's a tough one."

"You think it was the Skinner who attacked her?"

"It would make sense. Serial killers do that sometimes, taunt the police."

"But why try to kill her that way?"

"He might not have been trying to kill her."

"But why not? Why beat her up at all, instead of treating her as he did his other victims?"

Fedderman had asked himself the same question. He told Penny what he'd come up with by way of an answer. "Because he's crazy."

"Or maybe for some reason he doesn't want you to think he was the one who attacked Weaver."

Fedderman regarded her across the table. *It can make you smart, spending all that time in a library.* "Yeah," he said, "that's possible."

Penny sipped her cabernet. "Do you think he'd really try to finish the job while Weaver's in the hospital?" she asked, replacing the stemmed glass on the table.

"It's doubtful. I know it happens in books in the mystery section of your library, but in real life a hospital is a pretty secure place." He looked at her curiously. "Why are you so worried about Weaver?"

She seemed slightly surprised. "I'm not thinking about Weaver now. It's you I'm worried about, Feds. The killer might have to get past you to get to Weaver." She reached across the table and gripped his wrist.

Fedderman didn't know quite what to say. This woman often made him tongue-tied. He used his free hand to reach into a suit coat pocket and withdrew the small velvet-lined box from the jewelers. He held it out to her. It obviously contained a ring, and Penny realized it immediately and her eyes widened. She released his wrist and accepted the tiny box. As she slowly opened it, she peeked inside. She grinned at him.

"Is that a yes?" Fedderman asked. It sounded like someone else's voice. *Am I really doing this?*

"It's a yes, Feds! And this is beautiful!" She slipped the engagement ring on her finger. It looked slightly too large to Fedderman. Penny extended her hand and stiffened all its fingers, the way women do when displaying a ring. "Beautiful!" she repeated.

"So are you," Fedderman said, sounding as if he had a frog in his throat.

Penny got up from her chair, moved smartly around the table, and kissed his cheek. She sat back down. She had done all that in a crouch, and none of the other diners seemed to have noticed her maneuver. *Do women practice that?* Penny was still smiling. The Frank Sinatra imitator reappeared in their part of the restaurant. He seemed to sense something and drifted in the direction of their table. He was singing "My Way." Fedderman's marriage proposal and ring presentation were now drawing the attention he'd feared.

Penny was still grinning hugely, now in part at Fedderman's embarrassment.

"It might have been 'The Lady Is a Tramp,' " she whispered.

Fedderman knew that his life had changed forever.

Jock Sanderson stood waiting for the traffic signal to change. He'd wanted a drink badly all day but had made it through without touching a drop. He was proud of himself and dismayed at the same time. It was a weakness, this craving for alcohol, and Jock didn't like to think of himself as a weak man. Not in any respect. He was the one who was usually in charge of situations. He sensed weaknesses in others and moved in. That was what that prick the Skinner was going to realize one of these days soon—that Jock had moved in on him. He'd provided an alibi for the Skinner and made sure the killer knew that if anything happened to him, to Jock, the cat would be out of the bag. Letters could be left with lawyers, and in safety deposit boxes. The Skinner got the headlines, but Jock was in charge. The Skinner just didn't know it yet.

The light signaled walk, and he crossed the street with the knot of people who'd been waiting with him at the curb. He was wearing Levi's and a short-sleeved shirt he'd bought at the Wear it Again, Sam secondhand shop off Canal. There shouldn't be too many secondhand shops in Jock's future. Not with what he had in mind. He could go live someplace in South America, where there was no extradition treaty with the United States. Or maybe to someplace in the Caribbean. He'd heard that was where some people dropped out of sight and lived like royalty, on those islands. If he kept a low profile, he'd never be found.

He was so lost in his thoughts that he didn't notice the approaching figure that veered slightly so it was headed directly at Jock. When he did notice, he didn't pay much attention. Only a step or two away, Jock lowered his head, expecting the man to move out of his way, but he didn't.

Jock pulled up short to avoid a collision, and was about to say something. He found himself looking directly into the eyes of the Skinner. There was something in those eyes, something beyond cruelty and intensity, that froze Jock. The Skinner was smiling faintly, as if something far removed was amusing him.

"Jesus! You gave me a start," Jock said. They were standing so close to each other that he automatically dropped his gaze to see if the Skinner was brandishing a weapon of some sort. A guy this loony, he might not hesitate to kill someone even on a crowded sidewalk.

The Skinner's hands weren't empty. His right one was carrying a small white box.

Jock backed away. *Oh, God, not again!*

"Take it," the Skinner said. "Add it to your collection."

Jock's hands remained at his sides, pressed tightly against his thighs. "I don't have a collection. I don't want one."

The Skinner shrugged as if that were no concern of his.

"You're not going to do this . . . every time, are you?" Jock asked.

The Skinner seemed to consider. "Only if I deem it necessary," he said.

"Necessary for what?"

"Consider it a reminder." The Skinner moved the box closer to Jock, and something changed in his eyes in a way that scared the holy hell out of Jock. "People who wag their tongues out of turn risk the damndest things happening to them." He smiled broadly. "Not by coincidence, you understand."

"I understand," Jock said, and accepted the box.

"Maybe you'll become a collector, after all."

"I told you—no! There's no reason to keep doing this."

The Skinner ignored Jock's protests. "Keep that in a cool place so it stays fresh. The poor woman it belonged to was trying so hard to use it right up to the end that it might still have plenty to say." The Skinner put on an amused expression, toying with Jock. *Sadistic prick!* "Do you believe in life after death, Jock?"

"I'm not sure I even believe in life *before* death."

"Whatever you choose to do with those unfortunate appendages, maybe they'll talk to you in your dreams, or even sometimes during the day, when you least expect it. Especially Judith Blaney's tongue. I wouldn't be surprised."

"I would," Jock said.

"Ah, think where that tongue might have been when she was alive. Its many talents. She wasn't a chaste woman, our Judith."

Some of his initial fear had left Jock. He felt himself getting angry, or maybe frustrated. He couldn't tell which. He was the one who was supposed to have the whip hand here, and yet this asshole had the nerve to stop him on the sidewalk and give him somebody's severed tongue. Sick bastard!

Jock decided to try taking control of the situation. "Listen, you!" he said. "If you think . . ."

He let his voice trail off as the Skinner simply turned and walked away, glancing back for a final, smiling look at Jock, as if fixing him firmly in his mind.

Jock considered following him, laying a hand on his shoulder, and spinning him around, then handing him back his goddamned box. But he was paralyzed by what he'd seen in the Skinner's eyes.

He began walking, faster and faster, gripping the small white box in his right hand, digging his heels into the pavement with each step. He might be late for work now. He couldn't afford to screw up and get fired, all because of some psycho bastard who cut out people's tongues.

People's tongues!

The papers and TV news speculated about the tongues being removed because the Skinner was a cannibal and might consider them a delicacy. Jock might be the only one who knew better.

Of course, some other parts of the victims could have been removed and the police weren't telling the public. They did that sometimes, to weed out the screwballs that made false confessions. Maybe there was something to the cannibal angle. After dealing with the Skinner, Jock could easily believe it. Lord, right now he could believe almost anything!

Noticing a wire trash basket at the next corner, he veered

toward it and dropped the small box in it as he strode past. *There!* Maybe it would wind up in the same landfill as the first tongue.

He regained some of his confidence by reminding himself that he knew more about the Skinner than the pathetic psychopath imagined. The next time they met, that might be worth mentioning. It might keep the nutcase from giving him somebody else's tongue. Or maybe something more personal.

He reached his subway stop, and almost without slowing took the concrete steps down into dimness and dampness. Now and then he stole a glance behind him.

Maybe I should have wiped my prints from the box. Both boxes!

He wished he had a drink.

65

Vitali and Mishkin had been driving most of the day. Telephone checking could do only so much. They needed to drive to various retail and wholesale outlets and show people the drawing of the carpet-tucking knife, close cousin to the lower-class linoleum knife.

They had worked their way through Queens, then returned to the office and played with the phones some more to get some addresses, and had spent much of the afternoon in Brooklyn.

When they reported their wasted day to Quinn, he instructed them to widen their search to New Jersey. Which was where they were now, cruising along the highway in the Garden State toward a place called Underfoot Carpet Supplies, where maybe they sold carpet-tucking knives. Ordinary hardware stores sometimes had no idea what Vitali and Mishkin were talking about.

The car's interior seemed to be getting smaller and smaller, and Vitali was finding it more and more difficult to be cooped up and have to listen to Harold. Mishkin, in the way of people who could get under the skin of even a patient person like Vitali, seemed blissfully unaware that he was in the least bit irritating.

For the fifth time in five minutes, Mishkin mentioned to

Vitali that he was hungry. Like a mirage summoned by desperation, five hundred feet or so ahead loomed a sign advertising Doughnut Heaven.

"I guess that's where you go if you take your eye off the road to look at their sign," Mishkin said.

"It's where we're going to get some doughnuts," Vitali said, staring straight ahead and already starting to slow the car so he could pull into the doughnut shop lot.

Doughnut Heaven turned out to be not much more than a shack. It served only drive-through customers. There was a menu nailed to the wall near the serving window. It featured about a hundred kinds of doughnuts.

There were no other cars in line, which seemed ominous to Vitali.

"They make it almost impossible to make up your mind, Sal," Mishkin said, as he studied the menu.

"Give me a dozen assorted. Whatever's fresh," Vitali said to the skinny kid in the serving window. He was wearing a chef's cap that was cocked at an angle suggesting it might fall off any second. "And two coffees with cream," Vitali added.

It didn't take the kid long to exchange two foam cups and a greasy white bag for Vitali's money. "I added some doughnut holes as a bonus," he said with a snaggletoothed grin.

"Much obliged," Vitali said.

"We got a special," the kid explained.

As they pulled back out onto the highway, Mishkin added off-brand sweetener from one of the little green envelopes he always carried in one of his pockets. The cups didn't have lids, and coffee was starting to slosh over their rims in the car's plastic holders. Vitali took a careful sip and then replaced his cup quickly because the coffee was close to boiling temperature. He had burned his tongue. That didn't lighten his mood.

"What we oughta do is check the Internet for places that

sell carpet-tucking knives," Mishkin said, opening the dough-nut bag.

"I don't know how much good that would do, Harold. I mean, carpet knives aren't registered like guns."

"But I bet a lot fewer of them are sold than guns," Mishkin said. "Somebody might remember a fairly recent sale."

"Somebody in Bangadel, India," Vitali said, thinking how difficult it was to contact Internet-based companies on the phone. He saw that Mishkin already had powdered sugar on his bushy mustache.

"Where exactly is that?" Mishkin asked.

"India?" *Give him a little of his own medicine*, Vitali thought.

"C'mon, Sal, you know where I meant. Bangadel."

"I don't know, Harold. I made it up."

"Hmm."

They could hit this Underfoot Carpet place, Vitali thought, then maybe a few more, and head back to the city. Beside him, Mishkin stirred and the doughnut bag made rattling noises. This was the part of police work that drove Vitali nuts. He felt like pulling over and bolting from the car.

He saw a service station up ahead, glanced down at the dashboard, and found the car had less than a quarter tank of gas.

Even though they were hardly doing twenty miles an hour when Vitali steered off the highway and into the gas station, the tires squealed as if they were in a Grand Prix racer.

"You fill the tank, Harold. I'm going to walk over where I might be able to get a good signal and see if I can get in touch with Quinn."

Vitali strolled about a hundred feet away, near a rack of used tires.

Quinn answered his cell phone on the second ring.

"We're not getting anywhere driving around looking for

places that sell those tucking knives," Vitali told Quinn. "I think our time would be better spent just using the phone and the Internet. Calling carpet installers, seeing where they get them, if they even use them."

"I've got Jerry Lido prowling the Internet," Quinn said. "Pearl's been working the phone."

"Any luck?"

"Not so far. And some of the newer carpet-tucking knives look like straight razors, not the kind of blades that match the wounds."

"It's not a common item."

"No," Quinn said. "That's why it might mean something when we find places that sell them and keep a record. It's possible on the Internet, but not many are sold, and so far none in this area to anyone who could be a suspect."

"Internet, phone, and legwork," Vitali said. "Yeah, I guess that's the way to work it. And I'm in no way gonna underestimate Lido and his computer. If the guy didn't drink he'd be another Bill Gates."

"Or still with the NYPD. If you get no results today by driving, we won't waste any more time on it, Sal."

"Makes sense. Anyplace we can drive to, it probably has a phone."

"Yeah. And if the Skinner paid cash for the knife, it will probably be impossible to trace. And for all we know, he might've been in a hardware store looking for something else and simply bought the thing and there's no record of it because it isn't itemized, even if it was paid for with a credit or debit card."

"That's how I see it, too. But you never know; the information we need might be right on top and we'd kick ourselves if we found out later and hadn't touched that particular base. We can hit it tomorrow using national directories and the phone, if you want. Widen what Pearl's doing."

"Thanks, Sal. I gotta go now. Other phone's ringing. Anything else?"

"I might decide to murder Harold."

"Fight the impulse, Sal." Quinn broke the connection.

Vitali returned to the car. Mishkin had used a company card to pay for the gas at the pump and was already ensconced in the passenger seat. The car's windows were up and the air conditioner was laboring.

Vitali steeled himself and got in behind the steering wheel. He looked both ways, pulled back out into traffic, and accelerated fast so they could beat a tractor-trailer angling onto the highway from a cloverleaf ramp.

Mishkin looked over at him. "Anything, Sal?"

"Quinn says they hit a few places on the Internet that sell the knife we're looking for, but there's no record of any going to someone who'd be a suspect."

"It wouldn't surprise me, Sal, if we might be hitting the same places. Duplication of effort."

"Taxpayers would be pissed off," Vitali said.

"Like being back in the NYPD," Mishkin said.

They drove for a while.

"Doughnut holes, Sal. That make sense to you?"

"Not to me, Harold."

"A hole is like . . . nothing."

"Yeah."

"How's something like that get started?"

"I don't know."

"It's an oxymoron. Like jumbo—"

"Pass me one of those doughnut holes, Harold."

66

Tanya Moody emerged like a casual queen from the Breaverson Arms on East Fifty-fourth Street, wearing her navy blue shorts, armless blue T-shirt, blue and white sneakers, and carrying her sky-blue gym bag. She began perspiring as soon as she stepped from the cool lobby into the morning heat. She squinted and brushed a lock of her long brown hair back from her face. Today, she decided, was going to be even hotter than yesterday. After drawing a pair of Gucci knockoff sunglasses from an outside pocket of the gym bag, she began walking toward her subway stop at Fifty-third and Lex.

As she strode along the shaded side of the street, Tanya drew attention. She was five-foot-ten and lean and muscular. With each step her powerful thigh and calf muscles flexed. Her breasts were large, but too firm to bounce as she took the curbs. She was covering ground fast with her long, graceful strides.

Down the stairs to the subway platform she went, causing a man looking back at her to stub his toe painfully on a concrete step. Tanya heard the guy yelp and glanced back, amused by what had happened. He was gripping the tip of his shoe and glaring at her as if his mishap was her fault.

Tanya ignored him, fished her MetroCard from her pocket,

and headed for the turnstiles. She was well aware of the effect her appearance had on men and on some women, and was pleased by it. In her business, as a self-employed personal trainer, she was her own best advertisement.

She'd just left a fifty-year-old wealthy widow who still flaunted a fashionably trim figure. The woman had lost ten pounds and firmed up wonderfully since employing Tanya two months ago, and was especially pleased because Tanya planned and instructed physical workouts at her clients' homes. Most clients, encouraged by their initial progress, purchased their own exercise equipment—at a discount—from a company that gave Tanya a generous commission. All in all, Tanya was pleased by how her business had grown during the past few years.

She'd left the trim widow preparing herself for the dating scene, now that her husband had been dead over six months. She was doing wide-armed bench presses on a home weight machine, an exercise that built up the pectoral muscles that supported the breasts. Three sets of ten with moderate weights, every third day, had already added an inch to the widow's bustline.

Tanya was one of the first to board the train after the subway passengers exited. She found a seat near the back, where it would be easier to get out if the car became crowded as the train made its way downtown. As she settled in with her gym bag on her lap, the train jerked and squealed away. The motion caused her to glance to her left, and there was the man who'd been following her the past week or so.

Of course she wasn't positive he'd been tailing her. At least not sure enough to confront him. Besides, she was used to men sort of latching on to her presence and paying her particular and obvious attention. Some of them were married men, or men too shy to speak to her. If they were on more or less the same schedule, these men would appear on her periphery often. Only now and then would one approach her. Tanya knew they meant no harm. And in truth she was flattered by their presence.

But there was something about this guy that didn't fit the mold. He wasn't feigning disinterest and then sneaking glances at her, like most of her anonymous admirers. Instead he either completely ignored her or stared right through her, as if he could see her in outline and transparent, like one of those airport scanners, but she was about as important to him as an inanimate object. There was something creepy about that stare.

Other than the unsettling stare, he was an average-looking sort of guy. He always had a hat of some sort on, and seldom wore the same one two days in a row. As if he thought that by changing hats he was altering his appearance and making himself unnoticeable. Today he had on a Milwaukee Brewers baseball cap. Tomorrow he might be wearing a beret. She did pick up that she saw him mostly on weekends, when she did much of her work because her clients were free from their offices. So maybe he had some other job during the week. It was, she thought, smiling slightly, at least nice to be attracting men who were employed.

Thank God the man *didn't* look like Tom Stopp. Stopp was the man Tanya had mistakenly identified as her rapist ten years ago, not long after she'd moved to New York. Tanya had been at a club, drinking too much, with people she didn't know, and she passed out. She had never done that before and was amazed. Then suspicious. She didn't know whether someone had slipped a date-rape drug into her drink, or she'd simply not been used to so much alcohol in such a short period of time.

She had woken—or regained consciousness—the next morning with a man on top of her. She came alert and furious instantly, fought her way out from beneath him, and ran toward the door. Somehow she managed to snatch up her

Levi's and blouse as she ran, and in the elevator managed to yank and work her clothes onto her body. The physical action alerted her that she was sore where she shouldn't have been. She immediately knew what had happened.

My God! Was he the only one?

She scrolled through her memory and found blank spots. Vaguely, she recalled the three men and two women, her "new friends" she'd been drinking with at Arthur's Lounge on Sixth Avenue. Or was it Seventh? Her mind was playing tricks on her. Not natural.

A woman carrying a small brown dog got on the elevator when the door opened at lobby level. She'd looked at Tanya and said simply, "You've got no shoes, dear." The elevator door slid closed and Tanya made her way toward the street door. She heard hurried footsteps on the stairs and assumed Tom Stopp was coming after her.

Tom Stopp. I do remember his name.

In the street, she waved her arms wildly and a cab separated itself from traffic and came toward her. At the same time, Stopp broke from the apartment door, saw her, and started yelling and running toward her.

She could see the cabbie yammering in his radio as the taxi pulled up next to her. She threw herself into the backseat and pulled the door shut.

Stopp was there immediately, tugging at the cab's door handle.

"Doors, window, everything locked," said the cabbie in an accent Tanya didn't know.

Stopp started to beat on the window. For some reason the cabbie didn't drive away. He simply sat calmly behind the steering wheel, only now and then glancing over to be sure Stopp's efforts were in vain.

Then Tanya understood why the cab hadn't driven away. A police cruiser was double-parked in front of it. Two uniformed policemen appeared on either side of Stopp and pulled him away from the cab. Tanya twisted around and saw that another police car was parked close behind the cab.

Stopp was out of sight now. The cab's rear door opened, and one of the cops leaned in. "You okay, ma'am?"

Tanya was too confused to answer.

The cop looked at her more closely, smiled, then nodded. "Stay where you are for a little while, okay? Till we get this straightened out."

She nodded. Stunned by what had happened. By what must have happened last night.

Tanya told her story to the police. So did Tom Stopp. He claimed to have been home all evening, alone, in an apartment other than the one from which Tanya had escaped. The apartment where Tanya had awakened was down the hall from Stopp's. He'd heard a commotion, gone out into the hall, and seen Tanya fleeing. He went after her intending to help her.

The problem was that Stopp's fingerprints were in the apartment where Tanya was raped. It was an unoccupied furnished apartment and he maintained that he'd gone into it a week ago to examine it because he was thinking about renting someplace larger. The super confirmed this, but so what? The bed was unmade, sheets a tangle, and it was obvious that the rape had occurred. If it wasn't Stopp who'd drugged and attacked Tanya, where was the real rapist?

And who could substantiate that Stopp had been alone in his apartment, and not in the other that he'd known was vacant and had chosen as a convenient place to commit his crime?

Of course, Stopp's insurmountable problem was that Tanya positively identified him as one of the men she'd been with earlier that night at the bar. One of the bartenders, though less certain, had also identified him. A sympathetic jury, an enthusiastic prosecutor, an inept defense attorney, and the evidence, all added up to a fifteen-to-twenty-year sentence for Tom Stopp.

That had all happened ten years ago, to a young and naïve Tanya Moody. She was older now, a self-supporting woman with a business of her own.

Tom Stopp was older, too. He was a forty-year-old ex-con who'd been exonerated by DNA evidence collected at the time of Tanya's rape and stored for over a decade in an evidence box. He'd been released last year and was free.

Someone else had raped Tanya Moody, and he, too, was free somewhere.

The police had talked to Tanya about Stopp when he was released, and said he was living now in New Jersey and seemed to bear her no animosity. Also, he had alibis for at least two of the Skinner torture murders.

They warned Tanya to be careful, and to call them if she so much as caught a glimpse of Tom Stopp anywhere near her.

Only it wasn't Stopp who'd been following her lately. And she doubted if the man was her actual rapist. He looked nothing like any of the men in the bar that night, and he would simply have no reason to step back into her life after ten years. He could rape some other woman with much less risk.

The Skinner murders, and the strange man she at least *thought* might be stalking her, had brought back to the top of her memory the time of the rape. She'd assumed that she'd purged herself of that night, or at least left it as a part of the past she had no need to revisit. But the man she kept glimpsing on the subway, and on the sidewalks, had become a regular visitor to her dreams.

Tanya owned a small .22-caliber handgun that she used to carry in her purse. She'd obtained it illegally as a gift from a man she'd dated after the trial, and for years it had lain wrapped in an oily rag in a steel lockbox at the back of her closet's top shelf.

A week ago she'd gotten the gun down, checked it to make sure it was in working order, and again began carrying it. She knew it was against the law, but screw the Sullivan Act. When her life was at stake, the only law that mattered was survival. Tanya also had a tiny canister of mace in her purse, and she'd taken kickboxing lessons. But she knew the kind of uphill struggle the strongest of women might have with the weakest of men. The gun gave her comfort.

She didn't think she had enough evidence to contact the police about the man who seemed to be too often near her. And she didn't know how they'd find the man to talk to him, unless they assigned an undercover cop to tag along with her for days until she could point him out. Obviously they weren't going to do that. And after costing Tom Stopp years of his life, Tanya didn't like the idea of positively identifying anyone for any reason. The human eye was an unreliable partner to memory.

All Tanya could do was wonder if the man actually *was* following her.

And, if so, why?

And be ready.

PART 3

We know the truth, not only by the reason,
  but also by the heart.

—BLAISE PASCAL,
  Thoughts

I'll make my Joy a secret thing,
My face shall wear a mask of care . . .

—WILLIAM HENRY DAVIES,
  "Hunting Joy"

67

By noon Quinn had pretty much given up on tracing the Skinner through the recorded purchase of a carpet-tucking knife. The search was further complicated when they learned that building supply stores sometimes sold such knives as part of a tool set.

The good piece of news was that Weaver was being released from the hospital. She wasn't completely healed, but she was out of insurance and scheduled to become an outpatient. Aside from her mother in Pittsburgh, Weaver had a sister in Philadelphia who was a hospital administrator. Common sense and simple economics dictated that Weaver should spend the rest of her recuperation in Philadelphia.

Quinn picked up Weaver just before noon at the hospital and drove her by her apartment to pack, then to LaGuardia, where the good sister had reserved a seat on an American Airlines flight. He thought Weaver looked okay but still acted somewhat out of it. She kissed him on the mouth before she joined the security checkpoint line, and glanced back at him as she passed through the metal detector. Something about the glance suggested they would never see each other again.

All in all, her departure made Quinn feel like crap. Despite the hour, he used his cell phone to invite Jerry Lido to lunch. He knew what lunch was to Lido, and it was the kind of lunch Quinn felt like having today.

Quinn was supposed to meet Pearl for dinner before they went home to the brownstone. She sat alone at a diner table, sipping decaffeinated coffee that was catching up with her because she was on her third cup. Pearl figured three cups of decaf equaled about one cup of strong regular grind. Enough to keep her awake at night.

She knew Quinn had gone to lunch with Jerry Lido, and she knew what kind of lunch that could become.

Damn Quinn!

By the time she thought to check her cell phone, she felt as if she was swimming in coffee.

Uh-oh. Quinn had called and somehow she hadn't heard the phone. He hadn't left a voice message, but he'd called again and texted her. The text message mentioned his name, but after that made no sense whatsoever. Quinn hadn't used his cell phone for that call. She knew it was because he barely knew how to send a text message. She saw that the call had been from Jerry Lido's phone.

That explained a lot of things.

Pearl paid for the bottomless cup of coffee and went outside to hail a cab.

Pearl had to knock on Jerry Lido's door for a long time. A woman with an odd brown hairdo that made her look like a spaniel opened a door across the hall and glared at Pearl. Pearl returned the glare. The woman shook her head and ducked back inside.

When Pearl looked back she saw that her knocking had been answered. The apartment door was open. Jerry Lido stood there wearing pants and the kind of sleeveless under-shirt some people called a wife-beater. He was barefoot and smelled like gin. Behind him, across the living room, Quinn was snoring away on a sofa. He was dressed something like Lido but wearing a tangled tie. There was a Gilby's bottle on a coffee table. Three more bottles on the floor. Pearl felt as if she'd disturbed two hibernating bears.

"I see you had a party today," she said.

"More like a tête-à-tête," Lido said, surprising Pearl with his vocabulary and elocution. Especially since he was obviously still drunk.

"Looks more like you two rolled down a hill." She stepped inside and got another whiff of Lido's breath. "Are you still drinking?"

Lido shrugged. "A little hair of the frog."

"You mean dog. Frogs don't have hair."

"Nor do they bark."

Pearl went across the room and stared down at Quinn. He looked as bad as Lido, but his chest was rising and falling regularly. At least he'd stopped snoring.

"We were working on the computer," Lido said, as if in pathetic defense of his and Quinn's conditions.

Pearl could have guessed that. Quinn had been doing his job of getting Lido to drink so he could get in touch with and apply his tech genius to the hunt for the Skinner. Pearl wondered if the afternoon had been productive. She winked at Lido. "So what'd you learn?"

He eagerly led her to a long table on which was a big desk-top computer. A laptop was placed off to the side. There were two flat-screen monitors. One of them was blank. The other was showing that screen saver of what looked like PVC pipes that kept fitting together to form right angles unto eternity. That monitor came all the way to life when Lido sat down at the computer.

"We learned where carpet-tucking knives weren't," he said. "But when I was lying in bed, or on the floor, this evening, I thought of something else."

"What was that?"

"The fusion of time and geography."

"You're still drunk," Pearl said.

Lido gave the sheepish smile that made him look so human and pitiable. "A little, but not like him." He pointed toward Quinn, who had shifted in his sleep and appeared about to fall off the sofa.

"We know the murders are committed on weekends," Lido said. "Sometimes Mondays or Fridays. So what I figure is we can check New York hotel reservations around the times of the murders, maybe come up with the same name more than once."

So simple, Pearl thought. Like all products of brilliance. For the first time she saw and appreciated Lido's real genius on the computer. She could see why Quinn preferred him drunk when he worked.

Lido took a deep breath, like a concert pianist preparing to play. And he did play the keyboard like a musical instrument, roaming the Internet as if he invented it, pausing now and then to adjust something with the mouse as if fine-tuning or changing chords. There was no hesitancy, no altering of his strange body rhythm. His mind seemed to be one with the incredibly fast computer, somewhere out there in the ether, where Pearl couldn't follow.

An hour passed like a minute. There was a thump as Quinn rolled off the sofa. Pearl looked over at him, momentarily concerned. He seemed none the worse for his short drop, and was sleeping deeply and probably comfortably, on the floor. Pearl turned back to her work (rather, Lido's work) that Quinn should have been doing. Last night he'd followed Lido too far into the bottle. Pearl knew it wasn't the first time. This crazy plan of his had to stop.

But not yet, Pearl thought. Lido was drunk anyway, so why not make use of him?

There were two matches, both men, who'd been at hotels in New York at the times of most of the Skinner murders. Pearl watched spellbound as Lido used the Internet to learn everything about them. She knew that half the sites he visited were confidential. They were breaking the law as certainly as if they were burglarizing buildings.

Not the first time, Pearl thought.

Finally Lido sat back from his computer. One of the men was a seventy-two-year-old financial consultant who lived with his wife in Atlanta. He traveled constantly, visiting clients all over the country. The other man was a clothing designer whose Internet history made it clear that he was gay.

"The gay guy maybe, but not likely," Lido said, sitting back in his chair and obviously disappointed. He appeared to be sobering up. Pearl, still haunted by strains of youthful Catholicism, absently crossed herself as she located a gin bottle and poured Lido a generous drink. *Forgive me, for I know exactly what I do.*

He tossed the gin down like water.

"Has there ever been a gay serial killer who murdered women?" he asked.

"Not to my knowledge." Pearl poured herself a very small drink. "Not openly gay, anyway."

Lido worked the computer some more. "Uh-oh."

"What?"

"He's not only gay, he's married."

"Well . . ."

"To another fella," Lido said.

"Oh."

"And when Verna Pound was killed he was in Paris."

"Unless we have two killers, that leaves him out," Pearl said. She took a sip of her drink.

Lido looked crestfallen, but only for a moment. Then he suddenly came back all the way alive. The gin kicking in. "How 'bout another drink?" he asked.

"Let's work for a while, then I'll pour you one," Pearl said. *Carrot and stick.*

She felt terribly guilty to be using this guy. She felt no different from Quinn, who was over there sleeping on the carpet. She wanted to wring Quinn's neck, but she also wanted to wring yet more tech miracles out of Jerry Lido.

"I've got an idea," Pearl said. "Hotel reservations are one thing—if our killer even made reservations. They can be paid for in cash, or credit cards under different names. But if you travel alone and pay cash for an airline ticket, the authorities take note of you. And our killer wouldn't take a chance and use anything but a valid credit card when it came to Homeland Security. Maybe we should get into credit card files, if you can."

"Oh, I can," Lido said. "But it'd be easier to check flights into New York carrying passengers traveling alone, and who paid cash or with credit or debit cards."

Pearl knew he was right. "Only thing is," she said, "you're messing with Homeland Security, when you illegally hack into airline passenger information."

"Oh, I often get into—"

"Don't tell me, Jerry."

"I'll come and go without leaving any kind of electronic footprint," Lido said confidently.

"Jerry—"

"Sometimes I do it just for sport," he said, grinning. "LaGuardia, Newark, and Kennedy. I compare what all the passengers paid for their seats. Pearl, it's fun. God help me, it's fun!"

Pearl said, "You want another drink?"

*   *   *

It was past 2 A.M. when, with Lido's help, Pearl managed to get Quinn downstairs and into a cab. Within an hour, Quinn was in bed in the brownstone, and Pearl was curled next to him. Both slept deeply when they weren't dreaming.

In the morning, Pearl awoke to hear Quinn on the phone. He was doing what Pearl had heard him doing before—talking Jerry Lido out of suicide.

Pearl rolled onto her stomach and buried her face in her pillow, assailed again by guilt over having exploited Lido's vulnerability.

Later she felt the bed sag with Quinn's weight, and his big hand was gentle on her shoulder.

"Lido gonna be all right?" she asked, muffled by the pillow.

"I think so."

"I still don't feel right about what we're doing. I feel . . ."

"Guilty?"

"Yeah."

"Still the good Catholic girl," Quinn said.

"Sometimes, anyway," Pearl said.

She rolled onto her back and looked up at him.

"You've been crying," he said, and bent down and kissed the tip of her nose.

"There have to be rules, Quinn. Call them laws. Call them commandments. Call them whatever you want. But even in this screwed-up world, there have to be rules."

"There are," he said. "They bend."

Later that morning, when everyone other than Weaver was in the Q and A office, Fedderman stood up behind his desk and cleared his throat.

Every eye suddenly turned to him.

Every instinct told him he'd made a mistake.

He decided again that he and Penny would keep their engagement secret until after the Skinner investigation. Fedderman was sure he wasn't doing anything unethical, but why borrow trouble when there was so much of it already in the world?

He cleared his throat again and walked over and topped off his coffee.

Everyone else went back to what they were doing. Only Pearl looked at him strangely, sensing that he'd been about to say something.

Pearl would.

68

The police hadn't believed that Tom Stopp was trying to help Tanya Moody the night he was arrested. That he'd heard a commotion, gone to his door to investigate, and seen her come flying half nude out of the unoccupied apartment across the hall. She was struggling in a desperate dance to put on her clothes as she ran, somehow managing.

What had prompted him was blind instinct. She was obviously in trouble, running hard from something, and in need of help. He called after her, trying to get her to stop and explain what was happening. She'd glanced back at him, obviously terrified, running from *him*!

No! She had it wrong! He couldn't let her think of him that way. *He couldn't!*

He ran after her faster to help her, to explain to her.

They wouldn't believe him. Not at the scene in front of his apartment building, and not at the precinct house where he was read his rights and interrogated.

After a while in police custody, he could hardly believe himself. They paid no attention when he told them he'd tried to get Tanya Moody to stop, so he could convince her he wasn't whoever or whatever had frightened her. So he could help her.

Later, when she'd regained her composure and good sense,

she told them her story. Her concept of the truth. It was too late for Stopp then. There was enough circumstantial evidence against him to convict him ten times over.

The man who'd actually raped Tanya Moody was long gone. And Tom Stopp sat for the next several months listening to what he'd done, where he'd been, when in fact he'd been home in bed.

The more the prosecution, and the jury, heard his story, the less they believed it, and, strangely enough, that affected Stopp. He began to feel guilty. Maybe, when enough people didn't believe something, it could somehow become untrue. Who you were could seem little-by-little unreal, until finally you were someone else. Some person the system had created.

In prison they'd laughed at him. There had been times when he'd thought he was one of the guards, complete with uniform and authority. Laughter sometimes tilted to violence. He'd been badly beaten by other inmates when he'd tried to hurry them back to their cells.

If Stopp had experienced this problem before, being another person, he couldn't remember it. But that was the problem; that was how he became someone else sometimes, by not remembering who he really was or had been. The other person, waiting for an opportunity, would then take over. The one named Tom Stopp would recall what had happened, faintly through a veil, but not for very long. At least, from what other people said, that was the way it happened.

The prison doctor suggested mental illness, perhaps schizophrenia with multiple personalities. He was a general practitioner and recommended that a psychiatrist see Stopp. The prison authorities decided Stopp was simply putting on an act to better his circumstances and make his way back to the streets sooner.

Stopp saw no mental health professional. He simply remained convict 1437645. And one night when he decided *he* was a psychiatrist, it elicited more laughter than concern.

Now he was out of prison, wandering around unemployed, existing on welfare checks and whatever his brother and sister, living in California, sent him from time to time. Money he was going to pay back someday. Still. Even after his years in prison.

Stopp would find a way to pay his debts, even if it meant becoming a criminal, as they'd branded him all those years, and stealing the money. He owed that and more to his brother Marv the screenwriter, and his sister Terri the beautician. Tom Stopp was a man who paid his debts. Maybe someday his brother could write one of his TV movies about that. Stopp reflected that his life would make an excellent film.

But he knew his determination to pay what he owed was will rather than probability. Six months ago he'd been diagnosed with congestive heart failure. Which wasn't as bad as it sounded—but almost. Put simply, his heart couldn't pump out as much blood as it took in. A minor surgical procedure had helped, but not enough. The doctors told him he might live for years, if he didn't overexert himself, took medicine he couldn't afford, and slipped a tiny nitroglycerin tablet beneath his tongue if and when his heart started to act up.

There wasn't much danger of him overexerting himself, because in his circumstances, and with the lousy economy, he couldn't find a job. His stress mostly came from regret. He didn't blame the girl, Tanya. She'd been doped up and half mad with terror when he'd tried to catch up to her and been interrupted outside her cab by the cops. The bastard who'd actually raped her . . . well, Stopp could work up a hate for that guy, only he had no idea who he was.

So he kept his pills handy in his pocket and made it through his days. Time was misery and was killing him with exacting slowness. Years, the doctors had given him, if he was careful. Plodding along Canal Street, Stopp almost laughed, watching the vendors close the folding steel doors of their kiosks after selling tourists and phonies their knock-off brand merchandise. He was like one of those faux Rolex watches that looked good at a glance, but had a strict limit on how many ticks were in them before they quit running. He shook his head sadly. Reality was always in disguise.

Years . . .

Tom Stopp wasn't so sure. Something bad was going to happen to him, and soon. He could feel it. Like that time in Sweden when he'd been fired from his job as watch repairman.

He went home to his crummy basement apartment, stretched out on his bed, and watched the roaches. Outside, the sun began losing its battle with the night. Dusk moved in like an occupying army. After a while the apartment got dark, and Stopp could no longer see the roaches.

He wished he had some booze. He couldn't afford it, and he didn't like to beg. He'd tried panhandling once and decided it was less soul-smearing to write his brother for another loan. He felt like jumping up out of bed and leaving the apartment, walking the dangerous city streets. No, not walking. Running hard enough to outrace his tortured self.

Yeah, he'd had a lot of luck the last time he'd impulsively run from an apartment.

There was nowhere for him to go, anyway. No one he had to see or who wanted to see him.

He reread yesterday's newspaper, which he'd gotten out of a trash receptacle. Then he put the paper aside and lay quietly, outwardly calm, watching the shadows grow and listening to his heart.

Cannibalism.

Such rumors died hard.

The Skinner tossed his folded *Post* aside and sipped some more of his espresso. There was no doubt now that the rumors of cannibalism were started by Quinn, in an attempt to rattle him.

Quinn seemed to have rattled the women of New York even more. Before the cannibalism speculation, the Skinner could sense their uneasiness in dark or crowded places, in the subways or narrow streets, or chattering together as they strode in tandem along wide sidewalks. He walked among them and secretly enjoyed that rippling undercurrent of fear.

Now he saw in New York's women a quieter, deeper fear. They were scared shitless, and all thanks to Quinn. The media of course, had cooperated, but surely even they didn't truly make the leap from severed tongues to cannibalism. They pretended. That was fine with the Skinner. The whole world was pretense. Sometimes he thought he was the only real thing in it.

He glanced at his watch.

Tom Stopp was home sleeping, or perhaps in an alcoholic stupor. The Skinner had seen him negotiate the narrow steps to his pathetic apartment he shared with the roaches. Stopp wouldn't reappear until late tomorrow morning. That was his routine. He was where he was supposed to be, a game piece in its place on the board. And a move was about to be made.

It was almost time to leave the restaurant and do something very real.

Something Quinn could read about in the papers.

69

Edmundsville, the present

Beth was carrying groceries in from the car when Westerley's SUV, with its roof bar lights and sheriff's markings, pulled in behind her. Her car was in the garage, where it was shaded, but the opened trunk, containing the groceries, was in the sun.

Westerley got out of the SUV and smiled at Beth as he came around the front of the vehicle.

"I'll help you with those," he said.

She kissed his cheek as he relieved her of a bulging plastic bag that contained a half-gallon jug of milk, as well as assorted canned goods.

After placing the bag on the kitchen table, he made another trip to the car and got the rest of the plastic bags from the trunk. Juggling another heavy load of groceries, he slammed the trunk lid shut and headed for the door to the house.

The swinging wooden garage doors he left open; there was no way to close them with his SUV parked behind the used Kia Beth had bought when her old Honda finally refused to run. Westerley had helped her trade in the Honda.

She'd finished with the first load of groceries, but there were more on the kitchen table, and the refrigerator door still hung open. Westerley stood at the table and handed boxes, cans, and frozen vegetable bags over to Beth to put away in the nearby cupboard and refrigerator.

"Eddie home?" he asked, knowing the answer.

"He's in Iowa, taking summer classes at the university. Wants to make up some credits he lost when he had the flu last winter."

"Good for him. Where's Link?"

"Won't be home for a couple of days. There's a big numismatic convention in Kansas City."

"How come I didn't hear about it?"

"You don't hang around with people who save their wheat pennies."

"Link does love his coins."

Beth finished with the groceries, swung the refrigerator door shut, and leaned against the table. The kitchen was warm and she was perspiring. Westerley thought she was beautiful when her face took on a moistness that glowed and lent her a kind of life force. He moved closer and kissed her forehead. It was cool despite the moistness of her flesh. He even liked the taste of her when she perspired.

She backed away from him, as if she were still tired from lugging the groceries and didn't want one thing to lead to another. Not yet.

"Get any results back?" she asked. It had been two weeks since he'd sent the DNA samples in for analysis.

"Not yet," Westerley said. "The folks at the lab don't see it as top priority, Beth. I wish I had the clout to make them change their minds."

She smiled. "You got plenty of clout with me." She wiped the back of her wrist across her forehead. "Want something to drink?"

"Beer'd be fine. I'll get it. You go on in the living room and sit down."

"Fix me a glass of ice water, too."

He nodded and watched her make her way out of the kitchen; then he opened the refrigerator. A cold can of Budweiser was hiding behind the new plastic jug of milk. He worked the can out over the top of the milk and pulled the opener, feeling the cold fizz of beer on a knuckle. Beth was moving around in the living room. He heard the window air-conditioning unit kick on in there. He didn't hear her move down the hall, but a while later the bedroom unit started to hum. Westerley smiled and used the icemaker to clunk some cubes into a water tumbler. He ran in some filtered water from the refrigerator and carried the can and glass into the living room.

Beth was seated on the sofa with her legs curled under her. The flimsy skirt she wore had worked its way up. The sight of her tanned knees and thighs made something tighten in him. He handed her the glass of water and sat down beside her. Beth took a sip of water and then tilted sideways against him, as if her end of the sofa had lifted. She rested her head on Westerley's shoulder.

They sat silently for a while, sipping their respective drinks, enjoying each other's presence, and feeling the living room cool down.

"You think it's cool in the bedroom yet?" Westerley asked.

"Should be," Beth said.

"Let's do something about that," Westerley said.

Beth stood up first, and held out her hand as if to lead him.

They lay together afterward, nude and perspiring on Beth's bed, feeling the cool caresses of the window air conditioner breeze on their damp bare flesh. There was a slight variation in the unit's soft humming, almost like a three-note tune being played over and over. They both found it restful rather than irritating. The bedspread and top sheet had found their way onto the floor, and the wrinkled sheet beneath them was damp and still smelled of sex.

Beth's hand wandered over and lay lightly on Westerley's thigh. "I wish things would never change," she said.

They were both staring at the ceiling, maybe seeing the same pattern of cracks there.

"Except you want the results of those DNA tests," Westerley said.

"No. I mean, yes, I do. But I wish things didn't ever have to change from this minute. Ever."

"It'd be nice," Westerley said, "if the afterglow lasted forever."

"Be no wars or crime."

"Be no sheriffs."

Beth laughed and moved her hand, squeezing him slightly where he didn't want to be squeezed at all. "You are way too practical sometimes," she said.

"Somebody has to be." He turned to her, kissed her on the lips, and maneuvered to the side so he could sit on the edge of the mattress.

"You're not leaving already, are you?"

"Yeah. I'm afraid it's not that perfect world yet, Beth. If I don't leave and do my job, the county might elect somebody else."

She grinned. "Never happen. You're too good at your work to be replaced. I know that."

She reached for him but he stood up. "Seriously, Beth, I better shower and go give out some speeding tickets."

"Your deputy can do that."

"Billy? He doesn't like doing that to people. He's missing a mean streak."

"But you're not?"

"No. I'm perverse."

She got out of bed on the other side. "Not too perverse for me." The sheet and spread were tangled up with a stack of folded clothes that had been on the floor near the wall.

Westerley padded barefoot into the bathroom and took a quick, cold shower.

When he returned to the bedroom, the bed was stripped and the stack of clothes was on top of the mattress pad. Beth was wearing a pair of Levi's cutoffs and a blouse she hadn't bothered to button. Something to cover her until he was gone, then she'd take her own shower and get dressed. She was holding a slip of white paper out for Westerley to see.

"Is that a thank-you note?" Westerley said, still rubbing his hair dry with the towel from the bathroom.

"It's a restaurant receipt."

He stopped rubbing with the towel. "And?"

"It's from a restaurant in New York, dated two weeks ago. When Link was supposed to be in Houston."

Westerley took the receipt from her and looked at it. Someone had paid cash for a thirty-six-dollar meal at a restaurant called Dannay's on Tenth Street. He handed the receipt back to her.

"It was in the pocket of Link's suit," Beth said, motioning with her head toward the stack of clothes on the bed. There was a dark blue suit at the bottom of the stack. "I was gonna take it to the cleaners with the rest of those clothes and thought I should go through the pockets. Last time I took one of his suits to be cleaned, I left a ballpoint pen in one of the pockets and it made a stain."

Westerley handed the receipt back to her. "New York's a long way from Houston," he said.

"So how'd this receipt get in Link's pocket?"

"I don't know. Far be it from me to defend your husband, but things like that sometimes happen for reasons we don't imagine. I mean, maybe it's a national chain restaurant with New York headquarters, so they print all their receipts with the New York address so customers will identify them with the city. Like with Nathan's hot dogs. Or maybe the machine that printed the date was set wrong. Or maybe Link's having a secret affair."

"Do you really think that last one's possible?"

Westerley smiled. "Should we of all people doubt the possibility?"

Beth crumpled the receipt and tossed it in a nearby waste-basket.

"I'll go with the machine that's set wrong," she said.

"I'll bet on somebody else's old receipt, and Link picked it up with some other stuff and stuck it in his pocket."

"Yeah, that's a possibility, too."

But they were both thinking the same thing.

Maybe, when the DNA results came in, it wouldn't matter.

When Westerley got back to the office, Billy was hunched over the computer. The tip of his tongue was protruding from the corner of his mouth, where it always was when he was deep in concentration. Mathew Wellman was standing behind him, observing what Billy was doing. Mathew was smiling. He greeted Westerley with his usual politeness.

"Hi, Sheriff Westerley. Billy's got a good feel for this."

Westerley said, "I'm glad somebody in this department does."

"This software the state supplied you with is ideal for data mining."

"That's what we do," Westerley said, "mine data."

"Seeking gold nuggets of evidence," Billy said. "That's neat."

Westerley thought his deputy might be spending too much time with Mathew.

For a second Westerley wondered if Mathew could use

this wonderful new software to hack into the lab's system
and see what there was to see about the tests on the DNA
samples he'd sent them over two weeks ago.

But that would be illegal.

And he was the sheriff.

70

Quinn wasn't surprised when he picked up his desk phone and found himself talking with Nancy Weaver in Philadelphia.

He was the first one in the office, as he often was, and he suspected she'd phoned at the early hour to talk to him when he was alone, before things got busy.

Her voice had changed, he noticed, gotten huskier, and she seemed to be forcing her words.

"The news I'm reading and seeing makes it seem you're not making much progress," she said.

He smiled. "You call to chew me out?"

"No. To thank you, more than anything. You looked after me. Then you got me off the treadmill where I was running faster and faster but didn't realize it."

"Now that you've slowed down," Quinn said, "how are you doing?"

"I'm feeling better, but after the first whack on the back of my head, I don't remember much of anything until I woke up in the hospital. I lie in bed every night and work on it until I go to sleep, but I don't think I got a clear look at whoever attacked me. I can't say for sure it was Sanderson."

"It doesn't matter anymore—not to you, Nancy. You're

out of this one, and out of anything else, until you get back to being yourself."

"I'm enough like myself to view what's happening at a distance. It still looks to me like you've gotta pull out all the stops until you nail this asshole."

Quinn wondered whether the way she was mixing metaphors meant her mind still wasn't functioning at full capacity. Or maybe he was falling into the trap of playing amateur psychologist. "We're doing what we have to," he said. "We'll get him. You take care of yourself and let us worry about who gets nailed when the stops are pulled."

"Huh? You okay, Quinn?"

He grinned. "Maybe I need time off more than you do."

He heard the street door, then the office door open. Pearl had arrived.

"What's going on there?" Weaver asked on the phone.

"Pearl just came in."

"Tell her I said hello," Weaver said, and hung up.

Good buddies, as long as they're in different cities.

"Who was that?" Pearl asked, from where she was standing by the coffee machine.

"Weaver."

"Her brain still Jell-O?"

"More or less."

The street door made its clattering, pneumatic sound again. There were footfalls in the tile foyer, and then the office door flew open.

Quinn had expected to see Fedderman. Instead, Jerry Lido came bursting in. His khaki pants were amazingly wrinkled, his gray shirt was crookedly buttoned, and his tousled hair stuck out over his ears like wings.

Lido's eyes were swollen and bloodshot from fatigue, but his skinny body throbbed with energy. He was grinning with every snaggletooth and his face seemed to be illuminated from inside like a Halloween jack-o'-lantern's.

"I got something!" he almost shouted, his voice cracking as if he were a teenager grown too old for the choir.

"I hope to hell it isn't catching," Pearl said.

He aimed his glow of animated enthusiasm at her and then plopped heavily into her desk chair. "Pour me some coffee, Pearl."

She looked at him as if he'd gone insane. "I've got some boiling hot in this cup. Tell me where you want me to pour it."

Lido ignored her and turned his illuminated glassy stare toward Quinn. He sighed, as if he'd finally caught his breath. "I've got something," he repeated, only slightly more calmly.

"What have you got other than delirium tremens?" Pearl asked.

Quinn glanced at her and held out a hand palm down, signaling for her to lay off Lido so they could find out why he was so excited. He knew Lido and was sure that if he was this ecstatic he must at least think he had good reason. Besides, Quinn was sure that Lido wasn't drunk or hungover. Quinn recognized the symptoms. Lido was high on adrenaline while walking the jagged edge of exhaustion.

Lido beamed at both of them. "I worked the Internet all night, and I came up with a name."

No one moved or said anything for several seconds.

"The name we've been looking for?" Pearl asked.

Lido placed a cupped hand on each kneecap and nodded. "The name we've got for sure."

Pearl walked over to the brewer and poured him a cup of coffee.

Tanya Moody had overslept. Her first thought when she opened her eyes was that she shouldn't have taken that extra sleeping pill last night to calm her nerves. Daylight was streaming into the bedroom. She'd left the drapes opened wide and the window raised, so she could get some breeze during the first cool night forecast in weeks.

Tanya's second thought was that she was going to be late for work, and cascading behind that came the realization that something was wrong. She couldn't move. She became aware that she was breathing through her nose, and that realization made it suddenly difficult to breathe.

She tried to explore with her tongue, but even that was constricted. Her mouth was stuffed with material of some sort. Silk? She probed with her tongue's tip and found the backs of her teeth, managed to open her mouth slightly, and beyond the folds of material felt the tacky surface of . . . *tape!*

And the material jammed into her mouth *was* silk. . . .

She knew immediately what was happening. The open window she'd thought was far enough from the fire escape hadn't been far enough away at all.

She had a visitor.

Panic hit her as if she'd been Tasered. Her body vibrated and bucked, but she remained lying on her stomach, her wrists taped tightly behind her at the small of her back, her legs taped firmly together.

Finally the panic passed. The terror remained.

For some reason she thought of mermaids. Mermaids have no legs, only a single tail that they can flop around helplessly when out of the water. But mermaids could at least speak. With her panties wadded into a mass in her mouth, and her lips sealed with duct tape, Tanya could make only a low humming sound.

"I'm glad you're awake," a man's voice said.

She managed to swivel her head toward the sound, causing a sharp ache in her neck, as if she'd been jabbed with a needle. Outlined against the angled morning sunlight splashed on the white sheer curtains, she saw the dim silhouette of a man.

As he moved toward her she noticed something short and curved in his hand. She could tell by the way he was holding it—out away from his body and with respect—that it was a knife.

With an oddly delicate motion, he removed the thin sheet that was covering her.

Tanya was suddenly cold, and at the same time felt a spreading warm wetness beneath her as her bladder released. Until now, she had only thought she'd known fear.

He gently laid something over her head—the sheet—so that she couldn't see what was coming. She knew that he wanted each singular agony to be a surprise.

Two, three drops of liquid fell onto the sheet, and she smelled the acrid scent of ammonia. Then came a sound she recognized—the ratchet catch of a cigarette lighter—and another scent she knew. He'd lit a cigarette.

If there had been any doubt as to who had her, there was none now.

Tanya began to scream, over and over, sounding very much like a desperate bee trapped in a tightly sealed jar.

There was only one person close enough to hear her, and he wasn't going to help.

71

"So here's what I learned," Lido said, standing up from where he'd been seated in Pearl's chair.

Fedderman had come in. He stopped and stood still in obedience to Quinn's hand signal. The Q and A detectives were all there except for Vitali and Mishkin, who were still touching final bases in their fruitless search for the source of the killer's carpet-tucking knife.

Lido, drunk for a change on adrenaline rather than alcohol, began to pace as he spoke, three steps, then a quick turn, like a dance step, and three steps back. "I sifted through travel matches that occurred on or near the dates of the murders," he said. "Concentrated on male passengers between twenty-five and fifty years old and traveling alone."

"All this on the Internet?" Fedderman asked.

Lido glanced at him but didn't bother to answer. Quinn gave Fedderman a nod.

"Whaddya think, Feds?" Pearl said. "He was running around in Nikes?"

Lido ignored them all and continued: "This turned up a possibility. A passenger named Lincoln Evans flew from Kansas City, Missouri, into Hartford, Connecticut, on two occasions in the past three months. Hartford is only ninety-two miles from New York City. Both times the going and return flights bracketed Skinner murders, and both flights had layovers in St. Louis. Both times Evans paid cash for his ticket, and both times the airline made a note of his address for their database and for Homeland Security. Evans lives, or lived, in the small town of Edmundsville, Missouri."

Lido stood still and looked at them, as if expecting a reaction.

"Seems kind of spare," Pearl said.

"You don't get it yet?"

"No."

Lido grinned. "Only because I'm not finished."

Here was something Quinn hadn't seen in Lido—a flair for the dramatic. Probably a hopeful sign.

"I then went to work via the Internet"—Lido glanced at Fedderman—"on the car-rental agencies."

Quinn knew these were mostly questionable databases. He hoped no one would ask Lido about the legality of his Net searches. And how those searches would be used as evidence in court. Quinn was already thinking about how to put the monkey of illegal searches on Renz's back, where he could be sure methodology would never get in the way of results—or political glory.

"On both Hartford occasions," Lido said, "Lincoln Evans rented a Budget midsized car, paying cash and using his driver's license as identification. I managed to check deeper into the rental records."

"Hacked into them?" Fedderman asked.

"I don't like that term," Lido said, and ignored Fedderman. "Car-rental agencies keep scrupulous mileage records. Both times, Evans drove far enough to have visited New York City and then return to Hartford."

Lido sat back down in Pearl's chair and looked around, grinning in exhausted triumph.

Pearl returned his grin. "Now I do get it. Our killer's covering his tracks by not making any. He flies into nearby cities and then drives into New York."

"His killing ground," Fedderman said.

"And later he leaves New York the same way. I'm not finished checking other cities," Lido said, "but it'll be easier, now that we have a name."

"Lincoln Evans," Pearl said, as if the vowels left a bad taste.

"Great work!" Quinn said. And it was that, all right. Quinn knew that at the same time it might mean nothing other than that within the time frames of two of the Skinner murders, the same man, meeting their narrow criteria, visited a city within easy driving distance of New York. Maybe he was a business traveler with clients in Hartford and New York. Maybe he paid cash because he was a wise spender who didn't believe in credit. Maybe his credit had been revoked. Maybe he was a serial murderer trying to cover his tracks on the way to and from his kill zone.

Though what they had wasn't that much in and of itself, in the context of building a case, the information was specific.

Pearl was leaning a shoulder into the wall, obviously pleased by Lido's jittery but cogent presentation.

Fedderman was still standing stock still, working out in his mind what it all might mean.

The office had slipped into an anticlimactic torpor.

Quinn looked at Lido. "You had breakfast?"

Lido shook his head no. "Too busy to eat."

And too excited, Quinn thought. This was a major achievement for Lido. The discredited, ostracized alcoholic had come through with what might be the name of the killer. He had something to build on. But right now, Lido needed for his pulse rate to be brought down a few notches.

Quinn knew Lido must have done most of his work fueled on whatever was available to drink. This didn't seem the time to mention that.

Lido must have known what Quinn was thinking, because he smiled guiltily and shrugged.

"Time for real food," Quinn said. "Eggs, toast, sausages."

Lido knew that tone in Quinn's voice. It left no room for argument. He stood up out of Pearl's chair. "Okay, and some coffee."

"Decaf," Quinn said.

He was pleased to see Pearl smiling as they went out the door.

72

Edmundsville, the present

Edna Wellman was distraught when she phoned the sheriff's office, so Billy Noth passed the phone to Westerley. The sheriff and Edna's husband Joe had been hunting buddies before Joe's fatal heart attack five years ago.

"It's about my nephew Mathew," Edna said in a voice made soprano by . . . what, disbelief? Anger?

"He and I have met," Westerley said calmly, trying to slow down Edna. "He seems like a nice kid."

"Well, you wouldn't think so if . . ."

"If what?" Westerley wanted to get this call out of the way and tend to more important business, like surveying the week's traffic citations and felony statistics.

"If you come over here, I think you could better understand the problem."

Westerley sighed, hoping Edna hadn't heard. "Okay, Edna, I'll be right there."

The Wellman house, a 1970s brick ranch with two-car garage, was only three blocks from Westerley's office, on a tree-lined cross street of similar houses. Edna was waiting for him with the door open.

She was in her early fifties now, and had put on a lot of

weight since Joe's death. Her pretty, flesh-padded face was lined with concern. "Thanks for coming, Sheriff."

Not *Wayne*. A professional call.

"Somebody try to break in?" Westerley asked. There'd been a few house burglaries in the area over the past six months.

"Worse," Edna said.

She led Westerley to a small den where Joe used to go to smoke his cigars. The room hadn't changed much, except now there was a computer with a large monitor on the old maple desk.

On the monitor was a hefty blond woman having sex with a cucumber. Though he didn't know quite why, Westerley was glad to see that the cucumber was wearing a condom.

"This is mild," Edna Wellman proclaimed, looking away from Westerley and the image on the monitor, "compared to some of the other sites Mathew has been visiting."

Westerley coughed. "Well . . ."

"Isn't this kind of thing illegal?" Edna asked.

"It is if there are minors involved."

"Oh, I'm sure there are, on some of the sites."

"You've looked at other sites he's visited?"

"Yes, I thought I had to know what I was talking about, if I was going to confront Mathew."

"Good point. He's no dummy."

"I swear, Wayne, you wouldn't believe some of what goes on that a ten-year-old could visit if he swore he was twenty-one. There are safeguards to screen out minors, but there are also mere children who know more about computers than the people who designed the safeguards."

"Sometimes the people who produce this stuff use models who are of age but look a lot younger," Westerley said. He looked again at the woman on the screen. She didn't seem to be enjoying herself. "Mathew's what, twenty-two?"

"Just."

Westerley shrugged. "He's an adult, too."

Edna Wellman stared at him. "So what can we *do*, Wayne?"

"Where's Mathew now?"

"He left right after I walked in and found him looking at this filth. He's embarrassed, no doubt. He should be."

"I'm sure he is." Westerley moved the mouse along a series of blue numerals on the screen and clicked on one. A brunette with bangs was performing fellatio, not on a vegetable. She did look like a minor, but it was impossible to be sure. "I'll go look around, see if I can find Mathew. If I don't, and he comes back here, tell him I want to talk to him."

"I'll do that. And thanks." Edna shook her head. "He seems like such a normal young man."

"He is," Westerley said. "He's curious, is all."

"Then you don't think it's unusual for a boy—a young man—his age to visit these kinds of Internet sites?"

"It can't be," Westerley said. "Porn sites are the most visited places on the Internet."

"The women in those photographs, at least some of them, must have parents, husbands, maybe children."

"You left out money," Westerley said.

Edna looked disgusted. "Some world it's become."

"Some world," Westerley agreed.

73

Beth had used a brush to get around the edges of the porch floor with flat gray paint. That was the hard part, now that she was done with the scraping, and hammering in all the loose nails so they wouldn't stick up from the floor.

The floor had become so weathered that bare wood was peeking through the paint leading up to the door, and beneath the glider where people rested their feet. All she had to do now was pour paint into a tray and roll the floor. It wouldn't take very long, even though she'd be covering a large area.

She paused as she heard a car slow on the country road and turn into the driveway.

No, not a car—a truck. She could hear the rattling bass note of its big diesel engine.

As she watched, a gray, dusty truck cab parked near the short gravel jog to the house. It was one of the big rigs, with twin exhaust stacks protruding straight up on each side of the cab's sleeper. On the tops of the exhaust-blackened stacks were loosely hinged caps that bounced and danced as the engine idled. Behind the cab were only the greasy fifth-wheel connector plate, and air brake and electrical lines leading nowhere. No trailer, just the cab. There were numbers on the truck's door, meaningless to Beth. She stood and watched, the paintbrush forgotten in her hand.

The truck's door opened and Roy Brannigan swung down out of the cab.

Beth drew in her breath. Time seemed to collapse away beneath her, leaving her weightless and floating.

She and Roy hadn't seen each other in years. Beth was surprised by how her ex-husband had broadened, though he wasn't fat. More muscular, as if he worked out regularly in a gym. Or maybe driving, or loading and unloading trucks, had kept him in shape. She'd have known him at a glance, though, despite the buzz-cut hair and dark sunglasses.

He peeled off the tinted glasses and smiled at her, then took a few tentative steps toward the porch. He'd left the truck's engine idling. It sounded like a great beast's heartbeat, powerful, indestructible.

Beth walked to the top of the porch steps and stood looking at him. Somehow holding the brush gave her confidence, as if she might simply paint him out of her life again if he made trouble.

He moved a few steps closer so they could talk.

"Been a long while, Beth."

She said nothing.

"I'm driving a truck now, doing long-distance hauling. My route on this run took me close to where I knew you lived, so I thought I'd drop by and see how you were doing."

"I'm doing fine, Roy."

"Me, too, I guess."

"Eddie's fine, too."

At first he didn't seem to recognize the name. Then he said, "Good. I was gonna ask."

Sure you were.

"You look real good," Roy said, as if at a loss for words. He moved his scuffed black leather boots around on the gravel. "Look, Beth, I just wanted to let you know I was sorry about everything. What I did . . . how it happened . . . I upped and left you because of my religion."

"You still got religion, Roy?"

"I do, but you might say it's less severe. I mean, what I'm trying to say is, I wised up, like everybody does when time passes. I apologize for overreacting. You know, back when . . . it happened."

Beth chewed on her lower lip for a while, listening to the low, diesel beat of the truck. She didn't like this, Roy showing up this way out of nowhere.

"I've got a husband, Roy," she said.

He smiled. "I know you do. I checked on you. Fella in town mentioned Link's away on a trip someplace. That his name, Link?"

Mentioned it because you asked about him. "You know his name." Beth was beginning to feel the first cold touch of fear. "What is it you want, Roy?"

"It ain't to dig up the past. Except I would like to know that you at least sort of forgive me—no, not even forgive. I guess I'd like you to understand that I was more rigid in my thinking back then. Now I can't believe God would've approved of my actions. I've apologized to Him, and now I wanna apologize to you. I had no right to act like I did. I'm truly sorry."

She studied him. He did seem sincere. "All right, Roy. I can't forgive you, but I do understand." She wondered if there might be some way she could get into the house if he tried anything, hold him off long enough to phone Wayne Westerley. But, hell, Wayne was all the way over in Hogart. It'd take him just inside an hour to get here.

"I heard about Vincent Salas being released," Roy said. "Has that been making you uneasy in any way?"

"Not really," Beth lied.

"I'd be glad to go talk to him if you want."

"He wouldn't like that."

"You can't know for sure. His soul might need succor if not salvation."

"I'd prefer it if you'd just let all that drop, Roy. Let the past stay the past."

Roy seemed to think that over. "Okay, Beth, if that's what you want. But I got one question." Roy moved a few steps closer. "Even though things worked out the way they did, is it possible we could be friends?"

Beth got a firmer grip on the paintbrush handle. "I don't think I want that, Roy. I don't go around thinking ill of you every day, and I can't see where it does anybody any good to call up bad memories, or even good ones if they attach themselves to the bad. I've got a new life, and it looks like you do. Let's leave it that way."

Another step closer. "You sure that's what you want?" He squared his new, overpowering body to hers and leaned toward her.

Gravel crunched out near where the truck cab was parked, and Eileen Millvany, who lived with her mother two houses up the road, slowed her SUV and glanced over at Beth, then drove on.

Roy and his truck had been seen, and Roy knew it. That made Beth feel better, safer.

"I'm sure and I'll stay sure," she said.

Roy stood and stared at her, a kind of quizzical expression on his face, and then he nodded, turned around, and walked slowly toward his truck. The confused expression was one she'd never seen before. She remembered him being certain of everything when they were together. The younger Roy thought he knew all the answers before he'd even heard the questions.

He climbed back up into the cab, shifted gears, and the truck rumbled away. Nothing was left of it but a thin haze of dust and a final dying growl from the direction of the county road.

Beth tried to make herself believe Roy's appearance was

something other than an illusion. It was so strange and unexpected, him suddenly turning up here like that.

She looked down at the brush in her hand and saw that the paint on it had become tacky and the bristles were stuck together. It needed to be placed in the jar of turpentine, and then she could continue with what she'd been doing and roll the porch's paint-starved plank floor.

But not immediately.

She propped the brush in the turpentine jar and went inside the house.

She needed to make a phone call.

74

New York, the present

"At least a couple of days," Dr. Julius Nift said. "That's why it smells the way it does in here. But I've got other ways to tell: lividity, putrefaction in relation to ambient temperature—"

"All right, all right," Quinn said. He was the one who'd asked Nift how long the woman had been dead.

"Of course I'll be able to give you a more accurate estimate when I get her laid out at—"

"I know, I know," Quinn interrupted.

Pearl was standing dangerously close to Nift, looking down over his shoulder at Tanya Moody's corpse. Quinn caught her eye and gave her what he hoped was a cautionary look. Even in the initial stage of decomposition, it was obvious that Tanya Moody had been a gorgeous woman. Nift was almost sure to say something that might set off Pearl.

The CSU techs were busy in the front of the stylish but economically furnished apartment. There was a lot of polished wood and black vinyl. Tanya's dark tangle of hair seemed in some grisly way to go with the décor. She was nude, what had once been her lovely body marked by cigarette burns and intricate carving. Her gaping mouth was stopped with dried blood. A wad of material, probably her panties, that had been used to gag her, lay near her left shoulder. There was a lot of blood on the floor. The look on Tanya Moody's face suggested she'd died in unimaginable pain.

Quinn caught the slightest acrid whiff of ammonia. He leaned forward to confirm it was coming from the wadded panties and not from the contents of her voided bladder.

Nift had been watching him. "Very good, detective. That isn't the smell of urine. The killer must have brought Tanya back from merciful unconsciousness by applying a few drops of ammonia on the wadded panties in her mouth. She'd have to breathe in the fumes through her nose. A very effective method."

"Can you close her eyes?" Quinn asked.

"Why? She can't see one way or the other."

"Close her eyes," Quinn said.

Nift stopped probing and poking with his instruments and deftly closed the dead woman's eyes.

"Who found her?" Quinn asked.

A very tall uniformed cop standing just inside the bedroom door said, "A woman who lives across the street had an appointment at her place with the dead woman. Tanya never showed up, so she came over to see why not. When nobody answered her knock, she noticed the smell and called the super. They phoned, knocked, got no answer. Then the super used his key, and they found what you see on the floor. That's when they called us."

"What kind of appointment?" Pearl asked.

"Physical workout routine. The dead woman was a personal trainer. She made house calls, and also sold her clients home exercise equipment."

"I thought she might be some kind of athlete," Nift said, "with those legs."

"Where are the woman and super who found the body?" Quinn asked the uniformed cop, with a glance at Pearl.

"Super's in his basement apartment. Dianne Cross, the

one who was supposed to get the training, is down in the lobby. My partner's finishing up talking to her."

Quinn looked down at Nift. "What about Tanya Moody's tongue?"

"I probed," Nift said. "Preliminary finding is that it's been severed and is missing."

"May the bastard burn in hell," the tall cop said, to no one in particular.

Pearl said, "Amen."

"Can you turn her over?" Quinn asked.

"She won't object," Nift said. He carefully rotated the body, disturbing as little around it as possible. Rigor mortis had come and gone, so posed no problem. There were circular burns and complicated carvings on the victim's back, too. Her wrists were taped behind her, and where her fingers had rested near the small of her back was something she might have attempted to write in her own blood. The blood marks looked to Quinn as if they might mean nothing other than a doomed woman wriggling her fingers. Or the marks might spell out the letters *T* and *S*.

Quinn called Pearl over and pointed out the marks. They both stooped and looked more closely.

"What's that look like to you?" Quinn asked.

"I'm not sure," Pearl said.

"If I can join the Rorschach test," Nift said, "that looks like *TS*. A dying message."

"If she scribbled it behind her back," Pearl said, "she might have written the letters backward and meant *ST*."

"Then the *S* would be backward," Quinn said.

"Maybe," Pearl conceded.

Nift said, "I already checked the bathroom mirror. There's nothing written on it, or on any of the other mirrors."

"Playing detective again," Quinn said.

"Somebody's got to." Nift probed a flaccid breast with some kind of silver instrument. When its point broke the skin, Quinn had to look away. He heard Pearl's sharp intake of breath.

"It was no worse than her flu shot," Nift said, amused. "A mere prick."

"You're the biggest prick around here," Pearl said, "even if you're not the sharpest."

Nift looked at her seriously. "Have you had your flu shot?"

"Have you had your kick in the balls?" Pearl asked.

That was when Vitali and Mishkin arrived. Sal was his usual stubby and harried self, given to bursts of gravel-voiced comments and abrupt movement. Mishkin was quiet and looked slightly ill. The mentholated cream he used at homicide scenes lay glossy on his bushy mustache. Just standing near Harold could clear your sinuses.

Quinn instructed Pearl to fill in both detectives while he went downstairs to the lobby to talk with Dianne Cross.

He was on the elevator when his memory lit up. *TS.* He checked the tattered list he kept folded in his wallet and found that he was right. Those were the initials of Tom Stopp, the man who'd been released on DNA evidence after serving a prison term because of Tanya Moody's inaccurate identification.

Quinn wondered if Tom Stopp had an alibi for the time of Tanya Moody's death.

Can it really be as simple as this? The victim scrawls her murderer's initials with her own blood?

There would be ways to find out soon enough. They would find Stopp and lean on him hard. The truth would be in how he'd react, in what could be read in his eyes. Soon they would know if the awkwardly scrawled blood letters took their form coincidentally, or meant nothing at all.

Tom Stopp had an alibi, all right. Early the evening of Tanya Moody's murder, he'd been rushed to the hospital after suffering a heart attack. Surgery had been performed. He was still confined to bed.

"The elephant sat on my chest," he said, when Quinn visited him in his room at the Truman Rehabilitation Center. He grinned up from his bed. "That's what we heart attack survivors say."

"Have they found the problem?" Quinn asked.

Stopp nodded. "A weak left ventricle. They tried to fix it with drugs, but that didn't work, so they put in a little thingy that'll give it a jolt of electricity if it stops beating regular. That's what I think they said, anyway. I was still kinda groggy with whatever they gave me to put me out."

"I was you, I'd find out for sure," Quinn said.

"Believe me, I will." He stared up at Quinn. "You're here about Tanya Moody."

"How'd you know?"

"I watch a lot of news." His gaze flicked to a small television supported by a cocked steel elbow in a corner near the ceiling. "The world's going all to hell."

"Nothing new there," Quinn said.

Stopp raised an arm with an IV tube attached to it. "Listen, aside from having a perfect alibi, I'd never do harm to that woman. What happened to her, I mean the rape, was shitty, but I never had anything to do with it. Shook up like she was, she made a wrong identification. I don't hold it against her."

"You must a little," Quinn said.

"That's what I'd be telling you if I was guilty of killing her, trying to act the honest innocent. But the way I see it, serving time on a bad rap is just another example of the way my life's been screwed up and plagued by bad luck from the beginning, when I was a breech-birth baby."

"There are lives like that," Quinn agreed.

"It's almost enough to make you believe in astrology."

"Well, your stars were aligned right for this one. Your life was being saved around the same time Tanya Moody was losing hers."

"Her turn, I guess," Stopp said. He seemed to get no satisfaction from the observation.

Quinn nodded good-bye and moved toward the door. He turned. "By the way, is Stopp your real name?"

Stopp seemed puzzled. "Whaddya mean?"

"I mean, is it short for something?"

"Craps, losing lottery numbers, second-best poker hands, horses that stumble coming out of the gate."

"Really, what's your full family name?"

"Lance Thomas Stopp. That's it."

"No kidding. *Lance* has got some pizzazz. Your mom shoulda gone with that one."

"I dunno. For whatever reason, my mom and dad called me Tom, even when I was in diapers. The wrong name from the beginning. Maybe that's why my life's been all screwed up."

"That kind of thing can happen," Quinn said.

He wondered if Stopp had any brothers, and if so, what were their first initials.

"You got any siblings?" he asked Stopp.

"A brother Marvin out in California, and a sister Terri, is all. They don't talk to me anymore. Maybe because I owe them more money than I can ever repay."

Quinn asked himself if there could be so much self-pity in the room that it might be contagious. It was certainly suffocating.

"Take care of yourself," he said, and left before the walls closed in on him.

"It's way too late for that," Stopp said behind him as the door closed.

The phone call scared the hell out of Sanderson the second he recognized the voice. The call came in over his cell phone while he was walking along Central Park West. *Unknown Number,* it said on his phone's ID panel. And when he heard the voice he understood why.

"I don't like it when plans go wrong," the Skinner said.

Sanderson had stopped walking and stood leaning against a building in a shallow alcove where he had something like privacy. "What are you talking about? Tan—The job got done. It's all over the news."

"That's not what I'm talking about."

"I gave you your ticket stub, like we agreed."

"That's not necessarily enough. We also agreed on a patsy. You guaranteed me that Stopp wouldn't have an alibi, that he'd be by himself home in bed."

Sanderson was confused. He'd tracked Stopp. Knew his habits and routine. "Wasn't he?"

"No. I checked. I always check. When the woman we're talking about was losing her final battle, Stopp was almost losing his. He had a heart attack and was taken to the hospital in an ambulance. Lots of people that wear white outfits will testify he was nowhere near the apartment when the woman died."

"Heart attack? You serious?"

"Serious as . . . well, you know."

Sanderson's confusion was fast becoming anger. His fear was moderated by the fact that the Skinner was far away, on the other end of a phone connection.

Or is he far away?

Sanderson's gaze darted this way and that. *Unknown Number.* Any of the many buildings around him might contain a public phone. And there were cheap, disposable bubble-packed phones that didn't provide caller ID. "Listen, I couldn't know about a heart attack. I mean, that was something out of my control."

The laugh on the other end of the connection chilled Sanderson's blood. "Everything is out of your control. You're like the hunter who tracked a tiger to its lair and found out his gun wasn't loaded."

"Listen—"

But the Skinner had broken the connection.

Tiger . . . Lair . . .

Sanderson stood with his mind whirling. The hunter analogy had scared the hell out of him. This was terrible. Stopp had been intended as an insurance policy, a patsy held in reserve, a prime suspect with a motive to kill Tanya Moody, and no alibi. Between that and the Skinner's ball-game ticket stub printed with the time and date of Tanya's murder, the Skinner would have had a tight alibi. But instead of alibi insurance, what Stopp had provided was a heart attack.

That Sanderson could be blamed for not knowing about it ahead of time was vastly unfair. How could anyone have predicted a coronary event? Or was he supposed to have had a backup plan? Some way to maintain control of the situation?

Well, maybe . . .

Was the Skinner right? Did Sanderson have any control at all?

Of anything?

Sanderson couldn't stop looking around, searching with worried eyes. It had been a long time since he'd been so unnerved. He almost dropped his cell phone trying to slide it back in his pocket. It took a few minutes before his hands stopped trembling.

The Skinner walked away from the lobby pay phone in the Clarington Hotel. Across the street and down two blocks, he entered another hotel and went to the bar, where he ordered a Dewar's on the rocks with a splash of water and sat by himself three stools away from two men and a woman. They were watching an old black-and-white *Honeymooners* rerun on the TV over the bar. Jackie Gleason was bouncing around in his bus driver's uniform. Art Carney, as Norton the sewer worker, was patiently trying to calm him, but Gleason was fuming and out of control.

The Skinner smiled grimly. *Control.*

He reviewed in his mind his phone call to Sanderson. Sanderson had been right in that he, Sanderson, couldn't control something as unpredictable as a heart attack. That was the problem. It wasn't so much that the Skinner couldn't trust Sanderson; for now, he could be depended upon. But eventually, if Sanderson lost his fear, he might attempt blackmail even though he, himself, would be an accomplice to murder.

But all that was in a possible future. The problem with Sanderson now was that he'd become a complication as well as a coconspirator. *He* was something else that could go wrong.

The Skinner needed—no, *demanded*—perfection in planning and execution. Complete control. Imponderables made him uneasy. Sanderson was a parasite the Skinner hadn't so much minded, because he was useful. Not as useful as he thought, but useful. But Sanderson, by his own admission, couldn't control matters. Which meant that the Skinner couldn't control Sanderson.

On the other hand, if the Skinner eliminated Sanderson, it would open an entire new avenue of investigation, create a new vulnerability. And for now, Sanderson and his ticket stubs *were* useful. And who knew what kind of precautions Sanderson had taken? Were there Pandora's boxes that would automatically open if he were killed? There might be a sealed, incriminating letter in some lawyer's files, or video recordings lying in a safety deposit box, that would be examined upon his death.

Alice entered the drab apartment carrying a bag of groceries, and Norton quickly stepped between her and Ralph to protect her. Gleason, as Ralph, balled his right and righteous fist, rolled his eyes, and then sat down at a bare table and buried his head in his arms. He wept in frustration.

The Skinner sipped his scotch.

The people at the bar, watching the TV, laughed at something Norton had said sixty years ago.

The Skinner weighed his options.

75

Hogart, the present

"You want me to drive over there?" Westerley asked, after Beth had described Roy Brannigan's unexpected visit.

"No," Beth said on the phone. "He didn't actually threaten me, and he must have had to keep moving to stay on his route."

"If the whole thing wasn't a load of bullshit," Westerley said.

"I believed him about the driving job. I saw the actual truck. One of those big diesel things the drivers leave running even when they go in someplace for lunch."

"When's Link due home?"

"Not for two more days."

"I don't like it, you alone in that house, especially tonight when we know Roy's in the area. I could talk to the state patrol. Maybe they'd send a car around."

"They'd tell you there wasn't enough reason. Even I know they don't have enough people to protect every woman who suspects she might be in danger."

"True enough," Westerley said. "How'd Roy seem to you after all these years?" He was trying to get a feel for just how real a threat Roy Brannigan might pose. After all, the business about the rape and trial was a long time ago. If time didn't heal completely, it did tend to cool passions.

"Physically he looked about the same," Beth said, "only bigger and stronger than I remembered. And he seemed to be calmed down some when it came to his religious beliefs."

"Did his apology seem sincere?"

Beth hesitated. "I can't say, Wayne."

Westerley thought about it. "I could have Billy Noth drive out to your place and keep an eye on things till morning."

"Your deputy'd just love to spend the night sitting in a parked car," Beth said. "Or hiding in the woods."

"He could sack out on the couch, Beth. Billy's a light sleeper."

Beth didn't say anything for a long time.

"Wayne?"

"Yeah?"

"How 'bout you, after all? I'd like you to come over."

"Sleep on the couch?" Westerley asked.

"Don't try to be funny, Wayne."

Nothing out of the ordinary seemed to happen at Beth's that night. And Westerley didn't sleep on the couch.

When they got up the next morning, he took Beth to the Bob Evans near the Interstate cloverleaf and they had breakfast. Westerley had eggs and biscuits, Beth a waffle and sausages.

"I appreciate you coming here," Beth said, over their second cups of coffee.

"It's not like I got nothing in return," Westerley said with a smile.

There was a rumble outside the window by their booth, and they looked out to see a big eighteen-wheeler with a dusty black cab roll in. It parked some distance from the building with a hiss of air brakes. They stared and saw a short blond man climb down from the cab, stretch, and swagger toward the restaurant. He looked nothing like Roy Brannigan.

"I'm still jumpy," Beth said.

"I should come back tonight." Westerley said.

Beth smiled at him and stroked his bare forearm. It made the hairs on his arm rise up. "You'd do this all over again?"

He nodded. "I like the biscuits."

"I don't think I need anyone tonight," Beth said. "Roy's probably two states away by now. Besides, Wayne, you've got a job to look after."

"The Hogart Bank hasn't been robbed in forty years."

"Overdue, I'd say."

"Has Link got a gun?"

"His twelve-gauge shotgun's locked up out in the garage."

"I mean a handgun."

"Yeah. In the closet. An old Colt semiautomatic. I know how to use it."

"Keep it by the bed tonight."

"I'll do that. I promise."

Westerley did drive back to Hogart after breakfast, but not before making sure Beth was safely installed at home.

The first thing Westerley did when he got into town was to call his deputy, Billy Noth, into the office and give him the rest of the day off. Then he told Billy the situation with Beth and instructed him to drive to her place this evening and spend the night keeping an eye on the house without telling her.

"I can hardly recall what Roy Brannigan looks like," Billy said.

"Let's hope you aren't reminded tonight. By the way, Billy, Beth's got a handgun she keeps by the bed."

"Great," Billy said. Then he laughed. "You warning me away, Sheriff?"

"Get out of here, Billy," Westerley said.

When Billy was gone, Westerley called his contact at the state lab and asked if there was any progress on the DNA samples he'd sent in. There'd been a family killing in St. Louis that was put on top priority, he was told. It might be several days before he heard about his samples.

Westerley's next phone call was to his part-time clerk and dispatcher Bobi Gregory. He asked her to handle the phone and to call him if anything important came up. He wouldn't be far away, over in Jefferson City, where the Vincent Salas trial had been held.

Something about the time of the rape, and the Salas trial, was nibbling at the edges of Westerley's memory, but he couldn't identify it.

He spent most of the morning in the City Hall records room, reading the trial transcript. Salas seemed guilty again.

Only he wasn't. Not according to DNA.

Westerley went to another department and gained access to the section where evidence was stored from trials dating back years. He easily found the box containing the Salas trial evidence.

It angered him when he touched Beth's torn panties, the three empty Wild Colt beer cans. Salas had never reclaimed the contents of his pockets, which were in a separate brown envelope. When he examined the envelope's contents, Westerley understood why. The envelope contained a pocket comb, a cheap penknife, and sixty-two cents in loose change. A worn leather wallet held two one-dollar bills, a punch card that would earn free coffee at a restaurant in Flagstaff, Arizona, and an expired Missouri driver's license. One of the loose nickels attracted Westerley's attention. It was dated 1919, or maybe 1918. It was hard to tell, as worn as the nickel was. Westerley fingered the coin for a while, then dropped it back in the envelope with the rest of the contents, put the envelope back in the evidence box, and returned everything to its dusty space in the rows of metal shelves.

When he left it struck him as always how so much chaos and violence could be reduced to items in neat rows of boxes, and ignored to be rendered harmless by time.

76

When Westerley got back to Hogart and entered his office, Bobi Gregory was seated at the desk by the window. Across from her, Mathew Wellman was sitting in one of the padded black vinyl chairs with wooden arms. Mathew was pretending to read a supermarket tabloid. It featured the President of the United States smiling and waving as he boarded a flying saucer.

"My Aunt Edna sent me," Mathew said.

Westerley was thrown for a moment. Then he remembered Mathew's surreptitious viewing of pornography on the computer. He motioned with his head for Mathew to follow him into his office.

After settling in behind his desk, Westerley told Mathew to have a seat in a nearby chair that was exactly like the one he'd been seated in out in the anteroom.

Mathew looked down at the floor. "All I can say is I'm sorry about what happened, sir. I never meant for Aunt Edna to see that stuff."

"I bet you didn't," Westerley said. "Some of those women looked seriously underaged."

"Aw, they can make them look like that. You probably mean the one with the—"

"The sites are against the law," Westerley said, but he supposed they'd have to be looked at one by one to really determine that.

"Actually, they're—"

"I'll talk to your Aunt Edna and make sure she knows you were just satisfying your curiosity, and you're not a sex maniac."

Mathew seemed surprised by this sudden apparent termination of what he'd assumed would be a major and historic ass-chewing from an expert. He wasn't sure quite how to react. "I know pornography can become an addiction, sir."

"Yeah, yeah," Westerley said, noticing that Mathew was regarding him with a new attentiveness.

Mathew said nothing, sensing when to hold his cards close.

"You believe that stuff?" Westerley asked.

"About the addiction?"

"No. About the president and that flying saucer."

No fool, Mathew, knew that wasn't really the question. He said, "I don't dismiss it out of hand."

"You notice that computer on the table out in the other room?" Westerley asked.

"Sure, I did. Nice setup with plenty of power and storage. It's got that new chip that makes it unbelievably fast. If you wanted to play games—"

"I do," Westerley said.

Mathew grinned. "What kind of games?"

"Depends on what you and that computer can do. The state just bought it and I'm still lost on it. Probably always will be, to some extent. It's a generational thing. Seems that the younger people are, assuming they been weaned, the better they are with all this tech stuff."

"Weaned?"

"It's an old expression. Like *carbon copy*."

"You're funning me," Mathew said.

"Not really. People over a certain age have a difficult time getting the hang of computers. Bobi, out there, she mostly downloads recipes and sends e-mail and photographs, so she's not much help so far. Billy Noth might as well be flying the starship *Enterprise* for the first time. What I want calls for somebody who can make the most use of that expensive advanced technology. Really make it hum."

"That would be me," Mathew said.

"I'd find somebody younger if I could," Westerley said, wondering where the *sir* went.

"I'm in the right spot at the right time."

"That you are, Mathew. On the spot, you might say."

"I want to do something," Mathew said, "to repay you for keeping me out of trouble with Aunt Edna, and with the law. And for saving me a lot of embarrassment."

So young to be playing the game, Westerley thought. "I haven't done anything yet," he said.

Mathew nodded but said nothing. His bland, reassuring face was unreadable. The lad would go far.

"What's the expression used when you go where you aren't supposed to be on the Internet?" Westerley asked. "I mean, other than if you're looking at porn sites."

"Hacking," Mathew said.

"Do you possess that skill, Mathew?"

"It's more an art than a skill."

"So are you an artist?"

Mathew smiled. "Think Picasso."

Westerley stood up and came around from behind his desk. "Come with me to the other room and familiarize yourself with that computer," he said. "I'll send Bobi home to make a pie, and then go see your Aunt Edna. When I get back, I'll tell you what I need."

Mathew stood up, grinning. "I wonder what Aunt Edna would think if she knew we were partners in crime."

Westerley didn't smile. "You're going to have to learn, Mathew, not to pull my chain."

But Westerley knew Mathew wasn't exactly joking. He recognized the expression in the young nerd's face, the ironically dumb staring look in his eyes. Hero worship. Maybe it was the way the porno thing was handled. Maybe the uniform. Maybe the gun.

Westerley shook his head. *Terrific. I'm the idol of a kid smarter than I am.*

Link kissed Beth on the cheek when he came home. She tried not to react too obviously, but she wondered if he'd noticed her resistance, the slight drawing away and stiffening of her body.

If he did, he gave no indication. He sighed contentedly, like a man glad to be home, and carried his blue nylon suitcase into the bedroom. It was a roomy piece of luggage, a suit carrier that had lots of zippered pockets. It could be folded twice, and somehow managed to qualify as a carry-on and fit in an overhead compartment.

Beth followed him into the bedroom and watched him unpack.

"Add to your collection?" she asked.

He smiled as he tossed a pair of socks onto the laundry pile. "Not my personal one, no. But I picked up some valuable antebellum coins for the company." She noticed, not for the first time in the past few years, that Link had even begun to talk in a slightly different way, as if he were more educated. Not so much like the uncomplicated country guy she'd met years ago in a roadhouse with a parking lot full of pickup trucks.

Of course, he might simply have cleaned up his English to go with his suit-and-tie job.

"They should be pleased."

"They usually are, Beth. That's why they keep me busy

traveling. It looks like I'll have to be gone next weekend, too. Big numismatic convention in Denver."

"Nowhere near New York," Beth said.

Link stopped what he was doing and stared at her. "Why would you say that?"

"I don't know. You go to New York a lot, don't you?"

"Hardly ever. That place is too hectic, far as I'm concerned."

She shrugged. "Well, Denver next time."

He stopped unpacking and walked over to her. She stood very still as he gave her a hug.

"You don't think I like being away so often, do you?" he asked.

"I know you like to travel."

"Sure, I do. It's the being-away part I don't like. We're doing okay with me in this job, and later on I can transfer to something that doesn't involve so much travel. Or maybe even get another job altogether."

Beth made herself rest her head against his shoulder. "You're right, of course."

He kissed her forehead, as if that would make everything better, then went back to continue unpacking. "Heard anything from Eddie?"

"He sent an e-mail. I saved it for you. He needs money."

Link grinned. "Don't we all?"

He'd finished placing his blue oxford shirt, and most of the other clothes he'd worn during his trip, on a pile on the floor. Beth moved around the bed and scooped up the wadded clothes, using the shirt as a makeshift sack. "I'll put these in the washer."

"Thanks, hon."

"You might want to wear some of them on your Denver trip."

"Might," he agreed, grinning at her. "I'll check the e-mail, then grab a beer and sit out on the porch while the washer runs. Let me know when there's enough water pressure for me to take a shower."

"Sounds like a plan," Beth said.

These days, everything sounded like a plan.

77

New York, the present

The blue-eyed guy could mambo. Jane Nixon had to give him that.

He never seemed to get tired. They'd been out on the dance floor at Salsa Caliente for almost half an hour. She got to rest a bit during a merengue, but not much.

He was wearing her out, and nobody would say Jane wasn't in shape.

She spent most of her time at Davida's restaurant down in the Village, on her feet and moving as she waited tables. Most of her money she spent on dance lessons, and dancing here at Salsa Caliente or at Move On. Both clubs were only blocks from her apartment, easy walks. Since she'd taken up dancing six months ago, she'd lost ten pounds, and her slender body had acquired muscular definition.

But the blue-eyed guy was too much.

She stopped dancing and stepped back, breathing hard. The backs of her legs ached. She actually said, "Whew!"

"You okay?" he asked, looking her in the eye. He was on the tall side and built like a museum statue, if you could imagine a statue dressed in pleated black slacks and a bright red tight T-shirt with *Salsa* spelled out in sequins across the chest.

"Tired, is all," Jane said, smiling.

He walked with her back to a table where he'd been sitting with half a dozen of his friends. They were all up dancing now. The blue-eyed guy raised a hand to get the attention of a waiter and ordered them both Jack Daniel's and water. Each knew what the other drank, yet they'd never asked each other their names. They were here to dance, that was all.

"I'm all in," Jane said, after downing half her drink. "Time to go home and collapse."

He smiled at her. "We could collapse together."

"All I know about you," Jane said, "is you're a terrific dancer."

"That isn't enough?"

She laughed. "Maybe someday." She glanced at her watch.

"I'm Martin," he said, pronouncing it Mar*teen*. He raked his fingers through his sweat-damp blond hair.

Jane laughed harder. "You sure look Latin."

"Gerhardt Martin," he said.

"Yeah, so am I."

She patted the back of his sweaty hand and stood up to leave.

"Gonna be dancing tomorrow night?" he asked.

"Yeah."

"Maybe that'll be the someday. You know?"

She grinned. "See you, Gerhardt."

"See you right back, Gerhardt." He raised his glass to her as she walked away along the edge of the dance floor.

She'd checked her purse when she'd come in. After claiming it and glancing through it pretending to look for a tissue, but actually making sure nothing was missing, she went out into the lingering heat.

The streets were almost deserted, but she didn't have far to go. There was just about enough strength left in her legs to make it up the steps to her third-floor walk-up apartment.

She'd keyed the dead bolt and opened the door when she sensed movement behind her. There was no time to react. A hand shoved her between her shoulder blades and she went stumbling into the dimly lit apartment.

Jane had been raised in a tough area of Detroit and was no pushover. She didn't lose her head, and in an instant she was adrenaline fueled. Jane the dancer became Jane the fighter.

She heard the snick of the dead bolt. He was locking them in, not rushing, assuming she'd be disoriented and paralyzed with terror. Jane had been replacing her key in her purse when she was shoved. Her hand stayed in her purse as she stumbled across the room and fell.

She turned and he was coming for her, as she knew he would. A dark silhouette in the shadowy living room. There was something in his hand, a short, curved, and sharply pointed knife.

Christ!

She'd read the papers, watched the news, and she knew who this must be.

And for a split second she *was* paralyzed with terror.

The blue-eyed guy? Gerhardt?

No. Too small. And he didn't move like Mr. Blue Eyes.

She wished now she'd accepted the blue-eyed guy's suggestion that he come home with her.

As the dark form with the knife advanced on her, Jane made herself wait, made herself be still. Her hand that held the small aerosol canister of mace in her purse was perspiring. She slid the button forward to take the device off safety, and waited, waited. . . . The training she'd taken had made it clear that for this to work, her attacker had to be close. She hunched her shoulders, turned half away from him, as if cowering and helpless.

When he was almost close enough to slash with the knife,

she whirled and rose with a strength that surprised even her and extended her right hand that was gripping the mace canister.

Work! Please work!

The canister was only about a foot away from his face when she depressed the top button and a strong spray of pungent liquid struck him square in the eyes.

Surprise! You sick bastard!

He gave a strangled growl and flailed with his arm, striking her hard in the wrist and causing the hissing mace canister to go flying. She felt an immediate burning sensation in her eyes and when she tried to breathe, her nose and throat contracted and tears came. She knew she'd inhaled some of the mace when he knocked the canister away.

She could still see enough to find the bedroom door. She ran for it, got inside the bedroom, and slammed and locked the door with the knob latch. That should keep him away for about five seconds.

There was a lot of noise from the living room, and something—sounded like a lamp—fell to the floor.

The door to the hall opened and slammed. Footsteps like crazy descended the wooden stairs. Not rhythmically, but as if he was bouncing off the walls and banister.

He's not coming after me! Thank God!

Coughing and gagging, Jane crawled to the phone by the bed and yanked it by the cord down to the floor where she could reach it. That was when she noticed blood on her skirt. Her left forearm, which she must have unconsciously used to block the knife, was bleeding.

She saw immediately that the blood was coming from a small nick, a minor injury that probably wouldn't even require stitches. Looking at it, imagining what might have happened, sickened her. She sat leaning with her back against the wall, gasping for oxygen, and placed the phone in her lap.

Squinting to focus tear-blurred eyes, she tried to punch out 911 but kept getting it wrong.

78

The Skinner's eyes were still watering. He remained seated on a park bench, where he'd been for almost two hours.

Fortunately he had his sunglasses with him. Unless someone noticed the tear tracks on his cheeks, he wouldn't draw much attention. He was simply another New Yorker basking in a beautiful morning.

Last night had become a horror. How he'd even gotten to the park was a marvel of luck and ingenuity. Since the pepper spray or mace, or whatever it was, had struck him squarely in the eyes, he could barely see, and there was no way he could stop his eyes from watering.

At first he *could* still see, at least slightly, but once he was outside the building, he soon became blinded by the intensity of his tears. They were like acid.

He'd moved fast initially, bumping into things. He had to get as far away as possible from the screaming that was sure to follow.

And Jane Nixon did find her way outside and screamed. She screamed over and over. But by then he was almost a block away and barely heard. The lucky punch he'd gotten in before running must have dazed her for a while. Good luck to go with the bad.

Though he didn't remember actually working out the idea in his mind, he'd almost immediately dug the sunglasses from his pocket and pretended to be blind—legally blind. Why else would someone be wearing dark glasses on a New York street at two in the morning?

He'd managed to wave and attract the attention of a compassionate cabby, who pulled his taxi to the curb and talked him into the backseat step by step, like an air controller instructing a novice pilot how to land.

The Skinner put on a smile and thanked him, then gave him an intersection by Central Park as a destination.

After a few blocks, the cabby said, "How'd you come to be out wandering by yourself . . . I mean, not being able to see and all?"

"I've been blind since I was ten years old," the Skinner said, "but my eyes are the only parts of me that don't work well. Believe it or not, my girlfriend threw me out of her apartment."

"In the middle of the night? Morning? Whatever? Hell of a thing to do to someone sight impaired."

"It was mostly my fault. I picked a bad time to confess that once, in a moment of weakness, I made love to her . . . I'm almost ashamed to say this."

"Go ahead," the cabbie said. "I've heard everything. Taxis are like confessionals."

"I had sex with her mother."

The cabbie shook his head and laughed. "Pardon me. I know it ain't funny. But I can see how it could happen. I mean, my mother-in-law had a body made me wish my wife took after her and not her father. Why the hell did you tell her?"

"Conscience," said the Skinner. "I've always been plagued by my conscience. Don't make the same mistake. You can see where it gets you."

"Not to worry about me," the cabbie said. They drove in silence for a while. "I gotta ask . . ."

"The mother," the Skinner said.

The cabbie laughed again. "Makes sense. More experience." He made a left turn and headed toward the park. "I guess you won't make that mistake again, huh?"

"Neither mistake," the Skinner said, easing over to where the cabbie couldn't see him in the rearview mirror. He raised his tinted glasses and dabbed at his watering eyes with his shirtsleeve.

If he could make it into the park and stay out of sight, hide in the bushes or woods for a while, he should be able to wait until whatever Jane Nixon had sprayed in his eyes had worn off, at least to the point where he could see clearly and his eyes weren't so itchy and watery. It wouldn't hurt for it to be daylight out, either.

When the cab came to a stop and the cabbie called out the fare, the Skinner handed him what he thought was a twenty-dollar bill and told him to keep the change.

"You sure?" the cabbie asked.

"Sure," said the Skinner, and opened the cab door on what he figured was the sidewalk side.

"You want some help?" the cabbie asked.

"No. I'll just lean on that wall a little while and I'll be fine. This is my neighborhood, so it's familiar to me. I'll be able to figure out enough to make my way on my own."

"You positive?"

"Positive," the Skinner confirmed. "I don't want to seem stubborn, but I like to think I'm not completely helpless."

"Okay. I can understand that. Good luck to you, friend."

The Skinner waited until he heard the cab drive away; then he made his way not toward one of the apartment buildings behind him, but toward the park. Through his tears he could see oncoming headlights. They were some distance up the street, so he knew he'd be able to cross safely enough.

As for Central Park at night, that could be dangerous.
The Skinner had to smile.

Fedderman didn't feel like getting out of bed and going to work. Mostly, he didn't feel like leaving Penny. He looked over at her across the white plain of his pillow. It felt so natural waking up next to her, smelling her perfume, feeling the warmth of her. As if they'd been doing this for decades instead of days.

Penny was breathing deeply and evenly, her lips slightly parted. Fedderman couldn't know for sure, but he thought she might be smiling in her sleep.

It was ironic, Fedderman thought, how something so tragic could be the source of something as wonderful as his relationship with Penny. It would seem, since he was part of the investigation into her sister's murder, that the gruesome crime would be a barrier between them. Instead, it seemed to make them closer, as if sharing the knowledge of such a thing had created a bond. They understood intimately the fickle nature of death and appreciated each other all the more. That the death was so vivid and real made life all the more so.

His cell phone on the table by the bed began vibrating and buzzing loudly, bouncing on the smooth wood surface. Fedderman knew that if he didn't grab it fast it would dance off the table. If it missed the throw rug, it might shatter on the hardwood floor.

He located the phone by touch almost immediately, closed his hand around it, and drew it close to him. It pulsed again, like a live bird cupped in his hand. He was aware of Penny, a pair of sleep-puffed eyes. She was up on one elbow, curious to know who was calling.

Fedderman looked at caller ID and pressed the talk button, silently mouthing *work* to Penny. She let her head fall back on the pillow.

"Where are you, Feds?" Quinn's voice asked on the phone.

"Whaddya mean, where am I?" *Not that it's anybody's business.* Fedderman felt the light touch of Penny's fingertips on his bare stomach, then his thigh.

"Never mind," Quinn said. "Where you need to be is what concerns me. Come in to the office ASAP. Something interesting's going on."

Something interesting here, too. "What is it?" Fedderman asked.

But Quinn was no longer on the phone.

"Damn it!"

"Something wrong?" Penny asked.

"The only thing I know for sure is wrong is that I have to get dressed and leave."

Fedderman wouldn't mention it to Penny, but as he came more awake he felt a growing eagerness to learn the reason for Quinn's call. There'd been something in Quinn's voice, the controlled urgency of a predator closing in on its prey. Signaling the rest of the pack. Fedderman the predator had heard the message and caught the mood. Penny couldn't be expected to understand that, when Fedderman didn't himself.

He did know that over a week had passed since Tanya Moody's body was discovered. It was about time for the Skinner to take another victim, spill more blood. He was following a classic serial-killer pattern, striking more often and with increasing viciousness.

Fedderman climbed out of bed, stood on the cool hardwood floor, and looked around. He even stooped to glance under the bed.

Where the hell . . . ?

"What's going on?" Penny asked, propped back up on her elbow.

"Jockey shorts," Fedderman said, "if I can find them."

"Go ahead and take your shower," Penny said, getting out of bed. "I'll find your shorts. If I don't, you can wear something of mine."

It took Fedderman a few seconds to realize she was joking.

Out on the sidewalk, he felt an exhilarating disconnection from the people around him. They were on their way to work, maybe some of them with night jobs coming home from work, doing normal things, thinking everyday thoughts.

Fedderman knew he looked like one of them, but this morning he was different.

Behind him lay the woman he loved, sexually sated and alone, and he was on the hunt. Ancient blood ruled his thinking. If the tone of Quinn's voice was any indication, they were closing in on a killer.

Fedderman's wrist brushed his thigh, and his shirt cuff came unbuttoned. He didn't notice. He quickened his pace.

79

The office was warm but dry, and not much street noise filtered in from outside. Expectancy charged the air like high-tension electricity.

Quinn was waiting until Fedderman had arrived before going into detail for Vitali, Mishkin, and Pearl.

Fedderman entered the office and glanced around. "So where's the suspect?"

Quinn looked at Fedderman's eyes. *He's joking, but he's locked in.*

"You said on the phone you had something interesting," Fedderman said. "I figured there'd been an arrest."

"You seem pissed off," Pearl said. "Is there some personal reason you didn't want to come in a little early this morning?"

Pearl and her antenna, Fedderman thought. But then it didn't take a genius to know what was going on. Penny was attractive.

Quinn, knowing what Pearl was thinking, smiled over at her.

Damned Quinn!

Fedderman walked over to the coffee brewer as if he hadn't heard what Pearl said. He poured himself half a cup and added cream. Stirred with one of the plastic spoons.

Everyone waited patiently until he came back to join them. He leaned with his haunches against the edge of a desk. The four of them were perched that way, like birds on a wire. Quinn, behind his desk, was the only one actually seated.

"Late last night," he said, "a thirty-year-old woman named Jane Nixon came home alone from salsa dancing at a place down the block from where she lived. She unlocked her apartment door and started to go inside. That's when a man approached and shoved her all the way in, then followed her into the dark apartment and closed the door behind him."

"Our guy?" Fedderman asked.

"That's my guess," Quinn said. "He made sure the door was locked so she couldn't get out in a hurry even if she reached it, then he came toward her carrying what she called 'a curvy little knife.'" Quinn looked at his four detectives in turn. "This all happened within seconds. But while she'd been stumbling across the room after he shoved her, Nixon, who still had her hand in her purse after returning the keys when she unlocked her door, also had her hand near a small canister of mace she always carried."

"Tricky Nixon," Vitali said.

"Our assailant thought he had her cowed, and right where he wanted her. He was surprised when she waited till he was close, and then suddenly shot mace into his face from about a foot away. He got a snoot full.

"She spun and ran into the bedroom, and he made toward the door to the hall. He could still see well enough to get outta the building while Nixon was calling nine-one-one."

"What about Jane Nixon?" Pearl asked. "She get a look at him?"

"Not a good look. She was close when she let fly with the mace, and some of the stuff got in her eyes, too. She was half blind when the uniforms arrived at her apartment."

"Unhurt so far, though," Vitali said.

"Physically, she sustained only a small knife cut on her forearm."

"Poor thing's probably still scared stiff," Mishkin said.

"She'll be scared for a while," Quinn said.

"The knife sounds right," Fedderman said.

"Everything sounds right," Quinn said. "Right, and then fortunately interrupted."

"Did anybody see this sicko flee the premises?" Vitali asked.

"Maybe," Quinn said. "We got a cab driver picked up a guy near Nixon's apartment building in the right time frame. A blind man, no less, wearing dark glasses and bumping into things. No seeing-eye dog or cane, just blind faith. Cabbie said he drove the fare to an intersection near Central Park and left him there."

"He left a blind man near Central Park at night?" Fedderman asked.

"There are big apartment buildings on the other side of Central Park West, facing the park. The cab driver figured his fare was gonna enter one of them. The guy also gave him a line of bullshit about wanting to make it the rest of the way home by himself, so he'd feel self-reliant and useful."

"A man with pride," Vitali said.

"Those were the cabbie's exact words. So he drove away and left the guy."

"Smartest thing he ever did," Fedderman said.

"Or luckiest," Pearl said.

"He said he did glance in the rearview mirror when he was a little way down the street. The blind man was cautiously crossing the street, relying almost entirely on his sense of hearing not to be run down by some hard-charging motorist." Quinn looked at his detectives and didn't see optimism. "Nixon was raped six years ago and picked out her attacker from a lineup. The man she falsely accused got out of prison less than a year ago on new DNA evidence. He's all alibied up."

"Too bad Nixon didn't get much of a look at her attacker," Pearl said.

"She did say she thought he was average height and build. The word *average* came up a lot."

"It always does," Fedderman said.

"What about our guy Link Evans?" Vitali asked. "He was starting to look good for it."

"Different story. His wife in Missouri said he was at a big numismatic convention in Denver."

"That's coin collecting?" Vitali asked, to be sure.

Quinn nodded.

"In point of fact," Mishkin said, "he might collect other kinds of money, Sal, not only coins."

Vitali glared at him, still intolerant from his confinement in the car with Mishkin. "What the hell does that mean, Harold?"

"Bills. Paper money . . ."

"No. 'In point of fact.' What the hell's that supposed to mean?"

"In this case it means he was lucky," Pearl said.

"Not exactly," Quinn said. "Seems there is no coin show in Denver. Hasn't been one there in weeks."

Focus narrowed. Attitudes changed immediately.

Pearl stood up away from her desk. "We've got him."

"Not yet," Quinn told her. "And not for sure. We still can't be positive he's the Skinner."

"Maybe *you*'re not positive," Pearl said, "but I—"

The door banged open, and Jerry Lido came stumbling in.

One lapel of Lido's wrinkled sport coat was twisted inside out. His stained paisley tie was loosely knotted and flung back over one shoulder, as if he was battling a strong headwind in an open-cockpit plane. He needed a shave, and his eyes were reminiscent of stuffed olives.

"Don't you look like shit," Pearl said.

"Been busy," Lido said, shuffling his feet with nervous energy.

Pearl could smell the gin. She knew Quinn must, too. "Been at the bottle?" she asked.

"Just enough to straighten me out so I could come over here," Lido said. "I been at the computer." He flashed a lop-sided grin. "I found out a couple of things."

"I told them about the nonexistent Denver coin convention," Quinn said.

"Found something other'n that," Lido said. "Link Evans took a flight out of Kansas City two days ago, not to Denver, but to Philadelphia."

"So Denver was a feint," Vitali said.

"He rent a car in Philly?" Pearl asked.

"No," Lido said. "But he coulda taken a train right into New York City. It's an easy commute, and if he paid cash for his ticket, there's no way to check."

"Security tapes," Pearl said.

"Maybe. But that might take weeks. Months, even. And they might've missed him, or had a bad camera angle. You know security cameras."

Pearl did.

Quinn slowed Lido down enough to tell him about last night's attack on Jane Nixon.

"Okay," Lido said, still vibrating. "That dovetails. I think Evans trained into New York, and he paid Jane Nixon a visit. Then, after spending the night in New York, it was back to Philadelphia."

"Or somewhere nearby," Pearl said.

"I checked his round-trip ticket," Lido said. "He's due back in Kansas City at ten o'clock tomorrow."

"We can meet him when he comes through security," Quinn said.

"Call the K.C. cops," Vitali said.

"You're thinking like you're still NYPD," Fedderman said. "Besides, we've gotta be certain about this guy."

"If he gets a whiff of cop, he's gonna go underground and we might never get him," Vitali said.

"Pearl and I will fly to Missouri and meet him in Edmundsville when he comes home," Quinn said. "I want to talk to the wife before he gets there, be sure of our facts so we don't make asses of ourselves."

"If he's the Skinner," Pearl said, "wifey will know. She might not have admitted it to herself yet, but she'll know. And when she does admit it, we can be sure."

She smiled faintly at Quinn. Quinn and Pearl, thinking alike again.

"Get on the phone or Internet and get us airline tickets to whatever's closest to Edmundsville," Quinn told Pearl. "Let's see if we can get into a motel near there to use as our base, then drive in early tomorrow morning and talk to the wife before hubby arrives."

"I wouldn't give a plugged nickel for his chances," Vitali said.

Mishkin said, "I bet he knows exactly what one of those is worth."

80

Mathew Wellman was eating chocolate ice cream. He would spoon it into his mouth with one hand, and with the other manipulate the mouse and keyboard of Westerley's computer. With Westerley's permission, and charge card, Mathew had added to the computer memory chips and apps and features that Westerley not only had never heard of but still didn't understand.

Bobi had soon developed a liking for young Mathew and brought him snacks from time to time, even on days when she wasn't working.

Westerley sat at his desk and observed Mathew, marveling at how his gooey fingers danced. The sheriff couldn't see what was happening on the monitor because of reflection, with the sun angling in through the bamboo window treatments Bobi had bought. They softened the light somewhat but didn't keep it out.

After a while, Westerley voiced what he'd been wondering. "Is all this tech wizardry—which I heartily admire, Mathew—actually getting us somewhere?"

Mathew didn't answer until he'd swallowed the ice cream he'd skillfully transferred from bowl to mouth.

"'Es, sir," he said, swallowing. On the return trip to the

bowl, his spoon dribbled chocolate onto his blue Stephen Hawking T-shirt. Westerley had broken his rhythm.

"Where?" Westerley asked, somewhat surprised.

And Mathew Wellman proceeded to tell the sheriff everything that Jerry Lido had told Quinn and Associates.

When Mathew was finished talking, Westerley sat for a while thinking over what he'd heard.

He stood up and put on his Sam Browne belt, and the leather holster he wore on his right hip. Then he adjusted with movements of long habit the rest of the gear that was affixed to and dangled from the belt. The tools of his profession.

"Call Bobi and tell her I want her to come in," he said. He smiled. "You're doing a great job, Mathew."

Mathew beamed.

Westerley got his Smokey hat from where it hung on a wall hook. "If anybody needs me, I'll have my cell phone turned on. I'm gonna be at Mrs. Evans's house."

"I'll tell Bobi, sir."

Mathew watched Westerley go out the door and then observed through the window as the sheriff strode toward his SUV. He walked kind of neat, Mathew thought, with the uniform and thick belt across his back, and all that paraphernalia dangling from his belt. Holster, cell phone with GPS, key ring, leather notepad holder, telescoping billy club. Handcuffs, even.

Going to Mrs. Evans's house.

Mrs. Evans, Mathew thought with a smile. Was that kind of formality supposed to fool anyone? Not that Mathew blamed Westerley. He'd seen Mrs. Evans and thought she was hot.

Mathew called Bobi Gregory and then viewed some porn

from Sweden on the Internet. He could cover his tracks with a few clicks of the mouse when he saw Bobi coming. And what he was doing should be safe, considering he was using the sheriff's department's computer.

Sweden usually meant blondes. Mathew liked blondes.

81

Quinn and Pearl's plane lifted off from LaGuardia at six o'clock that evening. The closest airport to Edmundsville was St. Louis's Lambert International. From there they could rent a car, wend their way to Interstate 70, and drive west out of the St. Louis area.

In mid-Missouri, they could stay at a Hampton Inn just off 70, and in the morning drive less than an hour to reach the Evans house. If they left the motel about nine-thirty, they should easily arrive well before Link Evans. Evans's flight touched down at ten o'clock, and his drive from the Kansas City airport to home was slightly farther than theirs, leaving them plenty of time to talk to Beth Evans before her husband got home.

The flight from LaGuardia to St. Louis seemed longer than it was, maybe because of the infant in the seat behind Quinn that somehow kept managing to touch cold and sticky miniature fingers to the back of his neck. While they were deplaning, the kid looked over at Quinn from his mother's arms and grinned, as if they shared a secret: There were people, and then there were people who plagued them, and that was that.

Quinn and Pearl traveled with only rolling carry-ons. As

they made their way through the crowded terminal to where they could rent a car, Quinn said, "That kid behind us was driving me nuts."

"She was great," Pearl said. "She didn't utter a peep."

"How do you know it was a she?"

"Could have been the pink dress."

As they rounded a corner to leave the secure area, Pearl's rolling suitcase bounced over Quinn's toe. He was pretty sure she'd done it on purpose.

The drive toward Edmundsville was better than the flight to St. Louis. Their room was reserved at the motel, so there was no hurry. The sky was cloudless and tinted a deep purple. Though the day had been warm, it was so pleasant now that Quinn felt like putting down the Ford Taurus's windows. He didn't, though, knowing Pearl would complain about her hair blowing all over the place. She had no idea that he thought she was sexy with her hair all tousled by the wind. Or maybe she did know that, and she figured he was the one who'd made it clear that this was a business trip, so let him yearn. *There were people. . . .*

The motel was so well kept it looked as if it had been built yesterday, even though the architecture was a couple thousand years old. It had tall fluted columns that looked like the entrance to a Greek temple, with cars parked outside instead of chariots.

They checked into a room with a king-sized bed—Quinn's idea—then rolled their suitcases along a long hall toward an elevator to the second floor.

"I noticed they serve breakfast," Quinn said. "Means we can stay in bed pretty late tomorrow in case we don't get much sleep."

"Why would we not get much sleep?"

"We might be busy in a carnal way."

"You would think that," Pearl said.

"You'd be surprised what I might think," Quinn told her,

as he used the key card to unlock and open the door on only the fourth try.

The phone was ringing as they entered the room and deposited their suitcases on the bed. Quinn cursed inwardly. This didn't bode well. Not that Pearl seemed to be getting in the mood. But then you never could tell about Pearl.

Quinn snatched up the receiver, thinking he'd hear the voice of the desk clerk downstairs checking to make sure everything was to their satisfaction.

Instead he heard Fedderman: "Things have changed, Quinn. Lincoln Evans's flight tomorrow was canceled, so he booked another for this evening. He's in the air now. He'll change planes in Pittsburgh and will arrive in Kansas City at nine-thirty tonight."

"Which means he'll get home about ten-thirty."

"Roughly," Fedderman said.

Quinn glanced at the multifunctional alarm clock nightlight sleep timer radio on the dresser. "It's almost nine o'clock now."

"That nine-thirty is central time," Fedderman said, from far away in the eastern time zone. "Just so there's no mistake."

"We're in sync," Quinn said.

He felt a stirring deep in his hunter's heart. It was all coming at them fast now, the way it sometimes did. Any damned thing could happen, and they had to be ready.

"One other thing," Fedderman said. "Tom Stopp really does have a brother, and his name is Marvin and he's in California, writing for TV and the movies. Or struggling to, anyway. He's got a sister Terri, too. Beautician, unmarried, likes the ladies."

"Thanks for the confirmation, Feds." *So much for that* TS *possibility—if Tanya Moody actually* did *scrawl those two letters in blood.* "Call me on my cell if anything else happens. We're gonna be on the move."

"Good luck, and whatever else you can use."

Quinn placed the phone's receiver back in its cradle. Pearl was standing by the window, staring at him now instead of at the swimming pool below, knowing the game had unexpectedly changed. There was a special intensity in her dark eyes. He doubted it had anything to do with motel sex.

"We're checking out," Quinn said. "We've got more driving ahead of us tonight."

He explained to her about Fedderman's phone call.

Without having unzipped their suitcases, they got them down from the bed and headed for the door. They didn't talk as they rode the elevator down. Their minds were already an hour's drive away and on a dozen things at once. The endgame did that to people.

They didn't bother checking out. Probably it was done automatically tomorrow anyway. The clerk had already run the company charge card.

As they rolled the suitcases across the lobby's tiled floor toward the exit, Pearl said, "There goes that free breakfast."

She didn't sound as if she cared.

82

Wayne Westerley lay half asleep in Beth's bed. Her head was resting in the crook of his arm, and he could hear her gentle breathing. They were both lying nude on top of the sheets, letting the air conditioner cool the room after the heat of their coupling. Westerley absently decided that the gradually dropping temperature had reached a perfect level. He felt satiated and peaceful and could easily doze off.

His cell phone began to vibrate where he'd placed it on the nightstand. Beth stirred but didn't wake up. With his free hand, Westerley picked up the phone and glanced at it. The county sheriff's department calling. A good part of the county sheriff's department was here in bed with Beth. The thought amused him as he pressed the talk key and fitted the phone to his ear.

"Sheriff?"

It was Billy Noth, his deputy. "What's up, Billy?" Westerley kept his voice low.

"We just got a call from the New York City police."

Westerley snapped all the way awake, but he didn't stir. "'Bout what?"

"There's a warrant out for Link Evans to be arrested as a suspect in the Skinner murders in New York. You know, that nutcase who—"

"Yeah, yeah, Billy."

"I figured you'd want to know," Billy said.

"I did and I didn't."

"I know what you mean, Sheriff."

Westerley broke the connection.

He was dumbfounded. Still trying to put his thoughts together. Beth had told him Link wasn't due home until tomorrow from the numismatic convention in Denver. He played again in his mind his conversation with Billy Noth.

The Skinner?

Link?

Westerley considered contacting the New York police immediately; then he realized they'd be able to determine the origin of his phone call. Not only that, if his office got the message from New York, the state police and the Missouri State Highway Patrol almost surely received the same message. They might already be busting their balls on their way to see if they could apprehend Link here, where he lived, where Westerley was in bed with the suspect's wife.

He wriggled back on the mattress and sat up straight, waking Beth, and switched on the light by the bed.

Beth lay on her side and smiled sleepily up at him. "Something wrong, hon?"

"A few things," Westerley said.

Link Evans enjoyed being early. It didn't happen very often. His visit with the woman he'd gone to New York to see had taken less time than he'd expected. She'd provided the opportunity for them to be alone together almost as soon as he'd arrived in town. He figured that if his luck held, he'd be home before ten-thirty. Beth might still be awake. He could surprise her.

Link's luck did hold. The plane bounced gently twice on landing, then slowed rapidly with the engines roaring on reversed thrust. When the roaring dropped to a lower level, the pilot announced that they'd had a tailwind and were ten minutes early.

Deplaning was smooth and efficient. Link had no luggage to claim, so he was out of the main terminal fast. He'd left the pickup for Beth this trip and driven the Kia to the airport. The shuttle to the lot where he'd left the car was parked and waiting at the curb, as if just for him.

He was away from the airport and on the road in no time, driving fast toward home.

It was ten-twenty when Link slowed the car at the mouth of the driveway and let it roll to a stop. The house was dark. Beth must have gone to bed early.

Rather than wake her, he pulled farther into the driveway and left the car parked off to the side on the grass.

He wasn't going to bother unpacking tonight, and he didn't feel like lugging his suitcase all the way up the long drive. He left the suitcase in the trunk, then made sure the car was locked and began walking toward the dark house.

When he got closer, he saw the back end of an SUV that was parked behind the house, where it wouldn't be seen from the road or driveway. And the house wasn't completely dark. He noticed soft light escaping from where a shade hadn't been pulled quite all the way down. Silently, he approached the steady bar of light showing beneath the shade. He moved aside the branches of an overgrown forsythia bush that he'd neglected to prune. Crouching low, he peered inside through the window.

It was the bedroom window.

Quinn tried not to look at the dashboard clock or his watch. Beside him, Pearl squirmed. They'd been making good time before traffic had slowed, and then gradually stopped, on the

Interstate. Now they were creeping forward at less than ten miles per hour.

"Way it looks on the GPS," Pearl said, "we've only got a few miles before our turnoff."

"GPS tell us why we're crawling along?" Quinn asked.

"Not even if you asked it nice."

The highway curved, and ahead of them Quinn could see a long line of traffic and flashing red and blue lights. Though it was difficult to know for sure in the dark night, it appeared that traffic was being diverted to a single lane.

No. When he got a closer look, he saw that what had been a single lane was now realigning itself and again becoming two lanes.

There was a state patrol car parked just off the shoulder.

"Looks like an accident," he said, "and they finally cleared the wreckage off the highway."

Traffic began to pick up its pace.

They were doing fifty miles per hour and accelerating as they passed the twisted mass of steel that had been a car. A sheet or blanket covered a body that lay on the grass on the side of the road. Yellow lights flashed on the roof of a tow truck that was slowly bumping along, making its way against traffic by driving on the shoulder. A state trooper was frantically waving an arm in a circular motion, as if getting ready to pitch a ball underhand, urging drivers to keep up their speed. Quinn could hear a siren in the distance, probably an ambulance.

"No rush on the ambulance," Pearl muttered, craning her neck and staring at the body as they passed.

Quinn made no comment, and she said nothing more. Each knew the other considered the accident scene a bad omen.

Concealed behind the forsythia bush at the bedroom window, Link held his breath as he watched Westerley climb nude out of his, Link's, bed. Beside him lay Beth, Link's wife. She was nude and on her side, one knee slightly drawn up, her hip rounded and smooth, in a pose Link had seen in dozens of old paintings. She reached out and ran a hand languidly along Westerley's back as he straightened up.

Link clenched his teeth until his jaws hurt.

It was the way Westerley moved that got to Link—casually and comfortably, as he usually moved, with a well-muscled animal's grace and power. As if he was familiar with his surroundings, as if this was his home, his bed, his wife. Pretending might make it so, if you wore a badge.

Mindful to be silent, Link backed slowly away from the window. As he did so, dark clouds scudded across the moon, changing the shapes of still objects and seeming to set them into motion. When Link was in shadow, he moved farther away from the house, toward the garage.

Inside the garage was his steel gun locker with its combination lock.

Inside the locker was his Remington twelve-gauge shotgun.

83

Westerley managed to slide one leg into his uniform pants, but the other got tangled in material halfway in. He hopped around for a while on one bare foot.

By the time he'd gotten his other leg through and was buttoning and zipping up his pants, Beth had her nightgown on and was frantically trying to arrange the sheets and fluff his pillow so it would appear that she'd been in bed alone.

Finished with the bed, she went to the window and pulled the shade back slightly with one finger so she could peek outside.

"We'll hear them drive up," Westerley said, trying to reassure both of them.

"You've gotta be outta here before then, Wayne." Beth didn't sound reassured.

"Don't I know it." He plopped his Smokey hat on his head, knowing he looked ridiculous standing there shirtless and barefoot, but he didn't want to forget the hat. He could leave his shirt unbuttoned, work his feet into his boots without socks. The important thing was to back the SUV out from behind the house and down the driveway before the state police showed up. He'd have to do a hell of lot of explaining otherwise.

Beth, still at the window, said, "Holy shit, Wayne!"

Westerley stood frozen with his shirt in his hand. "What?"

"Link's out there! And he's got a gun. Gotta be a shotgun. He keeps one locked up in the garage."

"He's not due till tomorrow night."

"Whenever he's due, he's here!" She stared at Westerley with huge eyes. "Remember he's the Skinner, Wayne. He's a killer!"

What Westerley remembered was that he'd left his nine-millimeter handgun in its holster hanging by its belt over the back of a kitchen chair. He broke for the kitchen but took only two steps before tripping over his boots and sprawling on the floor.

He started to get up and dropped back down hard when pain jolted like electricity through his right elbow where he'd bumped it on the floor.

Funny bone. I get the message.

I'll be shooting left-handed!

He tried to stand up again and had made it about halfway when he heard the brass chain lock on the front door clatter. The chain rattled louder, Link testing the door.

Westerley barely made it out of the bedroom, and thought for a second he might make it to the kitchen and his gun, and maybe even out the back door. He would be armed then, out in the night, where he could formulate some sort of plan.

That at least might draw Link outside. Westerley wasn't going to leave Beth here alone with Link and his shotgun.

But the sheriff didn't have the time he thought he had. Link kicked the door open and stepped inside with the shotgun, looking at Westerley with eyes that might as well have been corneal transplants from a shark.

Quinn braked the Taurus and made a sharp right into the driveway. He almost hit the car parked off to the side, half on the grass.

"Ho, boy!" Pearl said, pointing ahead through the windshield.

They both saw the dark figure of a man kick open the front door and enter the house, carrying a rifle or shotgun.

"Let's go into the kitchen where we can sit down and talk about this," Westerley said. He kept his voice calm while his mind darted this way and that. He had to defuse this situation. "We can have us a couple of beers."

"I don't fancy one of my beers," Link said.

He racked the shotgun's mechanism and a shell popped out of the breech, bounced on the floor, and rolled in a half circle.

"I got more in the magazine," he said.

"Don't make a move," a man's voice said behind Link. It was an authoritative voice speaking slowly and carefully. "There are two guns aimed at your back, and we're too close to miss."

Link didn't move. The shotgun remained pointed directly at Westerley.

Westerley gave him a level look and said, "Stand down, Link."

Link said, "Get in here, Beth."

Quinn heard shuffling on a bare wood floor, then saw a frail-looking woman with a pretty but haggard face walk stiff-legged with fear from the bedroom. She was wearing only a nightgown and a pair of oversized fuzzy pink slippers.

Link Evans hadn't moved a muscle since Quinn and Pearl had entered the house. He remained still. "Come to me, Beth. Come to your husband."

"I wouldn't do that, Beth," Westerley said.

Link laughed. It sounded like a dog's single, guttural

bark. "She doesn't do it and I'll blow your heart clear out through your back."

"I think you're gonna do that anyway," Westerley said. So calm and easy it made Link want to kill him right then.

"This isn't a walk in the park, asshole!"

"We all know that, Evans," Quinn said. He kept his tone even, almost casual. Evans was revving up for something. On the keen edge.

Evans still hadn't turned and looked at Quinn and Pearl. In a way, he was dismissing them. In Link's mind they were part of the game but predictable and controllable. He was ready to lose his life, if that's what it came down to. Quinn knew that. Knew how dangerous Link Evans was right now.

Beth kept her gaze fixed on her husband and moved softly and slowly, as if she didn't want to wake something lightly sleeping, until she stood only a few feet from him. She was obviously trying not to tremble. Cold with terror.

"Got your car keys in one of those pants pockets?" Link asked Westerley.

Westerley nodded.

"Pull 'em out so I can see for sure."

Westerley did, holding the keys at waist level away from his body.

Smoothly and so fast it surprised everyone, the shotgun barrel moved to aim at Beth.

"We're gonna leave the back way, out through the kitchen," Link said. "You, me, and Beth. You lead the way, Sheriff."

Quinn and Pearl watched as the three of them went single file into the kitchen, the shotgun barrel steady and aimed at Beth Evans. Where she moved, it followed. It was a compass needle and she was magnetic north.

As soon as they were in the kitchen, Link Evans glanced quickly back at Quinn and Pearl. He actually gave them a thin smile as he pushed the kitchen door closed behind him.

Quinn heard the metallic cluck of a lock and what sounded like a chair being shoved beneath the doorknob.

He and Pearl were locked out of the kitchen.

Pearl looked at Quinn and silently mouthed an obscenity.

He motioned for Pearl to follow him, and they went out the front door fast and hurried around toward the back of the house, toward where he remembered Westerley's SUV was parked. He figured Evans would make Westerley drive, with Beth in the passenger seat. Evans would sit in back with the shotgun, making sure the two up front didn't misbehave.

As they crept cautiously along the side of the house, Quinn had that much figured out.

All he needed now was some kind of plan.

84

Link motioned with the shotgun for them to leave by the back door. It was such a small but unmistakable movement of the long barrel that the opportunity to jump him was here and gone in an instant, before Westerley could respond.

Beth was gripping Westerley's right arm now. Squeezing hard. That didn't help the sore elbow.

Link gave her a shove, and her hand fell away from Westerley. Link's effort made the shotgun barrel momentarily drop. Beth was fumbling nervously with the chain lock on the back door, momentarily diverting Link's attention from Westerley.

This time Westerley seized his opportunity. There was nothing to lose by rolling the dice. Link had come into the house to kill them. Now they were only alive because they had temporary value as hostages.

Westerley dived for the kitchen chair, where his holstered nine-millimeter dangled from its black leather belt draped over the chair's wooden back. The belt came free even though the chair toppled. Westerley rolled, trying to be as difficult a target as possible while he wrestled the heavy Glock handgun from its holster. He was vaguely aware of Beth screaming, of Link shouting something at him, but it all seemed to be happening dreamlike and at a distance.

He was in a pocket of time and place that moved slowly as he slid the gun from its holster and began raising his arm to take aim at Link.

Westerley's arm was still throbbing where he'd banged his elbow against the floor in the bedroom. His heart plunged as he realized he was raising the Glock slower than Link was swinging the shotgun around to point at him. Westerley fired a shot, but he was too eager and the bullet went into the floor. The arc of the shotgun barrel was as inexorable as fate.

There was an explosion and a blast of light. Something like a train crashed into Westerley's chest and right shoulder. The floor hit him in the back, and he was staring up at the ceiling and kitchen light fixture. The ceiling wouldn't stay still; it was like the underside of a floating rectangular object in a heavy sea. Westerley turned his head to the side and watched Link Evans get the back door to outside open and shove Beth through it ahead of him. He didn't bother glancing back at Westerley as he rushed out into the night.

Westerley suddenly realized that his head, which he'd raised slightly so he could watch Link and Beth leave, was incredibly heavy. He let himself go limp, and the back of his head struck the floor. The kitchen, which had been dim to begin with, was now completely black.

Westerley understood why Link Evans hadn't bothered glancing back at him as he was leaving. Link had already mentally subtracted Westerley from equation of what was happening this dreadful night. For that matter, probably so had Beth.

They think I'm dead or dying.
I think they're right.

Quinn was ahead of Pearl when he heard the roar of the SUV's big engine. The vehicle skidded around in the gravel in reverse until it was pointed down the driveway. Quinn dropped to one knee, holding his vintage police special with both hands and aiming carefully. He was aware of Pearl doing the same beside him, on his right side and back about a yard.

The SUV's knobby tires threw gravel as it sped down the driveway and past them. A few small pieces of rock struck Quinn's right cheek, stinging and causing him to squint.

It didn't matter anyway. The angle was bad. There'd only been a second or two when Quinn or Pearl had even a difficult shot at Link Evans, who was on the far side of the SUV and crouched low behind the steering wheel. Beth Evans was in the passenger seat, between them and her husband. If they had managed to fire over her and hit Link, his frantic return fire with the twelve-gauge might have struck Beth. She was sitting forward, braced with both hands on the dashboard so hard that her elbows were locked. Not having her seat belt buckled was the least of her concerns.

The SUV had passed Quinn and Pearl so fast it left only what seemed a still photo in their minds: the speed-blurred vehicle, the driver bent over the steering wheel, the rigid figure of Beth, her mouth open wide in a silent scream. A study in speed and desperation.

Quinn remained kneeling but deftly switched positions and got off three shots at the SUV's rear tires. He heard Pearl's Glock bark twice. She was also trying to hit a tire, lying on her stomach in the dirt and gravel, keeping down so her bullets would follow a low trajectory.

The SUV didn't seem affected by their gunfire. When it was near the end of the driveway, brake lights flared, as Link slowed to turn onto the state road.

Quinn and Pearl were already up and racing toward the parked Taurus.

Not that they'd be able to catch Westerley's SUV, which doubtless had the police package and could outrun any rental.

They piled into the car. Quinn drove down the rutted driveway. Pearl dropped her gun and had to bend down and retrieve it where it was bouncing around on the floor. As she straightened up, she bumped her head painfully on the dashboard.

Quinn made a right turn out of the driveway, behind the SUV.

Once on the county road, it became obvious that the rental didn't have the horses to catch the SUV. Quinn could see its taillights ahead like amused red eyes watching the Taurus recede.

The SUV took a curve and disappeared, then reappeared up ahead when Quinn followed in the Taurus. He lost control when the rental car's tires broke contact with the road, and the car might as well have been on ice. Quinn wrestled with the steering wheel and mashed his foot down hard on the accelerator, powering out of the skid and causing the car to swerve from one side of the road to the other. Pearl had slid forward and was out of her seat.

He stole a glance over at her. "Put on your damned seat belt, Pearl!"

She scooted back into the seat, tucked her Glock beneath a thigh, and managed to buckle up. When she looked over at Quinn, she saw that he hadn't fastened his seat belt.

Finally he regained full control. Beside him, Pearl was bone white, but she said nothing.

The state road straightened out where it began its approach to the Interstate highway, but the SUV's twin red eyes were farther ahead and pulling away. Quinn kept the accelerator pedal flat to the floor, and the Taurus's speed began to edge up. They were doing over ninety now. They couldn't catch the SUV, but they might manage to stay reasonably close.

Red and blue flashing lights appeared up ahead. Something coming in the opposite direction. And coming fast.

Quinn figured that would be the state police, speeding toward the Evans house.

Quinn began flashing the Taurus's headlights.

The state cops caught on fast. They had to. Westerley's SUV passed them going the other way at over a hundred miles an hour. As Quinn watched, two state patrol cruisers made sweeping U-turns and gave chase.

Another showcase of dancing red and blue lights exited the ramp from the interstate. Another highway patrol cruiser. It was headed directly for the oncoming SUV. The two vehicles would pass or collide within the next twenty seconds.

The patrol car suddenly went into a skid and stopped so that it formed a roadblock in the narrow county road. To get around it in the SUV, Evans would have to leave the pavement.

As they neared the scene, Quinn sized up what was happening. He saw the uniformed highway patrol cop jump out of the cruiser, leaving it with its lights on and angled across the center line, and dash from the car toward the side of the road as Westerley's SUV approached.

The SUV's brake lights flared and it slowed. Quinn and Pearl were closing fast. Then the SUV built up speed, and Quinn knew Link Evans was going to try driving around the roadblock.

Link sped toward the parked highway patrol car. He left the pavement to drive around the cruiser, and chose the side of the road where the uniformed patrolman had run to take cover and wait.

Bad choice.

As Quinn and Pearl watched, the SUV veered off the road and around the parked cruiser. Quinn saw what appeared to be muzzle flashes, and the SUV made it back onto the road but was swerving drastically. What looked like chunks of tire flew into the night.

The other state patrol cars, and Quinn and Pearl in the

Taurus, were closing fast when the SUV left the road on the opposite side.

"He's lost it," Pearl said.

The SUV bounced off the shoulder and sailed into the dark woods. Its headlight beams went crazy among the trees.

The scene ahead came at them even faster, and then they were a part of it.

"Stop this damned thing!" Pearl yelled.

Quinn was already standing on the brakes.

85

Quinn brought the Taurus to a halt at a steep list toward the passenger side, its two right wheels off the road. He had to climb up out of the car. Pearl opened her door and simply tumbled out.

Around them were half a dozen parked state patrol cruisers with lights flashing. Moving figures crossed the blocked highway and ran into the woods.

Quinn hurried around the front of the Taurus and helped Pearl to her feet.

"Still got your piece?" he asked calmly.

Pearl held up the Glock and showed him.

"Ready?" Quinn asked.

But Pearl was already running with the others toward the woods. Jaws were clenched. Everyone was intent. There were sounds of heavy breathing, but no one spoke. If the state cops were giving orders, they were using hand signals.

Broken branches and crushed underbrush marked the SUV's path, making it easy to find.

No one knew exactly what would happen when they found it.

* * *

Beth was aware that her left side hurt. Then she realized she was lying in an awkward position on top of Link.

Westerley's SUV lay on its side. If Beth wanted to exit, she'd have to climb up to the broken-out window on the vehicle's right side. If she could force the door open, maybe she wouldn't have to climb through the window and risk being cut by remaining glass shards.

She remembered the SUV leaving the road, then rolling over and over. Link, belted in, was still in the driver's seat, but he was flopping around, unconscious or dead. Beth had been bounced back and forth violently. She had no idea how seriously she was hurt.

She moved her body parts tentatively and tried to take inventory. No doubt she was badly bruised, and there was a painful bump above her right ear. It was the pain in her left side that was intense. Every move made her suck in her breath in agony. Maybe a broken rib. Maybe it had pierced her lung.

She managed to change position so she had one leg beneath her and could gain some leverage. She clutched the cushion of the bucket seat above her and tried to pull with her arms.

Something was in her way, blocking her left arm.

Link's shotgun.

It posed no danger now. She gripped the barrel and shoved it away.

A little more room. She got her foot braced on the steering wheel, gripped the seat cushion, and started to raise herself so she could squeeze out through the window. She smelled smoke. She could hear fluid dripping and could also smell gasoline. Any second now, the SUV might catch fire. Burst into an orange fireball the way wrecked cars did in the movies and on television. She had to get out of here before that happened. She thought about Link. Maybe he was dead. Beth found that she didn't care, not considering what she knew about him now. What he'd done. And he'd killed Wayne.

My God! He killed Wayne!

She drew a deep breath and found the strength to elevate herself. The pain in her side flared, but she made progress. She actually managed to close her hand around the door's padded arm rest. Something to grip, to use to wriggle higher and see if the door handle worked.

Link's hand closed like a trap on her ankle.

The overturned SUV hadn't exploded. Not yet, anyway. But it was burning. Oil or gas in the engine compartment was sending out gray smoke that disappeared quickly among the canopy of leaves and the dark sky.

Quinn and Pearl stopped advancing with the contingent of state police, when Beth Evans staggered around from behind the big vehicle lying on its side. She dropped to her knees.

Quinn nudged Pearl and motioned with his head. They moved to the side as the state patrol advanced cautiously on Beth. It took only a moment to determine that the overturned SUV was unoccupied.

Pointing to a glimmer of blood on a dark leaf, Quinn struck out in a continuation of the way the vehicle must have been moving when it rolled onto its side.

"They always keep going the way they were moving," he said.

"That Quinn's law?" Pearl asked, keeping up with him.

"Link's gotta be shaken up, not thinking straight. But one thing he knows, even if he hasn't admitted it to himself, is that it's over. His mind'll clear and he'll get tired enough or ache enough that he'll stop running. It won't be worth it to him to buy a few more minutes, or even hours. He'll be played out."

"Then what?" Pearl asked.

"He'll stop. He'll turn around. He'll give himself up, or he won't."

Another siren yowled to silence nearby. Link had to know he was sewn up tight. There was no escape.

Quinn kept leading the way through the trees, his clunky black shoes crunching and snapping undergrowth as he cleared a path for Pearl. Mosquitoes started to bite. Branches started to scratch faces and bare hands and arms. Even though he was soaked with perspiration, Quinn found himself wishing he hadn't left his suit coat in the car. A mosquito tried to fly into his ear. He slapped at it and it tried to fly up his nose.

A sound he recognized made him stop. He stood still, other than to slowly extend an arm to his side as a signal for Pearl to stop beside him.

"He's got a pump shotgun," Quinn whispered. "I heard him rack a shell into the breech."

Pearl said nothing but stood stock still. She even ignored a mosquito drawing blood from her right arm.

They stood near the edge of a small clearing. Quinn figured Link Evans was concealed on the other side, and his running was over.

There was a lot of noise, and small branches snapped behind Quinn. The state police keeping up. One by one they appeared along the line of trees, on either side of Pearl and Quinn.

A trooper named Gulliver, who seemed to be in charge, approached where Quinn and Pearl were standing in cover and concealment behind two trees grown close together. Gulliver was a spindly guy with a big Adam's apple; he had long, skinny legs that accounted for most of his height.

"I think he's straight ahead," Quinn said softly, "and he's got a shotgun."

"We know about the shotgun," Gulliver said. "It was missing from the SUV."

"The wife gonna make it?"

"Yeah. Busted up some, but my guess is she'll recover. She said Evans was holding her hostage, and they were getting ready to set out through the woods, when we arrived. She was talking to him, she said, trying to convince him to give himself up, and when she turned around he was gone. He deserted her."

"She's hurt and she'd slow him down," Quinn said. "Leaving her alive and injured slowed you down."

"Yeah. It sure wasn't an attack of compassion." Gulliver surveyed the clearing and surrounding trees, and the darkness beneath the trees.

"He's run to ground," Quinn said. "Had enough. I think if we talk to him right he'll give—"

He stopped talking and stared in disbelief as Link Evans emerged from the trees on the other side of the clearing. His shotgun rested in the crook of his arm with the barrel pointed at the ground, as if he were starting out to hunt rabbits. He knew there was no hope and he was going to end it his way.

"He don't look like he wants to be talked out of anything," Gulliver said.

Quinn felt Pearl snatch at his arm as he moved into the faint moonlight and stepped out into the clearing.

Link Evans looked exhausted. His shirt was torn and hanging half off at the shoulder. His face was stained with sweat and dirt so that his eyes looked dark and hunted, the whites showing all the way around his pupils.

"You're making the wrong move," Quinn said.

Link shook his head. "It doesn't matter when the game's over."

Quinn said, "Still and all . . ."

That was when Wayne Westerley stepped from the trees

into the clearing. He was covered with blood and was no more than thirty feet from Link, and he held the twelve-gauge riot gun from his patrol car aimed at Link's midsection. He was bloodstained and looked ready to collapse, but he held the shotgun steady.

Link managed a wide grin. "Sometimes prayers are answered."

"Some folks pray and go to hell anyway," Westerley said.

"You can't pull that trigger," Link said. "You're too honorable a fool to kill the husband whose wife you stole. It'd be against your code. You know you did wrong once, and it's not in you to do wrong again."

Westerley said nothing from behind his mask of blood.

"I'm gonna shoot the shit outta you now, Sheriff Westerley, and fine and honorable man that you are, you're not gonna do a thing about it. That's 'cause you know you deserve it."

Westerly's shotgun roared through the night. He'd squeezed the trigger twice. From such close range Link caught most of the pellets in tight patterns. His body looked as if it might separate in half as he staggered back three wobbly steps and then folded up like a cloth puppet.

Westerley stood still and watched the circle of police slowly close in on what was left of Link Evans. Then, using the shotgun for support, he lowered himself so he was seated on the ground. He looked up as he saw Quinn and Pearl approach.

"I guess he had me wrong," he said.

Quinn said, "He had you about right."

86

In a pole tent the state police had set up as a temporary base of operations near Beth and Link's house in Edmundsville, Quinn stood with a forensic expert named Wellington and examined the contents of Link Evans's wallet. There were Visa and American Express cards, a Missouri driver's license, three simple business cards with Evans's name on them, an AAA card, medical insurance card, and eighty-six dollars, mostly in twenty-dollar bills.

In the single piece of luggage in the trunk of his car, a scuffed leather suitcase, they found his airline boarding pass and confirmation of his flight from Philadelphia to Kansas City.

It was the last flight he'd ever take.

Caught outside the structure of his planning and ritual, the Skinner had gone out in the inglorious blaze so many serial killers covertly sought. Their grand exit, and one last chance to outwit the hunters who were closing in on them.

Winning the game the hard way.

Beth awoke in a hospital bed in Jefferson City. Her ribs were wrapped, and her right knee was in a white plastic cast that made it impossible for her to straighten her leg beyond a thirty-degree angle. That was okay with her, because any effort to move the leg resulted in terrific pain.

She knew she must be under the influence of some kind of drug, because she couldn't quite piece together the fragments of her thoughts. She remembered last night—if it had been last night. The fear and the horror of seeing Wayne shot. The ringing in her ears, and the smell of cordite. Then the jolting chase with Link in the SUV and the accident. After that it was blank. Here she was, staring up at an IV tube and clear plastic bottle, and with a spasm of pain every time she breathed.

A large man in a wrinkled gray suit came into the room. He had a bony, somehow handsome face with a crooked nose, and straight brown hair that needed a trim. His smile was surprisingly charming as he pulled up a chair so he could sit near the bed. His bulk, the scent of him, suddenly dominated the room. Beth closed her eyes, trying to fit him into the incomplete fragments of last night. He'd been there, at the house and at the scene of the accident. She was sure of that.

She could hear him breathing and knew he was watching her, trying to decide if she was awake and lucid enough to carry on a conversation.

"I'm Frank Quinn," he said. "A detective from New York."

"I've got painkillers in me," she said, not opening her eyes.

"I know," he said. "The nurse told me you were aware enough to hold a conversation, if you weren't too tired."

"Is Wayne . . . ?"

At first Quinn didn't understand who she meant. Then he did. "Sheriff Westerley? He's badly hurt but alive. The doctors say he's going to make it."

"My husband tried to kill him," she said. "Link. I really think Link was going to kill me, too."

"Probably."

She opened her eyes and stared into his. "Where is Link? I don't remember anything after the accident. There's a lot I need to know."

Quinn moved automatically to pat the back of her hand but drew back when he saw the IV needle taped to it.

"I have a lot to tell you," he said.

Westerley was released from the hospital first. The shotgun blast had sent pellets into his right chest and shoulder. Most of the damage was done to the shoulder and his right upper arm. A single pellet, diverted by bone, had barely missed his heart. Another had creased his skull above his right ear.

When he came to visit Beth in the rehabilitation center where the hospital had sent her, he was wearing a brown short-sleeved shirt and faded Levi's. Brown moccasins that he could slip on and off easily. His right arm was in a sling. They'd talked on the phone, and she knew he might never regain full use of the arm.

Beth struggled up from the chair she was sitting in when Westerley arrived, and he held her in the crook of his good arm and kissed her. When she looked up at him she was crying.

"If only I suspected . . . about Link, I mean."

"No way you could have," Westerley said. He helped her sit back down in the chair and extend her injured leg. Then he dragged over a nearby chair so he could sit close to her.

"They tell me if I don't respond to treatment here I might need an artificial knee," she said.

"Your leg, my arm," he said. "We can live with that."

"I don't like thinking about that night."

"Then don't."

"Easier to say than do. Sometimes I think it was better when I couldn't remember anything about it."

"No," Westerley said, touching her arm lightly with his left hand. "It's better to face it and put it behind you. You did nothing wrong, have nothing to be ashamed of. What we both had was bad luck, but we lived through it and we're together."

"You're right. We could be dead, like those women."

"I don't waste much time on what might've been," Westerley said. "It's time now to think about what's gonna be." He stood halfway up, so he could lean over and kiss her on the lips.

When he sat back down, he reached into his shirt pocket and withdrew a letter-sized white envelope that was folded in half. "Billy Noth gave me this, Beth. It came in yesterday's mail. The DNA results from the samples we sent to the lab." He gave her a look she couldn't fathom. "You wanna see the results?"

"Do you know them?"

"Yeah. I talked to the lab on the phone." He shifted his weight, wincing when he leaned on his injured arm. "Trust me, there's no reason you need to know any of this now, Beth."

She smiled. "Didn't you just tell me it's better to face the facts so we can put them behind us?"

He returned her smile and shook his head. "Seems I did say that. But I didn't say always." He reluctantly handed her the envelope.

She accepted it but didn't open it. "Just tell me what it says, Wayne."

"Salas's DNA, Link's, Eddie's, and the DNA sample from the rape scene—none of them match except Eddie's and the rape scene sample, Beth. There's no way Link could have been Eddie's biological father."

"Or that Vincent Salas raped me."

"But you already knew that, Beth."

"I didn't really in my heart. Not for sure. Not until now."

Beth sat back, relieved. But now she was angry with herself. "All that mess and pain because of my imagination," she said.

"Your imagination's what got me looking into Link," Westerley reminded her. "And it's what brought us together."

"It's all so goddamned confusing," Beth said.

Westerley shrugged. "It's a mixed bag, Beth. Like most things in life." He glanced down at the envelope in her hand. "You wanna keep that, in case of any future doubt?"

She crumpled the unopened envelope and squeezed it into a tight ball, which she handed back to Westerley.

It was about the past. She didn't need it.

Westerley had been sure Beth would take his word rather than look into the envelope herself, and pretty sure she wouldn't look in the envelope at all once he'd told her about its contents. The envelope had contained two folded blank questionnaires he'd picked up at the nurse's station when no one was looking. The actual DNA report, the one that confirmed Link Evans was Beth's rapist and the father of her child, was folded in quarters and tucked in a back pocket of Westerley's Levi's. Before leaving the rehab center, he'd duck into a restroom, tear the report into small pieces, and flush it down the toilet.

Beth didn't need to know Evans was Eddie's biological father.

And Eddie sure as hell didn't need to know it.

The sad fact of the world, Westerley mused, was that sometimes the best way to deal with the truth was with a lie.

87

Quinn sat in his usual booth in the Lotus Diner and absently sipped his third cup of coffee. He didn't notice its bitterness. Nor was he paying attention to the pedestrians streaming past outside the window, hurrying to make the walk signal at the corner. His thoughts were elsewhere, in a place he wished they hadn't gone but kept revisiting.

Harley Renz, and apparently everyone else involved, was satisfied with the result of the Skinner investigation, but the assumption that Link Evans was the Skinner kept jabbing like a needle into Quinn's mind. It would wake him in the middle of the night, and he'd lie motionless and listen to Pearl's breathing and let his mind work like an Internet search engine roaming the vastness of the ether. How could it come up with the right answers when he kept asking the wrong questions?

Something was wrong. He knew it but didn't understand why.

Maybe it was because too much didn't make sense to him.

The attempted murders of Beth Evans and Westerley must have been impromptu, and the Skinner never did anything impromptu.

It was difficult to believe Link had planned the murder of

his wife, which he then planned to pin on Vincent Salas—or would have planned—if he really was the Skinner.

And where was the carpet-tucking knife the Skinner was going to use to remove Beth's tongue? A careful planner like the Skinner wouldn't have relied on a kitchen knife. It was probably ritualistically important to him to use a particular knife, his special knife that served no purpose other than to carve the flesh of his victims. The ritual knife was nowhere to be found in or around the Evans house.

Adding to Quinn's doubts, Beth would have been the first Skinner victim to be shot to death.

The case might have been declared solved, but those were a lot of leftover pieces.

With Jerry Lido's help, Quinn began to dig. It wasn't that difficult, now that the Pandora's box of Link Evans's secret life was wide open. Lido used his legal and illegal skills to trace Evans's movements during his New York visits. Everyone who moved about on this earth left a trail, and Lido was an expert at finding and following those trails, be they old or new, hot or cold, paper or electronic.

It was time-consuming, assiduous work, but when it finally brought results, things fell into place in a hurry.

Gas receipts, as well as restaurant and motel charges, turned up from an area of Long Island. One of the motel databases had the license number and make of the car Evans and a woman were driving when they checked in. It didn't match the make or number of Link's rental car; they must have used the woman's car that night. A mistake that Lido, months later in a quiet room, pounced on like a famished predator.

A license-plate number was as good as a birth certificate to Lido. It rapidly opened door after door after door. The woman's name was Julie Flack. She was forty-three years old, lived on Long Island, and was married to a circuit judge.

Then it got easier. She had a Facebook account.

There was her photograph. She was an attractive blond woman with a sly smile. She had a daughter by a previous marriage, liked to sail, shop, and dine out. Her favorite food was Indian. Her all-time favorite movie was *An Affair to Remember*. Her all-time favorite TV series was *Sex and the City*. She hated everything about *The Sopranos*.

Hated *The Sopranos*?

Lido found that odd.

Within five minutes after his phone conversation with Lido, in which Quinn learned these facts, he made a phone call to Julie Flack.

Her area code indicated she was on a landline, so he identified himself.

"I was expecting the pool-maintenance man," she said.

"He'll still turn up," Quinn assured her. "In the meantime, you have me."

"Why?" There was a hint of suspicion, maybe alarm, in her voice.

Quinn decided to hit her with it immediately, while she was off balance. "We need to talk about the Skinner murders, and your relationship with Lincoln Evans."

Silence.

"You *do* know him," Quinn said.

"I'd rather not talk on the phone." Nothing in her voice now. Little Miss Neutral. *Probably already thinking about lawyering up.*

"I could drive out there," Quinn said. "We could sit by the pool and chat."

"I don't think so. The pool-maintenance man will be here for quite a while, making repairs."

"Fixing leaks?" *Too late for that.*

"No, the filter's causing problems. Letting in the darndest things. Some of them through the phone."

"We could meet somewhere," Quinn said.

"Fine. The bar at the Medford Hotel? Say six this evening?"

"That would work."

"Please be on time."

"What's really wrong with your pool?" Quinn asked.

But Julie Flack had hung up.

Quinn sat back and smiled. She was a cool one, Julie Flack. Though she had to have been horrified by his call, she'd stayed calm, and in fact managed to stay on top of the conversation, as if *she'd* called *him* and casually imploded his life.

Quinn could hardly wait to meet her in person.

88

But it was Julie Flack who was late for their meeting at the Medford. It was already ten after six and she hadn't appeared.

The hotel's lounge wasn't crowded. There were three men and two women at the bar. They looked like business travelers. Others were scattered about the place, alone or in small groups, at the tables or in the black leather upholstered booths.

Quinn had chosen a secluded booth where they could talk privately. He sat where he could see the door, and waited.

He'd made his way through half a martini, when a pudgy white-haired man in an obviously expensive blue suit swiveled on his stool at the bar and walked toward him. He wore a kindly smile and an elegant blue and gold tie. He carried his drink—scotch or bourbon on the rocks—carefully balanced in his left hand.

Quinn realized the man must have been studying him in the back bar mirror.

When he was standing next to Quinn, he extended his right hand. "I'm Morris Henshaw, Ms. Flack's attorney. She sent me to meet you as her representative."

Quinn wasn't surprised, the wife of a circuit judge.

"For all practical purposes," Henshaw said, "I'll be Ms. Flack."

Quinn shook the cool, dry hand and motioned for Henshaw to sit down. Henshaw scooted into the seat across from Quinn in the booth.

"How long have you been sleeping with a serial killer?" Quinn asked.

The kindly smile didn't waver.

"You said you were Ms. Flack," Quinn reminded him.

"You seem the sort of gentleman who'd buy a lady a drink," Henshaw said.

Quinn laughed. "Okay, Mr. Henshaw. I'm assuming Ms. Flack isn't here because she has something to hide."

"Or she doesn't want to be embarrassed. Or frightened."

"Or arrested."

"Do you have the authority to do that?" Henshaw asked. And of course, no attorney asks a question without knowing the answer.

"I have the means."

"How would she know you're who you claim to be? She has every right to suspect an attempt at blackmail, since you seem to be under the impression that she's vulnerable."

"Fair enough." Quinn fished out his ID and showed it to Henshaw.

"Actually, I know who you are," Henshaw said, barely glancing at it. "I've long admired your work." He leaned forward over his drink. "Why don't you state exactly what you want of my client, and perhaps we can help you."

"I think your client is in deep trouble, Mr. Henshaw."

Gray eyebrows rose curiously. "How so?"

"It seems she's been involved in a love affair with a serial killer, who planned on using her as an alibi if he were to find himself in a tight spot."

"This serial killer, if there was one, is dead?"

Quinn nodded.

"Then why should my client's name be dragged through dirt? I can assure you she knew nothing of her hypothetical lover's . . . extra-extramarital escapades. Her husband happens—"

"I know who he is. Circuit Judge Aaron Flack. Are you also *his* attorney?"

"I'm the family attorney," Henshaw said, sipping his drink. He stopped smiling. His pale blue eyes bore into Quinn. "Is your motive for doing this political?"

"Not in the slightest," Quinn said. "My motive is simple. I want to know the truth."

Henshaw settled back farther in the booth, smiling and shaking his head. "Such an elusive thing."

"In your business."

"Oh, we usually manage to pin down one version of it or another."

"I'm going for my version."

"You would wreck a marriage and ruin a fine man and an honest judge in the process?"

"It would depend," Quinn said.

"You talk like a man with a price."

"I'm not."

"So you're an idealist."

"Hell, I don't know."

"But you see yourself as a just and good man."

"I try. And I do understand the delicacy of the situation."

"Might I appeal to your reason?"

"Oh, probably not."

"Is it useless to quote a number?"

"Useless."

Henshaw finished his drink and placed the glass on the table. "Then there's nothing I can do here." He extracted some bills from a beige leather wallet and laid them on the table, enough to pay for the drinks and a more-than-liberal tip. His jovial smile was back. He extended his hand to Quinn. "It's been a distinct pleasure, sir."

"I'll look out for your clients, Mr. Henshaw."

"I will tell them, Detective Quinn, that they should be reassured."

"Within reason," Quinn said.

"Everything within reason," Henshaw said. "Everything."

Quinn recalled the victims he'd seen, the artful carving in human flesh, the torture wounds, the hope no longer hope, the futures no longer futures.

Not everything.

89

Quinn decided his wisest course of action would be to continue his investigation quietly, so there would be a minimum of interference.

Badgering Julie Flack would provoke plenty of interference. Morris Henshaw would see to that, especially if Renz or the media learned what Quinn was doing. Besides, Henshaw had left little doubt that he'd take the case to the wire to establish that his client was unaware of her purpose in Link Evans's activities. It wouldn't matter anyway, if Quinn was right and there was more to the Skinner murders than had been uncovered so far.

The next step, Quinn decided, should be what he or one of his detectives would have done if the debacle at the Evans house in Missouri hadn't occurred. If the investigation hadn't ended in gunfire. He decided to question the man who'd wrongly gone to prison for the Jane Nixon rape. Who had motive to try to kill her.

His name was Scott Trent, and he'd been living in New York since his release from prison a year ago. He was employed by something called Amalgamated Cartage, and had an apartment on the Lower East Side.

* * *

"He's at work," Trent's neighbor said, when Quinn was knocking on the door to Trent's walk-up apartment. It was on the second floor of an old brick building that was bare on one side where the adjoining structure had been torn down. There was a faded advertisement for Rheingold Beer on the exposed and discolored old bricks.

Quinn turned to see a woman at least in her eighties leaning out from the partly opened door of the adjoining apartment. She was wearing a gray robe dusted with crumbs, had long gray hair in a style better suited to the head of a twenty-year-old, and a face as wrinkled as dollar bills that had been in circulation too long.

"I'm Cranston," she said, peering through narrowed eyes at Quinn. "*Mrs.* Cranston."

"At work where?" Quinn asked.

"Could be drivin'. Could be preachin'."

Quinn flashed his identification in its leather folder, letting her think NYPD. Her eyesight obviously wasn't much good anyway.

"That a wallet?"

"Sort of."

"You offerin' me some kinda bribe?"

"Showing you my identification."

"I don't care a fig about your education."

"Who I am."

"I don't give a flyin' fig who or what you are," Mrs. Cranston said.

"Be that as it may," Quinn said. He looked for a hearing aid in either of Mrs. Cranston's ears. Didn't see one.

"No say or nay about it. I don't much like Trent, and I don't much like his friends. Wish to hell he'd quit rehearsin' his sermons late at night, loud as if he had an audience of thousands. If I could afford it, I'd buy me a hearin' aid just so's I could turn it off and use it as a plug, so as not to hear all that rantin' and ravin' about goodness, and not takin' into account an old woman's sleep."

"Hypocrisy," Quinn said.

"Hippopotamus?"

"Where does he preach? Other than his apartment?"

"Street corners. Says he found religion in prison. Like somebody accidentally dropped it and he could use it. Found new ways to steal from good folks, too, I bet. All prison is anyways is a college for criminals."

"Which street corners?"

"Who the hell cares?"

Quinn tried Trent's apartment door and found it locked. Better not let himself in, with Mrs. Cranston keeping a constant if clouded eye on things.

"Do you think he's working today?" he asked.

"Worming?"

"Working. At work. Working."

"Who gives a fig?"

Quinn thanked Mrs. Cranston for her time and left the building. He was relieved to see that his car hadn't been stolen or vandalized. He thought he saw Mrs. Cranston peeking out from behind a curtain as he set out for Amalgamated Cartage.

It was just off Eleventh Avenue, not far from the docks. A billboard-size, weathered sign proclaimed that the flat, almost windowless brick and cinder-block building it rested upon was Amalgamated Cartage. The blacktop lot was surrounded by a tall chain-link fence topped with razor wire, but a wide gate was open. There was a line of overhead doors along a truck dock running the length of the building, broken only by a flight of wooden stairs leading to a gray-painted steel door that allowed access by foot.

Half a dozen truck trailers were backed into loading doors. Trucks were hooked up to two of them. The overhead doors where the trailers had truck cabs attached were raised, and Quinn could see in past the sides of the trailers. There was activity inside the building, men walking, orange fork-lifts moving back and forth, clanking over the steel bridges that allowed access to and from the trailers. The trailers dipped and rose as the lifts ran in and out, depositing or re-moving pallets of freight. A driver sat in one of the truck cabs, a dusty blue Peterbilt, engaged in some kind of paper-work attached to a clipboard. He seemed to be paying no at-tention to Quinn.

Quinn climbed the sturdy wooden stairs and found the door unlocked. He opened it and stepped through into a vast warehouse whose steel shelving seemed to contain mostly long rolls of something covered with brown paper.

The men involved in loading rolls into two of the trailers glanced over at Quinn but didn't show much interest.

A hefty redheaded man in too-tight jeans and a black muscle shirt emerged from what looked like an unpainted plywood office and swaggered toward Quinn. He had a full-sleeve tattoo on his beefy right arm. In his right hand was a clipboard.

"Help you?" he asked, without a smile.

"You can if Scott Trent works here."

"He does."

Quinn showed his ID. It didn't seem to impress the man.

"You the boss?" Quinn asked.

The man nodded.

"I need to talk with Trent, is all. Won't take more than a few minutes."

"His minutes belong to the company during working hours."

Quinn moved closer to the man. "I'm working under the auspices of the NYPD, and I didn't come here looking for a pissing contest, but I can win one."

Something in his voice made the Amalgamated boss look closer at Quinn and then blink. He shrugged. "Okay. Makes me no difference. He's out sitting in that truck cab, checking over his manifest. At least, he damned well better be."

"I noticed him when I came in," Quinn said. "Tell me about him."

"Ain't got the time."

"Are you sure you can't find the time?" Quinn asked, in a way that prompted the boss to think about it.

"Aw, screw it," the boss said. "There's not much to tell. Trent's been working here about a year as an over-the-road trucker. He ain't got much seniority so he takes the long runs, delivering on Thursdays or Fridays, and has weekends to himself before turnaround. That's so the company doesn't have to pay him overtime on weekends. So he has weekends off here in the city, where he lives. Listen, the man's an ordained minister of some sort. The cops have already been here talking to him. He wouldn't attack anybody. He'd pray for them instead."

"Amen," Quinn said, He nodded to the boss and moved toward the gray steel door.

"Don't take up too much of his time."

"Not to worry," Quinn said. "I know it's money."

He walked the length of the trailer that was hooked up to the blue Peterbilt truck, then around to the driver's side of the cab. He rapped on the metal door with his knuckles. A man about forty, wearing gray work pants and a black T-shirt like the boss's, only with AMALGAMATED lettered in white on the chest, opened the door and looked down at him.

Quinn flashed his ID as he had with the boss. Trent gave it only a glance.

"Let's have a talk," Quinn said. "I cleared it with your boss."

"I don't have much time. Gotta be in Georgia tomorrow with this carpet pad."

"Everybody here is in a rush," Quinn said.

Trent set aside the clipboard he'd been holding, tucked a pencil in the T-shirt's saggy pocket, and swung down from the cab.

Quinn saw that he was wearing brown Doc Martens boots. He was slim and muscular, slightly shorter than Quinn.

"This about Jane Nixon?" he asked.

Quinn said that it was.

"I already talked to a police detective," Trent said. "They accepted my alibi." He dug into his hip pocket for his wallet and handed Quinn a ticket stub for *God Is My Sales Manager*. The address on the stub was in Lower Manhattan.

"This is what?" Quinn asked.

"A motivational talk. I was there listening to it the night Jane was attacked," he said, as if that settled the matter and now he could get back to work.

"Truck drivers do much selling?"

"No. That's the problem. It's why I'm thinking about getting into sales."

"You know the name Lincoln Evans?" Quinn asked.

"Sure. It's been all over the news."

Quinn's cell phone abruptly vibrated in his pocket. He drew it out to silence it, but when he glanced at it and saw Pearl's name, he thought he'd better take the call. He excused himself and moved a few steps away, half turning his back for privacy but leaving enough angle so he could keep an eye on Trent.

"Whadya got, Pearl?"

"I did more checking on Jane Nixon's exonerated rapist, like you told me," Pearl said. "He's been mixed up in some bad stuff, and used forged papers and different identities, buying and selling stolen goods. The name Scott Trent is an alias he was using at the time of his rape conviction, and he's been using that name in New York since his release."

"You don't say," Quinn said, trying to sound casual in case Trent was tuned in.

Quinn suddenly remembered Trent's words: *"Gotta be in Georgia tomorrow with this carpet pad."*

"Quinn, he's also Beth Evans's former husband, Roy Brannigan." Pearl gave Quinn a few seconds to absorb what she'd said. "He supposedly raped Jane Nixon not long after he left Beth in Missouri and found his way to New York."

"And the DNA evidence that sprang him?"

"He was convicted on blood type and Nixon's identification. Turns out it wasn't his blood."

"Then he really was innocent."

"That time, anyway," Pearl said. "Like a lot of those other guys who've been set free thanks to DNA."

Quinn kept his voice low and told Pearl where he was. She'd know what to do.

"Be careful," he heard her say, as he broke the connection.

Trent—or Brannigan—hadn't moved while Quinn was talking, but there was something different about his stance, a subtle tenseness. How much had he overheard?

Quinn smiled and stuffed the phone back in his pocket. "I do have a few more questions about Jane Nixon," he said, letting Trent think the conversation wasn't about anything he had to fear. "The woman you were convicted of raping."

"I was later exonerated. DNA don't lie."

"Far as we know." Quinn worked his way closer.

"What's that supposed to mean?" Brannigan's eyes were beginning to roam. Quinn knew the signs.

"Listen, Scott—"

Brannigan hit him hard in the stomach with his fist, and then slammed the clipboard into his head.

Quinn shook off the clipboard blow easily enough, but he sank to his knees trying to catch his breath. Brannigan was on the run, and he had a stride like a deer's.

When Quinn was just beginning to suck in air, the steel door opened at the top of the steps and the big boss peered down at him.

"What the shit's goin' on here?" he asked.

Quinn tried to speak but only made a squeaking sound. He raised a forefinger for the boss to give him a few seconds.

The boss came halfway down the steps and leaned so he could get a better look at Quinn.

"The employees park in this lot?" Quinn managed to wheeze.

"No. They park in a lot out front."

"That the only gate?" Quinn tried to motion with his head, but his head didn't move.

"That's it," the boss said.

"Lock it," Quinn said.

"Says who?"

"Me," Quinn said, and drew his police special from its holster. "And when you're finished, go back inside and lock that door."

When the boss was headed toward the chain-link gate, Quinn worked his way to his feet. Holding the old revolver at the ready, he began moving cautiously along the line of trailers, now and then pausing to peek beneath them. He tasted blood trickling down from the clipboard cut on his forehead, but it was Roy Brannigan's blood that he smelled.

90

Roy Brannigan was terrified. If he managed to work his way along the building and get to a section of fence where he thought he could wriggle beneath it, he might be okay.

He'd known who Quinn was the second he'd seen him, and he couldn't let the big detective catch him. He'd hit Quinn hard and heard the breath rush out of him, but he didn't know how long he'd be down.

It was amazing, Roy thought, how suddenly everything had turned to crap. Jock Sanderson had been blackmailing him about the ticket stubs, and Roy was increasingly reluctant to pay. Sanderson's threat to expose Roy and then live large in some country where there was no extradition treaty was losing credibility. It was easier to *talk* about setting yourself up as a wanted blackmailer and accessory to murder, and taking refuge in a foreign land, than it was to actually take the step.

But it wouldn't hurt for Roy to have alibis in case the police happened to connect the dots. The stubs would be plausible. Some men let ticket stubs and the like build up in their wallets or on their dresser tops. The stubs would make it difficult if not impossible for him to be convicted of any of the Skinner murders.

At least, Jock Sanderson had convinced him of that.

And after the death of Link Evans, Roy thought he was completely safe.

Roy had latched on to Link Evans's extramarital adventures while spying on him because he'd taken Roy's place as Beth's husband. Never one to ignore opportunity, Roy coordinated his Skinner murders with Link's clandestine visits to New York to see Julie. Roy knew that Link would draw suspicion away from him, and also deny being in New York at the times of the murders. If push came to shove, Julie would provide Link's alibis, but Link would do almost anything to avoid that eventuality. Not to mention that women in love make lousy witnesses.

Roy's boot toe caught on a crack in the asphalt and he stumbled and almost fell. Another reminder that things could go wrong. His heart felt like a bird beating its wings in his chest.

This isn't supposed to be happening! This isn't fair!

Roy had wanted only to rid the earth of destroyers of innocent men. Such women gave false witness and were possessed by the devil. Like his own wife Beth, who'd ruined the lives of two men and bore the son of the devil that possessed her. Roy hadn't anticipated Satan working through a blackmailer to torment and defeat him. Or unleashing on him a cop stubborn enough to follow every lead and learn the answer to every question.

Roy felt a joyous pang of hope. He should never have doubted his special blessing and mission as God's blade of vengeance. He was almost there. The parked trailers made good cover. He could see the misshapen corner of the fence and the scooped-out area of dirt where kids, or maybe a large dog, had squeezed beneath it. Roy was lean and strong. He knew with certainty that if he made it to the fence, he could escape from the lot, escape Quinn.

He was dashing the final fifty feet toward the break in the fence when the blast of a gunshot temporarily froze him. He spun and saw Quinn about a hundred feet away, trudging around the nose of a parked trailer. His movements were deliberate. His head was down, but his eyes were trained on Roy. He looked like doom itself.

Roy began dancing backward toward the fence corner, watching Quinn, watching the muzzle of the gun. It wasn't aimed directly at him, but pointed to the right and down.

Quinn fired again. This time Roy didn't flinch at the shot, but he heard the bullet zing off the chain-link fence. There were buildings outside the fence, on the opposite side of the street. He knew Quinn would have to be careful shooting at him, making sure where his warning shots would go.

His warning shots.

Quinn could safely fire a bullet into him and not worry about collateral damage, but only when he got close enough.

Keep moving! Keep moving!

Roy kept walking backward with the grace of a ballet dancer, almost skipping. He couldn't look away from Quinn, who was coming at him slowly but relentlessly, angling like a boxer cutting off space in a ring, cornering his prey.

Roy knew now that he'd never have time to squeeze beneath the fence. When he got to within ten feet of the chain-link corner and its sturdy steel post, he wheeled and at the same time slipped his Amalgamated shirt over his head, whipping it inside out. He tossed the shirt up over the razor wire that topped the fence and launched himself after it.

For a few seconds it worked. Then the razor wire came through the thin material of the shirt and sliced into Roy's arms. He glanced back and saw Quinn still coming, and he panicked, flailing his arms and desperately trying to gain enough grip despite the pain so he could pull himself up and over. It was pure primal reaction now. *He had to escape!* The razor wire was like fire. He was surprised to see one of his fingers sliced almost all the way through and dangling limply by a flap of skin.

He heard Quinn calmly say his name behind him.

All right! Enough . . .

Roy released his grip on the razor wire. Part of his shirt ripped away and fell with him like a bloody flag as he dropped from the fence and slumped exhausted with his back against the chain link. He cradled the section of ripped shirt wrapped around both bleeding hands.

Quinn holstered his revolver and knelt beside him, as if to administer an act of mercy.

But what Roy saw in Quinn's eyes wasn't mercy; it was curiosity.

"Where'd you get the ticket stub?" Quinn asked.

"Same place I got the others," Roy said.

"You gonna tell me now, or later?"

Roy told him, and then told him everything else, not liking it at all, but not minding what was going to happen to Jock Sanderson, thinking ex-wives, what a pot full of trouble they are.

Quinn thought it was over. He shifted his weight so he was squatted near Roy, reaching out to adjust the bloody strips of shirt wound around his injured hand.

That was when Roy pulled the carpet tucking knife out from the bloody rags with his good hand. The wickedly hooked blade flashed through the narrow space between the two men. Quinn got his arm up right away, or the blade would have severed a carotid artery, and Roy would have had the pleasure of seeing him bleed to death. The gash in Quinn's arm gushed red as he backed away, drawing his revolver from its holster. He slashed sideways with the gun and knocked the knife out of Roy's hand and away, on Roy's second attempt to kill him.

Quinn got up on one knee, laid his gun on the pavement, then removed his shirt and tied it around the gash in his arm.

He used his belt to make a tourniquet, which he yanked tight high on his bicep.

Roy had his injured hands together again inside the blood-coagulated mass of material that was his shirt. On his knees and elbows, he was crawling toward the knife lying on the blacktop. Quinn knew what Roy wanted. It was what almost all the sick animals who became serial killers wanted—to exit in a blaze of glory. Fame and finale at last! Quinn would have to kill him, if Quinn himself hoped to survive.

Sirens were sounding blocks away. The NYPD wolves closing in. Roy didn't have much time. But it was enough to get his wish.

They were across the street from a boarded-up building. Parked trailers blocked vision from the warehouse.

When Roy had almost reached the knife, both his hands still wrapped tightly in the packed layers of his shirt material, Quinn picked up his revolver and aimed carefully. Three bullets ripped through the bloody mass of material, and through Roy's hands.

Roy stopped crawling, then rolled over on the hot blacktop and stretched his jaws wide in a silent scream of terror and frustration. He drew up his knees and hugged his ruined hands tightly to his body.

"Self defense," Quinn said. "You came at me again with the knife."

"Not fair!" Roy yowled. "Not goddamn fair! Shoot me! Shoot me in the heart!"

"You've got no heart," Quinn said. "And you won't harm another woman with what's left of those hands, in or out of prison."

"You're goin' to hell!"

"Maybe we'll do this again there," Quinn said.

91

"Roy Brannigan all the time," Renz said from behind his vast, uncluttered desk. "He did his Skinner murders between out-of-state truck runs delivering carpet, and he used Link Evans for a patsy, while Evans was using those same weekends in New York putting it over on his wife with Julie Flack."

"Jock Sanderson had it worked out almost from the beginning," Quinn said. "He used Roy to kill Judith Blaney, the woman who'd wrongly sent Sanderson to prison. Sanderson even provided Roy with an alibi. But all the time, he was planning on taking it further with blackmail. The little bastard decided he'd rather be a rich fugitive in South America or someplace else with a favorable exchange rate, living high where there was no extradition treaty and he couldn't be touched by the law, than be an impoverished janitor in this country."

"He didn't get to the airport quite fast enough," Renz said. He opened a desk drawer and withdrew an aluminum tube. He unscrewed the tube and produced a cigar, which he fired up with a lighter from the same drawer, puffing so that his jowls expanded and made him look like a bullfrog working up to a good croak. Instead of croaking, he said, "There's a certain judge wants to take a bite out of your ass, Quinn.

His wife is pretty much out of legal trouble, but she's embarrassed as hell."

"I did what I could."

"He puts people like that away all the time."

"The incredibly popular police commissioner will protect me," Quinn said.

Renz smiled around the cigar. "Thash true." He removed the cigar from his mouth and held it up. "You want one of these? Against the rules, but so what? We're celebrating the arrest of the real Skinner."

"No, thanks."

"You're gonna go home and smoke one of your Cubans. That's okay. I'm gonna hold a press conference this afternoon, talk about how our policy under my administration is never to give up on a case until all avenues are explored and all questions answered. We owe it to the public."

"I'll be watching on TV," Quinn lied. He'd already seen Renz blow enough smoke for one day.

"You did a good job, Quinn. If you were still in the department, I'd present you with a commendation. But you can understand why I won't mention your name or Julie Flack's in the press conference."

"Sure. It's your press conference. Your political ass."

Renz smiled and blew more smoke.

Quinn and Pearl stood and watched the workmen put the finishing touches on laying the brownstone's upstairs carpet. The gray-haired man doing the artful and delicate trimming around the baseboard finished with his tucking knife and then stood up and grinned, admiring his work. He glanced over at Quinn and Pearl.

"Beautiful," Quinn said. The spread of beige carpet lay wide and pristine, a geometrically perfect blank space awaiting an identity. Outside the tall windows, their panes distorted by the years of three centuries, the city hummed and bustled, but the old building's thick walls reduced the sounds to subtle punctuation.

"It makes a hell of an improvement," the carpet layer said.

Quinn agreed.

Pearl gave Quinn's arm a squeeze. "It looks like home."